# Beaches, Bagels & Babes

## By Nat Paga

Book Cover by Nat Paga

Illustrations by Nat Paga

1st edition 2025

## Content Warnings

This book contains mature plot points and elements that some readers might have difficulty with. For their sake, here is a list of that content. Spoilers follow.

.

.

.

.

- *Graphic depictions of sex*
- *Traumatic loss of parents*
- *Alcoholic parent*
- *Emotionally abusive guardian*
- *Homophobia*
- *Being sexually outed in a traumatic manner*
- *Kidnapping and imprisonment*
- *Coercion with explicit material*
- *Gun violence*

*Dedicated to the worriers,*

*the ones who get in their own way for life and love.*

*Let it be, ride the sea...*

# CONTENTS

# PROLOGUE

*Wonderwood, New Jersey – 2004*

### *Daisy*

T he shoreline glimmered like an ocean of diamonds as the sun bore down on the water's surface. It was a gorgeous sight, the kind some people dreamed of seeing their whole year, maybe their whole lives. It wasn't the Florida Keys, California coastline, or some tropical island paradise. Even so, "shoobie" vacationers paid good money to take a break from their regular routine and experience the New Jersey coast like this.

For Daisy, this was as regular as things got.

At twelve years old, she had more responsibility than your average pre-teen. More than some adults, too, leaving her jaded before she knew what the word meant. However, her parents' business on the bustling Wonderwood Boardwalk needed all the help it could get.

Thankfully, the menu was simple enough that just about anyone could keep the place running—bagels, plain hot coffee, and cold fountain drinks. Only the basics, but they did the basics well. The stall was simple, too. A single countertop set with four plush pleather stools, a refrigerated display window, plus a prep area and register, all painted bright 90's fluorescent greens and pinks.

Despite its small scale, Bagel Bombs! had been an institution of the community for years. Her parents worked hard to make the place popular with their unique take on the humble breakfast food and, once she was old enough, Daisy did, too.

Usually.

Today, things were dragging.

After waking up at the crack of dawn, she pulled herself out of bed and biked to the boardwalk from her parents' bungalow on the far side of the island. That alone left her panting since it was "soupy," as her mom called it. Hot and humid with breezeless air, it was the kind of day that started with everything covered in a thick layer of dew.

Still, by the time the first glimmers of dawnlight peeked over the horizon, the boardwalk was teeming with people. Bikers and runners getting their morning exercise, beachgoers looking to claim their prime spot, and your average amblers taking in the sights streamed past the mostly-shuttered boardwalk storefronts.

It might be soupy, but Daisy could tell right away it would be packed.

As soon as she hauled up the security chain and flipped on the styled *"DA BOMB!"* neon open sign, she was met with a line of hungry customers. Like a true pro, she powered through the morning rush to the lunchtime pop. Nothing out of the ordinary happened apart from running out of sesame bombs. She served one *very* cranky lady who perked right up once she got her coffee, but that was as exciting as things got.

Now, there was nothing to do but wait until shift change.

Her mom, who was busy running errands and doing adult business during the day, would arrive soon to take over for the rowdier night crowd. Then, Daisy could go be a normal kid. Not that she was normal in any sense of the word, but it might be nice to pretend.

What would she do with her freedom, though?

The brand-new fishing wharf-turned-amusement pier, Perry's Pier, was across the boardwalk. All day, *all summer,* it blasted her with a barrage of arcade sounds, rushing coasters, and other people enjoying themselves. Maybe she could join in the fun.

Then again, by the time she closed up, she would be even more tired. What was the point of paying to ride a ride she would fall asleep on? She would probably go home, nap, and get roped into helping her dad pre-make more batches of bagel bombs. Just like yesterday and the day before.

Daisy didn't mind too much. She loved it when her parents praised her or when customers told her how good she was. She loved being responsible and independent. Getting paid helped, too. But, sometimes, she felt bitter about being one of the only kids in a vacation town not having fun.

A yawn escaped Daisy's mouth.

The rolling churn of the waves was hypnotizing. Back and forth, a great rush followed by a crashing release. Everything else, even the intermittent, screeching gull calls, faded under the soothing rhythm.

Daisy's head bobbed in her hand. Slowly, her eyelids drooped past the point of no return. As she imagined all the excitement going on at the pier, she joined in hazy half-dreams.

First, she played *Dance Dance Revolution.* They had real machines, unlike the other boardwalk arcades with their knock-off diagonal arrows. After that, ice cream was a must. She heard their Kohrs Bros stand had *six* different soft serve flavors as opposed to the normal three, and, of course, she would have to sample each one.

She would ride all the rides, saving the best for last: the

Mouse Kart. Secretly, heights scared her, so the tiny two-person coaster was right up her alley. Or, she thought it would be if she ever got the chance to ride.

*ClackClackClack...*

The clanging of the coaster gears made its way into Daisy's dream.

Up, up, and up, Daisy could feel herself inside the goofy-looking mouse ascending the track. At the top, it paused, and she saw the endless, glimmering ocean.

Was this what shoobies felt like? Full of hope and carefree bliss?

However, Daisy wasn't on vacation. She was at work. Her budding customer service instincts snapped her back to focus as someone approached the counter.

And, by snapped, it happened literally. The arm Daisy had propped against the counter gave out, dropping her chin onto the hard, peach-pink laminate. It hurt. Yet, the girlish giggle from her would-be customer brought an extra sting.

At least Daisy was wide awake now.

With her jaw buzzing, she garbled out, *"Canni-takyerurder?"*

The girl giggled even harder while Daisy flushed.

They had to be about the same age. That, though, seemed to be the only thing they had in common.

People used the word "gawky" to describe Daisy. She was the tallest in her class, with muscle from trekking all over the island and a distinct tank-top tan from her work uniform. Her angular face was one her parents promised she would grow into, made more awkward by her most recent haircut. She'd asked the stylist for "Trinity, from *The Matrix*," and ended up more like an athletic Julia Robert's Tinker Bell thanks to her ash blonde hair.

This girl, meanwhile, was the complete opposite. She looked like a doll, tiny and cute, with silken ringlet curls tied into effortless pigtails. Her entire outfit was like something from a pre-teen fashion magazine, with low-cut whitewash jeans, a matching halter top, sunflower yellow Converse sneakers, and expensive-looking big movie star shades. Her smile, with perfect, pearly teeth, made Daisy feel all squirmy.

In an instant, the girl's expression dropped. She covered her mouth and spoke through her fingers with polka dot-painted nails.

"I'm sorry! I didn't mean to laugh. Are you okay?"

"Um, yeah. I've got a hard chin."

*DUMB. Dumb, dumb, dummy!* Daisy's internal voice chanted. She swallowed the lump in her throat and willed the transaction to move faster.

One of the girl's eyebrows arched.

"But, like, you're bleeding."

Daisy did not know why, but the words failed to register. She stared at the girl, and the girl stared at her like they were waiting for someone to tell them what to do next.

Then, the girl figured it out.

Dropping her Coach purse onto the countertop as if it weren't a $500 bag, she dug until she found a pack of tissues. She reached out, offering one.

They stood there like that until Daisy remembered how to be a not-awkward, hormone-ridden mess. She took the tissue and pressed it against her chin. Thankfully, the damage wasn't too bad; she dabbed away the worst of it and slapped on a bandage from the emergency first-aid kit. The dull, throbbing pain was a distant afterthought as she fell back into service-mode.

"Er, thanks. I think I'll live. Can I take your order?"

"Oh! Um…" The girl bit her lower lip, messing up her shiny gloss. "I'm sorry, I was just looking. I don't have any money. I have to ask my uncle if I want stuff."

Daisy followed the girl's hesitant gaze to a group of adults near but not in line for the fun pier's ticket counter. They did not look like shoobies; they looked like businesspeople in their definitely-not beach wear. Something about one tall, stark blond-haired man was familiar, but his back was turned, so she could not see his face.

Without thinking, Daisy offered, "How about a free sample?

I'm allowed to give away one per customer."

"They *do* smell good. But…"

The girl cast another furtive glance back at the adults. She propped her sunglasses on top of her head to look at the bagel bombs under the counter window, revealing bright seafoam blueish-green eyes.

"You'll eat it in one bite," Daisy promised. "I'm no narc, they'll never find out."

"Well," the girl asked with an interested tilt, "what *are* "bagel bombs?"

"They're like bagels, but *DA BOMB!*"

Daisy spun in place and snapped her fingers, doing a little dance just like her parents taught her. Again, the girl giggled. Daisy's heart, which had not stopped its wild beating, kicked up even harder. Normally, she hated putting on a show, but she liked making this girl laugh.

In a rush, she added, "They're like mini hot pockets or doughnut poppums. Bite-sized bagels stuffed with different cream cheeses or jellies. We've got savory and sweet, your standard favorites, along with the random flavors my dad feels like trying out."

"Poppyseed, cinnamon raisin, lemon glaze… *'Peanut butter and jelly?'*" The girl read with an arched eyebrow.

"Oh. I made that batch. Yeah, I know. PB&J is a little kiddish, but I thought it would be fun and—"

"I *love* PB&J! It's my favorite. What kind of jelly did you use?"

"Um, it's blueberry and cream cheese mixed with chunky peanut butter. It's best toasted."

"Mmmmm… Okay! As long as it won't get you in trouble, I'll try one."

Daisy put the girl's sample bomb into the big, industrial toaster oven, plus an extra one for herself. While they waited, Daisy shifted nervously. It was hard to decide whether she wanted the moment to go faster or if she wanted to 'accidentally' drop the bombs so the girl would have to stay longer. The latter option felt pretty nefarious, but if it worked…

She was surprised when the girl started making conversation.

"You really made them all by yourself? And you work here, too? That's so cool!"

"'Cool?'"

"Yeah! I mean, you're in charge, right? So you can talk back to adults or do whatever you want. It must be fun."

Daisy had never thought of her conscription that way, but she supposed there was something nice about it.

"I guess so. I get to keep tips. And yeah, I sometimes come up with flavor ideas when my dad says we need something new. My PB&J is pretty popular."

"See? That's cool! I wanted to get a summer job, but my uncle says I'm not allowed, ever, since I'd just mess it up. He told me to marry rich if I want money."

Daisy deadpanned, "He sounds like a jerk."

This time, the girl did not giggle. A small, forced smile tugged away her true one.

"He tries. He might say things like that, but he cares about me."

"Until the rich husband?"

The girl snorted, looking less than enthused.

"Or not," Daisy backtracked. "Maybe you'll be rich, and your husband'll ask you for money."

*Or-or,* Daisy's internal voice whispered, *ditch the husband and get a wife!*

While same-sex marriage was still illegal in the United States, with the recent ruling in Massachusetts, it was technically possible. For Daisy, who was just starting to realize her lack of interest in boys, that possibility was very appealing.

The glow returned to the girl's expression. She rocked back on her heels, musing, "Maybe."

Seconds later, the toaster oven buzzer went off. Daisy gathered the bagel bombs in paper baggies, one for her and one for the girl. Their fingers brushed as she handed it over, a happy accident that wasn't so accidental.

"Thank you," the girl said. "My name is Candace, by the way."

"D-Daisy." Her voice cracked as she realized she might never see this Candace-girl again. She blurted out, "Are you on vacation? There are a lot of places only locals know. I'm about to close up so I can show you around. Um, if you want."

Candace hesitated. Again, she chewed her lip.

"I'm not. Visiting, I mean. But I'd—"

"*Candy.*"

The single, icy utterance made both girls stand bolt-straight. It was the blond man. Daisy had been too preoccupied to notice the business people walk over. He came up close to Candace and placed a tightly gripped hand on top of her shoulder.

Fear struck Daisy as she realized who the man was: Peter Perry, the owner of Perry's Pier. Her parents pointed him out and told her to be extra careful if she ever served him. Not that he would ever be caught dead patronizing their "eyesore" of a cafe, as he called it, but just in case. Her mom said he was "a powerful man with powerful friends who weren't afraid to be bad."

Daisy clocked him as trouble just by looking at him. Full of swagger, like he owned the place in his Tommy Bahama button-down and linen slacks, he was the type who was all fun and games as long as he got his way. If not, he'd do everything he could to make you miserable. His bright smile, contrasted by the tanning-bed bronze of his skin, was shark-like.

He repeated the infantilizing nickname, this time in a sickeningly sweet tone. "Candy. Baby, I told you to wait."

"Sorry, Uncle Perry. I saw this girl here, and we started talking. She's really nice."

For an instant, the man regarded Daisy. His eyes were impossible to see behind his aviator Ray Bans. Even so, his disdain was plain as day. A smirk cocked the corner of his mouth as he joked to his friends.

"Huh, child labor is alive after all. I told you these South

Jersey towns are hick country."

Heat radiated from Daisy's face as she bit her tongue. There was nothing she could say that wouldn't get her in trouble. Candace, however, went on excitedly.

"It's cool! She bakes some herself, and she gets to keep tips. Look—" Candace showed him the PB&J bagel bomb, "—she gave me a free sample."

It was unbelievable. Faster than either girl could process, Perry snatched the bagel bomb and tossed it to some seagulls. The scavengers greedily gorged it in milliseconds.

He chided, "Don't spoil your appetite with trash food. If you're hungry, I'll buy you a salad. Or not, if you keep acting out."

He laughed, and his friends went along with him like starving a child was some hilarious joke. In an instant, the happy, giggling girl was gone. Candace wilted as she trained her gaze on the splintery boards under her shoes.

"Sorry..."

"Good girl. Now, c'mon. We've got better places to be."

With the hand still clenched over Candace's shoulder, Perry steered her around. She cast one last backward glance at Daisy. Her eyes were watery with disappointment.

It was wrong.

Daisy couldn't leave things like this. She spotted Candace's forgotten purse on the countertop. Her hands moved on their own, bagging up and shoving the second PB&J bagel bomb inside. She banged on the wall that separated Bagel Bombs! from the caramel popcorn stand next door. In a single breath, she bellowed, "John! Watch my stuff!"

Then, she bolted.

It was almost impossible to catch up with them. Dodging and weaving around the ceaseless flow of foot traffic was like an extreme game of *Frogger* with more cursing. However, just as they were about to take the street ramp, Daisy managed to close the distance. She hooked a hand around Candace's arm, stopping her and Perry in their tracks.

*"How dare—"*

Daisy ignored Perry, telling Candace, "I thought you might want this back."

It was like the tissue all over again. This time, though, it was Candace who stared in awe at Daisy. And was that *blush* on her cheeks? It could be the heat, but the idea that it was thanks to Daisy made her own skin feel like magma.

Eventually, Perry tore the bag away himself.

"What're you waiting for? A tip? Here."

Peter Perry slapped a piece of paper into Daisy's palm. It was a single-ride ticket from the man who owned them all. As he cracked more rude jokes to his chortling posse, he once again forced his niece to walk.

This time, when Candace looked back at Daisy, her eyes were harder to read. The sadness lingered, yet there was something else, too. Defiance sparkled in those seafoam depths, powerful like the waves crashing on the shore. She would be okay because she was stronger than she looked.

Daisy watched until the girl was gone from view. Candace Perry, her first crush and future heartbreak.

# CHAPTER 1

*Wonderwood, New Jersey — 2025*

## *Candace*

The summer season was right about to kick into high gear at the Wonderwood Boardwalk. It was a jewel of a May day that promised record profits for the businesses situated along the coastal strip. Perry's Pier was especially packed, which was sure to make Candace's uncle happy. She, meanwhile, was having a terrible time.

It was nostalgic to be back in Wonderwood, but not in a mushy, nice way. The beach town was a salt taffy promise—a pretty but fake place filled with uncomfortable memories and a bitter present. The minute Candace drove over the old island drawbridge, she wanted to turn back, to go somewhere, anywhere, else.

But this was it.

At thirty-three, an age where she should be in the prime of

her career, Candace was unemployable. After a key client of the consultancy firm that Candace worked for complained about her for reasons that were still unknown, no one would give her a chance. She tried everywhere: other big competing firms, small firms, private business accounting, and mom-and-pop operations. She even put in applications outside of her field, but nothing panned out. Word of her supposed transgressions followed wherever she went. She was out of money, and her credit cards were maxed. So, she had to stoop to begging her uncle for help.

Candace replayed their phone conversation in her head and cringed.

*"I'm traditional,"* he told her with his trademark joking-not-joking tone. *"If you want something, you ask in person. But don't worry. You know I've always got sugar for you, Candy."*

Another cringe rippled down her spine.

Peter Perry was a button-pusher. He enjoyed making other people squirm, saying whatever he wanted, being intentionally insensitive, even with his own flesh and blood. However, all of it was under the guise of "fun." He would not even let him call her by his first name like a normal uncle; he was 'Uncle Perry,' Wonderwood's favorite wild, wacky public figure. It was his brand, and he was very protective of it because of the goodwill it bought him.

Candace knew that all her uncle really cared about was being the top asshole at the local marina. Everything he did was for power and prestige. He had both in droves, but it was never enough.

He liked to be petty with it. He told Candace to be at the fun pier's office building under the Manta Coaster at 8 AM sharp. Even though there was no way he would show up anytime close to then, he would check the security tapes to make sure she did.

So, Candace waited.

And waited.

*8:30* flashed on her phone screen as she checked it.

Candace stifled a yawn. She hadn't had time to make coffee this morning in her motel room's little single-serve maker. There was a perpetually brewed pot in the front office reception room, but that would've been a dangerous gamble; she was sure it hadn't been emptied, let alone cleaned, in decades.

Best to avoid negotiating with a time bomb in her stomach.

Candace shifted in the sunken, mildewy seat. Her nose crinkled. Most of the place had a musty smell. It was not a surprising problem for a business built over the ocean. Even so, with regular maintenance, cleaning, and upgrades, it was somewhat mitigable.

*Regular* being the important word.

Candace's uncle had better things to spend his money on, like impressing his rich friends or expanding his empire. Knowing him, he was probably out to breakfast at one of the local big-wig haunts, rubbing elbows with the police chief and mayor. Her suspicion was confirmed when her uncle's long-time secretary poked her head into the office.

"Miss Candy," the older woman, Janice, chirped, using Candace's hated nickname. "Mr. Perry called to say he's at an urgent meeting, so he won't be able to make it. He had me wire money to your account and said that he'd talk over the details with you later."

Candace resisted kicking the rusted desk in front of her only because it would have scuffed her white wedge sandals. Instead, she flashed a smile that bared teeth.

"Oh, of *course*. I know my uncle is busy. No worries."

*Fresh-caught farm-to-table scallops over Eggs Benedict at Ferdinand's?* Candace wondered. *Or maybe a showy platter at the Seashore Diner, a king among the commoners?*

Whatever the answer, Candace played her uncle's game and got what she wanted. Almost. She checked her banking app, and the balance was just enough to get her out of imminent financial ruin. She might even be able to treat herself to something other than a microwave dinner. Still, the idea that her end of the bargain remained undisclosed sat as poorly as that coffee would have.

Candace fled from the office feeling uneasy. She exited the building out to the damp sub-level and was immediately assaulted by sensation. The blast of humid heat as she left the air-conditioned space; the Manta Coaster overhead, shaking the whole place; the salty smell that clung to everything.

It brought a rush of memories, too. Some good, some bad. All of it made the pressure in her chest worsen.

Candace kept it together while she was in view of her uncle's security cameras. With practiced poise, she wove through the surprising amount of people already queuing for the first rides of the day and made her way to the main boardwalk. There, she braced herself against the railing with her eyes trained on the glimmering ocean horizon.

Candace hated this place. She managed to avoid it for so long; it was fitting that she had to come here when she was at her lowest. Everything about it brought her back to that first awful summer she spent with her uncle after he took her in. At twelve years old, someone had to, and he was the best option. Her only option. She felt like that powerless, scared girl again because *she was.* Wonderwood had not changed in all this time, and neither had she.

She would, though. Candace would get back on her feet and go where she wanted to be. Once she figured out where that was, since her bridge in the financial sector had apparently been burned. For now, she was stuck.

In and out, Candace breathed. She drew deep, full breaths into her belly—held at the top—then, released great, throat-cleansing exhales. Slowly, her breaths synced to the rise and fall of the waves spilling out over the beach sand. Her mind calmed.

After a time, with a little sigh of relief, Candace's breathing returned to normal. Her best friend and yoga teacher, Demi, taught 'pranayama breathing,' centering the body and mind by breathing along with an internal wave. The more metaphysical sides of yoga, limbs of practice beyond the physical workout, were a bit beyond Candace. But techniques like this helped to quell her occasional bursts of uncontrolled emotion.

Most of the time.

Candace's stomach, though, was another story. It grumbled so loudly that a group of passersby on a four-seater surrey bike turned their heads to look at her. She waved with a forced smile as they continued on their way, laughing amongst themselves.

*Could this day get any more humiliating?*

Candace should have known better than to ask.

Turning, she leaned back against the hot metallic rail that separated the boardwalk from the beach dunes below. At least her card would not be declined if she bought a coffee. But where?

Perry's Pier was coming to life with its kitsch-themed fast-casual dining options, carnival food stands, and more. Presumably, one of them sold coffee. Still, Candace loathed the idea of giving her uncle's money right back to him, even indirectly.

It had been fifteen years since the last time she walked the boardwalk's two and a half miles of splintery planking. She recalled hearing that a chain coffee shop had opened, but it was nowhere in sight. There was Zeus' Torch, the long-operating 24-hour Greek diner run by Demi's relatives, which had the best gyros in the area. Even so, the place was a stiff hike to the far side of the boardwalk. As far as she could see, there were T-shirt shops, soon-to-open candy stores, and novelty goods, but no *real* food.

Aside from one place, right in front of her, that she had been staunchly hoping to avoid.

Bagel Bombs!.

It looked exactly the same as the last time she saw it, except not. The place seemed clean and cared for, but there was noticeable wear.

The neon pink and lime of its '90s pop aesthetic had faded to dingy russet and sludge green in the harsh salt air. Its styled *DA BOMB* open sign struggled with a flicker, and the overhead one needed de-rusting. Four stools were now three, and it looked like a gamble to sit on any one of them. Compared to the newer stores on either side, the place was in bad need of a makeover.

Some things stayed the same, though.

The smell of freshly toasted dough and roasting coffee beans that carried over from the cafe was a memory wrapped in a scent. Even after all this time, Candace could taste her first bagel bomb. Warm, nutty bread with a satisfying outer crust and a soft, gooey center. It had just the right amount of peanut butter, jam, and cream cheese filling. Sweet and savory in perfect balance.

Candace licked her lips at the thought.

After that first sample, she was hooked. Unfortunately, getting the bagel bombs had been difficult. Once her uncle gave her a credit card, he read her statements like it was a sport. If he knew she was stuffing herself with "garbage food from a garbage girl," she would have never heard the end of it.

Yet, Candace couldn't resist. Not entirely. Purses, makeup, clothes, shoes... She traded whatever her friends wanted in exchange for getting her fix. It wasn't the best system, but it worked for the years she had to be sneaky.

Now, things were different. There was nothing stopping Candace from picking up one foot after the other, walking up to that counter, and ordering for herself like a big girl.

Well, almost nothing.

*Was* she *there?*

Through the busy rush of foot traffic, Candace could not see who was working the cafe's counter. She strained, balancing on her wedge tips even if it meant scuffing them, but it was impossible. Unbeknownst to Candace, her legs started taking her across the boardwalk.

*She couldn't be here,* Candace told herself. *That girl probably sold the place years ago, went to college, moved away...*

Except, she had not. The girl—woman, now—was exactly

where Candace last saw her. In what felt like slow motion, the crowd parted enough for Candace to see her standing behind the cafe counter.

*Daisy DeMarco.*

She, too, had changed and not. Her figure had always been impressive, so tall and toned that it put the roving bands of beach bros to shame. As a teen, it made her stoop and try to lessen herself. Now, she stood as confidently as a model.

Or, more accurately, some kind of punk rock-baker.

In a printed black tank top and athletic shorts, Daisy's multiple piercings were plain to see. The sleeve tattoo she bore of a seafoam-colored jellyfish was also prominent, with fanning tentacles that twined with seaweed all down her bicep to her forearm. The addition of a flour-covered apron over top, and her short-cropped, ash-blond hair tied under a turquoise bandana, looked effortlessly cool, as if she knew exactly who she was.

*Strong.*

*Confident.*

*Sexy.*

Candace could not stop herself from staring. And Daisy stared right back at her.

Pranayama breathing turned to short, panicked puffs of air. It was like some sort of awful, slow-motion nightmare. Candace's legs refused to obey her and continued towards the one place she *really* had not wanted to go. All the while, she argued with herself in an internal monologue.

*It's been fifteen years. There's no way she remembers you or what happened. You were both hormonal teenagers. It didn't mean anything, it was just—*

"Good morning," Candace greeted on autopilot once she reached the point of no return. She flashed her best customer's smile, which often got her exceptional service and the occasional extra goodie. "I'd like a large coffee, and—"

Daisy did not reply. Granite-faced, she reached for the *DA BOMB* sign. The fluorescent flickered out, along with Candace's hope that her day would get any better.

# CHAPTER 2

*Daisy*

The tide was a tricky force of nature.

Ebbing and flowing by the moon's rule, it tugged at the world's watery domains like magic. The gravitational dance was predictable, a known quantity to live and move by. Yet, in acts of prestidigitation, sometimes, the tide could produce unexpected curiosities.

Lost treasures from vessels sunk long ago...

Terrific creatures from unexplored depths...

Today, it brought trash.

Or, more specifically, a trash person named Candace Perry. Even after all this time, it was unmistakably her. For years, Daisy had the biggest crush on the girl and thought she could do no wrong. A mistake, as it turned out. That crush was dead and gone, leaving them here.

Salesperson and customer.

Daisy could count on her hands the number of times she turned someone away. Between vendor bills and the rent she owed King Wonderwood himself, Peter Perry, she wasn't in a position to be choosy. It was a last resort reserved for the most irate, detestable customers—the bottom feeders and walking-algae scum that somehow ended up with sentience enough to place a coffee order.

So, Candace definitely qualified.

Saying nothing, Daisy started closing up shop while the trash stood there gaping.

"Excuse me? I asked for—"

"I heard you," Daisy cut her off. "We're closed."

"It's not even 9AM yet. Your coffee pot is still on, and you just served this man here."

Daisy's attention flicked to Norman, her die-hard regular seated atop the one stool that didn't yet wobble. He was an old fart in the best way, always outfitted in a classic suit and tie because that was how people from his generation dressed when they came onto the boardwalk. He kept reading his newspaper, ignoring or, more likely, not hearing the exchange.

With a shrug, Daisy folded her arms and did her best club-bouncer impression.

"Well, we're closed now."

The woman switched tactics. She flashed a dazzling smile that had probably never failed to win someone over.

"Please? It's not like I'm asking for much. I'd be grateful."

Daisy scowled. Mainly because she knew that if it hadn't been for their history, the plea would have worked. Candace Perry had grown into the gorgeous archetype of femininity and poise she was always meant to be. The creamy white, belted and collared romper she wore was a business cut, yet the material could not help contouring to curves that gave Sydney Sweeney a run for her money. Matching wedge sandals added a couple of inches to her height, but that pristine smile and all the warmth it radiated seemed to lift her up on a pedestal. Anyone would fall to their knees before such a sight.

Which made Daisy stand even straighter.

"I don't care what you're asking for. I said no. Why don't you go to the fun pier, *Candace*? I'm sure your uncle will buy you a coffee."

"You... um... remember me?"

Daisy scoffed. "Yeah. Yeah, I do. You were a mean girl bitch. Now, screw off to someone who will put up with your shit."

Stunning eyes that used to make Daisy's knees weak went wide with... anger? Shame? It was hard to tell because the woman's expression remained the same. Still, her admittedly attractive face turned bright crimson.

Daisy almost backed down. Sure, she had daydreamed this hundreds of times. Seeing Candace Perry again, after all these years, and being able to turn her away. Just like she should have the last time they saw one another, when Candace broke Daisy's heart.

But maybe Candace had changed. It was a small town, and locals gossiped about each other on the regular. Daisy heard that Candace went out of state for college, finally breaking from under her uncle's thumb to make her own way. She got out, moved on, and was living her best life—an accountant or something that had to do with money. She likely did not remember the "bagel girl" she met so many summers ago. Not in the way Daisy remembered Candace.

The idea that Daisy could simply be forgotten stung. She hid it under a blank expression, determined not to fold.

And she didn't.

Candace, however, did. Like a fast summer storm, a downpour descended on her cheeks. Full-on, uncontrolled emotion unleashed in a wild torrent. Passersby slowed to watch. If Candace didn't pull it together soon, she'd end up as a meme on someone's social feed. Worse, Daisy might, and her struggling business didn't need that kind of exposure.

"We're good here," she called to the teens already starting to record the scene. "Shoobie stepped on a nail. Anyone wanna help?" Thankfully, the threat of humanitarian work got the rubberneckers to move along. She breathed a silent sigh of relief.

Daisy might be bitter, but she wasn't heartless. She pulled a napkin from the counter dispenser and handed it over. An awkward beat passed while Candace tried, and failed, to clear her clogged nose with dignity.

"Hey," Daisy started. "I'm not going to apologize, but are you oka—"

"*No!* I'm not okay, not even close! I *hate* Wonderwood! It's an awful place."

"Huh. You're allowed to be wrong, I guess. If it's so terrible, go somewhere else."

Another fresh flood found its way to Candace's face. She mastered her emotions herself this time with a few controlled breaths. Her wounded expression soured.

"If I had any other choice, I would."

Candace huffed for emphasis and tossed her sunflower locks over one shoulder. Daisy didn't watch how the light caught on the sleek strands, and she *definitely* didn't feel a rush as the scent of lilac shampoo hit her nose. When Daisy said nothing in response, Candace slumped.

"Not that you would care, but my life is a mess. I got fired from my dream job, and now I'm unhirable."

"Oh. Bummer."

"Yeah, 'bummer.' So this is my last option. I have to suck it up and beg for help from the one person I swore to never go to again."

"Hitting up Uncle Moneybags, huh? Must be nice."

"No," she snapped, but seemed to catch herself. She took a deep breath through her nose and added, "Sorry, but it's not 'nice' owing Peter Perry, even if you're related to him. It might even be worse because he feels like he's somehow *allowed* to make me miserable because we share some DNA. He'll hold this over me for the rest of my life."

Regret hit Daisy. She recalled the scared young girl she met so long ago and imagined what their home life must have looked like. She started to apologize. With a shake of her head, Candace stopped her.

"It's alright. Privilege with strings is still privilege, I know."

"Yeah. But it does sound like it sucks. You're allowed to complain."

"Thanks. Everyone thinks he's wonderful. 'Wonderwood's Wacky Uncle,' who revitalized the boardwalk. Living with him, having the same name, is different."

Plainly, Daisy said, "He's an asshole, and this place would be better off if he fucked off."

Candace giggled in a musical burst. A rush of deja vu hit Daisy, and her heart did a little skip.

"He is, isn't he? It's nice to hear someone say it out loud. I'm not just taking his money, to be clear. I'll pay him back every single cent as soon as I can. I might not technically be a banker anymore, but I can still manage money. In the meantime, I get to relive some of the worst years of my life."

Pausing, Candace snatched another napkin from the dispenser and blew her nose; unladylike, a little gross, and wholly human, which was disarming for Daisy to see.

She continued, "That's the reason for... whatever this was. I've been burying a lot of emotions, and being here dredged them all up."

" 'Tide 'tis time's temptation; let it be and ride the sea.' "

Candace looked at Daisy like she had two heads because why wouldn't she? It was an old fisherman's limerick, something Daisy's mother used to belt in a silly, sing-song voice whenever Daisy was having a bad day. She could not remember the last time she thought about the phrase, but words left her lips before she registered it happening.

In a rush, she explained, "It's a sailor's saying. Weird, I know. It's—"

"I like it." A small, thoughtful smile curved Candace's lips. She mused, "It's a bit like saying 'go with the flow,' which I need to hear sometimes. Thank you."

"Yeah."

Candace's smile flickered and shifted from a genuine action to a practiced one. She started to turn away. "Well, then. Sorry for bothering you."

Daisy couldn't say why. On impulse, she filled their largest insulated to-go cup with coffee and placed it on the counter before Candace. The woman blinked her somehow still perfectly mascaraed eyelashes at the steaming object before her.

"On the house," Daisy offered with a shrug. "I know a thing or two about owing Peter Perry money. I get it."

A beat passed. Candace took the cup, carefully, between both of her hands. In a small voice, she said, "Thanks... Daisy."

It felt as if a bolt went through Daisy's chest. What was happening here, and why did she want it to continue? Nerves abuzz, Daisy motioned for Candace to sit. When she did, Daisy busied herself putting things away and tried *so hard* to quash the desire to keep Candace talking.

Then, curse him, Norman went and did it himself.

"Good morning, miss," he greeted. "Beautiful day, isn't it?"

"It's lovely, yes."

"Are you in town for the horseshoe crab exhibit?"

"T-the what?"

Candace stared at the old man blankly. On anyone else, the woman's deer-in-headlights look would have been cute to Daisy. Instead, it irked her. Or, maybe, *because* she found it cute it irked her.

She mocked, "What a shoobie. You don't know about the horseshoe crabs? They're what Wonderwood is famous for—or was, before the boardwalk took all the attention."

"I know what those nightmare-fuel sea spiders are," Candace shot back. "I just hadn't heard anything about an exhibit. Also, isn't this cafe located on that attention-grabbing boardwalk?"

Almost, very nearly almost, Daisy swiped the cup Candice was drawing to her smugly upturned, peony pink lips. Rather, she found herself watching the subtle shifts as they met cups' top, imagining what they would look like pressed against...

Daisy was rescued from her daydreams as Norman continued.

"It's a hoot! Those little critters are an important part of the ecosystem and medical science, so the wildlife center decided to do a little publicity campaign." He rifled through the local newspaper propped on his lap and handed over a page that detailed the whole affair to Candace. To her credit, she feigned interest.

"How cute! It looks like the wildlife center went all out. I appreciate you letting me know. I'm not exactly here as a tourist, but if I have time, I'll take a look."

They chatted a bit longer about the upcoming summer, how the farmer's almanac said it was going to be a stormy end of the season, and other simple things. Daisy listened with begrudging gratefulness. Although Candace would never know it, she probably made Norman's week since he loved nothing more than chatting up fellow counter-sitters. Nowadays, though, people were too glued to their phones for idle conversation.

*Could Candace have changed?* Daisy wondered. *Or is this all some weird rich-girl ploy?*

Not too long later, Norman finished his coffee. He neatly folded his paper with a crisp $20 tucked inside (overpaying as always) and went off with a tip of his suede fedora.

Daisy waved, saying, "Thanks, Norm. See ya tomorrow."

There were few things she could count on, but the old man perched on that stool was one of them. Daisy cleared his cup and the paper wrappings from his breakfast, keenly aware that Candace watched her all the while.

The silence was deafening. Not even the sounds of bustling vacationers, the roaring fun pier, or the ambient crashing of waves could cover Daisy's internal scream of *SAY SOMETHING!!!* Candace was the one to give in, and her tone was stilted as a first-time line-read.

"You must enjoy this. Running the cafe, I mean."

*Enjoy it?*

Daisy almost laughed. The metaphorical (sometimes literal) blood and sweat she put into keeping Bagel Bombs! alive was immeasurable. Scrimping, saving, spending all her waking hours doing whatever she could to keep the place in business...

'Enjoy' was the last word Daisy would use to describe her circumstances. But, she wasn't about to complain to Candace Perry.

"It's a job. Pays the bills, mostly."

"Ah, I see. I wasn't sure if you would have sold it after..."

Candace trailed off, but Daisy guessed what she was about to say. It was delicate; a tragedy that the whole island, even semi-locals like Candace, knew. One rainy day accident sparked a whole public safety campaign with shiny new signs to indicate the town bridge's status. They even made up a mascot, Slippery Sally, to make learning about car hydroplaning fun for kids. For Daisy, it changed her whole life.

"You mean," Daisy finished, "after my parents took a swan dive into the bay?"

Candace choked on her coffee. She came close to staining her romper but managed to catch the liquid in her free hand. She shook her fingers to the side to dry them.

"I was going to say after high school. I'm so sorry. I only meant I was surprised to see you here. You were always drawing in that, what was it...? A field journal? I thought you would've become a marine biologist or write a nature comic book."

This time, Daisy was the one to falter. Her thumbs hooked into the loop of her apron tie, tugging anxiously at the knot.

"You remember that? Well, plans change. Some bridges go up in flames, others get icy when wet. After the accident, the cafe fell on me, so things just kind of worked out this way."

Pity filled Candace's eyes. It made Daisy uncomfortable, reminding her that she *was* pitiable. In a rush, she added, "Plus, my parents put their hearts and souls into this place. I could never forgive myself if I shut it down. Might not be my choice sooner rather than later, but I'll keep the lights on as long as I can."

"Oh? Have things been difficult in the bagel business?" Stumbling, Candace backtracked. "I'm sorry. If you'd rather not say—"

Daisy let loose a snort. She panned a hand around the dingy cafe space, saying, "I think this speaks for itself. Once the fun pier opened up its own breakfast options, offering discounts with ride purchases and points for season ticket holders, my numbers never recovered. Every year I manage to stay open is a surprise."

Candace gasped.

"That's criminal! The food on the fun pier is gross, processed, over-portioned crap bursting with grease and high fructose corn syrup. Your bagel bombs are better by miles!"

"Hm? I don't remember you ever buying my bombs."

Again, Candace's face shifted to that adorable 'you've caught me' look. She fished for an excuse and mumbled something about friends ordering. "I enjoyed them in passing, once or twice. But it's been a long time."

Biting her tongue was the only way Daisy did not break out into a full grin. She always knew that Candace Perry was a secret customer. The confirmation was beyond satisfaction, closer to catharsis.

With a forced air of cool, Daisy crossed her arms. "You're damn right. My bagels are fucking delicious, so I'm not giving up without a fight. Where else could someone get their fix of pimento, creme brulee, Nashville hot chicken, or—"

"Or peanut butter and jelly?"

Candace pointed to the neat placard inside the refrigerated display as she spoke. Her face was impassive, like she was asking about the weather. Even so, there was something in her eyes, a glimmer, that spoke of summers' past. There was something else, too; unmistakable against her bright clothes, a crimson flush flooded her winter-washed skin.

Was she *flirting* with Daisy? Over *bagels*?

*Impossible.*

Did Candace even admit that she was attracted to women these days? For her part, Daisy had no intention of flirting with the woman before her. Regardless of how nice (or attractive) Candace was at present, she hurt Daisy. Maybe that was why Daisy wanted to tease her now. She braced herself against the countertop and arched over Candace's seat so the woman would be forced to meet her eye.

"Yeah," she answered in a low rumble. "I've got that. Want a sample?"

Candace squirmed under Daisy's shadow. She swallowed hard, and her mouth bobbed with an inaudible response.

"What was that? Couldn't hear you."

The flush crept further up Candace's neck, all the way to her ears.

"I—"

*RIIIING*

"I—"

*RING RIIIIIING*

Eyebrow cocked, Daisy asked, "You gonna get that?"

"Oh, um..." Fumbling, Candace withdrew her blaring phone from the expensive clutch looped over one shoulder. Disappointment mixed with dread morphed her features once she read the caller ID. Finally, resignation.

Daisy guessed, "Uncle Moneybags?"

Tight-lipped, Candace nodded. "I need to take this. Can I... I mean, would it be alright, if—"

"Here." Daisy tossed Candace a baggie with one peanut butter and jelly bagel bomb. "You'll have to eat it cold. Let me know if it's as good as you remember."

"... I will."

For one last lingering moment, Candace kept her eyes trained on Daisy. Then, with a vicious thumb-swipe, she answered her phone and spun on her heel. As she power-walked away, her voice, which raised to an impossibly sweet tilt, carried with her.

*"Uncle Per-per! Thank you for—. Yes, I understand. Of course. Be there soon."*

Daisy watched until the woman was swallowed up by the bustling throng. Candace Perry, who looked like a picture-perfect businesswoman but was, in fact, jobless and down on her luck. She probably deserved it, Daisy thought. She'd done something or pissed off someone, and that was why the woman was forced to this "awful" place.

Still, it was a difficult position to be stuck in. Wonderwood was a paradise for most people, but for Candace, it was a punishment. While everyone else was having the time of their lives, she couldn't wait to leave.

Daisy understood the feeling.

# CHAPTER 3

## *Candace*

"*C*andy," Uncle Perry started right in, cutting off her greeting. "*Meet me at Ferdinand's in a half hour and we'll catch up. Don't forget to change out of that PTA Karen outfit. Give the boys something nice to look at.*"

Phone conversations with Peter Perry were one-sided, frustrating exercises in steamrolling. With Candace, calls always followed the same script: a curt confirmation he was speaking to whom he wanted, what he wanted, and when he wanted it.

End call. No hello, no goodbye.

The man treated his family like business and business like family. It was his right to conduct his relationships as he saw fit. Even so, it rankled Candace to be nothing more than a pretty prop to parade around his friends. She cringed at the knowledge that he was judging her outfit through the pier security cameras, yet she expected nothing less. He was a control freak through and through.

To change into the "something nice" her uncle demanded but still meet him on time, Candace needed to book it back to her motel room at the Comfort Clam Inn. It was off-island in Cape Crest, a small town on the mainland bay where vacationers who were looking to save on accommodations flocked. Not that it was cheap by any stretch, but it was less expensive than the mini mansion rentals or hotels built up along the boardwalk.

Most importantly, it was what Candace could afford. It was also a fifteen-minute drive across the bridge and another ten from there to the marina—far too tight for comfort, which her uncle no doubt knew. She bowled through boardwalkers towards her car like she was aiming for a high score.

It was a beach day miracle. Candace was not blocked from getting out of the overpriced car lot by families unloading their horde of hyper children, nor did she hit a single sun-sapped pedestrian as she worked her way through town to the traffic-free bridge. Choosing an outfit that her uncle would approve of turned out to be the most difficult part.

When the dire reality of her jobless and unhirable position set in, Candace sold what she could to cushion her finances. The majority of her designer clothes, expensive yoga gear, and other non-sentimentals were fair game when it came to keeping up the buffer between herself and groveling to her uncle.

Ultimately, though, it was moot. Candace was still standing in her stuffy motel room that was either blazing hot or bone-chillingly cold (nothing in between), sorting through an old Lululemon tote bag stuffed with what was left of her wardrobe.

Candace knew what her uncle was looking for: that careful mix of sexy but not *too* sexy. Enough for Peter Perry to show off that his niece was "fuckable," yet too pure to touch. Something that wouldn't "embarrass" him. In the end, she settled on a stylish sundress.

It was a classic look and fit, quarter-sleeved, falling a little below her knee and cinched around her waist with a thick, bow-tied belt. The base dress was navy, and it had an outer, modest layering dotted with white polka dots in a breezy chiffon-like material. She completed the aesthetic by lacing her hair into a loose French braid that fell over one shoulder; cute, but practical. Candace gave herself one last survey in the mirror while the bathroom vent sputtered death rattles overhead.

She could do this. All she had to do was dress nicely, smile, and pretend a cadre of rude, morally dubious humans were likable. If she could do that, she could get on her uncle's good side. Then maybe, *just maybe*, secure some gainful employment out of him rather than relying on occasional handouts.

Candace knew that his in-house accountant, Mr. Leary, had recently passed away. He would never trust her to take over the books, not in a million years. But maybe, at least for the appearance of giving her something to do, he would let her take over while he looked for someone permanent.

And if she could prove she could do the job...

Again, Candace shuddered. The idea of working with her uncle full-time, moving back to Wonderwood, filled her with dread. However, handling an account as mountainous as the pier, even for a little while, might buy her back the credit she needed to work elsewhere.

It had to.

The wanna-be macho man valet at the marina parking lot was less than pleased having to take Candace's car. It was a limited-edition sunflower gold (with a little *actual* gold) convertible BMW, and the one expensive possession she had not been able to part with since it had been a present to herself after years of careful planning.

Candace loved her car. It was gaudy and ridiculous, unapologetically existing in a world that had gone dark and gloomy. Without it, she would have nothing to show for her hard work.

Plus, the speedy gal got her to the marina right on time.

If Candace weren't terrified of tripping her heels through the gaps in the plank deck, she would have sprinted. As it was, she did a sort of hopping dance in her mad dash to reach Ferdinand's beyond dozens of busy boat slips.

Thankfully, she spotted her uncle right away. He was seated on the popular brunch spot's sunny oceanside veranda. There, surrounded by his friends at an umbrellaed circular table laden with neat bourbons and artful canapes, he looked like a king holding court. Candace's mouth watered at the sight of crispy gnocchi-olive-chorizo skewers, tartlets filled with savory bacon and tangy cranberry cheddar cheese, and some kind of creamy, dill-dusted smoked salmon pate surrounded by an array of fancy crackers.

The local celebrities who were her uncle's friends picked at the gourmet selection. They were businessmen, politicians, and law enforcement, all useful relationships built on parasitic symbiosis. She heard they even managed to start their own 'non-partisan' political party, "Wonderwood Works," and get a mayor elected. Life was a game to this group, and in the small oceanside hamlet, they were cleaning house.

Candace had known most of her uncle's regular associates since she was a teenager, meeting them at various galas and public events she attended at his insistence. Growing up, none of them paid attention to her until she was old enough to leer at. Now, they did not even try to be discreet.

"Candy!" Tim Burgson, who had hopped from a position on the town council to big-wig county executive despite several sexual harrassment suits from his secretaries, greeted, "I'll be damned! Here, have a seat."

Without waiting for a reply, the man rose and offered Candace his wicker chair—mostly, she thought, so that he could have the excuse to hover and look down her dress. He continued. "We didn't believe Pete when he said you were coming. A pretty woman like you has better things to do than spend your time with a bunch of old men."

A candid, "I do," slipped out before Candace could stop herself. Without missing a beat, she added, "But it wouldn't be half as fun! Nice to see you, Uncle Tim. And everyone else, too. It's been ages."

One by one, Candace said her hellos to the table. She wanted to remind them both that she was not some airhead, and that she knew who to file charges against if they decided to get fresh. Uncle Perry tipped his bourbon at her.

"Welcome home, Candy. I knew you wouldn't be able to resist Wonderwood for too long."

Candace worked her grimace into a toothy smile. "Spot on, as always. Happy to be home."

From there, Candace hoped to fade into the background. She would laugh at the occasional off-color joke, throw out some pleasantries, and bide her time. When they were alone, after she took whatever mocking she had due for the loan, she would ask her uncle about a job. Beg him. She would frame it as her getting into the family business, something wholesome he could play up with his friends and fans. His ego was huge, so there was a chance he would go along.

Unfortunately, the group's attention stayed stuck on Candace.

"You were up in New York City, weren't you?" Ed Cando, the former police chief, probed, "Are you visiting for the summer, or is *Real Housewives: Wonderwood* getting a new cast member?"

"Oh, the housewives and I are getting our nails done tomorrow," Candace said, flipping the misogynistic joke. "They've got to catch me up on all the gossip with you boys. But they couldn't afford my full-time fee. I'm a guest star."

"Is that so? Too bad. See, we heard you might be making a more permanent move. I was going to set you up with my boy. He could use a good woman like you."

Even with the sun landing right on her, it took Candace considerable effort to contain her shiver. She popped a ham and cheddar croquette into her mouth to give herself time to think of a reply.

Although they had not gone to school together, the 'boy' had been a part of her extended friend group during her time spent on the island. It was difficult to imagine he had matured much from the obnoxious beach bro he was back then. Ted Cando would never be the one for her. She wouldn't be interested in him even if she were interested in men, and there were *no* ifs when it came to that—she'd tried.

Across the table, Uncle Perry eyed Candace with something that was a cross between disdain and amusement. He'd known she was a lesbian from reading her journals and monitoring her internet search history when she was forced to share a roof with him. He knew, and his biggest concern was that she did not embarrass him by confirming it to mutual acquaintances. Now, because he had no desire to broach the topic of his niece's sexuality with his conservative-leaning cohort, he came to her rescue.

"Your boy needs a saint to fix him, Ed. Don't put that on my poor Candy." The group chortled heartily at the insult. Even Ed, despite the tensing of his expression.

Candace took extra long chewing the appetizer that barely needed any. She added, "I'm flattered, really. But with everything I have going on, dating is the last thing on my mind."

"Oh?" Ed asked with the sharp eyes of a former investigator, "What keeps a girl like you busy if it's not dating or sun bathing with the girls?"

Candace forced herself to take a breath instead of letting out her snapping retort.

*Because of course those are the only things 'a girl like me' would be interested in. Ass.*

As she took a second breath, her silence gave Uncle Perry room to torment her.

"See," he added with a devilish grin, "the working-world has been a culture shock for my girl. I tried to warn her that she's better at spending money than keeping track of it for others, but she's stubborn."

The local rotary president, Sal Rocco, ribbed, "That's the pot calling the kettle!"

Uncle Perry waved him off.

"For me, it's focus. Drive. When I dig my heels in, it's because I know I'm going to win. My girl Candy just doesn't like being told no."

Candace fidgeted in her chair as the group laughed.

"I was—*I am*— good at my job."

Uncle Perry asked, "If you're so good, why were they so quick to let you go?"

"I… I don't know."

To his friends, he jeered, "That's familiar. The half-brain teens I fire for lighting up in the ride booths say the same thing."

"That's unfair. I worked hard to get where I was, and I never stopped. It's possible I made a mistake, but it was not something my superiors were willing to discuss at my exit interview. If you listened to me, you'd know that."

The edge in Candace's voice surprised even her. Discomforted glances were shared around the table. The conversation had turned too personal, too real, even though these people were the ones who had been prying.

Almost imperceptibly, Uncle Perry turned the class ring on his finger.

That ring was the only jewelry he wore, unless one counted

his watch collection. When Candace was a child, he used to turn that gaudy hunk of metal whenever she set off his temper. Uncle Perry never raised a finger against her, but the threat worked well enough. Even now, she had to hold back from flinching.

In a gross, patronizing tone, Uncle Perry soothed, "Candy, baby. I'm on your side. I only want you to be realistic about what you can do."

"Then let me prove it to you." The words left Candace's mouth, and she could not take them back. Steeling herself, she barreled forward. "I heard about Mr. Leary. You need someone you can trust to take over the pier's books."

"... You... want *me* to hire *you*?"

"Give me a chance to help with the family business. If you find someone else, go with them. But, I promise you, I can do this."

Candace felt her uncle's laughter before she heard it. Years of derision, insults laced with levity, made her keen to his moods. As the rest of the table echoed his amusement, she shrank. She tried to defend herself, but her voice came out small and wavering.

"I'm as qualified as any other candidate. I know the pier inside and out. If you just—"

With a handwave, Uncle Perry cut Candace off. He flagged down their server. Gesturing to Candace, he asked the young, nervous teen, "Has this woman paid her bill?"

"Uh... I haven't closed out your table yet."

"But will she? A big girl pays her own way, right?"

"Uncle, please..."

Candace wanted to disappear. He loved making her look small so that he could look big. "No. I've got this, and whatever else you need. All you've got to do is ask, Candy. And you know how I'm able to do that?"

Uncle Perry waited painfully long while his cronies snickered amongst themselves. Candace squirmed, which was exactly what he wanted.

Defeated, she gave in. "I don't know, uncle. How *do* you do it?"

"I stay in business, whatever it takes. I make deals and moves. In fact, I've started preparations for a massive expansion. Gift shops, new rides, a resort-quality hotel with a multi-level parking garage... Millions of dollars in contracts, meetings with multiple banks and investment firms, miles worth of financial documents... Which means I'm going to find the right man for the job. Or, hell, I'd even take a woman. If a pierced, tatted up dyke can handle the pressure, they're in. Unlike you. See? You can't even be told no without tearing up."

Candace wanted to leave. She wanted to so badly, but she knew it would only make things worse. As long as his money was lining her account, she had no choice but to take whatever he spewed.

Her voice was foreign to her ears as she agreed with her uncle. "You're right. Yuck. That's way too much responsibility for me. Congratulations on the expansion."

From there, the conversation went on without Candace. She became the pretty background feature her uncle wished her to be. After ordering herself a mojito from the still-hovering server, she at least had that to focus on. While she sipped at a drink she was sure had been upgraded to a double, the others offered their well-wishes for her uncle's upcoming business venture.

"So, it's all coming together, then? You secured the funding and you got your permits sorted? If not, I know a gal in the planning office who might be able to move some paperwork along."

The person who spoke, Rhonda Moss, was the only other woman present. In her early fifties, she'd spent her most early career clinging to a middle management county government role in Wonderwood's planning office. She cozied up to her uncle's ilk and, like magic, she ended up managing the whole department.

If Candace's spirit weren't in tatters at her feet, she would have laughed at the small town Deep State they had going on. Instead, she took a long, loud sip from her mojito. Idly, she wondered where her uncle was planning this grand expansion. The pier was already overdeveloped, so he'd have to build a whole new one. Or, take over half the boardwalk, but both of those options would be crazy. Her ears tuned back into the conversation as a name caught her attention.

"—few holdouts," Uncle Perry told them with annoyance. He turned the ring on his finger while he spoke. "Pests, that's all."

"Can't just throw on the ol' Perry Pocket Change charm and convince them to sell? How much could it cost to buy a couple of tee-shirt shops out?"

"Those were the first ones to fold. It's the family business that's giving me trouble." He said the term 'family business' with a sneer that turned gleeful. "No matter what, I'll get my way soon enough. They're out at the end of the season. No way that bagel bitch can match the terms I've set in her lease."

At that, Candace could not stop herself from letting loose a dull-sounding, "What?"

That same sneer stayed on her uncle's face as he answered her with the patience of an adult speaking to a child.

"A lease is something that says a poor person owes someone like me money. I have a very well-worded stipulation in my leases stating that if my tenant's business doesn't make a gross profit of a certain amount by the end of the boardwalk season, I am free to terminate our agreement. It's going to be a blowout summer for her, just not the kind she'll enjoy."

Candace gaped.

"How... How is that legal?"

By the table's uproarious laughter, you'd think Candace told a spectacular joke. Uncle Perry's lawyer, Vinny Lamarka, was the loudest of everyone. But, the humor never reached his eyes. Still grinning, he answered, "This is a bit technical, but it's a breach of confidence clause. The courts can't expect your uncle, a businessman, to rent to a failing business. It's just, well, bad business. Right?"

"I..."

Candace's head felt muddled and not from her drink. Uncle Perry was going to force Bagel Bombs! to close so that he could have room for another gift shop, parking lot, or some flash in the pan oddity. Spite was also a likely possibility. He hadn't liked Daisy DeMarco since that first time they met. He never made it a secret how he felt about her business being a stone's throw away from his lofty empire.

So, he would force Daisy to close.

It wasn't right. It probably wasn't legal. Yet, Peter Perry would get away with it because his type always did.

Vinny's attention was fixed on Candace. His expression regarded her like the others, as if she were the token ditzy blonde. His gaze, though, was sharper—daring her to question the legality a second time.

The man was dressed in a plaid button down and tan dockers, plain and casual, as if he bought the outfit off a department store mannequin. You would have trouble picking him out of a lineup of the other mid-fifties, late Gen X men currently dining on the veranda. Unassuming, he had an easy smile and was always eager to talk about his big family's Sunday pasta dinners.

Candace had known him longer than anyone else at this table and knew very well to tread lightly. He was Uncle Perry's lawyer, but he was also his fixer. Through methods legal or otherwise, troublesome business associates and the people who stood in Peter Perry's way had a habit of kowtowing after a visit from Mr. Lamarka. If she ever really stepped out of line, she knew he would fix *her*.

The white hot, angry fire inside Candace shrank to a simmer. She took on an airy tilt, saying, "I understand I'm in over my head with all this boring talk."

"Good girl," her uncle dipped his aviators and winked. "Like I said, this is all too complicated for you. Don't worry. Let me handle the business side of the family, and the good times will keep going."

*Good times.*

The phrase echoed inside Candace's head, mocking her.

If Candace worked for her uncle or continued to take his money, she was a part of it. HIS, at the mercy of a reprehensible man's morality. Whatever he did with his liability nightmare, money-gouging behemoth—destroying more pieces of Wonderwood history and bullying his way into success—would fall back on her.

Is that what Candace wanted? The grand revelation of a question echoed on repeat inside her head.

"Why don't you put her on a billboard?" Ed Cando suggested. "A mascot like her would draw in all the boys."

Mock aghast, Perry told him, "I run a family establishment! We don't need sex to sell tickets. Although…"

More jokes and ribbing went around the table. Ideas of how the fun pier could age up its attractions, from plausible to cringe-worthy pitches worthy of an early 2000's exploitation reality show, were met with raucous enthusiasm.

All the while, Candace nursed what might be her last drink in a long while. She thought of it as such because she'd come to a conclusion. Tuning out the piggish banter, Candace waited for the brunch's conclusion. At her car, she made a show of thanking her uncle for his generosity. She buttered him up, became the besotted, blithering idiot he wanted her to be. Then, she retrieved her convertible from the grimacing lot attendant, and floored it back to her motel room.

Candace did not have a moment to lose. She had research to do.

If Peter Perry wanted to make it his business to break down another person, Candace would make it her business to build them up.

# CHAPTER 4

*Daisy*

"Zee? Hey, Earth to Zee!"

Rio, Daisy's reliable part-time employee (reliable in the sense that they would occasionally arrive on time for their shifts), tried to get her attention. It was a futile effort.

Daisy had been distracted all morning, and it had nothing to do with a certain blast from the past that had come barging up to her counter the day before.

*Nothing at all.*

But, in her musings, Daisy did wonder how Candace's meeting with her uncle had gone. Did she cozy up to the man and get what she wanted? Would she really come back and tell Daisy how those bagel bombs were? Why was she still *so damn hot?*

Daisy's mind wandered on that twisting track as she cleaned for shift change. It was not until a bagel, thrown with expert precision, hit her square on her forehead that she realized she was being spoken to.

"Er, yeah." Daisy guessed, "You can have Tuesday off."

"That was two conversations ago. And you're damn right I can have off. Without me, you'd be screwed. Which is why I was offering to post online about a job. You need to hire someone to pick up the slack around here."

"Dotty is—"

"Dotty is a gem of an old, but she sleeps through half her shifts. We need some life around here."

For emphasis, Rio set down the box they were stocking the display freezer with, and crossed their arms. The move was far from intimidating coming from a person who looked like Frodo Baggins' cousin, just as short, complete with canvas overalls and a mop of adorable raven, springy curls. The wide, rainbow-rope secured shimmer-frame glasses added a bit of Elton John to the mix, and their array of graphic tees gave a dash of nerd. Today, they wore a print of something called *Avatar: The Legend of Korra*.

Rio was unabashedly themself, and always spoke their mind. Usually, Daisy listened. But this wasn't going to be one of those times.

"Look, I hear you," Daisy told them. She continued packing, aware that if she got caught up in the dinner-time pop, she would get home late tonight.

If she got home late, she wouldn't have time to catch up on the dough she needed to make. If she didn't make the dough, she wouldn't be able to make more bombs. And if she ran out of bombs...

Daisy scrubbed harder at the mystery gunk that had melted onto the display window. She did not look at Rio as she continued talking.

"I know it's been busy. But busy is good, it means we stay in business. You have a lot going on with your degree and your internship at the Wetlands Institute, so just let me know when you need off. I'll cover it, no questions."

"What about you, Zee?"

Daisy flinched. The nickname Rio used, which was actually what everyone called her now, sounded odd after hearing Candace use her given name.

They pressed, "When was the last time you took a real day off? Where you didn't do bagel prep or bookkeeping?"

A peek at Rio showed that their mouth had drawn into a narrow line, making them look like a disapproving librarian. Daisy looked away again, frowning as well. For an employee and boss, their relationship was too murky.

Rio had started working at the bagel cafe right before the start of their freshman year of college at a nearby university known for environmental studies. The two bonded over their love of local ecology and marine life, plus some general shared taste in books, movies, and games. Daisy did not leave herself much time for hobbies, so most of what she knew about popular culture came from the far more socially in-tune Rio. Oftentimes, they forced Daisy into fun activities. Apart from Norman, they were the only other person Daisy might call a 'friend.'

But they were in different life stages.

Currently, Rio was enrolled in a master's program that involved an internship with the local Wetlands Institute's technology department. They were a whiz with computers and had a passion for nature, so they combined the two. After that was through, though? The world was open to wherever they wanted to take their hard-honed skills, while Daisy was stuck here. She would be lying if she said it did not sting. Still, she was excited for Rio, which was why she would not let her friend-ployee worry about some dead-end summer job.

Putting on an air of bravado, Daisy waved Rio off.

"I had the whole winter to hibernate. I'm all good."

It was a lie. Even during winter, while the pier and most other places on the boardwalk shuttered for the season, she kept the cafe open. That period was arguably more difficult since she handled the shifts, minus Dotty's handful, herself.

She had to keep the cash flow coming if she was going to make rent. Even if she could find someone willing to take over some bagely burden, she could never afford them. She'd have better luck training Horace the Horseshoe Crab as her newest employee.

But those weren't concerns she could share with Rio.

"Really. Don't worry about me."

Rio might have argued more. Thankfully, a few customers approached the counter and put a pin in the conversation. From there, inventory tally overtook Daisy's attention.

*Everything flavor was popular today,* she mentally noted. Followed closely by cinnamon crunch and spinach/feta. The last one was a rotating flavor Daisy only occasionally made, but it sold out within days the last few times she made a batch. If she let people know ahead of time when the flavor was available, maybe it could drum up some much-needed interest.

Daisy tapped her pen against her tally notebook as she racked her brain. They sold a decent number of bombs during the morning shift, but not nearly enough. They needed to do better. *She* needed to do better, but that would involve business planning and online posting and all sorts of things she was *not* great at. With most schools still in session, Wonderwood's prime season was just a few precious weeks away. Her time to enact any daring, brilliant business strategies was running low.

What could Daisy do to turn things around? Nothing she could think of seemed anywhere near drastic enough. She lost herself in thought, terrified and, deep down under a sticky layer of guilt, thrilled at what failure would mean for her.

Cutting through Daisy's mental spiraling, a familiar, valley-girl voice reached her ears.

"Is Daisy here?"

"'Daisy?'" Rio asked with confusion, "You mean Zee? She's—"

"Here!"

Too fast, Daisy shot up from where she'd been crouched. Once again, her ex-crush was standing before her looking like she'd stepped off a runway. Daisy cleared her throat and forced an air of nonchalance.

"'Sup, Perry. Back already?"

"Yes," Candace exhaled the word, seemingly breathless. Or, rather, she appeared preoccupied as she looked around the cafe with narrowed eyes, muttering to herself. "I've seen worse. Paint, a new sign, functional seating, social media campaigns... It would be difficult, but possible."

Perplexed, Daisy shared a look with Rio. She felt a jolt as the woman's attention fell on her once more.

Serious-faced, Candace asked, "What's your overhead like? Employee costs? Rent?"

Daisy started to answer the questions until her brain caught up with what she was doing. "Wait, why am I telling you any of this? You wanna finish me off by reporting me to the IRS or something? I might not have some fancy degree, but I know how to file my taxes."

"It's nothing like that! I want to help!"

Daisy cocked an eyebrow.

"'Help?'"

"Yes," Candace repeated. "Can we speak in private?"

The woman's cheeks began to flush, and she cast a nervous backward glance at the long line forming behind her. Of course, it was simple psychology; passersby noticed a bombshell like Candace ordering from the cafe, and were drawn like moths to a flame.

Rio caught Daisy's eye.

"I got the register. You hear out Princess Peach."

Daisy snorted at the nickname. Rio was a gamer, specifically a Nintendo stan, and they'd made endless jokes about Daisy being Mushroom Kingdom's chapstick lesbian princess. Thank the stars Daisy went by "Zee" in her day-to-day life, so the nerd eventually ran out of steam. Or, Daisy thought they had.

If Candace caught the nickname, she did not mention it. She clutched a three-ring binder to her chest with both hands like it was the one thing that grounded her there.

*What's she so hopped up about?*

Candace's entire presence was different from the weepy, depressed woman Daisy met the day before. Wired was the best word to describe her. Intense. No, Daisy was sure she'd missed Rio's joke because her attention was fixed on whatever she had to say. Her aura was like an accelerant that kicked Daisy's pulse up to match.

But she tried not to show it.

Flatly, Daisy told her, "Alright. You've got until I get bored." She lifted the counter divider between them and motioned inside the stall. "C'mon. It's too hot out here, we'll talk in the office."

Wedged between the gigantic chest freezer that housed their back inventory, the back exit, and the washroom, the 'office' was a glorified closet. A window overlooked the employee lot, and an overstuffed desk was jammed up underneath it. There was a single fold-out chair that had long since abandoned any pretense of being padded. Since there was not enough room for two full-grown adults to stand comfortably in the space, Daisy plopped her butt on the desk. Papers, years-old tax documents and receipts, crinkled under her rump.

Candace, meanwhile, perched herself atop the chair as if it were covered in needles. The binder was still clutched to her chest. She took in the office, and Daisy, with assessing eyes.

The temperature was, of course, worse in the stifling space. Sweat started to bead at Daisy's temple, captured by the bandana she wore. The heat building inside her was not helped as she looked down at the too-close woman. She noticed that Candace was wearing a dress today. It was pink, Princess Peach Pink to be exact, and although it was still a tame, short-sleeved cut, it was far more revealing than her romper.

The woman had to work out. Daisy's gaze traveled the sharp line of Candace's neck, down to taut traps and defined collar bones. Micro-movements that tensed her muscles promised more beneath the distinctly feminine exterior. More muscle, more sleek curves contrasted by strong angles, more—

Daisy grimaced. She ripped off her bandana and mopped her brow.

"My bagels were so good you just had to come back, hm? Or is there something *else* you're after?"

Confusion flashed over Candace's features as the words registered. It was hard to tell if the implication made the woman flush because she had not stopped. Her fair skin was close to the same shade as her dress, and her chest thrummed with quick breaths.

Finally, she replied with a simple, "Yes."

"Yes, and...?" Daisy pressed, and could not keep the suggestion from her tone. "I swear, Perry... I haven't seen you since *that* night, and now you come barging back into my life like you own the place. Really, what gives?"

"I..."

Now, Candace *definitely* flushed redder. Daisy was starting to feel herself flush too, but not with embarrassment. Bitter resentment soured every thought.

Just like all those years ago, Candace Perry waltzed into Daisy's life and demanded attention. She would coo and fawn, and be so *damn* lovable. Then she would leave, like every other customer and person, abandoning her to endless, lonely drifting. So, this time, Daisy would beat her to the punch.

Arms crossed, Daisy propped one flip-flopped foot on the edge of Candace's seat, close to the woman's thigh.

"Yeah," she continued. "Then and now, you're too chicken to say what you want, but too hooked to stay away."

"You're right. I was afraid, but I'm not anymore."

"Uh-huh. I'd congratulate you, but growing a spine at thirty-three is a little pathetic."

Hurt cracked Candace's expression, so profound Daisy thought the woman would start weeping again. She did not. Instead, she rose to the challenge in Daisy's voice—literally. On her feet, which practically brought them crashing into one another, she thrust the binder forward.

"W-what's this?" Daisy had to try hard to keep the waver from her voice as Candace's sweet lilac scent, tinged by a hint of heady sweat, washed over her. She took the binder if only to have a barrier between them.

"It's how we're going to turn things around at Bagel Bombs!, and beat my uncle."

"Your uncle? He's a shit landlord, but I manage fine."

It was an obvious lie that Candace easily spotted. The woman reached around Daisy to leaf through the near-toppling stack of bills and blank employee pay slips.

"Is that so...?"

"Okay!"

Daisy growled, throwing herself as far away from Candace as she could get. Which was not much, considering there was a window behind her. Her back landed against the dusty glass with a smack. Candace seemed to take the hint and pulled back.

"Fine," Daisy conceded. "Maybe things have been tough the last few years. Or more. But what makes you think I want your help? Why should I trust you?"

"Because you're right. I love your bagel bombs. Ever since that first one I had, the peanut butter one you were so nice to give me, I got them every time I could. But I was a coward, and I never told you. I let my fear of my uncle keep me from something I liked... But I'll be damned if I let him take it from me now."

Daisy blinked.

"I give up. You've lost me, Perry."

Were they even talking about bagels anymore? Memory of a starlit beach... the cool, smooth sand that spilled over her feet contrasting with the wet, warm tongue exploring her own... Trembling hands that slipped under her tank top to touch—

Daisy swallowed hard. She watched that once-familiar tongue give an anxious swipe across Candace's lips.

"He's going to take it."

Daisy exhaled a shaky breath, saying, "Just get to your

point."

"My uncle is going to use a clause in your lease agreement that gives him the ability to toss you out at the end of the season. If he has his way, Bagel Bombs! will be a fun pier car lot by this time next year."

Daisy did not respond. Could not, as shocked numbness spread throughout her whole body. At least it doused the discomforting tingle that had flared up alongside memories better left dead and buried. The logical part of her brain, the one that looked at dwindling bank accounts and unpaid invoice piles, had known things were dire. Perry had made vague and not so vague comments that indicated he wanted her gone. But, with her lease locked for the next three years, she thought she had time. If she kept her head down, kept working, she could hold on until... She was not sure what she was even holding out for, but this was not how she expected things to go. In her silence, Candace continued.

"He and his friends think they own this town. Anyone with less money, or who isn't a part of their little club, is fair game to fuck over. It's never going to be enough, either. They won't stop until this whole town is ruined. I don't want that to happen."

"Oh? Is this how you're going to save Bagel Bombs!?" Too aggressively, Daisy flipped open the binder. "You think you know a single thing about running a business? I've been doing this my whole life, I was born into it. There's no way you—"

Daisy trailed off. She had not intended on looking. However, she could not help it. There was real, genuine effort put into Candace's proposal. Cost projections based on comparable businesses, government tax rebates they might apply for, renovation mock-ups, and so much more. There were even cute, breakfast-themed stickers for color-coding. It was, damn herself for even thinking the word, impressive.

*How the hell did she put this together so quickly?*

As if she knew what Daisy was thinking, Candace explained, "This is my job. Er... was my job. I was technically an accountant, but my role was more specialized. I plan, and I'm damn good at it. At my firm, I learned everything I could about our clients' businesses so they could stay in business. I saw what made them fail and what made them succeed. If you let me help you, Bagel Bombs! will have a fighting chance. Trust me."

"Why should I?" The words came out quieter than Daisy meant to say. Weaker and betraying the fear she very much felt. "Last time you promised me something, you ended up leaving me high and dry."

*Literally.*

Candace spun on her heel, and Daisy was sure she would run away just like last time. She did not. Instead, she retrieved her phone from her handbag and pulled up her banking app.

"Look," she offered. "I'm broke. I need this to work as badly as you do."

"So... What? I would be your boss?"

Frankly, Candace said, "No. Partners, if you're comfortable with that. You would still own the business and make final decision on everything. But, on paper, I would be your partner and financial advisor."

"I can barely pay you minimum wage."

"And I can make that work. The one benefit of staying at the illustrious Comfort Clam Inn is the locked-in room rate."

Daisy's nose wrinkled. She was no posh posy, but everyone knew that motel was on the sprouted side of seedy.

"You're staying in that dump? Doesn't strike me like your kind of scene."

Candace shrugged. "It's not. But, like I said, I can make it work. Once the season is over, we can renegotiate based on how much profit I helped to generate."

"You sound awfully confident there'll be a profit."

"I'm confident in your bagel bombs. I did my research. Even without an online presence, people post about coming to this boardwalk *specifically* for Bagel Bombs!. They say it's the best, and they're right. So let me help you prove it. All we have to do is put this place out there more, and people will come."

*Will they?*

Daisy was not sure which she was more afraid of: that people would come, or that they would stay away. Both made her feel queasy.

"This is nuts. Maybe you have business experience pushing papers, but have you ever worked a job like this? Because if I'm paying you, you're going to be behind the counter pulling your weight."

Candace rolled her eyes. Still, Daisy could see a tightening in the woman's posture.

"If a bored preteen can keep this place running, I'm sure I'll be fine."

"I'm not teaching you how to mop."

At that, Candace gave a mock huff. "I know how to use a mop. And how to balance a register. The cafe I worked at through undergrad would've fired me real fast if I didn't." Smiling, she added, "I'm not all that helpless."

"No. Maybe not."

Thick, swelling heat radiated around them. Still, both women faced each other coolly. Despite the impending news of doom, Daisy felt a surge of excitement—of something new.

Daisy asked, "Can I sleep on it?"

A flash of disappointment fell over Candace's face. It was gone just as quickly, back to business.

"Of course. This is a big decision, I wouldn't want to rush you. I included a standard partner contract in the binder, along with my contact information. If you have any questions or concerns, I'd be happy to discuss things more."

"I'll read it."

Daisy was surprised that she was being honest. She would look through this grand business proposal of Candace Perry's. Maybe, *just* maybe, she would consider it. If this was going to be her last summer running Bagel Bombs!, she might as well go out with a bang.

Plus, a signed, legal document that gave Daisy permission to boss around her former crush was dangerously appealing.

Mental image of Candace on all fours scraping tile scum made Daisy feel smug... among other things.

"Well," Candace exhaled. "I'll be waiting."

Candace turned to leave.

On impulse, Daisy reached past the woman and held the door closed. They both froze, looking at one another with bated breath.

"My bagels," Daisy whispered. She scrubbed her short, bandana-dented locks, suddenly self-conscious. "You really think they're good?"

Candace's lips parted, then curved into the gentlest, most sincere smile.

"I don't think that, I know it. And I want everyone else to know it, too. I won't let my uncle run you out of business without a fight."

Candace departed for real, then, leaving Daisy stupefied. She should not, and did not want to care. A gnawing, distrustful voice inside told her not to believe a word Candace said. And yet, she did. Far more than she was capable of admitting. The woman's compliments burned in her ears. It was not until Rio poked their head into the room minutes later that Daisy snapped out of her thoughts.

"So? What was that about? Is Princess Peach my new mom?"

Daisy opened her mouth to make a witty retort. She knew, though, that if she seemed defensive, it would only add fuel to their insufferable fire. And, if they ever suspected that Daisy had a past with Candace...

Shaking her head, Daisy gave Rio a noncommittal grunt. She offered the binder, warning, "She's trouble."

"Hm," they mused, flipping through Candace's proposal with an expression that showed escalating interest. "There's bad trouble and good trouble. Both can be fun, and, girl, you *need* fun."

Daisy wanted to argue, but again, she closed her trap.

"Yeah," she answered after a beat. "We'll see."

The tide brought Candace Perry back into Daisy's life. Now,

it was her choice whether or not to toss the woman back in. Regardless of what she did with Candace, Daisy needed to read through her lease with Peter Perry, like, *yesterday*.

It was barely the beginning of the summer season, and it was already shaping up to be a blast. Daisy just needed to figure out which kind it would be.

# CHAPTER 5

## *Candace*

T he steady, whirring hum from the Comfort Clam's decades-old air conditioner unit droned on through the night. It might have kept Candace up if she were not already wide awake, staring at the popcorn ceiling. After the humiliating meeting with her uncle and his cronies, Candace spent all the rest of that day and night working on her proposal to save Bagel Bombs!.

It was not just to spite her uncle. The more she researched and found online about enthusiasm for the Wonderwood institution, the more she truly believed in Bagel Bombs!'s marketability. Franchising, food trucks, frozen supermarket meals… if they played their cards right, the potential was limitless.

That is, Candace knew, if Bagel Bombs'! owner wanted them to be a 'they.'

Daisy DeMarco did not trust Candace. She had every reason not to. If she took Candace's proposal and used it herself, she'd be justified. Even so, Candace wanted to help. Needed to, really, but that was aside from the point. Whether or not Daisy trusted Candace, she hoped the woman could see that she was willing to give it her all.

This time, she would not run away.

For a while, Candace texted back and forth with Demi. Even before yoga teaching came into her best friend's life, she had always been a calm, exceptionally kind person. Demi was balanced, which often led to her giving great advice. Candace explained her plan, much to the woman's surprise.

*Demi: WOW*
*Bagel Bombs??*
*Like, Daisy DeMarco-you've-had-a-massive-crush-on her-forever-BB???*

*Candace: I do NOT. We hooked up once and never talked again.*
*Anyway, I don't think she remembers that part*

*Demi: Yeah.*
*Sure she doesn't lol*
*Did YOU forget?*
*Anyway, what about your uncle?*
*I thought you were getting ready to sell your soul to him*

*Candace: It turns out I don't have one <3*
*New plan!*

*Demi: Like catching up with a certain bread-beauty....?*

*Candace: NO.*
*Get your head out of the gutter.*
*If Daisy accepts my proposal, we're going to have to work together. We'll be partners.*

*Demi: Uh-huh.*
*        Partners ;)*

*But seriously. Are you sure this is a good idea?*

When that last text came through, Candace tossed her phone onto the vacant pillow beside her. She was too exhausted to defend herself. Demi would be going to bed soon, most likely. She had an early vinyasa class to teach. Meanwhile, Candace had no idea what her next day would hold.

It probably was a bad idea. It was impulsive, risky, and, worst of all, *sentimental.* Business decisions made on feelings were the first step towards bankruptcy—that was what her uncle said.

Even so, when Candace's phone buzzed sometime later at 1:57 AM with a text from an unknown number, she felt an electric jolt.

— *I'm gonna need you to prove it*

Candace swiped the phone up so fast that she ripped the charger from the wall along with it. Before she could type up a response, the three-dot typing indicator popped up. She waited, heart hammering like a bongo in her chest.

— *If Candace Perry says she can mop, I'm gonna need to see it to believe it*

Right away, Candace texted back.

*Candace: Prepare to be amazed.*

Candace waited an impossibly long time as the dots sputtered in and out with Daisy's apparent deliberation. It was only after the text sent that she realized the woman might not have expected her to be awake. The dots continued their dance, so Candace sent what she hoped would be an icebreaker.

*Candace: I've heard the best way to mop is mixing bleach with whatever you find under the sink Works every time!*

When Daisy did not reply right away, Candace furiously clarified.

*Candace: Just kidding. I don't really think combining toxic chemicals is a good idea.*

*Daisy: I dunno. The floors at BB are a crime, so we might need to commit one to get them clean.*

Candace sank back against her lumpy pillow, sighing with relief. A word stuck out to her.

*Candace: Oh? 'We?'*

It took an eternity for Daisy to text back. Five minutes, actually. But that might as well have been an eternity in texting time.

*Daisy: Bagel Bombs!. Dawn.*

Candace waited, but it seemed the conversation was over. She 'thumb-upped' the text and forced herself not to press for further details. They would come soon enough. A quick check of her weather app showed that dawn was a few precious hours away.

Candace shut her eyes and attempted to calm her heart. She was not sure when, or why, it had started thundering in her chest. She only knew that the thought of seeing Daisy DeMarco, working with her in that tiny stall over the next several months, made it kick up even faster.

*The metallic, gunpowder tang from the fireworks filled Candace's nostrils. It burned, along with the eyes that watched them. So many eyes, filled with judgment, ridicule, and worse. She had to do something, say anything, to make it stop.*

*She could feel Daisy's eyes on her, too. Their warm, rich amber with flecks of gold that calmed her like a summer afternoon.*

*But it was not summer. For now, Candace was still Candy. If she ever wanted to be anyone else, she had to pretend. The lie left her tongue like black ink, spilling out to mark their future paths...*

When Candace left Wonderwood behind, packing

away the bad memories and traumas with practiced compartmentalization, it included Daisy. She rationalized what happened between them as high school drama and minimized her actions. Even now, she could not fully acknowledge the gravity of what she had done.

But, deep down, Candace knew that it was monstrous.

Reckoning with this was not why Candace had come to Wonderwood. But, it might be what she needed. Could Candace find her path for the future while also making up for past mistakes? She had to try.

It was selfish. Vain. But Candace worried over whether or not Daisy hated her. Maybe, even if she did, saving Bagel Bombs! would be enough to change her mind.

# CHAPTER 6

*Daisy*

W orking with Candace Perry was, as it turned out, not the trainwreck Daisy predicted.

She'd been waiting when Daisy pulled her golf cart into the car lot behind Bagel Bombs!. Her figure on the back steps was murky in the early morning haze, hunched as she hugged her sleeveless frame against the clammy chill. The instant she saw Daisy, she snapped to her feet. They exchanged painfully awkward greetings.

Then and there, Daisy said and internal "fuck it."

Last night, after stress-baking a literal mountain of bagel bombs, Daisy dug out her lease with Peter Perry. Candace had been telling the truth. Despite her lease technically spanning for another three years before she needed to renew, she was screwed. Tucked into a clause about "tenant responsibility," in legalese Daisy might not have understood without Candace putting it so plainly, was Peter Perry's trump card. If she did not meet a ridiculous gross profit backed by financial documents she was obligated to provide by an arbitrary date at the end of August, he was free to kick her out.

It sure did not seem legal. But Daisy's signature on the document was plain as day. She did not have the time, let alone money, to fight a man like Peter Perry in court. His lawyer, Vinny Lamarka, was well-respected around town, but it was rumored that he had shady ties and even shadier tactics.

So, fuck it.

Maybe Candace was as self-serving as ever and was just looking for the first boat she could cling to. At the same time, the woman seemed to legitimately loathe her uncle. If she wanted to expend her time and effort to help Daisy stand her ground?

Fine. Done deal.

Still, determining if the woman could be trusted to run Bagel Bombs! without burning the place down seemed important. It was not complicated: take the order, put the bombs in the toaster oven, fill beverage, done. There were other, more complicated things like inventory stocking and rotation, but Daisy had a special system and it was better if she handled that part.

All while Daisy showed her the ropes, Candace took notes.

"... and you'll want to make sure to *ease* the button in," Daisy told Candace as she explained the industrial toaster that was older than either of them. "Be gentle, and don't rush her. But that's all there is to it. This ol' gal might not look like much, but she's good for it."

"Hm," Candace mused. A wry smile curved her lips. "The oven and I have a lot in common."

Daisy almost laughed. She managed to turn the sound into a neutral grunt, not wanting to give the woman an inch.

"So," Daisy started. "I looked over your master plan some more. A facelift and social media blitz are easy enough to spitball, but they're out of the question right now. Even if I had the money to renovate, I can't afford to close the place long enough to do it. And I tried social media, but I only ever got traffic from trolls and lost grandmas."

Candace held up her pocket notebook, hiding her mouth. Her eyes, though, danced mischievously.

"Just leave all that to me."

Daisy crossed her arms. In the background, the toaster oven ticked with their breakfast bombs. Asiago and chive cream cheese for Daisy, and cinnamon for Candace—she liked sweet things, go figure. A woman used to a sugar-coated world, accustomed to things simply working out for her. Well, Daisy thought, this time it wasn't just Candace's taste setting the tone.

"Really," Candace assured. "I told you, I know what I'm doing."

"Is that so? Well, why don't you take your first customer?"

With a flick of her wrist, Daisy turned on the fluorescents and officially opened her haven for the hungry. Dawnlight was just starting to brighten the beach and boards, bringing with it the first wave of breakfast goers. This early, their patrons consisted mainly of runners and bikers, the athletes of Wonderwood. These types were happy to have something mobile like bagel bombs. Small, in sealed little baggies so they stayed warm, the bombs could be eaten on the go, or taken back to family still sleeping in vacation rentals. They were a reliable, steady customer base.

Except today.

It was a slow morning. Minutes ticked by, and not a single passerby stopped to glance at Bagel Bombs'! window display. In a hyper-aware sort of way, Daisy could sense Candace's apprehension growing—her own certainly was. Daisy could not say why, but she started to feel embarrassed. Doubly so as Candace grew so bored that she took out her phone.

When they finally did see some life, Daisy had to nudge Candace with her flip-flop. It was not the best start. Even so, watching the woman with customers was like a switch flip.

Daisy was a good salesperson. She was informative, able to upsell, and, most importantly, knew how to make her customers happy.

Candace, though, made every person who visited Bagel Bombs! her best friend. Old or young, shoobie or local, and every personality type, no one seemed immune to the Pier Princess' charm.

Least of all Daisy.

Stoically set like a statue before the backroom curtain, Daisy observed Candace. Her outfit, a silk, cropped halter top in a shade of vibrant emerald that highlighted the subtle green of her eyes, was a poor choice. Sleeveless, the top was cinched in a cute (but impractical) collar that looped behind her long neck. The undershirt she wore beneath it was creamy white, like her jeans and stylish pumps. It was an outfit better suited to an office or, more likely, schmoozing at a fancy event with clients.

Slinging hot dough and coffee in a sweltering box?

Not so much.

Her hair was tied up into a long ponytail, which was also not the most practical style, with its ribboning tresses left free to fly. The locks that framed her face were constantly getting in the way. Pretty, though. Like liquid gold, it bounced and curled artfully. All of her, every detail, was pure poised perfection.

Daisy was staring. She told herself it was to catch any slip ups... that she was an owner watching a potential hire. It was a lie, and she knew it. But that was better than admitting the truth.

In a frustratingly astute read, Candace turned to Daisy between customers. She winked, saying, "Pretty incredible, I know. I worked at the campus cafe all through undergrad."

Daisy did not bother to hide her disbelief. "Yeah, right. Why would you need to work?"

A flash of hurt, a downward tug of her lips, showed the comment stung Candace. Yet, her rebuttal was light and haughty.

"You don't know me as well as you think, Daisy DeMarco. My

regulars cried when I left."

"Yeah, yeah. You're the hero of the morning rush. Also, you've got cream cheese on your tit."

Candace let loose a pomeranian-sized yip that might have been the most adorable sound Daisy ever heard. Without even realizing it, she laughed louder and more honestly than she had laughed in a long time.

"I'm glad you find my ruined blouse so amusing!"

Daisy snapped her mouth shut. What was wrong with her? She handed the flustered woman a damp towel, just as flustered herself.

When another round of customers arrived, Daisy turned away from the one-woman bagel ballet before her. She busied herself sorting items that were already where they were meant to be.

After a time, the morning pop settled down, and they were left with scattered sustenance-seekers. Candace played on her phone between customers, which was only slightly annoying. Daisy was glad that it kept them from having to make small talk.

*Anything* but that.

Candace said Daisy did not know her, and that was fine. Past this grand scheme to save Bagel Bombs!, she did not *want* to know her.

Not her past as a rich girl working at a campus cafe, regardless of the questions it raised. Or why she was so ready to turn on her uncle for a stranger. Or even her favorite color (although, definitely, it was something bright like a warm, sunflower yellow).

The rest of the shift was a strange combination of dull and the most anxious four hours Daisy ever spent working. She was thrilled when Rio arrived to take over for the evening. Immediately, she set to packing her things.

It was stifling inside the bagel stand. No matter where Daisy went, Candace was within arm's reach.

*Too close.*

Had the place always been this small? Before she could make a clean escape, Candace stopped her.

"Wait!" Candace looked confused. She had difficulty getting her words out. "You… Um, you've decided, then?"

*Had she?*

Daisy spent the whole morning on edge. Not even a mid-shift stop from Norman had helped since he was thrilled to have Candace on the other side of the counter. He adored her, like everyone else. Just like deep down, Daisy was afraid she would if she let Candace stay.

Daisy glowered. She could not wait to get home, smoke a blunt, and bake the inventory she needed to replenish her depleted supplies.

*Very depleted*, she noted. Even after the slow start, this was one of the best days they'd had in a long while. Maybe Rio was right. Bagel Bombs! needed new blood. A talkative, attention-grabbing presence like Candace could be just what the doctor ordered.

Daisy scanned Candace, not bothering to hide her measure. Once, years ago, she let Daisy down. Would she do it again? And, more importantly, would Daisy let her?

"You know what time we open."

# CHAPTER 7

## *Candace*

S weat streaked down Candace in artful patterns. Sheening, slick, and result of the best release of endorphins she had in months. It was intense. Passionate, even. The only thing better would have been sex. Unfortunately, it had been ages since she managed *that* kind of release. This activity was the best alternative she could get.

Hot yoga was one of the few places Candace let herself descend into disarray. She had only started practicing a few years back, having been dragged to a class by Demi during one of her many visits to New York. But, after forcing herself through some rough initial sweltering forays, she fell in love.

It was glorious. She sweated, huffed, and put on muscle that her uncle complained about being "mannish." Despite a lifetime of obsessively worrying about what everyone was thinking of her, she only paid attention to what was happening on her own mat. Today of all days, it was exactly what she needed to recenter herself.

The pep talk Demi gave her afterwards was less helpful. After showering at the yoga studio, the pair headed out for a late dinner at her family's restaurant. A cacophony of clinks and casual conversation filled the bustling Greek diner. Candace was glad to see the place so busy, as much as it used to be years ago when she would visit Demi while she waited tables. Just like back then, the woman could not help fussing over her. Demi leaned over the faux marble laminant tabletop towards Candace, and her bold, arched brows knitted with concern.

"So, you're really doing this?"

"Eating a whole gyro? After that workout, yeah, I think I can manage."

Demi blew her drink straw paper at Candace, missing by a mile.

"Don't play dumb. I'm talking about this scheme of yours. You and Daisy have history. *Complicated* history. It sounds to me like she doesn't even want your help."

"Who said anything about scheming? I've been suggesting. Emphatically, because I'm right. Whether she wants my help or not, she's dead in the water without me."

Snorting, Demi joked, "There's that famous Perry humility. I'm glad to see your ego is back." The comment and tangential comparison to Peter Perry rankled. As Candace winced, Demi was perceptive as ever and noticed. Her hand found Candace's atop the table. "Sorry. It's a good thing, I mean it. I was worried after—"

"Don't be," Candace cut her off. She did not want to hear the word 'fired.' Being in limbo for her next job was bad enough. She pulled her hand away and crossed her arms, trying her best not to sound defensive. "Look. Who helped you write your business plan for the studio? Or put together that elaborate doppelganger story to get your ex off your back?"

"You," she conceded in a huff.

"Yep, me. As long as you've known me, I've always had a plan. And this is a golden one."

"For you, or for her?"

"What's that supposed to mean?"

The bangles on Demi's wrists jingled as she held up her hands in defense. "Nothing. I just want to make sure you're doing this for the right reasons... Not because you feel guilty over what happened between you two."

Leave it to Demi to cut to the heart of things. She knew Candace better than anyone else, making it difficult to hide from the truth. Thankfully, one of Demi's young cousins chose that moment to drop a whole tray of fountain soda drinks. The thunderous crash made the entire place fall silent.

Under her breath, Demi mumbled something in Greek and sidled out of the booth. To Candace, she ordered, "Hold that thought."

Candace could not help smiling as she watched the scene. While the girl, Tina, cried over her clumsiness and ineffectively dabbed at the mess with her lone towel, her family set to action. There was a lot of bickering and opinions on the best way to mop. Demi looked like she wanted to slap her cousin Leo when he suggested using paper towels. It was like something out of a comedy skit. Most importantly, though, they rallied around each other when one of them needed help.

South Jersey Greek diners had a distinct vibe. It was pure chaos, a perfect dance of synchronized service. Always family-run, and staffed with every extended relative capable of wiping down a sticky menu. From backline cook to hostess, they knew that they could rely on each other for support.

But who did Bagel Bombs! have? Who would step in to help Daisy? Candace knew what it was like to not have a big family support system.

When Demi came back, she brought their food with her. Two heaping platters, gyros (pronounced *YEE-roh*, not JAI-ros, as Demi would firmly correct), one lamb for Candace, the other falafel for Demi, looked like little food mountains atop the table. The scent of warmed pita, dill, and other spices sent a flood of saliva into Candace's mouth.

Before she tucked in, Candace ignored Demi's question and asked one of her own. "What do they say about Daisy? She must have friends and hobbies…. Go places in the off-season. I know you hear things from your yogis."

"Oh yeah, I hear a lot of things. But I'm no Gabby-gossip."

Laughing, Demi tossed her petite frame back against the plush, pleather maroon booth backing. Small and curvy with a deceptive amount of muscle thanks to her yogic pursuits, she had shoulder-length, curly auburn hair that she most often confined in a loose (yet effortlessly artistic) bun. With big, colorful, beaded earrings and an airy, floral print creamy white dress, she set a particular boho vibe. In a lineup, she would be the first person you would point out as the owner of a chic, small town yoga studio. However, her cute, festival girl appearance hid that she was a shrewd businesswoman like her restaurant-owning relatives.

Over the last several years, Demi turned her little shore town yoga studio, Downwood Dog Yoga, into a vacation destination. Candace gave her a few financial pointers, but really, the woman earned her success. With special classes on the beach, teacher training, and more, shoobies and locals alike loved her. She had clientele from all walks of life, young and old, rich and poor… Bagel-eaters…

She had to have heard something of Daisy DeMarco.

"Demi," Candace urged. "You can't ask me if I'm sure, then clam up. What's the deal with her? Her bagels are delicious, she's good at what she does, but she seems…"

*Overwhelmed? Alone?* Or, maybe, Candace was just projecting.

Demi gave a belated answer after taking a heaping bite of her gyro. "If you ask me, she's stuck."

"'Stuck?'"

"Well, think about it. Zee has been tethered to that bagel

stand since her parents' accident. Before that, even, with how much she worked when we were kids. Like you said, she's good at it. But I don't think her heart has been in it for a long time. And..."

"What?"

Demi bit her lip, looking uncomfortable. "They say she won't leave the island."

"You mean she's a homebody?"

"No. I mean, she hasn't left Wonderwood in over a decade. She keeps to herself."

*Completely to herself, or...?* Candace plugged her mouth with a hot, salty steak fry before she could embarrass herself asking about Daisy's dating history.

Swallowing, she mused, "Maybe she just needs help. With the right push, I think Bagel Bombs! could take off. Then, I could start to put my life back on track."

"You will. Even if this isn't your path, you'll find your way, Can-can. No matter what, I'm here for you."

Candace grimaced at the nickname. Demi knew she hated it and only whipped it out when she was trying to be particularly annoying or earnest. An uncomfortable tightness pressed Candace's chest in a physical manifestation of how trapped she felt. This *had* to work, otherwise...

To cover her unease, Candace navigated taking a bite of her gyro. The burst of flavor was a welcome distraction. Earthy herb-spiced lamb, juicy beefsteak tomato, crunchy red onions, lettuce, and feta crumbles were ensconced within warm, pillowy pita in an irresistible combination. Her shoulders lost some of their tension as she chewed, and she did not rush to wipe the tzatziki sauce dripping down her chin.

Face pinched with worry, Demi cleaned Candace herself. "Honestly. Just because your life is a mess right now doesn't mean you have to eat like one."

Candace gave a ditzy shrug. "I might be a mess, but at least I'm cute. Look at you. Just can't help taking care of me after all these years, can you?"

"Brat. And you won't even tip me these days."

Candace stuck out her tongue, then took another graceless bite. Demi smiled fondly and pulled another wad of napkins from the dispenser. Dependable, loving Demi; Candace knew she would always have her best interests at heart.

They met shortly after Candace came to Wonderwood, during the brief period that Uncle Perry and his friends were trying to court Demi's aunt for some project they wanted greenlit. Along with being a long-time restaurateur, the indomitable woman was also a town council member. She was not amused by their brownnosing and made it known that all they were buying was her delicious food.

Uncle Perry was disappointed and carried on his vendetta to this day. Candace, meanwhile, had gotten a best friend.

"How's your Aunt Anathea?" Candace watched the woman behind the diner's wrap-around counter and noted, "She hasn't changed one bit. You mentioned things have been awkward since the divorce?"

"That's a word for it," Demi mumbled. She filled her mouth with gyro, looking sullen. It was *very* awkward. Introducing her aunt's husband to his future affair partner, one of her studio's other yoga teachers, no less, had been an accident. Even so, it put a dent in Demi's once-close relationship with her aunt.

After making eye contact from across the diner, Aunt Anathea stopped by their table for a hello. To Demi, or Demitria as she greeted formally, there was a distinct coldness. Candace was a different story. Never one for physical boundaries, the woman bent into the booth and yanked Candace close for a side-hug.

"*Omorfi mou!* It's been too long! You're so grown up and lovely, but you still have an appetite!"

"Thank you, Ms. Panopoulos. I've missed your cooking. New York gyros don't have anything on yours."

Pulling back, big, gleaming teeth flashed with the woman's smile. The physical resemblance between her and Demi was strong, like looking at future or past versions of the same person. Especially their eyes; their kind, brown warmth they both possessed was like warm cocoa on a chilly day. She pinched Candace's cheek, chiding, "It's '*Theia* Thea' to you. Are you visiting?"

"No, I'm... um..."

"She's sussing out some new opportunities in the area," Demi answered for Candace. "In the meantime, she's a Jersey girl again."

*Theia* Thea did not look at Demi, but she nodded with understanding. "Well, Wonderwood is lucky to have you back for however long you'll be here. This booth has your name on it whenever you want a good, home-cooked meal—as long as you don't bring that bastard uncle of yours."

Candace hated that no matter where she went or who she spoke to, that man somehow wormed his way in. Forcing a smile, she assured, "Don't worry, I'm a one-top. I'm sorry for all the trouble he's given you."

"Nothing I can't handle." *Theia* Thea waved a hand with long, nicely manicured nails in the air as if it cleared the thought. "His type is a dime a dozen. He's just a big baby who doesn't like hearing 'no.'"

"Well, still, I'm sorry."

A sincere, knowing smile tugged the woman's full, dark red lips. "Family is more than blood. You might not have picked him, but the Panopoulos' pick *you*. Don't be a stranger."

With that, *Theia* Thea went off to take care of any one of the million other things that demanded her attention in the bustling place. It was odd. A warm, contented feeling filled Candace as her gaze followed the motherly woman set to work. It was a familiar sight, but one she had not seen in so long. Was this what other people felt like when they returned home? For the first time since she came back to Wonderwood, pleasant memories stuck out over the bad.

After finishing what they could of their platters and wrapping the rest to go, Candace begrudgingly let Demi pay their tab. It was cheap thanks to a family and friends discount, which made her grateful heart grow to bursting. She waited while Demi hugged her cousins goodbye, fighting back happy tears.

The pair left Zeus' Torch and exited onto the boardwalk. Despite the slight chill of the May evening, the place was packed with people crammed from storefront to rail. Candace watched the bustle with awe. In just a few short, weeks schools would let out, and the shoobies would arrive in full force. More so than ever, she was sure this would be a record-breaking summer.

Down the boardwalk, too far to see, Candace wondered how Rio was doing at the bagel cafe. Daisy had to be long gone. It was nearly closing time, and they had both been up since well before dawn. Longer, in Candace's case, since she had never been able to fall asleep. She could not believe she had gotten through that whole shift, a yoga class, and was still standing. After stuffing her face, all she wanted to do was crash.

And yet, her eyes lingered in the direction of Bagel Bombs!.

Beside her, Demi gave Candace a peck on her cheek. "If there's one thing I'm sure of, it's that you know how to get what you want. Business-Candace has her time and place. But, if this is really what you're after, you might need some sweetness to draw them in."

"You're probably right."

Candace cringed. It was time for Candy to come out and play.

# CHAPTER 8

## *Daisy*

The last days of May melted away until the metaphorical pressure cooker was set and locked. Memorial Day, the unofficial kickoff of the summer season, was coming up fast. Daisy was surprised, confused, and (she realized with a fair amount of annoyance) glad when Candace continued to show up. Aside from the shifts helmed by Rio or Dotty, the woman jumped right into Daisy's admittedly grueling schedule.

Every morning, as Daisy pulled up to the back lot, the woman was waiting there with a bright smile and her arms open to help carry the inventory. Apart from a mild phone addiction, she was a model employee. Great with customers, a multi-tasking wiz, and never complained about sidework.

It was the bare minimum for someone who wanted to have a personal stake in the business, Daisy reminded herself. All that effort was not for *her*. Candace worked for Candace's interests.

Even so, it was hard to ignore the excitement bubbling inside her. The chance of something new, the chance for change... Daisy knew that she needed to be careful, or she would get burned.

It was a particularly hot day, the hottest of the season so far, that things boiled over.

Daisy could not believe how busy they were. From the minute she opened, the pair was met with a line of hungry customers. While Candace handled the register, Daisy danced between the ticket spike, the freezer, and toaster oven fulfilling orders. It was close quarters, with multiple bumps and accidental brushes against her would-be partner. However, they both soldiered on.

The business did not let up even as Rio arrived for their evening shift. Daisy stayed on to help, and so did Candace without even being asked. A mix of concern and giddiness struck Daisy as she noted that they had nearly blown through their whole inventory. A problem, but a welcome one.

In a lull between customers, Daisy took over the register while Rio and Candace cleaned up. Despite her uptight demeanor, the woman was not afraid to get dirty. On her hands and knees, Candace scrubbed the disgusting gap between the floor and the oven.

Like her first day and every other day, she was not dressed for the job. Her top was a form-fitting but modestly cut plum-colored blouse. It buttoned and tucked neatly into a snug pair of high-waisted creamy white slacks, secured with an accenting black belt. White pumps lifted her calves and tensed the muscles underneath.

Crouched as she was, squatted like a frog to avoid staining her clothes, Daisy again noticed her subtle athleticism. Despite her awkward position, she balanced with ease on the balls of her feet even as she furiously worked away grime.

There was something else Daisy could not help noticing.

Candace faced the opposite direction. Her belt pulled taught at the linen pants, creating a gap and, although her shirt was tucked, it lifted while she scrubbed. Lifted, and revealed the smooth and lily white skin underneath... along with the trace curve of a thong's purple lace.

Unconsciously—with no subtlety—Daisy craned her neck up, angling to see more. Why did such an awful human have to have such a perfect peach of an ass? It wasn't fair. Daisy thought she remembered the woman mentioning yoga in one of her overly familiar customer chats. Did yoga sculpt butts? Daisy had no idea, but if that's what Candace wanted, the results were plain to see.

It was only Rio's voice, wry and tilting, that broke Daisy from her lechery.

"I see why you've wanted to work all these shifts with her. She's like a nice Regina George."

"She's still training," Daisy shot back in a low hiss. Rio gave her a pointed look. "And she's *not* 'nice.'"

"Uh-huh. I remember you leaving me to work this place alone after one day."

"What can I say? You're a star."

Daisy's attempted brush-off fell flat as Rio crossed their arms over an old *Power Rangers* tee.

"You're gonna tell me the story between you two, right? Cause I looked her up, and there's no way Wonderwood's Pier Princess woke up one day and decided to go to bat for you."

"You're reading into things."

"And *you're* a terrible liar. You're both the same age. She didn't go to Wonderwood Public, but her best friend did. And, judging by some past social media pictures where she looks *very* cozy with some pretty ladies, I'm gonna bet she's in the rainbow brigade like us."

"Ladies—?! Where did you see that? I mean, *there's nothing!*"

Daisy snapped loudly enough that Candace paused her scrubbing. They all stared at one another for a beat. Blessedly, a customer chose that moment to materialize, and Daisy rushed to greet them.

The group was your average post-sunset roving band, a half

dozen college-aged fun-seekers. They looked like they might be with some kind of sorority, with a few of them wearing matching logo shirts. Their apparent leader was a tall, tanned, gorgeous young woman wearing a sheer white saran over an eye-poppingly red bikini. She tilted her head at Daisy, tapping a black painted fingernail against her plump lower lip.

"You're not the person I messaged?"

"Um, no. But I can help you. What would you like? Our special flavor of the week is strawberry cream cheese, it's homemade with local berries."

"Oh, I'll have one of those," she said with confidence. "And three Bomb Bonanzas."

Daisy stared at the girl. Individually, the words made sense. Yet, she had *no* idea what they meant in this context.

"Three... what?"

The group shared confused glances. The young woman frowned, saying, "The deal you have? The Memorial Day Bomb Bonanza, every flavor bagel you have for a discount. We talked to Candace online about how our sorority was throwing a breakfast party. These bombs are going to be perfect."

Like a springboard, Candace popped up beside Daisy.

"Yes! Marta, from Delta Sigma Pi. I was starting to think you lost your appetite."

"Never, *mamacita*! Especially if it's cooked up by you." She giggled at something her friend whispered, and batted her long, enhanced lashes at Candace. "But first, you promised to tell me about your sorority days..."

"Well, it was a little wild..." Elbows on the counter, Candace leaned in and dropped her voice low. Whatever she said next made 'Marta' throw her head back with laughter. The girl's magenta, purple, and blue bisexual flag earrings jingled as she not-so-subtly played with one.

Daisy could not take any more. Scowling, she stepped back while the pair flirted through the painfully long order.

"Huh," Rio once again Iago'ed in her ear, "that answers that question. Maybe I have a chance to be her Birdo after all.

Unless... there are any other takers."

"*Hell no!* This princess is staying far away from that castle."

Daisy had been looking at Rio while she spoke, but she turned her gaze to find Candace right in front of her.

"Um..." Candace tried to sidle past Daisy, very deliberately avoiding her eyes. "Excuse me."

She ducked into the back room and returned with three packed containers from the freezer. Marta and her friends took the boxes, but not before slipping in a few more suggestive comments Candace's way. Meanwhile, Daisy ground her teeth.

When they were out of sight and, most importantly, fully paid, Daisy forced Candace to face her. Arms crossed, she demanded, "What the hell was that?"

"Hungry customers? I don't know what the problem is. Are you mad at me for making a sale?"

Daisy stared her down, but the woman was unfazed.

Candace was a good liar. There was no quaver to her voice, no hint of doubt. Just confidence that *she* was the one being wronged and how *dare* Daisy for doing it.

"You're my problem, you—"

"Oh, shit," Rio exclaimed. They looked at their phone with awe. "Princess Peach brought us into the 2010s."

"What?"

Rio angled their phone towards Daisy, who promptly snatched it. A vein throbbed in her forehead as she scrolled. Instagram, Threads, Facebook, BlueSky, TikTok... Bagel Bombs! had a profile on each app, and probably more.

When Daisy told Candace she'd tried social media, she'd been lying; she never got traction because she refused to post. She hated everything about it. Candace, though, had no such qualms.

Post after post, memes, daily affirmations with bagel themes, and *so many* customer interactions that were just... wholesome. And, yes, the so-called 'Memorial Day Bagel Bonanza' ridiculous promotion that just wiped what was left of their inventory. The scale of it made Daisy dizzy. Did the woman never sleep? The timestamps for her posts and messages were all over the place. She supposed she now knew what the woman had been up to all those times she was glued to her phone.

In a nervous rush, Candace explained that this was all a part of her plan that was detailed in the binder. *Her* plan, which hinged on a strong online presence.

A feeling nagged at Daisy. So dusty from being buried away, she did not recognize the hope bubbling inside her as she read comment after comment from people excited about her bagels. Instead, it made her nervous. She felt the pressure building, and with it came anger. She was supposed to be grateful? To *thank* Candace for making her feel this way?

*Fuck that.*

Through gritted teeth, Daisy asked, "You didn't think *any* of this was worth running by me, the owner of this place? Shit, Candace. You just do whatever you want, don't you?"

"But I didn't—"

Daisy thrust up a finger, cutting Candace off.

"I never approved any of this."

"C'mon, Zee," Rio urged. They pried their phone back and continued scrolling themself, saying, "I've been begging you to let me run some profiles for years. She's already got a ton of followers."

Daisy snatched the phone back.

"Of course she does when this is the kind of thing she's posting!"

Eye-rolling puns about filling holes.

Hashtag "BagelBoobs" under the image of a two pack that... yes, looked surprisingly like boobs with a single sesame seed nipple planted just so. But that was not the point. They were a bagel stand, not some kind of joke. Worst of all was the picture that seemed to garner the most attention because *of course* it did.

Thirst traps were pretty popular.

While Daisy's face could not be seen, it was undoubtedly

her. Taken from behind as she stood before the counter, she wore her usual Bagel Bombs! branded tank top, athletic shorts, and flip flops. Her arms were raised in mid-pull, drawing up the metal security cord as they opened for the day. The black and white filter Candace applied to the photo pushed contrasts to their most extreme, highlighting a side of Daisy even she had never seen.

She looked strong. Cool. Sexy, even. And Candace had noticed. So, too, had a parade of commenters under the photo.

It was too much.

Too much like back then, with the messages, the eyes, the attention. Daisy could feel the blood pounding in her temples, the bitter dryness stinging her throat. She thrust Rio's phone back into their hands.

"This isn't okay."

Candace said nothing, but looked guilty as hell. Frustratingly, Rio shrugged. "It's good. You can't even tell it's you. Honestly, it looks like a model promo." To Candace, they praised, "Well done. Professor Oak would be pleased."

"I can't take any credit. Daisy... I mean, Zee, is the perfect subject."

Daisy's nostrils flared. She tore her apron off and popped the counter up so that she could escape the confining place. If Candace wanted it so badly, she could take care of it for a while.

# CHAPTER 9

## *Candace*

C andace messed up. She knew it as soon as Daisy started scrolling. All at once, she was sure it was... a lot... seeing the scale of what she'd managed to build in a couple of scant weeks. Even she was impressed by herself. However, she had years of experience managing her college cafe's social media pages. With some recycled memes and bagel-themed puns, she'd been able to get engagement going with no trouble.

But Candace realized that she had overstepped, especially with the picture of Daisy.

It was an accident. She had been checking her notifications while the woman's back was turned, and happened to look up as she hauled the chain open. A single moment that seemed suspended, waiting for Candace to open her camera app. She snapped the picture, then almost deleted it just as quickly to avoid feeling like a dirty old man.

Rio said it, though. It was too good to relegate to the trash bin's ether. Candace had told herself she could use the shot because of how prominent the Bagel Bombs! logo was on Daisy's tank top. Loose, with long, wide arm holes that showed a tantalizingly large amount of the woman's toned side, if she turned the angle of the shot just a little more... Commenters were asking where they could get their own Bagel Bomb! apparel, or the blonde in it. Candace tried to delete and ban the creeps, but a few slipped by. All of which Daisy saw.

Again, Candace let her down. Maybe this was as awful an idea as Demi seemed to think after all. She sniffled, but refused to cry. Instead, she gathered her things. Rio watched, arms crossed.

"You're seriously leaving me to clean up this mess?"

Candace stopped before the backroom partition. Mumbling an apology, she set her things back down and picked up a rag.

"That's not what I meant."

"What should I do? I'm pretty sure that kind of exit means she's had enough of me."

"Frankly," Rio suggested, "you could start by apologizing. Don't get me wrong, what you did was impressive. But Zee is touchy about this kind of stuff."

"What 'stuff' specifically?"

"Attention, maybe? I'm not sure. She almost fired me when I tried to set up an Insta a while back."

"Wow... I thought you were close."

Shrugging, Rio admitted, "We're closer now. I might be one of the *only* people she's close to, between you and me. It's taken time for us to get to this. And even then, she puts up walls."

"I see..."

An ache for Daisy thrummed inside Candace's chest. Loneliness and isolation were things she understood all too well.

Rio continued. "To be honest, I thought Zee had given up. She's worked herself to the bone and burnt out. Nothing gets her excited lately. Nothing, until you showed up."

"If by excited, you mean furious. Making her mad seems to be my specialty."

With a wink, Rio said, "Maybe. But who doesn't root for a good enemies-to-lovers story?"

Scoffing, Candace shot back, "It's *definitely* not that."

*No*, her thoughts echoed, *this isn't that kind of story. Not after what I've done.*

At the very least, Candace knew Rio was right about her needing to apologize. Even if this was the end of whatever business partnership she and Daisy might have, she did not want to leave things between them on a sour note.

Not a second time.

Candace took a bolstering breath. She cast Rio a guilty look, but the helpful human waved her off.

"I've got things here. Not too much to do but close up when we're sold out. Which is probably also part of why Daisy is pissed."

"I don't understand. Isn't being sold out a good thing?"

"Not when Zee's the only one making these things. From shopping cart to oven, she's a one-woman show."

*"Really?"*

"Yep. She keeps an inventory system that even I can't make heads or tails of. Your deals are great, but they upset the balance. Now that you've wiped her daily inventory and her backup freezer stock here, we're down to whatever she has prepped at home."

Candace blanched. Her hand flew to her blouse, where she anxiously played with a button. "Oh no..."

"Yeah. Zee's got some work to do thanks to you. At least it's a Dotty/Me day tomorrow, but there goes her day off."

"I really messed up. You're right. I need to tell her I'm sorry. Do you have any idea where she's gone?"

Rio tapped a finger to their elfin, angular jaw. "Well, she didn't head out the back, so she couldn't have gone far without Otto." By Candace's blank stare, they must have gathered her lack of a clue. They clarified, "Her golf cart. She doesn't have a car, but she uses Otto to get around."

"Ah."

One mystery solved. Candace noticed Daisy pull up in the golf cart decorated with streamers, local Wonderwood regalia, and Bagel Bomb! branding. Probably not street legal, but it suited Daisy. Candace could picture her, aviators on and hair whipping in the open air, looking like she owned the island. It brought a smile to her face without even realizing it.

"Oh!" Rio slapped their hand on the counter, startling Candace from her mental image. "I bet she went to visit Horace!"

Horace, as Candace belatedly recalled, was the name of the horseshoe crab star of the boardwalk nature center's new summer exhibit. Thankfully, the satellite center was not far, unlike the larger Wetlands Institute research facility that was located out in the mosquito-infested marshes. It was built into the boardwalk storefronts past the convention hall pier, between an adventure mini golf course and a jewelry shop.

A seaweed-covered, rusty diver robot waved at passersby while an audio recording belted out sea life factoids in a chipper, Flo-from-the-Progressive-commercial voice. The building itself was, like Bagel Bombs!, in bad need of a makeover. Candace supposed state funding and donations only went so far. Even so, the place had a sort of kitschy charm.

It seemed to be closing time. The ticket counter was vacant, and the pull-down metal gate was half-shuttered. With practiced privilege, Candace ducked inside. From there, Daisy was not hard to find.

The building itself was composed of artful, creatively placed glass cases that were teeming with local flora and fauna displays. There was a long, low table where kids could paint hermit crab shells alongside a beach hut-themed enclosure that teemed with the critters.

A hilly sand dune line was replicated in a detailed miniature scale model, and tiny plaques explained their importance; distantly, Candace recalled someone telling her the very same information. Someone familiar, with ashy hair and warm, amber eyes...

As the star attraction, Horace's enclosure was in the very center of the hall. A sign explained that despite the masculine name, Horace was an elderly female crab who had been a subject of the nature institute's research program for years. Thanks to her blood, the scientific community gained valuable research knowledge. Now, Horace was retired and had a nice setup made to look like the New Jersey bay where their kind liked to nest.

A see-through plexiglass barrier that was a few feet tall encircled the exhibit, giving a raised view of the angled marsh recreation. There was a deep section of water planted with marsh reeds, a muddy bank, and even a sandy beach scene complete with a mannequin family beneath an umbrella. It looked like the nature center had picked up a piece of the bay and plopped it right here in the building.

Candace found Daisy seated on a bench that surrounded the enclosure. She made no attempt to hide her approach, yet the other woman ignored her. Daisy's attention was trained on the horseshoe crab, where the creature was burrowed into the faux bank. Candace held back a cringe as she looked at its weird carapace body. She noticed the tiny Go-Pro strapped to it for the enclosure's so-called "Crab Cam" live YouTube feed, but could not imagine what it possibly showed apart from sand. In her nervousness to fill the silence, she made the comment aloud.

Daisy took notice of that, and not kindly.

Still facing the display, she said, "It's not 'nothing.' It's important research on a unique, close-to-endangered species. If the right people in the medical community took notice, it could make Wonderwood the ecological hub it's meant to be. But why would you care? You hate it here."

Slowly, Candace sat on the bench, a little more than an arm's length from Daisy. "I thought I did. But I think it's more complicated than that. I hate the memories that get dredged up when I'm here. Wonderwood isn't without its charms, though."

"Oh? Like what? Those sorority girls?"

Was that *jealousy* Candace detected in Daisy's voice?

*No way, that would be crazy.*

"They certainly don't hurt. But there's more."

Quiet settled between them. However, Daisy did not tell Candace to go, so she went on.

"I forgot how much I missed the salt air. In the morning, when everything is covered in mist and dew, no one else around, it's otherworldly. With sound and sight muted, the tinge of brine in every breath, it's like something out of a scary movie. But it's somehow peaceful at the same time. Great for the skin, too."

Daisy made a 'you would say that' snort.

"I missed the way Wonderwood moves at its own pace. It's not like the city. People put their guards down, and they're not in as much of a rush. Yes, I liked talking with Marta and her friends... They're nice, and they spent a good chunk of change. But I like talking with Norman and the other Bagel Bombs! regulars just as much."

Quietly, a begrudging slip, Daisy asked, "Anything else?"

"Your bagels. I've really, really missed your bagels. Sweet or savory, any flavor—it doesn't matter, I love them. You... Your bagel bomb was the first good memory I made here after a lot of bad ones. But now I've gone and messed everything up. I should have asked about starting those accounts. And before I posted your picture. I'm sorry."

Without turning, Daisy said, "You cut me out of my own business. You posted *as* me, saying things I'd never say. Plus, you totally fucked my inventory."

"I know. Or, I know now. Rio explained that you have a system."

Daisy grunted.

"I made a mistake," Candace pressed. She hated the whine creeping into her voice, but she was desperate. "Can't we just… start over?"

"Start over? You think we can *start over?*"

Now, Daisy hauled a leg around the bench to straddle it, facing Candace. Anger drew her features tight, along with hurt. Emotions Candace wished she were not responsible for. But when they were staring her down, she had no choice but to face all she'd done.

Shoulders slumped, Candace answered, "No. You're right. If we didn't have the history we do, I wouldn't be here."

Surprise shifted Daisy's expression for a moment. Then, right back to anger.

"Well, good. At least if you get that, you can go back to—"

"No. I won't," Candace resolved. She straightened, meeting Daisy's fierce gaze with one of her own. "Because of our history, because we *both* need this, I'm not giving up. Besides, barring our little inventory hiccup, my campaign worked."

"You can't be serious…" Daisy shook her head. "This is some crazy rich girl shit."

"I showed you my bank account. You know I'm one missed paycheck from living out of my car."

"It's a mentality. Can't you get it through your head? You're trash to me, Candace. Pure garbage. I don't want anything to do with you!"

*Garbage.*

For a beat, they looked at one another, letting that declaration hang between them. The truth stung Candace. More than stung, as her pride and heart took simultaneous critical blows. Yet, it was not as if she were unaware of Daisy's feelings. Although the woman had thawed somewhat over the last two weeks, she never lost her frostiness. Still, it hurt to hear aloud, and to know that she deserved it.

Daisy was the first to falter, dropping the arms she raised in the air for emphasis. She slapped her palms onto her thighs and let loose the breath she'd been holding.

"Okay. Look, that was harsh…"

"But fair," Candace conceded. "I'm sorry that's how you see me, and that there might be some truth to it. What's also true is that if you want your business to survive the summer, you need me. Garbage or not."

"Why? To screw me over again? Thanks, no thanks. I'm going to have to spend my whole day off food prepping because of you."

Candace angled on the bench to face Daisy. Legs together and slanted, ladylike, as her grandmother taught her, to try and project the poise she did not feel. She agreed, "My verbal communication could use some improvement. Previously, I worked with boomer-banker types who live in the technological stone age. I'm used to being the 'young one' who implements any strategy that has connection to computers or the internet. However, if you read the binder I gave you, it clearly outlined my individual steps to getting Bagel Bombs! up and running, which included how I planned to start our social media push."

"Like that stupid Bomb Bonanza? Was that in your binder?"

"No. That came from a customer feedback thread." She paused, and cocked her head. "You know what their biggest complaint was?"

Candace could see it; the chink in Daisy's armor. Interest, fear, and, maybe, a bit of excitement. She wanted to know.

Smiling, Candace revealed, "They wish they could have more. So, I offered to give it to them in a limited promotion with every flavor. That wasn't the first bonanza we sold today, and it won't be the last."

Pulling out her phone, Candace showed Daisy the barrage of

comments and private DMs she'd gotten from people about the woman's little counter cafe.

"They *love* Bagel Bombs!. So many people have reached out to share family vacation memories that involve eating your food. Some people mentioned that they might come back to Wonderwood for the first time in years to try and recreate some of that nostalgia. Meaning, they want to give you money."

It was hard to tell what Daisy was thinking. The message she currently read was from an older widow who used to visit Wonderwood with her long-grown children. The woman talked about getting a "Bombtastic-Bob-Box," and riding bikes along the boardwalk. Daisy stared at the message long enough that Candace felt the nervous need to talk.

"It's a cute name for a promotion. That woman remembered it after all these years."

In a far-off voice, Daisy told her, "Robert… Bob… was my dad's name. That was his special—one each of Boston cream, Nutella and strawberries, plain, and a mystery pick. For some reason, he'd pick sundried tomatoes for the random one like 50% of the time if he made up the box. Used to drive my mom crazy because it was a specialty flavor. It's been so long, I'd forgotten about it."

"That's a sweet memory. It sounds like your parents had a lot of fun running the cafe."

"They did."

Daisy gave Candace her phone back. The fingers that brushed hers were cold and shaking, so much so that she almost steadied them with her own. She hesitated, though, and instead clutched her phone to her lap.

For a while, they both watched Horace. The crustacean was half-buried in the briny water, having scuttled itself up to the human-made shoreline. The simulated waves that lapped up over its carapace shell were soothing, cutting through the silence.

Candace wanted to apologize again. She knew that she had

to, more explicitly, for everything she'd done.

'Daisy," Candace started softly. "Or, Zee, if that's what you prefer."

"Daisy is fine." She said it quickly, as if she surprised even herself. "You're not my friend, you call me Daisy."

Candace swallowed hard. "Okay. Daisy, then. About what happened between us... I—"

"I'll tell you. From my perspective, I'll tell you what you did to me."

# CHAPTER 10

*Wonderwood, New Jersey — 2010*

## *Daisy*

For many, senior year of high school is the precipice of a new chapter. A year of exciting change, new horizons, and previously unreachable bounds coming within sight. For Daisy, it was when her world stopped.

That year, one rainy October night, Daisy's parents were in an accident. As the pair drove across the lone bridge that connected Wonderwood to the mainland, their car went over the guardrail into the bay. The police report said there were signs of speeding. Considering the bad weather, they deemed it an open-and-shut case. Her parents were gone.

At first, Daisy was in a haze. She hardly remembered the first few months as a handful of teachers and her school counselor guided her through the funeral. Since she was a newly minted eighteen-year-old, she was essentially on her own. Her father had been estranged from his family, and her mother's half lived on the other side of the country. She did not have any friends because she had always been so busy working. Very suddenly, she was on her own.

Daisy was raised to be independent. Even if she had people to ask for help, she did not know how. So, she did the one thing she knew: she worked.

Keeping Bagel Bombs! open became her number one priority. The place meant everything to her parents, and they would have been devastated if it ever closed. Plus, Daisy needed the money. The cozy bay cottage bungalow she inherited was paid off, but she had regular bills and daily expenses. It was also not long before Peter Perry, along with his strongly worded lawyer letter, informed her of the imminent rent payments she had coming for Bagel Bombs'! space on the boardwalk.

Daisy was in over her head. There was so much paperwork, all of it in terms she could barely understand. Her parents had taken a lackadaisical approach to teaching Daisy about the business side of running Bagel Bombs!, and it was not like she had wanted to learn. Now, though, Daisy had to figure things out. She could not afford to stop. All day, every day, she pushed herself to exhaustion until the only thing she could do was sleep.

By June, a bit of relief was on the horizon with Daisy's upcoming graduation. Wonderwood Public was a small school, and her teachers had been more than lenient with her about turning assignments late (or not at all). Still, it was one less thing she had to worry about with the summer season kicking into high gear. She would not have to hear her peers talk excitedly about fun plans, big graduation parties thrown by their loving families, or upcoming college adventures.

Or, so she thought.

One Friday after school, the week before graduation, Daisy worked yet another shift at Bagel Bombs!. It was primetime for sunbathers to get their last bit of beach lounging for the day, and usually a lull time for the bread business. She was neck-deep in the fountain soda freezer, scraping a thick layer of frost, when *they* approached the counter.

The girls were local teens like Daisy, all high school seniors, too. They were the children of well-off Wonderwooders, and they attended the expensive private school on the mainland in Cape Crest. The girls' blue plaid skirts and white polo shirt uniforms made them easy to tell apart, along with the air of superiority that followed wherever they went. Their money was as good as anyone else's, at least.

Brushing ice chips from her arms, Daisy stood before the register and waited.

The girl who stepped forward for the group was the only one not wearing a Holy Mother Prep uniform. Daisy recognized Demitria, "Demi," Panopoulos, with her dark olive skin and her lion's mane auburn hair that was pulled into a bun. She attended Wonderwood High with Daisy and was also a member of the "child labor club," thanks to working at her aunt's restaurant on the other end of the boardwalk.

Demi was not too bad. She had an easy smile and was friendlier than most. When they passed each other in the hallways at school, she waved despite being a part of the popular crowd. Despite being *best friends* with the Pier Princess herself, Candace Perry.

*Was she here?*

Since that first hot summer day they met, Daisy sometimes caught glimpses of her. She watched Candace from afar over the years, heard the town locals fawn over Peter Perry and his darling charge. The pair were Wonderwood royalty, with eyes that followed wherever they went. She never ordered directly from Bagel Bombs! again, but, every so often, they would run into each other around town and exchange polite hellos. Candace was kind and courteous to everyone, after all. It was Daisy's imagination that the girl's eyes shone brighter and attention lingered longer on her.

*Right?*

Not that it mattered. Even *if* she were somehow right about Candace having an interest in her, Daisy would never have the metaphorical balls to act on it. Daisy was far from out about her sexuality. It was not that Wonderwood was unsafe. She did not necessarily feel the need to hide her attraction to other girls. Yet, there was a prevailing "don't ask, don't tell" sentiment that the locals seemed content with. South-south Jersey was, as her mom used to say, just under the Mason-Dixon line, so social attitudes trended conservative. Plus, like any other teens, her peers were jackals with gossip. After her parents' accident, the last thing she wanted was more attention.

So, Daisy would not look for the girl she *definitely* did not have a crush on.

Deadpan, she asked Demi, "Can I take your order?"

It was a large list, and years of customer service training kept Daisy focused on writing it down. Until Demi paused and called over her shoulder. "Oh, shoot! Can-can, what was the last kind you wanted? Can-can? Hey!"

*Can-can?* Daisy tried not to snicker at the nickname. Then, amusement was replaced by a distinctly different feeling. It was *her.*

Matching her schoolmates, Candace wore the same collared white polo and blue plaid skirt uniform. It was not like the Catholic School, over-sexed getups they showed on TV. The polo shirt was plain, with an elastic hem that made the garment relatively formless on both male and female bodies. After years of students rolling their skirts to make them shorter, the school switched to longer versions that looked like they belonged in a church choir. And the penny loafers were straight out of *Grease.*

*How does Candace look **so** much hotter?*

Maybe it was her legs. Candace had grown into a tall bombshell over the last few years. The navy knee high socks she wore did *things* to Daisy's imagination, a swell of salacious thoughts that would have landed her in a confessional if she gave a damn about that sort of thing. No, she would keep these fantasies between herself and the vibrator she got at *Spencer's*. The flecks of ice that covered Daisy melted as she started to sweat.

Candace was beet-red by the time she worked her way through the boardwalk throng. In a hiss of a voice, she admonished Demi. *"I told you not to call me that!* It's Candace. *Can*–DACE. And what are you talking about? I didn't want any."

The girl's eyes slingshotted from Demi, to the bagel display, to Daisy in record time. They lingered, looked so long on and deliberately on Daisy, that she could not have imagined it.

Demi huffed. "You're ridiculous, you know that? It's not like he's watching… right now, at least. Order the damn bagel, Candace."

The Pier Princess faced her friend defiantly. Stone-like, she said, "I don't know what you're talking about."

The pair had a staredown while Daisy was held hostage at the register. Not that she wanted to look away. The excuse to observe her crush this closely when *she* was not being the weird one was a rare opportunity. Even so, she was confused, and then a bit grumpy. Who was this "he" they talked about? Daisy heard that Candace dated some boys from both Wonderwood Public and the prep, but the relationships never seemed to last long. If this newest guy was trying to control what she ate, Candace needed to dump his ass.

Feeling testy the more she thought about this hypothetical boyfriend, Daisy goaded Candace. "C'mon, the carbs aren't gonna kill you. But I might die of boredom if you take any longer."

Guilt surged inside Daisy as Candace's attention flashed to her. Embarrassment, maybe even anger, drew her fair features tight. She snapped, "Fine. Two cinnamon, two asiago, two peanut butter and jelly." Before Daisy could comment on the amount—not that she ever would—Candace added, "I need to eat before the bonfire tonight."

"Ah. Okay."

Daisy retrieved the requested bombs from the freezer and set them to toast.

"Are you going?" Demi asked Daisy, and Candace gave the girl a practically audible side-eye. "It seems like our school and the prep are going all out to promote 'unity,' or whatever that means. There'll be fireworks."

Daisy grimaced. She was not fond of school events and had been glad to have the excuse of the bagel stand when her teachers tried to encourage her to go.

"Eh, I'm going to have to pass. Gotta work."

"Really? That sucks."

Shrugging, Daisy repeated, "No can do. I'm the only one who can provide Wonderwood with its bagel fix."

"Are you sure? You can't close for one night?"

It was not Demi, but Candace, and she sounded *disappointed*. She looked as if she had not even realized she spoke aloud until everyone's attention shot to her. Her mouth shut like a steel trap, and she made a show out of grabbing napkins from the dispenser.

While Daisy's heart beat furiously to the echo of those words, the teens moved on to talking about what they would wear to the bonfire, and whose house they would party at afterwards. Candace joined in the conversation, back to her usual, bubbly self. But, more than once, her regard drifted back to Daisy. When the oven buzzer went off, it made them both jump.

Once Daisy dolled out the group's order, they began to amble off. Candace, however, lingered. Releasing the lip she chewed on, she suggested, "You should come tonight."

"Do you want me to?"

For a long beat, the Pier Princess held Daisy in the churning depths of her impossible-to-read gaze. She repeated, "You should come."

It took Daisy three tries to leave her house before she managed to keep going. Even then, it was only out of sheer stubbornness. She knew her neighbors watched her waffling, and eventually, one of them would come outside and comment on it. They were well-meaning, but nosy. Ever since her parents' accident, people she hardly knew wanted the details of her personal life when they had been perfectly content to ignore her before.

So, Daisy did her best to keep a strong outward front. She did not want their pity or whatever help they offered to make themselves feel better. Daisy was fine on her own, and she would prove it. She was a normal teenager, going to hang out with other normal teenagers.

Like Candace Perry.

Why did she tell Daisy to come? The idea that Candace thought of her, ever, past their brief interactions, seemed impossible. But maybe, just maybe, she remembered the first time they met. Maybe, some impossible maybe, Daisy was not crazy, and the attraction she felt was mutual. It could not be that.

And yet...

Daisy was glad that she had a somewhat long walk to the beach cove so that she could calm her anxious fretting. Her parents' bungalow—her bungalow, now—was on the south side of the island with the other blue-collar worker homes, closer to the bay than the boardwalk. It was a walkable distance, but it gave her some time to think. Or, more likely, obsess.

Until the very object of her fretting appeared once again.

Demi, driving her old Jeep Cherokee with its sides open, pulled up alongside Daisy. Her boyfriend, a band kid who also attended Wonderwood Public, was seated in the passenger seat. Candace, of course, was in the back.

"Hey again!" Demi greeted in a chipper tone, "You're coming to the cove after all! Need a lift?"

Daisy forgot how to speak. She looked from Demi's expectant gaze to Candace. The other girl did not meet Daisy's eye. However, as she unbuckled herself and scooted over to make room, it was all the permission Daisy needed. Thanking Demi, she scuttled into the jeep with the grace of a hermit crab.

"All good?" Demi asked.

The seatbelt was like a slippery noodle in Daisy's shaking grip. A hand, Candace's hand, helped to steady her. The contact went on long enough that Daisy could marvel over how velvet-smooth the other girl's skin was. Long enough that it felt intentional, like Candace, too, was conducting her own covert investigation.

Then, she withdrew as if it were nothing.

"T-thanks," Daisy told her, and Candace nodded, tight-lipped.

After she started driving, Demi glanced back in the rearview. "So," she asked, "are you going to college, Daisy? I start at Rowan in the fall."

"No, I've got to run the cafe."

"Oh, um... That's—"

"But I don't think it's for me anyway," Daisy added in a rush. "My grades were never all that great, so it'd be a waste of money."

She did her best to keep her tone light. Dismissive of the idea. That did not stop the sting, though. Just like the rest of her life, everyone else was allowed to go off and do what they wanted. Meanwhile, she was stuck here.

Daisy tried to move the conversation off of herself, saying, "I hear Rowan is a nice school. What are you going for?"

"Art and design. I want to move to Cali and work in a big-name animation studio. Just don't tell my *theia*. She thinks I'm going to work at the diner forever. You still make art, too, right? We had that class together where you put together that driftwood and seaglass sculpture."

"Um, not recently. Been a bit busy."

*What happened recently?*

Daisy could feel them think, and realize that she meant since her parents' accident. Awkwardness spread like a miasma. Needing to dispel the tension, Daisy kept talking.

"Er, Candace. Where are you going to school?"

"Columbia, for business accounting," she answered succinctly with her eyes trained on the floor.

"Wow. That's really impressive. You must have worked hard."

Finally, briefly, Candace locked eyes with Daisy as a small, shy smile curved her lips. "Thanks. I did."

"And I hate it!" Demi whined, "You're not allowed to leave me all alone."

Demi's boyfriend grumbled, "You've got me..."

"Are you Can-can? No. But I guess you'll have to do."

The pair continued their bickering all the way to the cove. Candace, meanwhile, stayed quiet, sitting stiff as a board. Out of the corner of her eyes, Daisy could not help watching her. She'd changed from her school uniform to a sunflower yellow crop top and black mini skirt, which showed far more skin than Daisy's suppressed libido could handle. Very acutely, Daisy wished she'd picked something more stylish than her faded, ripped jean shorts and plain black tank.

When they were close, Demi parked on a side street, and they continued to the cove on foot. It was packed with teenagers. There were a few adult 'chaperones' hovering, but they did not seem the least bit concerned with the rowdy goings on around them. In fact, Daisy saw the football coach from the prep carrying a beer pong table with her school's theatre director. If unity—or, more accurately, a gigantic party

—was what the two schools were hoping to achieve, they succeeded.

Twilight had given way to darkness, but once they passed the duneline before the beach, light from the bonfire engulfed them. The central fire was large enough to light a vast space, and smaller ones surrounded by individual groups were also spread out amongst the area.

Wading into the chaos, Daisy was glad for the excuse to stay close to Candace. She seemed to know everyone, with happy greetings called out in their wake. Her responses were just as enthusiastic, but Daisy sensed something.

The way Candace was with them was different. She was bright and cheerful, almost ditzy compared to the shy, high-achieving girl from the car. They called her 'Candy' and Pier Princess, and maybe that was who she was around these people. When she looked over her shoulder to see if Daisy still followed, though, her eyes were all Candace.

It made Daisy's heart leap.

The sound of Kesha's "TiK ToK" song blared from a speaker on a nearby temporary stage. Red Solo cups were all around, doing the bare minimum to disguise their alcoholic beverages. It was bold of them to drink at what was technically a school event; however, as long as no one went overboard, the Wonderwood police would look the other way. When half of the attendees were the children or relatives of cops or other well-connected locals, a blind eye was the simpler solution.

So, as Demi passed her a cup filled with a hoppy-smelling beverage, Daisy took it. The only other times she'd had alcohol were tastes of her parents' occasional adult drinks. But, she did not want to turn it down when Candace accepted her own.

"C'mon," Demi urged. "Let's find the others."

The "others" were the rest of the group who had been tagging along at the boardwalk earlier, plus a few extras. All popular, rich, connected (or some combination of the three) students from both schools. Not the loner outcasts she generally drifted to when forced to attend social gatherings with her peers. Daisy could feel their surprise seeing her in tow. If Candace had not offered her a seat on the fireside driftwood log that two boys eagerly cleared, she might have run away. Instead, she sat, caught between terror and elation as her knee brushed against the one reason she wanted to be here.

Of course, the main topic of conversation centered on everyone's future plans. This person got accepted to Yale, that person had a full ride to two separate universities, someone else was getting into modeling after signing a contract with some fashion line... it went on and on like that until Daisy wanted to disappear. Before she knew it, her drink was empty.

Candace was going to leave Wonderwood and never look back. Maybe she would visit, a tourist who flitted in and out of Daisy's life while the years passed. And she seemed so happy. When she detailed her plans to the group, it was the happiest Daisy had ever seen her. Happy and ready for a future far from here.

Daisy wondered what it was like. She loved this town, she really did. But she hated not having a choice.

"So," one girl, Amanda, asked, "are you going to work for your uncle once you get your degree? Bet it's a nice gig. Must be nice to be the Pier Princess."

Candace scoffed. "As if. I don't ever want to set foot on that pier again."

"Boo!" Demi hooted, "You're just afraid I'll beat you at air hockey."

"It's not fair! Your reaction time isn't human!"

"True. I'm the abomination produced by endless male cousins. At least I only heckle when I beat you. They write 'loser' on my forehead."

One of the girls' boyfriends asked, "Didn't the pier just open a new roller coaster?"

Candace nodded. Because she was close, Daisy also caught her eyeroll. "There was some building code issue, but I hear your mom at the permit office greased things along."

The kid missed the obvious disdain in Candace's tone as he high-fived with the other thrill seekers beside him. Talk of particular rides prompted the group to share their favorite pier activities, from the teacups to the new ghost bayou attraction. Even Candace admitted to loving the carnival games, and she readily shared the tricks to beating them.

Daisy was lost in her thoughts, thinking how cute Candace's button-nosed profile was, when she felt all eyes turn to her. "Um..."

Across their group's baby bonfire, Demi looked comfortable under her boyfriend's arm. She clarified, "Everyone else said their favorite thing about the pier. Don't hold out on us!"

*Make something up!*

Daisy tried, but her mind went blank. She could not think of a single ride. When a painfully long time had passed, she managed to admit, "I don't know what my favorite ride is. I've never been."

The groups' incredulity seared Daisy hotter than the flames in front of her. She took a swig of her drink even though it was long empty.

"Never...?" Candace's small voice was equal parts wondrous and pity-filled. "But you're *right* across the boardwalk."

All Daisy could do was shrug.

"Wow," one of the boys quipped, "your parents must not love you."

A metaphorical lead balloon socked Daisy right in the gut. The rest of the group exchanged wide-eyed shock, apart from the oblivious boy who'd spoken.

"What?" He asked, and one of his friends leaned in to explain.

"Bro... the people from that freak bridge accident. That's their kid."

"Oh—shit, yo... Sorry. That's messed up."

Daisy could not look at him. She could not look at the others as they echoed his sympathy in mumbled discomfort. She knew that she had to do something, say the words from the grief-script she'd found herself forced to repeat over and over. She felt trapped, suffocated despite the crisp May evening air. Without realizing it, she got to her feet.

"Um," she droned out. "I'm out of beer."

Pivoting, Daisy all but bolted from the group—from the party entirely. She earned more than a few dirty looks as she barreled through the crowd. Mumbled sorries were the best she could do.

It was only as she made it to the dune line, almost back to the streets and her solitude, that Daisy realized she was being followed. Hearing the sound of sand shuffling behind her, she whirled.

The other person came to an abrupt stop. So abruptly that they crashed into Daisy because of how close they'd been.

They were in a darkened corridor between the beach bonfires and the street lights of Wonderwood's civilization. It might have been impossible to tell her pursuer's identity. Even so, the airy gasp she let loose as Daisy steadied her, the scent of lilac and, most tellingly, the way Daisy's heart started hammering at their skin contact, gave Candace away.

"Are you alright?"

Daisy tried to play it cool. She released Candace and stepped back.

"You're the one who nearly face-planted a dune. I'm good."

"You said you were getting more beer."

"I never said I was getting more. I said I was out."

Daisy could not see Candace's frown, but she could feel it.

"Are you leaving?"

Was that disappointment in her voice? Why did she follow Daisy?

"He's an ass," Candace blurted out when Daisy did not— could not—respond. "Dumb as a bunch of rocks. No, a single rock, and not even a cool one. Just a big, dumb boulder. I told him to get lost."

"You didn't have to do that. It wasn't his fault he didn't know."

"Well, now he does, and he can go be stupid somewhere else. If you want to come back, no one will say a word."

Daisy considered it. She was happy that Candace wanted her back. That she'd stood up for her. Still, she'd had enough and she said as much.

In a sugary sweet tone that made Daisy's knees wobble, Candace pleaded, "But the fireworks are going to start soon."

Somehow, Daisy managed to feign indifference. "I can see them from here."

"I suppose that's true. Alright, then. I'll watch them here too."

"What...?"

Candace huffed, but it was somehow a gentle sound. "I want to watch them from here now. Is that a problem?"

"N-no."

Daisy sat at the foot of a dune that was at least triple her height, letting her back rest against the hard-packed sand, and Candace followed suit. An awkward silence settled between them while a million different thoughts flitted through Daisy's racing mind.

What was this? Why did Candace want to stay with her? It was pity, right? That was what it had to be. But this didn't feel like pity. There was something here, a charged current running between them. Like magnetism, if Daisy could just move even the slightest bit, she might—

"We could climb the dune to get a better view?"

Daisy's daydream vanished. She automatically answered, "Can't. It's illegal."

Silently, Daisy cursed her inner nature-nerd. However, she could not stop. In what could only be considered word-vomit, she explained the importance of sand dunes to the shore ecosystem, both for the creatures of the beach and for their function as a natural storm barrier for raised water levels. Thankfully, the interest in Candace's response seemed genuine.

"Oh, wow! I had no idea how important they are. My uncle

calls them wasted real estate, but he's wrong about most things."

"Really wrong. If a hurricane hit and these dunes weren't here, Wonderwood would be in trouble. Er, sorry. I don't mean to be boring."

"It's not! Boring, I mean. I'm sorry for being clueless. Very shoobie of me. You've lived here all your life, though. Right?"

"Yep. Wonderwood local here. I'm half sand, half bagel, all dork. And you're not a shoobie. The Pier Princess is royalty around here."

They both laughed. In Candace's though, Daisy heard some discomfort.

"You don't like that name," Daisy thought aloud. "Or nicknames in general."

"No. Not really, if I'm being honest. Growing up, my parents never called me anything other than my name. Now, people forget what it is half the time."

Daisy didn't know anything about Candace's parents. She wanted to so badly, but she could not bring herself to ask. As if she felt the question regardless, Candace went on.

"My mom... she died when I was little. An aneurysm."

"I'm sorry."

It was strange. All the sympathy Daisy had gotten since her parents' deaths over the last year, all the 'I'm sorrys' she hated to hear, but that was her automatic response now. She wanted to ask Candace if it ever got easier, but held back as the other girl continued.

"I don't remember her all that well. My dad went from being the best dad in the world to a complete wreck of a person. Then he met his new wife. She wanted nothing to do with me, so they sent me to my grandparents on my mom's side."

"What a cold witch."

Daisy's eyes had adjusted to the darkness enough that she thought she could see the slightest shrug of the girl's shoulders.

"You can't make someone want you. That just makes

everything harder. My grandparents tried, at least. But they were too old to take care of me."

"So that's how you ended up here with your uncle."

"Mm-hm," Candace confirmed with a sigh. "He's my mother's brother. I've been stuck with him in Wonderwood, where they call me anything but my actual name. Shoobie fits, though, because I've never really felt at home here. I can't wait until I get out."

Daisy knew Candace could not see her, but she shook her head with awe. She had no idea. All this time, the happy-go-lucky girl who had been the center of town gossip and adoration since her arrival six years ago was living through so much difficulty.

Memory of that anxious, beguiling girl she met one hot summer day came to Daisy. How sad she seemed, how out of place she was. She came to Wonderwood as an outsider and had only ever been welcomed on its terms.

All at once, Daisy snapped out of her thoughts and scoffed. "You know what? Shoobie is a dumb name, anyway. You're Candace Freaking Perry, and no matter where you are, nothing and no one is gonna hold you back."

"Thanks, Daisy."

Since the darkness hid Candace's face, Daisy could not read her expression. There was something there, though. The sand beneath them vibrated with tension.

A moment passed. Back at the bonfire, the sounds of partying carried over in an odd juxtaposition to their heavy silence. As if she the felt need to fill it, Candace admitted, "I've seen you around, you know."

"You have? I mean, I guess with the pier right across the boardwalk, it's a given."

"No, not just at the cafe." The sound of sand shifting alerted Daisy to Candace's movement. The inky darkness of her figure turned, almost craning over Daisy's reclined form. "You hang out around under the convention hall. And near the westside jetty. I've seen you with your sketchbook, scribbling away.

Demi says your art projects are always the best in class. But I don't know much about you."

It was more than Daisy expected. Her pulse pounded in her veins at the thought that Candace ever noticed her as anything apart from the girl behind the bagel counter.

"You want to?"

The words tumbled out of Daisy's mouth like marbles, clattering between them and rolling along. She felt so *stupid*. And needy. And—

"I do."

It came out in a rush. Daisy told Candace about herself, from working at Bagel Bombs! to the driftwood art she made for class. She explained more nature facts, going off on a rant about how the people speeding on Route 9 endangered the nesting turtles. Candace giggled at Daisy's passion, but offered to bring up the issue to some bigwig on the town council.

It was a boomerang conversation, going from inane topics to heavy ones in an instant. Candace talked about wanting to get away from her uncle's controlling tendencies and gave a lecture about building a diversified investment portfolio. She surprised Daisy when she made a reference to a show it turned out they both loved. They proceeded to make a series of inside jokes in mock-imitations of the four-fingered, yellow cartoon characters.

Daisy came as close as she could to admitting that she'd been struggling. The weight of it all as she talked about it, the pressure she couldn't escape, seemed to shrink as Candace's hand found hers in the darkness.

Eventually, their talk reached a natural lull. It was like coming up after a long dive. They spoke for so long, Daisy forgot all about the fireworks. The party, the other people, were background noise. She was here for Candace, and Candace...

"I'm glad you came tonight. I'm moving right after graduation, so I wasn't sure I'd see you again before I left."

Inside her chest, Daisy's heart performed wild somersaults. What could she say to that? A grand revelation that was as glorious as it was disappointing. Candace wanted to see Daisy, but she would be gone soon. Was there a way to make this moment last forever?

"I'm here," Daisy whispered, almost to herself. "What were you hoping would happen if I came?"

The sand shifted. Shadow swallowed Daisy as Candace's form moved over her. Then, atop her lips, she felt a subtle, soft press.

*Candace's lips.*

It was Daisy's first kiss. She felt herself lift up, catapulting into a stratosphere of sensation she'd only dreamed of, while her toes curled into the cool sand to keep grounded. It was a vain effort.

The kiss lasted all but a few seconds before Candace pulled away. But it happened. She wanted to know Daisy in *that* way. Not only was she interested in women, she was interested in *her*.

Breathlessly, and so adorably unsure, Candace asked, "Was that okay?"

"I dunno… We'll have to try again."

Nervous, giddy laughter escaped them both. A beat passed, a mutual intake of bated breath. Then, their lips collided.

It was awkward and unrefined. More fumble than finesse, as they tested each other's bounds with clipped kisses and tentative touches. Yet, before long, they eased into a rhythm, soft and swaying like reeds in the wind.

Candace relaxed over Daisy as they both sank against the dune. The grit of the sand, the annoying places it slipped into, was a distant afterthought compared to the yielding press of flesh. Daisy never knew how warm it would feel to be held like this, how goosebumps would rain over her skin with every needful shift.

The first slip of Candace's tongue along Daisy's lower lip caught her off guard. Daisy was ready for the second, and she met Candace's tongue with her own. Sweet saliva tinged by mystery alcohol swept her on a journey of forbidden taste. She was not sure if the moan came from her throat or Candace's, but she was unable to stop herself from adding another.

—followed by a gasp as fingers slipped under Daisy's tank top collar and moulded around her breast. Breaking their lips, Candace asked Daisy in a hot puff of breath, "Do you want to slow down?"

*"Fuck no!"*

Daisy did not want to waste a single moment. She found Candace in the darkness. The pulsating thigh that her fingers grazed against was a drum beat urging her on. She ghosted her fingers from that low point, up and up, until she reached the miniskirt's hem. As Candace kissed her again, Daisy took it as permission to go further. She did not want to overthink, or worry, or wonder. She wanted to know Candace, too.

However, the side she saw next was the worst part.

Being with Candace Perry should have elated Daisy. It should have made her belly flop, and her heart flutter. Instead, before she could enjoy any of those sweet sensations, an explosion rumbled the air. As the fireworks burst into bright, beautiful colors, sparks rained down below. Sparks that illuminated the bonfire attendees, Daisy and Candace included.

Over the crowd's general "oohs" and "ahs," a shrill voice cut above them.

*"Oh my GAWD.* Is Bagel Girl trying to **kiss** Candy Perry?!"

It was impossible to tell who said the words as a wave of eyes turned to Daisy and Candace on the dune. So *many* eyes. Fellow students, teachers, and even Candace's own Uncle Perry watched the pair like they were on a stage.

Daisy did not look at them. Her attention was locked on Candace, who sprang up so fast you'd never think she was the one who made the first move. Successive fireworks showed flashes of emotion over the girl's face like photographs as she looked down at Daisy.

Embarrassment.

The lingering flush of lust.

Fear.

And total, gut-wrenching sorrow.

Yet, with the crowd looking on, it was like she became a different person. Tossing her hair back, she boasted, "Can you blame her? Who wouldn't want a piece of me?"

Daisy stammered under her breath, "But you... I—"

"It was brave of you to make a pass, but I told you, I'm not that kind of girl."

"Yeah," some Pier Princess defender jibed, "keep dreaming, lesbo."

Then, they laughed. Candace joined in, laughing along with her friends and both of their schools, while Daisy felt like she was sinking into oblivion.

It was only thanks to the finale, and all its glorious, attention-grabbing glory, that Daisy was able to escape. Scrambling through the sand, she stumbled up and away from the beach as fast as her shaking legs would carry her.

Where she got was here: Lonely. Directionless. And, worst of all, right back where she started, sitting next to the person who hurt her most.

Daisy shook her head to clear the past. The nature center and the simulated waves that lapped against the sides of Horace's enclosure helped to ground her.

"You know why I don't like social media?" Without waiting for a response, Daisy explained, "I was outed to my whole school. Hell, the whole island found out. They harassed me for years for trying to get with the Pier Princess. It was humiliating, and I just had to take it. You, though... You got to fuck off to New York like it never happened. So, Candace... If you were me, would you want anything to do with you?"

# CHAPTER 11

*Candace*

C andace did not have an answer to Daisy's question. She did not want much to do with herself after hearing Daisy's side of that shameful night.

At the bonfire, Candace's queerness exploded after years of repression. She had agonized over inviting Daisy, and even more so over what she would say if they were ever alone. Kissing her had never been a part of the plan. But it happened, and it was more incredible than she could have ever imagined.

Then, just like those fireworks, she fizzled out.

Candace had been a coward. Under the threat of her uncle's condemning eyes, fearful that he would punish her and make her stay in Wonderwood, she threw Daisy under the bus. Candace lied. Yet, it had driven her to be more honest and open once she escaped.

Throughout college, and up until her recent drought, she'd

had an active sex life with several partners. No deep romances, since she had not had the time for anything beyond surface level when her career was her focus. Even so, that agonizingly brief taste of requited feelings with Daisy gave her the push to pursue who she wanted as an adult.

That moment, so many summers ago, changed Candace's path for the better. It had been a life-defining, monumental event for her. For Daisy, it caused nothing but hurt. And Candace, somehow, thought she might have forgotten.

*How stupid…*

Garbage was a kinder description than she deserved. She liked to think that she was more than the vapid, oblivious girl so many people thought she was. But with this, the evidence was irrefutable.

Candace did something terrible, and no amount of growth she'd experienced since negated that. There was no excuse, no explanation good enough to justify the ridicule Daisy faced.

However, the words still needed to be said. Simple as they were, without frills or fuss.

Candace told Daisy, "I'm sorry. I'm sorry for what I did to you and what you had to face because of me. It was wrong. I was wrong, and I would do anything to take it back."

"… Okay."

Daisy was impossible to read. Her posture was tight, her strong features set in stone. Even so, Candace swore she saw a softening in the woman's smooth caramel eyes. It was all she needed. Acknowledgement, if not acceptance, would have to suffice.

Sucking in a deep breath, Candace released it in a shaky exhale. Idly, she admitted, "It was my first kiss too."

Candace caught a dubious, interested eyebrow quirk before the woman's face turned back to granite.

"Your first kiss with another woman, you mean."

"No. In general."

Daisy scoffed. "You're lying. I heard you dated the prep's football captain."

"My uncle set us—no, he told me to date Lary. I never kissed him, though. He got grabby, and it gave me the excuse to dump him."

Daisy seemed unconvinced.

"You don't believe me? What reason would I have to lie about that?"

"I don't know," Daisy admitted. Sounding annoyed, she added, "You can barely call it a kiss anyway. I've had burps that last longer."

Candace winced. She was not sure why, but the dismissiveness in Daisy's tone was the deepest cut in this knife-sharpening conversation. She felt like a human whetstone trying to take the blows. But, comparing a kiss she'd dreamt about, fantasized endlessly over what would have happened if they went further, drove the metaphorical knife right through.

Evenly as she could, Candace got to the point. "So. If this kiss meant nothing and everything, where does that leave us? Where do we go from here?"

For a long while, so long that Candace was beginning to think she would not reply, Daisy kept quiet. At a deliberate pace, she nodded. Her voice was confident.

"You said you'd do anything to make up for what you did to me? Fine. Help save Bagel Bombs!. I can't guarantee I'll forgive you or be nice, but I can work with you. And, as much as I hate to admit it, you know what you're doing."

Candace's spirit soared. She could not keep the smile from her face as she exclaimed, *"Really?!"*

"Yeah, but wipe that grin off your face. You get one more chance, and this time, I'm gonna ride you *hard.*"

Daisy seemed to know her phrasing was off the moment she said the words. The woman flushed, and her face scrunched as if she'd eaten something sour. Candace, however, did not miss a beat.

"Good. I'm counting on it."

At 8 AM on the dot, Candace pulled up along the curb in front of Daisy's house. She considered pulling right back out. Last night, after Daisy and she snuck out of the long-closed nature center following their sort-of reconciliation, they parted on better terms than she thought possible.

Not *good,* but better off than they were when everything was left unsaid.

Now, it was time for Candace to put her metaphorical money where her mouth was.

Candace checked her reflection in the vanity mirror before exiting her car. Worry stared back at her as all the ways she messed up and *still could* mess up played in an endless loop through her imagination cinema. She hated this movie, the one where she was the villain in Daisy's story as well as her own.

*What if I get in the way?*

Chaotic as it was, Daisy had a process and method to managing her business. Would she be angry at Candace trying to insert herself again? Think she was being pushy?

Or was Candace just making up excuses because she was afraid of rejection? A therapist session was in her future, but for now she had to move forward. Daisy was counting on her.

Send the script back for rewrites, Candace told herself. She was the one in charge of her actions, and it was time to take responsibility.

Sighing, Candace closed the mirror shutter with a snap. At least costume department was doing their job for this metaphorical movie. Despite her limited wardrobe, there were a few pieces she kept from her regular rotation in case she had a special occasion… such as surprising her boss/partner in a desperate bid to garner goodwill.

Candace almost felt like her old self wearing her favorite sleeveless blazer and pencil skirt. Seafoam tweed with gold accents, it matched her eyes and was tailored to fit her like a glove. She pulled her hair up into a tight, no-nonsense ponytail, with two elegant locks left free to frame her face. In this outfit, strutting in her tan kitten heels, she'd never failed to turn heads and leave slack jaws in her wake.

Maybe it would be enough to stop Daisy's scowl.

Walking up the mismatched stone pavers to the gray-blue slatted wood of the bay cottage's tiny covered porch, Candace could feel her heart pound harder. Not in a nice, fluttery manner, but like a trapped animal. Her step faltered as she missed a paver thanks to her shaking legs. Stopping, she took a moment to collect herself.

Candace had always felt emotions intensely. It was her Scorpio energy, Demi said. Her uncle berated her for it, called her weak and a typical woman. So, over the years, she had gotten better at controlling the outward display.

Breathing techniques were a helpful part of her coping arsenal. Through yoga, therapy, and a zealous need to research everything that interested her, she picked up several different types over the years. Alternate nostril breathing was her favorite for centering. To start, she shimmied her skirt up so that she could sit down on a paver, cross-legged. She set the coffee caddy on the ground, then pinched her nose with her thumb and pointer finger. Then, she alternated which nostril she plugged as she breathed in and out at a timed pace.

Thankfully, Daisy did not have a doorcam to catch the odd behaviors. No bell, either.

Once she gathered herself, Candace tried the brass knocker and waited.

And waited.

As long as Daisy had not moved from her childhood home,

Candace was sure she was at the right place. Years ago, Demi pointed it out to her while wearing a sly, knowing grin.

Daisy's golf cart was nowhere in sight, but the house had an attached garage, so it was reasonable to assume it was stored there. The landscaping was minimal, with tall bay grasses and shrubbery like prickly holly bushes. Nothing was too unkempt, but there was little personality—not even a garden gnome. The place seemed so... *bland*. Not like the cool, witty, artistic Daisy she knew.

Maybe she was wrong, or...?

*No*, Candace thought. *This is it.*

In the end, it was the smell that made Candace certain.

A familiar, bready scent caught Candace's nose. Her empty stomach rumbled with anticipation. She took a long, savoring breath of toasted flour as she followed the invisible trail around the side of the house. There, past a narrow yard where the only thing of note was an outdoor shower stall, she continued to the back.

It was a small area. Just as sparse as the front, it was secluded by a high wood fence and tall spruce trees. A double-panel glass sliding door with no curtains or cover allowed Candace to see right inside.

Her jaw dropped.

*Holy bagels.*

It was an open lower level, so from where Candace stood she could see straight through from the kitchen to the living room to the locked front door. A TV faced her on the far wall, playing an old rerun of *The Simpsons*.

The main appliances, countertop, and sink were located in the right corner of the room closest to the sliding door. Every burner of the stove was active, from big boiling pots of water to what looked like curry in a saucepan. A behemoth, rustic farmhouse central table took up the majority of the space, and each inch of it was occupied by a bagel bomb or bagel bomb component in various states of completion.

The bread-stravaganza was impressive. Candace counted

ten trays with at least twelve different flavors. That, however, was not what she stared at. Once her eyes found Daisy, she could not look away.

And not just because the woman was half-naked.

Daisy was like some kind of bagel gladiator, chopping, slinging, and gliding her way through the kitchen like she was grand champion. Lean muscles rippling, she whisked a perfect roux, kneaded a tough-looking glob of dough, and retrieved a pan from the oven in the space of a minute with expert precision.

All while wearing nothing but a gray cotton bralette and matching bikini bottoms. Her short hair was pulled up into a top tail that stuck up like a horn, with some spilling out in a spiky mane around her face. A face that was drawn tight with concentration, focused and set with self-assurance that was so *damn* sexy.

*Holy bread babe,* Candace thought. She watched, slack-jawed and embarrassed by the needful pulse between her legs.

Then, by being caught.

Daisy saw Candace. Her curse was muted, but the crash of her dropping the pan she held was thunderous. An avalanche of bagels spilled all over the floor.

After a stunned moment, Candace snapped from her stupor. Thankfully, the sliding door was unlatched. She rushed through, greeted by Daisy's yelling.

*"The FUCK, Perry?!"*

"I'm sorry! I'm so sorry!! Shoot—!"

Candace scrambled to join Daisy picking up bagels and forgot about the coffee caddy she was holding. She caught the tipping cups right as they were about to slosh hot liquid all over herself and the classic black and white linoleum floor. Setting it aside, she did her best to corral the rolling balls while Daisy continued railing at her.

"Candace! What the hell are you doing? Why are you in my house?!"

"I promised I would help! I thought you might need an extra

pair of hands for bagel prep, and—*Oh...!*"

Candace's attention shot from the bagels to Daisy, who was still half-naked. And, now, that nakedness was a *lot* closer. After she turned off the stove burners and muted the TV, she moved to tower over Candace. Once again, the woman was an imposing gladiator with her arms crossed beneath her bralette.

Candace could not help noticing the way her piqued nipples poked through the sheer material, or the under-view of soft swells from the slightly-too-small garment. Her gaze plunged lower, past abs that her fingers wanted to spend days climbing, before settling on the valley between Daisy's thighs. They were parted by her strong stance, just enough that Candace could see a few ghosting curls and the barest definition of her—

All at once, Candace realized how much of a creep she was being. She covered her eyes and blurted out another emphatic "Sorry!"

Long, agonizing seconds passed. Candace's entire body radiated so hot she thought she might burn a hole through the floor. She could not see Daisy's face, but eventually heard her snort. There was the sound of movement, and she felt Daisy's soft mouth press against her ear. A shiver coursed down her spine as the woman spoke in a hot, heavy puff of breath.

"*Out.*"

Startled, Candace fell back onto her butt with a yip. She found Daisy's face once more to discover a wry expression. Her tone was a mix of exasperation and smugness.

"You really are something else, you know that? Let's try this again."

"W-what?"

"Get out and go knock at the front door like a normal, not privileged princess. I'll put some clothes on. If you're going to help, I can't have you drooling like an idiot the entire time."

A few minutes later, Daisy let Candace into her home through the proper entryway. She wore a fresh pair of navy blue joggers and a black T-shirt. It was not much more than her usual tank top and shorts, but it seemed like a pointed shift.

Candace felt like she'd been caught with a hand in a cookie jar... A tall, tanned jar that she'd love to lick the inside clean and—

Clearing her throat along with the lecherous thoughts, Candace coughed out a good morning.

One of Daisy's dirty blonde brows cocked as she surveyed Candace. She took a sip of coffee—the coffee Candace had brought—and stepped back.

"Mm-hm. Good morning for Peeping Toms."

"I tried knocking! You didn't hear me over Homer Simpson."

The dubiousness of Daisy's expression was broken by her smirk. She apparently liked to see Candace squirm, which was a frustrating find. At least she was not angry. Daisy led Candace to the kitchen.

Like other bay cottages, it was not a large space. They passed a narrow stairway that appeared to lead to a single room upstairs, and a short hallway with two ajar doors. She got a peek of a retro pink tile bathroom and a bedroom strewn with clothes. When Daisy saw Candace's eyes linger on her bedroom, she shut it from view.

"I wasn't expecting company," Daisy grumbled.

"It's homey. And I guarantee my place at the Comfort Clam is no showroom."

Overall, the thing that stuck out most to Candace was how

dated the place felt. Like the outside, it was maintained and clean, but worn. Daisy's house reminded Candace of the set for an old sitcom. With its fully carpeted living spaces dominated by caramel tones, wood paneling on the lower half of the walls accented by squiggly line wallpaper overtop, and chunky, faded furniture, the place was straight out of *Malcom in the Middle*.

But this was not a TV set. This was where Daisy lived, where she grew up, and the evidence was all around. Candace spotted a hand-knitted throw blanket with loops loosened by years of use; interesting shells and sea glass tossed in a bowl by the door; tons of hanging family pictures that showed a completely different Daisy from the one Candace knew today. Ones that showed the Daisy she remembered from their teens, from before the hurt and distance filled up an ocean between them.

Candace forced herself not to look overlong. She could not bear to, despite how adorable little-Daisy was. She stuck to the present.

The only modern items were the appliances. Now that she was not focused on bagel retrieval or ogling a nearly-naked woman, she saw high end brands like Kitchenaid and Bosch wedged among old, natural oak cabinets and butcher's block countertops.

An array of stand mixers were arranged in a row along one section of the counter, and all of the pans were shiny stainless steel. She supposed a baker needed proper tools to produce on the scale that Daisy did. That massive table with its bagely bounty took up most of the floor space, extending right to where the kitchen linoleum and den carpet met.

Like a well-oiled machine, Daisy set back to what she was doing before Candace interrupted. The woman had so many metaphorical plates spinning (and some burning), it was clear that she could not afford to stop. She knew what she was doing, though. Despite being thrown off her game, the experienced baker adjusted her timers and set to task again.

Candace was totally out of her element. She could read directions and assemble food, but *this* was really cooking. Trying to take initiative, she started to finish cutting up a half-chopped onion, but dropped it as Daisy said it was the wrong type of cut.

Standing there, Candace felt an overwhelming surge of shame. Why did she always complicate things? She kept trying and trying, but maybe she was as incompetent as everyone thought. This was her fault to begin with, and now—

"Dish duty!"

"Excuse me?"

Brushing past Candace to grab a big pair of yellow rubber gloves, Daisy lightly whapped her arm with them and pointed to the sink. "I have too much going on to teach you how to make the bombs now, but you can do the dishes. That would help me out."

"Right!"

Out of every household task, Candace honestly *liked* doing dishes. Growing up, after her mom died but before she was shuffled from her grandparents to her uncle, most of the household tasks fell to her. They had to, since her father had other priorities. Candace was rarely, and then never, included in his plans for a happy home. Even so, he did thank her for keeping their place clean in the brief, dark period before he was able to find a new woman to take care of it.

In the vague recesses of her childhood memory, Candace recalled how the trash and bottles piled up. Her grandparents on her mother's side would come to check on them (her), and Candace did not want her father to get in trouble. So, she would clean up the evidence of his drinking and neglect.

Afterwards, her father would praise her and promise to do better. She lived for those slivers of attention. It was the only time she felt wanted. But it was not enough for him to keep her when she did not fit into his new family.

Candace frowned as a sudsy frying pan slipped from her grasp. It had been years since she thought of her absentee father. Of all the stressors and pain points in her life, he was a trauma she'd long packed away into a neat little box. Or, at least, she thought she had. She supposed seeing all the pictures of Daisy's happy family sparked it.

Trips to the beach where they posed with melty ice cream cones; Daisy, with the most bashful grin on her face, holding up some kind of driftwood sculpture; all three of them standing proudly before Bagel Bombs!. She looked like a complete mix of the two, having inherited her mother's kind brown eyes and her father's impressive height.

They were the perfect family.

The kind of family Candace always wished she had. Daisy's parents seemed to genuinely love her. No wonder she was reluctant to give up on the business they worked so hard to build.

If the napkin numbers Candace ran last night were right, they were on track. Not the best one, but one that might mean surviving the season. Provided she could build significant momentum with a few more promotions, and her uncle did not pull any more dubious legal moves, they had... not a chance, but a chance of a chance.

Candace finished washing the frying pan and moved onto a proving container crusted with old dough. As she scrubbed and scrubbed, bubbly water sloshed dangerously high. It was under control—

—until Candace happened to catch sight of Daisy videoing her. In her surprise, she leaped and the water came too, splashing all down her front.

"*Shit!*"

Candace let out an unusual-for-her curse and rushed to dab the material with a nearby rag. If she didn't dry it fast, she would never get the watermarks out.

For her part, Daisy burst out laughing.

"I'm glad you find this so funny! My favorite outfit is ruined!"

"Consider it payback for you paparazzi-ing me all over

social media. And it's what you get for always dressing like you're going to a client meeting. Do you even own a pair of sweatpants?"

"What's wrong with a little style? Besides—" Candace clamped her mouth closed. Daisy didn't ask for an explanation, and she probably would not care for one either. "It doesn't matter. You just go ahead and keep laughing it up."

With an annoyed grunt, Daisy set her phone on the table. She left for a beat, then returned with a tank top and shorts.

"Here. Minus some boobage, we're about the same size. Give me those and we'll see if the dryer can salvage things."

"Permanent press setting," Candace confirmed. "No fabric softener." She finally stopped her anxious patting, though her heart still hammered as she took Daisy's clothes into her arms. With a shake of her head, the woman laughed again.

"Of course, m'lady." Daisy pointed, saying, "I'm not undressing you, too. Bathroom's over there."

Red-faced, Candace bolted.

Her life continued to run from one humiliation to the next. But, she thought as she closed the door behind her, it was nice to see Daisy smile. Unconsciously, she held the bundle close. The summer scent of beaches and bagels filled her soul.

# CHAPTER 12

## *Daisy*

*W*hat a weird day.

*No, what a weird person,* Daisy thought while tossing said person's sopping clothes into the dryer.

Candace was taking a long time getting changed. She was probably inspecting the state of the bathroom's tile grout. Or fixing her perfect hair. Or making fun of... something. Daisy saw the way the woman's eyes scanned every detail of the house, judging it. Judging *her* and the way she lived.

*Whatever.*

Daisy did not give a shit what Candace thought about anything, least of all herself. She could stay in the bathroom the rest of the day for all Daisy cared. No one asked her to come barging over in the first place. Like always, though, the woman did what she wanted.

Daisy swiped her coffee from its place on the table and took a generous gulp. It was black, just the way she liked it, and the bean roast was that perfect blend of earthy bliss. Recollection hit her mid-draught that Candace had brought the drink. She dropped the cup with a grimace, stubbornly set on refusing to enjoy any part of the intrusion.

What Daisy needed was a nice, long nap. But naps were for closers. Or, for business owners/bakers who caught up on their inventory issues. Thanks to Candace, Daisy was a ways off.

Apart from a brief rest when her dough was proofing, Daisy had been up all, night locked into an endless cycle of mixing and measuring and making. She felt like she was going to be scraping dough and cream cheese from under her fingernails for days. She made so much, she'd run out of key ingredients.

And she needed to do more.

She was waiting on her finished bombs to cool down. Then, she would bag, vacuum seal, and freeze the pocket treats. It was a process that was almost as meticulous as the baking. One mistake now meant a major headache (and customer complaints) later.

Like her dad used to say: *"Do it once, do it right, it won't come back to bite."*

Daisy proceeded to rearrange her workspace. She cleared an area to seal the bombs, prepared her reusable bags, and carefully wrote out each label in big, clear-to-read blocky letters.

*Plain.*
*Whole Wheat.*
*Sesame.*
*Everything.*
*Cinnamon Raisin.*
*Asiago.*
*Chive cream cheese and bacon.*
*Maple French Toast*
*Cheddar Jalapeño*
*Chocolate Chip*

*Japanese Curry*
*Italian herbs and cheese*
*Chorizo & Cotija*
And,
*Peanut Butter & Jelly*

Daisy stared at that last label. The flavor was not one she made often. Maybe once every few months, if that. Having it prepared when Candace first came to town had been pure coincidence. But, since then, Daisy had found herself making them a part of her regular batch bakes.

It was not because the flavor was Candace's favorite. Consistently, the peanut butter bombs that did not end up in the woman's mouth sold out. She just happened to have good taste, and Daisy would make whatever sold well.

That's all there was to it.

Daisy tossed her marker aside with a curse. Candace *always* got her way. How had she known where Daisy lived, anyway? Even when Candace was being helpful, she barreled through obstacles as if they meant nothing to her lofty self. It would be impressive, if not for the frustration.

*What a steamroller of a woman.*

Daisy looked up to see the object of her thoughts emerge from the bathroom. And she kept looking because *goddamn*.

It was just a Bagel Bombs! tank top and loose athletic shorts. The type of outfit Daisy threw on each day with little to no thought. She'd worn this particular combination hundreds of times. Daisy was certain, however, that the clothes did not look like *that* when she wore them.

It was rare to come across another woman as tall as Daisy, but, in her kitten heels, Candace came close. Her long, toned legs filled out the Under Armour shorts *too* well; with their flared and slight side part, it looked almost like a black mini skirt. The tank top, meanwhile, was too small. Daisy did not need much to cover up her petite bust, while Candace and her hourglass proportions demanded the next size up. Her chest practically popped under the tight neckline, and the hem lifted, exposing a pale sliver of midriff.

The irony was not lost on Daisy that their roles were reversed from earlier. Unlike the naked, obvious lust Candace showed, Daisy thought she did a good job of keeping her outward display neutral... in spite of actual, annoying arousal that spiked inside.

"See?" Candace mumbled, "This is why I don't wear this sort of thing. It looks so trashy on me."

Daisy gaped.

"You think you look *trashy*?"

Candace crossed her arms as if she were trying to hide her shame, gaze trained on the linoleum. As she curled the lock of hair framing her face behind her ear, Daisy saw the deep pink flush that scored the other woman's cheeks.

"I can never get casual clothes to fit me right. It looks like I'm just trying to get attention by showing skin."

A frown replaced Daisy's open-mouthed disbelief.

She flipped the logic, clarifying, "You think I'm trying to get attention when I wear my everyday clothes? You think *I* look trashy?"

"*NO!*" Candace met Daisy's gaze with her shout, but broke as she went on. "I don't think that at all. You always look so *cool*. It's just... that's what my uncle used to say whenever he saw me in these sorts of clothes. He once told me that hoodies and sweatpants were for poor people."

"That's the dumbest bunk I've ever heard. Don't you do yoga? What do you wear, a business suit?"

Daisy could not help picturing what Candace might wear to one of her classes. How she might bend, twist, and...

*NOPE.*

Daisy gave herself a mental slap and turned back to the ridiculous conversation at hand.

"That's different," Candace countered. "You wouldn't understand."

"No, I think I've got things figured out."

They were separated by the length of the table. Crossing her arms, not to hide but to project strength, Daisy closed the distance between them.

She explained, "Your asshole uncle is weird about how you dress, so now you're weird about it. And it pisses me off, because *what the fuck?* It's a tank top and shorts, they're totally normal clothes. What kind of chode gets worked up about that?"

A ghost of a smile flickered on Candace's face at Daisy's choice of insult. Her reply was a sober, long-considered conclusion.

"The kind of person who views you as an extension of themselves, subject to their morals and standards. In his eyes, I'm supposed to draw attention, but only the *right* kind of attention. He's fine with dressing me up in a bikini to promote the pier, but if I wore something like this around the house, his comments would be less than kind."

"So he's a hypocrite and a gross control freak who sexualizes his own niece."

The more Daisy heard about Peter Perry, the more she hated the man. Candace's eyes popped open at the bald-faced truth. Then, she deflated. Her arms dropped to her sides with her reluctant shrug.

"Yeah. That's the gist of it. I'm sorry for being weird."

Daisy shook her head. "Don't apologize to me. Apologize to yourself for internalizing that horseshit. You're hot, princess. You could wear a potato sack and make it look like a designer dress. That doesn't mean you're out for attention."

"No," she confirmed with a shudder. "The last thing I want is to be front and center. I've just gotten good at putting up with it to make him happy, and for my job. But it's difficult. Which is exactly why I should have known better about taking that picture of you without asking. Sorry again."

Daisy scratched the back of her head, unsure of what to say. She had not been expecting another apology for the social media snafu. In fact, she'd been sort of excited by how positive a response it got. She read over the comments last night and even screen-shotted a few for when she needed an ego boost.

"I appreciate you saying that. We're good."

"Really?"

"Really."

The hopeful shine of Candace's eyes was almost bright enough to make Daisy squint. Instead, she loosened up. She transferred her weight to one leg and leaned a hip against the table. Musing aloud, she said, "You know, if it'd been a promo shot with you, we'd have gotten an even better response."

"You think?" Candace considered with a coy tilt, "What about both? That way, you and I have an equal share of the spotlight."

Candace pivoted on her heels so that they faced the same direction. She retrieved her phone from her pocket and held it up selfie-style. Her back brushed against Daisy's front as she adjusted her placement in the frame.

With her thumb hovering over the capture button, she asked, "Is this okay?"

A sense of deja vu hit Daisy. They were the same words Candace said right after their fateful kiss. The same spike of anticipation shot through Daisy as well. Before she'd even processed the action, she saw her reflection on the screen nod.

It was over in an instant. Candace snapped the picture and maneuvered away in one smooth, swift twirl. For all of Daisy's apprehension, it had been painless. Even so, the idea of strangers seeing her share a frame with Candace Perry filled her with a different kind of worry.

What if it was not a good picture? Could they do better? '*Do it once, do it right, it won't come back to bite.*' Daisy had creative control, so it was time she exercised it.

She pitched, "How about a video? I need to finish bagging these puppies up and set my next batch of dough to proof before I make an ingredient run. You need to learn how to do this so you're not useless. It might be good marketing material to show how the gravy's made."

Candace stuck out her tongue. "I wouldn't call doing the dishes useless. But I love the idea. Hm..." She thought for a moment, then grinned. In a decisive swipe, she grabbed a gloop-covered spoon and held it up to her mouth like a microphone.

"I'm the interviewer, you're the expert."

Daisy snorted. "Damn right I am. Let's see if we can get you up to speed."

That being said, they started slow. While packaging the finished bombs, Daisy did her best to give Candace an overview of the process.

For Daisy, it was like explaining how to breathe. She'd been making bagel bombs since she could reach the countertop with her step stool, helping her dad with small tasks until she could handle larger ones. He always made her feel like the best helper, and every new technique she mastered was a celebration. So, she tried to be patient with her own would-be helper... even though she had to show the woman how to properly set a kitchen scale.

"What can I say?" Candace defended herself with a nonchalant shrug. "The campus cafe I worked at only served premade pastries."

Daisy did not hide her eye roll.

Baking was an exact science, without room for error. The bagel bomb recipe started with portioning out the cream cheese filling. Each dollop needed to be exactly the right size, and the right weight, so that it would fit inside of the bagel bomb. Too much, and it would burst during the boil step. Additional elements—from bacon grease to Candace's beloved peanut butter and jelly—brought the complication of extra moisture.

There were many points of failure. A complete novice for a helper added another.

Daisy had to prevent a pouting Candace from adding more to just about everything she portioned out. She was slow thanks to keeping up her mock-interview bit. And messy. And

Daisy was concerned she was going to chop her fingers off thanks to her poor knife technique.

But, to her credit, she was trying.

Once Candace got the hang of how to prepare the fillings, Daisy was able to leave her to it while she started the dough. Dry ingredients went into the stand mixer, followed by water. At this point, she knew what she wanted by sight and feel; she would work the dough until she got it to the proper elasticity, then place it in a proving container to rest for about an hour.

It was while Daisy was kneading her last dough—manually —that she noticed Candace watching from behind her phone camera with a strange expression.

While tiring, working dough by hand was fun. There was nothing like taking your frustrations out on a soon-to-be edible mound of putty. Daisy needed her stand mixers to produce on the scale she did, but she still liked to mix the occasional batch by hand. Just like when she used to make art, she liked the tactile feel of creation.

"What?" Daisy shot Candace a look, but did not stop her methodical moulding. "You wanna try?"

"*Me?* Won't I mess it up?"

"It's almost there," Daisy assured her. Stepping back, she washed her hands and took Candace's still-recording phone. "Just do it."

With clear trepidation, Candace did as she was told. Daisy watched through the phone screen as the woman eased her delicate fingers into the dough. *Too* much ease. She looked like an awkward teenage boy going for their first tit.

"Am I doing it right?"

"No. Harder. C'mon, I *know* you can grope better than that."

Candace sucked in a short breath. Her motions became even more fumbled.

With a sigh, Daisy stepped in.

"Here. Like this—"

Sidling up behind Candace, Daisy positioned herself so that she could guide the other woman's motions. Her right hand enveloped Candace's while her left raised the phone high to keep recording. She pressed in close to keep them both in frame.

As Daisy threaded her fingers with Candace's, she noticed the woman's nails were painted a blue-green color that would have matched her former outfit. They were already chipped in places, but that somehow made the effect cuter. It was the effort; Candace always put in a huge amount of effort to look nice, but she was not afraid to get her hands dirty either.

Daisy wondered if it was personal pride or if there was someone the woman wanted to impress.

At Daisy's urging, she massaged the dough's smooth surface. Their fingers disappeared into the pliable mound, then back out. They started out at a slow rhythm, but quickly picked up pace.

"That's good," Daisy praised. "Don't be afraid to put some muscle into it."

"It's harder than it looks!"

Candace grunted with effort, but she matched Daisy's intensity. Their bodies pushed and pulled in tandem while they settled into a sort of rocking motion. Daisy was not sure which of them giggled first, but once it started, they could not stop.

It was silly.

Fun.

Then, it felt like something else entirely.

Candace put her full self into the task. The motions were innocent, fueled by a desire to do well. Each successive, strengthened thrust ground Candace's firm rear against Daisy's hips. The sensitive spot she brushed was accidental, and yet—

*Once.*

*Twice.*

Daisy sucked in a sharp breath that romantics might have called a gasp. The scent of lilac curled around her awareness, sweet enough to lick. She felt a deep, aching want in the pit of her core. A desire to throw the phone across the room, thrust a hand down Candace's shorts, and knead her like she was dough until she—

*HELL NO.*

Disgusted by her daydream, Daisy leaped back. Her heart pounded in horny protest but she ignored it.

Daisy set the dough in a proving container, saying, "It's done."

And so was she, until she could get her libido in check. An awkward beat passed. When Daisy could take it no more, she did the only thing that came to her mush-mind.

"I need a shower."

"O-okay," Candace stammered. She might have said more, but Daisy did not wait to hear it. The bathroom door slammed shut between them. She tore off her clothes, turned on the shower, and jumped in while it was still cold.

Daisy emerged sometime later with a much cooler head (and body).

She concluded that what she felt was a natural physical response. Candace was attractive. Sexy, even. It was pointless to pretend otherwise. However, just because she was attractive and Daisy happened to notice did not mean she was attracted *to* her.

There was a difference, *damnit.*

Daisy needed to get laid. The last time she had the bandwidth for anything beyond surface-level dalliances was... too long ago to remember. One-night stands suited her more, but even then, it had been a bit of a dry spell.

Quite literally.

What was her name? Francesca? Flora? She was a vacationer visiting with her brother and sister-in-law, in desperate need of some adult attention after helping corral her niblings all week. Daisy had been more than happy to give it after listening to her complain during a bagel order. The fact that her bed was empty the next morning (and every other morning) was fine.

She was completely fine and in control of her emotions. Enough that the sight of Candace only filled her with annoyance. It was not cute the way she draped her legs over the couch's arm. Or how she cuddled under Daisy's favorite blanket, watching the now-resumed Simpson episode. Her laugh at Lisa and Bart Simpson fighting over being on separate hockey teams was grating. Daisy swiped the remote from its place on the coffee table and turned the TV off.

Startled, Candace swung her legs back to their proper place and sat up bolt-straight. She apologized, saying, "Sorry. It's one of my favorite episodes, so I thought I'd watch while I waited."

"Mine, too," Daisy found herself grunting. Arms crossed, she and Candace stared at each other until the latter looked away.

"Growing up, I was alone a lot. I used to watch this show to feel a little less that way... like I had a big, dysfunctional family with siblings and parents who would do anything for me. You said it was your dad's favorite, right?"

Daisy frowned. When had she mentioned that?

Reading her, Candace offered, "You told me that night at the bonfire."

"Oh, yeah," Daisy hazily recalled. She did not mean to keep talking but thought aloud. "Before streaming was a thing, it was our nightly ritual to eat dinner while we watched, then start baking. His whole routine would be thrown off on days the network didn't air on schedule. I put it on when I bake now for background noise."

Otherwise, it was too quiet. When it was silent, and all that she could hear was the clatter of cooking and her own mumbling of baking calculations, she could hear something *else.* A thought, half-formed but fully mature, that demanded answering.

*WHY?*

Why was she still doing this? The struggle, the frustration... What was *any* of it for, other than keeping the dream of her parents alive?

Whenever it was too quiet, and she was alone with only herself for company, that thought nagged her. Daisy hated it and herself for letting it creep in.

So, up the TV volume went.

"I tried to straighten things," Candace told her, breaking Daisy's dour descent. "I'm not sure where everything goes, but I did my best."

Daisy saw when she came out of the bathroom. The kitchen was cleaner than clean, like a tidy army had descended upon it. The items that could not be put away were arranged neatly. What had once been a mountain of food-crusted implements was now sparkling and stacked by cookware type.

If Daisy were being honest, it was a better job than she would have done herself. Honesty, though, was beyond her when it came to this woman.

"Okay."

The flicker of disappointment that crossed Candace's features was replaced by practiced business professionalism.

"You said you need to go ingredient shopping before the dough finishes proofing?"

As Daisy nodded, Candace rose in a smooth motion and went for the door.

"No time to waste, then."

"You're coming?" Daisy did not like the hint of excitement she heard in her voice. Flatter, she said, "I don't need you to do that."

Candace stood before Daisy, at least an arm's length between them. She cocked her head as she spoke and it spilled her ponytail over one shoulder in a perfect cascade.

Daisy had the urge to pull it.

"Maybe not," Candace agreed. "But don't you want me to?"

Her expression remained neutral, as did her tone. Even so, the directness of her gaze, the way she crossed her arms behind her back and leaned into Daisy's space, felt like a challenge. Or a flirtation. In either case, both needed to be shut down.

"Yeah," Daisy scoffed, leaning back as far as she could. "Like I need a root canal."

With a shrug, Candace replied, "Proper dental care is important. And four hands are better than two. Let's go."

Rolling her eyes, Daisy locked up the house behind Candace. She opened the garage door with her key fob to reveal Otto and settled into the driver's seat. Candace, looking dubious, hovered by the passenger side.

"My car is right over there," she said. "Why don't I—"

"No way am I riding in that ridiculous eyesore. Get in or go home."

Pouting, Candace took her loss and belted into the passenger side. Daisy did not bother to hide her smirk.

The grocery route Daisy followed was as practiced and finely-tuned as her bagel preparation. Even her vehicle was outfitted for the task, with its back seat converted to a grocery-toting icebox. No, her golf cart was not street legal in the strictest sense. However, through the lesser-traveled side streets that ran along the bay and alleyways parallel to the major streets, she could zip by without too much trouble.

As long as she did not go driving on sidewalks or take the cart off-road, the police were content to let her pass with the occasional talking-to. They had bigger fish to fry (and ticket revenue to pursue), and some of the older PD members had known her since she was a little girl. Some had been on the scene of her parents' accident and were the ones to deliver the news to her.

That was the thing about Wonderwood. It was a modern town, in constant flux thanks to the vacationers that came through year by year. Yet, when the summer season died and only the locals were left, it became something different. In off-season, Wonderwood was the type of small town Americana only shown in movies. If you were a local, people knew you or of you.

And, they knew Daisy well enough to leave her alone.

The open air rushing past Daisy filled her lungs with the scent of the shore, of nature, and the promise of freedom. Unconsciously, her death-grip on the steering wheel loosened. Being outside had always helped to stabilize her. When the weight of everything and her responsibilities seemed too heavy, this was what she needed.

Candace commented, "Wow. I didn't know you could look so relaxed."

"I'm a goddamn Zen master, Perry."

With a laugh, Candace pulled out her phone and started recording once more. "Teach me your ways, O' wise one!"

First was the Produce Pavilion for fresh vegetables and fruits. Daisy preferred to stock up at the bi-weekly farmer's market, where local vendors set up with far more reasonable prices, but she had to make do in the meantime. She grabbed an extra case of strawberries since they were in season and looked a gorgeous shade of ruby red—strawberry cream cheese was always popular. And, as Candace moaned out an idea for chocolate bagel bombs filled with the sweet and savory mixture, Daisy had to admit it was a good one.

Next, they went to Carnie's, the local butcher shop. While the place was more expensive than your run-of-the-mill grocery store, they stayed in business because they had the best cuts of meat in the area.

Daisy loaded up on bacon, pork roll, and scrapple. It was important to cook out as much liquid as possible from her ingredients, and the greasy breakfast meats were a challenge. Well worth it, though, since plain bombs loaded with meat were by far her best sellers.

At the big-box grocery store, Daisy picked up her bulk general items like flour, yeast, and eggs. Candace offered to be her second set of hands, so Daisy stacked her like a human mannequin. She only laughed a little when the woman toppled and nearly dropped the whole load.

Last on Daisy's route was Marin's Crab Shack for lump crab meat, scallops, and lox. The trifecta were "toppings" she offered along with the other breakfast meats. It was a little bougie, but she had some die-hard regulars like Norman who got them with every order. Daisy liked to give her customers what they wanted, so she kept it up. Even if the only way she could keep stock was thanks to Marin's special prices.

Which, it seemed, were about to end. While Daisy was paying up at the register, she broke the news.

"So, you hear about Mort's?"

Feeling an ominous pang of foreboding as she stuffed cash back into her cross-body bag, Daisy shook her head. Mort's was, for a time, one of the most popular seafood restaurants of all the New Jersey shore towns. They sourced their ingredients from local fishers and were known for their top-quality, high-priced dishes. Unfortunately, local gossip said that times had been tough for the business. Last Daisy heard, the place was barely scraping by.

The old salt confirmed it.

"End a' July, they told me. Just put their last order."

Annoyingly, Candace threw her two cents in.

"That's so sad! I used to go there all the time when I was little. They had the best clams casino that was so buttery, it would just melt in your mouth like… mmm!!" She had the grace to flush as she either remembered her current company or caught Daisy's sour look. "Sorry, I skipped breakfast."

The crow's feet around Marin's eyes crinkled with her hearty chuckle, giving her sun-leathered face a craggy quality. "No need. I'll take it as a compliment. I work hard to harvest those buggers. Or, worked, I suppose."

Pausing, Marin sighed, puffing an escaped wisp of salt and pepper hair from her face. The sinking feeling in Daisy's stomach became a black pit.

Candace asked, "Why are they closing? People used to call

weeks ahead of time to get a table. Well, not us, but other people."

Before Marin could offer a more diplomatic answer, Daisy shot back, "You wouldn't need to wait, would you? And for your information, one of your uncle's friends bought the place and ran it into the ground. Poof, onto the next town institution they can ruin."

Understanding seemed to dawn on Candace. She knew the games her uncle and his rich friends played. With the right maneuvering, with their holdings under shell corporations or patsies, people like that could make money strip mining and bankrupting businesses. They were greedy vultures, unlike Marin, who had worked for everything she had.

The fisherwoman continued.

"It's a kick in the teeth. Mort's was my last big customer left. Between that and all the other headaches in my life, I think it's about time I cut anchor. My daughter has a room for me, and with the minnows needing babysitting, it'll work out for both of us. You understand, dear."

Through a mouth that had gone desert-dry, Daisy managed, "Yeah."

"Sorry. I wanted ya to hear it from me." In a nervous rush, she added, "Now, I know you don't like to go off-island, but I have a friend who owns a market right across the bay. He doesn't have quite the same stock, and he might not be able to cut you as much of a deal, but—"

"I'll figure it out," Daisy snapped. She regretted her tone seeing Marin's hurt, but could not help it as white-hot panic flooded her veins. "Thanks for the heads up."

Saying a quick goodbye, Daisy fled from the fish market and all but ran for her cart. She did not look back to see if Candace followed, but heard the woman scramble behind her.

It felt as if a black cloud followed them the entire drive back to the house. Occasionally, Candace would try to make small talk, commenting on places or pedestrians they passed. Daisy, though, was lost deep in thought.

One of her earliest memories was of going to Marin's with her mom. Clear as day, she remembered picking out the meanest, snappiest crabs for dinner... How Marin, with far less salt and pepper in her hair, gave Daisy a glittery rubber worm tackle that caught her eye... How she and her mom nearly flooded the kitchen when the boiling pot toppled, which ruined part of the linoleum floor.

That was a long time ago.

If Marin's closed, she would have to say goodbye to some core menu items. Norman was going to be heartbroken. Even if, and it was a big *if*, she could manage to get her ass over the bridge, there was no way she could afford even a slight price hike.

Why couldn't things just stay the same?

Every time Daisy got used to the status quo, or thought she might have figured it out, some new, fresh hell emerged to complicate her life. Something had to give soon.

*Right?*

Ahead, the street light turned red, and Daisy was so preoccupied she did not notice. She kept her foot on the gas, barrelling right for the intersection.

*"Daisy!!"*

Candace's yell brought Daisy back to Earth. As she slammed on the brakes, the cart came to a lurching stop. Most of their groceries were thankfully locked in the cooler compartment, but a loose bag of apples went flying. The bottom-only seatbelts kept the women in place, but their upper halves still jerked forward. Were it not for Candace's quick reflexes, Daisy might have broken her nose on the steering wheel. Instead, the woman brought her forearm up to block the impact, and they both yelped in mutual pain.

"What the hell?!"

"You were going to miss the light!"

"No," Daisy growled, "your arm! Are you stupid? I could've broken it! I didn't... Did I?"

A pained grimace was plastered on Candace's face, and she

held her battered arm close. Even so, she shook her head. "I'm fine. Are you okay? You've been spacing out the whole drive."

Daisy wanted to respond with a snappy retort. A flippant quip to dispel the sudden, very palpable tension. But Candace was not clueless. She could read the situation even if Daisy did not say it.

Another, smaller part of Daisy also whispered that Candace needed to know how this would affect business. She might even be able to help and, damn her, Daisy *wanted* it. She was relieved to finally have someone else to share the burden of figuring things out. The realization hit her with more force than the break slam.

Before Daisy could say any of that, a car horn behind them blared.

"*Rude*," Candace shouted back. To Daisy, she asked, "Want me to go ruin their day?"

Daisy started driving. "How? You'll send 'em to a dungeon, princess?"

"The pier *does* have a holding cell for roughhousers and drunks. It's nice and moldy."

"Yeah? You're cute when you're scary, you know that?"

Almost too quiet to hear, Candace countered, "I'm *always* cute."

Daisy couldn't argue.

At the house, Daisy parked in the driveway. Before she could start unloading the groceries, Candace stopped her.

"Can we sit for a minute?"

Daisy grumbled but made no motion to leave. It was a fucking gorgeous day. The kind where you could take a big beach towel, grab an umbrella, and sleep outside lulled by the sounds of the sea. Daisy wished she could have a carefree day like that. Instead, her head swam with worries.

Candace's voice cut through.

"We can figure out where to source new product. I kept the receipts from today so I can compare prices and see if there's anywhere I could save us some cash. There have to be distributors we can work with to buy in bulk, and this friend of Marin's—if they're right across the bay, we can—"

"*I can't!*"

The declaration shot out like kettle steam. Once Daisy started, she couldn't stop.

"None of the local distributors will work with me anymore. They're all either connected to your uncle, or I've already run through my credit. I do my bookkeeping, I make sure to pay Rio and Dotty on time... ish. But the truth is, I'm a shit business owner. I lose track of things. I make promises, forget, and disappoint people.

"I don't have enough space in my head for the details I need to keep track of. Bagel Bombs! is falling apart, and it's taking everything I have to keep it together. The only reason I've managed to keep things running this long is thanks to people like Marin, like *you*, taking pity on me.

"All that, and I still don't have a life! No hobbies. No friends. The idea I'd ever have time for a girlfriend is a joke. Not that anyone would ever put up with me. I can't even leave the island because of that damn bri—"

Daisy clamped her mouth shut. Her stomach churned, and a cold sweat began to trickle down her back. She did not want to talk about this. She never did because she was so ashamed of her weakness.

It was a bridge. At the height of the summer, thousands of people crossed it every day. Other than a boat trip across the bay, it was the only way on and off the island. And Daisy, mired in her unresolved trauma, had not crossed it since her parents' deaths.

Every time she came close, even the thought could send her spiraling. Like now.

Again, Candace's voice brought Daisy back.

"Turn towards me and close your eyes."

"What? Why?"

"Humor me. Please, Daisy."

Daisy was not sure why, maybe because she liked the

desperate tone of the other woman's voice, but she listened. Seconds passed, yet it might as well have been an eternity to her keyed-up self. She flinched as Candace's hands grasped both of hers. With deliberate care, Candace placed one set of their combined hands over Daisy's heart and one overtop her belly. Then, she spoke.

"Breathe in through your nose, out through your mouth. In. Out. Fill yourself completely and release it all back."

"C'mon," Daisy complained, eyes open. "I don't have time for this."

"You don't have time for breathing?"

Daisy scoffed. She wriggled, but Candace held fast. Eventually, she gave in and shut her eyes once more.

From there, Candace guided Daisy through her first-ever breathing exercise. It was silly. And a little weird. But with each breath, as she scraped the back of her throat and the bottom of her lungs with life-giving air, she found herself calming down. Candace's words were an anchor. Not one that dragged her down, but a guiding line back to the surface.

*Reassuring.*

*Focused.*

*Kind.*

Candace's voice was a mesmerizing mantra. It made Daisy feel like she could face her problems. She might not overcome them today, not tomorrow, but they would not control her forever. As long as she kept breathing.

When Candace finished, she told Daisy to go at her own pace. To take in the sounds, smells, and energy around them. Then, release. Seconds trickled by as they sat in contented silence.

After a time, Daisy cracked an eye open to observe Candace. She was a far cry from the woman who ended up bawling in front of her cafe. Dressed in Daisy's clothes, her hair let loose from its usual ponytail or bun, she looked like a different person. But, also, one who Daisy had known most of her life.

It was funny. Their reunion seemed like a lifetime ago but,

in reality, not even a month had passed. Candace washed back on Wonderwood's shore, and showed no sign of leaving. Not when she kept twining herself with Daisy.

Metaphorically and literally.

Overtop Daisy's own hands, she became keenly aware of Candace's. The fingers that almost threaded with hers, hovering over the valleys between them; stiff, like divers at the edge of a pool. With each breath Daisy took, her chest and abdomen expanding, their skin brushed ever so slightly.

It would be easy to turn the tables, an internal, devilish voice told Daisy. To take control and move those hands where she *really* wanted them to be. They were so close, if she just...

As Candace murmured Daisy's name, shivers shook her core.

"Daisy, it's going to be okay."

"I-I know."

"Your heart is beating so fast. I understand what it's like to feel overwhelmed. I got so used to shoving those feelings down, and it made me the worst version of myself. If there's anything else I can do to help you feel better, I'll—"

Daisy pulled back. Not roughly or in a panic, but with gentle ease.

"I'm okay. Really."

Worry filled Candace's gaze as she opened her eyes and searched Daisy's face. Whatever she saw seemed good enough, thankfully. A smile curved the corners of her lips. If she knew the direction Daisy's thoughts had *actually* turned, she gave no indication.

Needing to fill the air with something other than buzzing tension, Daisy asked, "Where did you learn how to do that?"

Candace's hesitant smile bloomed, and it made Daisy feel uneasy all over. It was gorgeous; *she* was gorgeous. But who could inspire her to make that kind of expression?

"Do you remember Demi Panopoulos?"

Daisy fought her grimace into a flat line. How could she forget Candace's old right-hand minion? She'd heard gossip that they were still friends. In fact, Daisy often saw the woman floating around town in her hippie skirts. She might have been the one person to show some humanity after Daisy was outed. Even so, when they ran into one another, Daisy did her best to turn the other direction.

She supposed she would have to say hello, now.

"I remember her. She owns Downwood Dog Yoga here in Wonderwood, right?"

"Yep! She's the best person I know, hands down. She taught me not to keep things bottled up and how to manage when I feel out of control. I don't know where I'd be without her."

"Touching."

"Demi's also a fabulous designer. She put together the mock-ups for Bagel Bombs!' remodel."

That was news to Daisy. Her first inclination was to be mad that she was left out of the loop again. However, as Candace pulled out her phone and showed a series of designs to Daisy, her irritation vanished.

It was perfect.

There were multiple variations, but each mock-up centered on maintaining the retro '90s vibe of the hole-in-the-wall cafe, while updating the layout and materials. Fresh neon lime and green accents; a multi-leveled countertop with more (and functional) plush swivel stools; new, shiny signs and displays.

Also, it was as weird-looking as it was functional. With curves and odd shapes, the design was reminiscent of the kooky character that fast-food joints had before corporate investors took over and went with the least offensive designs possible. Walking along the boardwalk, it would be impossible to miss in the best way.

Candace was a bubbling brook of excitement while Daisy soaked in the digital drawings.

"I wanted to wait for the right time to show you. Demi emailed them over while we were cooking earlier, and, to be clear, nothing is even close to final. This is some spitballing she humored me with. We'll meet with her to talk about any ideas you have, and if this isn't what you want, we'll scrap—"

"I want it," Daisy heard herself say. Less intensely, she added, "There are a couple things I might change for practical reasons, or restaurant code. But I... My parents would have loved it."

Softly, Candace told her, "I'm glad."

A beat passed, and she continued. "We're in this together, all the way. Not but because I pity you, because I believe in you. Let me handle inventory logistics. It doesn't mean you won't have a say in it, since you'll need to tell me what we need. But I'll get us the best bang for our bucks, and make any field trips we need over the bridge. What grumpy distributor could say no to me?"

For emphasis, Candace winked and tossed her hair over her shoulder with a flippant wave. Daisy rolled her eyes, but she could not stop the smirk that cocked her mouth.

"Alright. But if you over-order on peanut butter, you're eating it."

Candace let loose a groan and held her stomach. "Glaaaaaadly. I'm starving. Do you *know* what kind of self-control it took for me to not eat the inventory earlier?"

"Your loss. I had a few while we were packing them up."

"You didn't tell me I could do that! Here I am, wasting away!"

Daisy laughed. Not at Candace, but with her, and it felt impossibly good.

*Right.*

Then, of course, she was reminded of how wrong it was.

"Well, you need to eat," Daisy said with a mock-scoff. She paused to pick her words and to get over the sudden thickness of her tongue. "It'll be dinner time once we wrap up this last round of bombs. If you've got nothing better to do, we can order takeout. Anything that isn't bagel-related. There's a decent Vietnamese place that opened up last year. It'll be my treat, and—"

"I'm sorry," Candace cut Daisy off. "I have a date."

"A... date?"

Daisy's mind whirled.

*Candace.*

*Date.*

Why was that such a wild concept? There were customers who ordered from Bagel Bombs! specifically for a chance to flirt with the woman. It was a wonder that Candace was not already locked down by the first person who caught her eye. But she had never mentioned a potential girlfriend or anyone she was interested in.

The protective, possessive surge that Daisy felt shocked her. Still, she forced an air of indifferent cool.

"I get it, no biggie. Have fun."

Looking horrified, Candace blurted out, "Not a date-date! I swear, Bagel Bombs! comes before any romance in my life right now. It's my uncle. He set the stupid thing up, and I'm only going because I still owe him for bailing me out when I first got to Wonderwood."

Daisy sneered.

"The same uncle who objectifies you, keeps you down, and wants to destroy my business? *That* uncle?"

"You know I can't say no." Candace wilted. She broke from Daisy's gaze, saying, "He wants a favor with the old police chief, and going on a date with the man's son will get it."

With air quotes, Daisy jibed, "And then you'll be 'paid off'?"

Candace shrugged.

"Maybe. When he asks for something, it's best not to turn him down. If he finds out I'm working with you—"

"That vulture owns the pier across the goddamn boardwalk. Of course he's going to find out you're working at Bagel Bombs!. Or are you ashamed of it?"

"What? That's not true at all! I don't want him to retaliate before we're ready for it. The longer I can make him think it's business as usual, the better."

"Yeah, yeah," Daisy jibed. She could feel the caustic venom seeping into her words, but she could not stop it. "Wouldn't want to piss off Uncle Moneybags, right? Gotta make sure to play both sides, even if you don't bat for that team. I wonder how far this date will be expecting you to go?"

With none of her usual charm or cheer, Candace reiterated, "It's dinner. *Just* dinner. And I don't appreciate the implication otherwise. Let's go. There's nothing productive happening here, and we need to unload those groceries before we finish the rest of the bombs."

In clipped, efficient movements, Candace started to fill her arms with grocery bags. Daisy all but yanked them back.

"I've got it from here."

"Daisy, please... Don't be like this."

Scoffing, she shot back, "No, you go get ready for your date. I don't think he'd appreciate you showing up in something so *trashy*."

Throwing the insecurity back in Candace's face, the words hit their intended mark. Too well, perhaps. The woman hugged her arms to her chest while a deep, scarlet flush radiated over her fair skin. Daisy hoped for anger, maybe even a little embarrassment, to shame Candace.

The raw hurt was surprising.

By the time Daisy opened her mouth to walk the comment back, it was too late. She went for a swipe and landed a gut punch. Who would stick around for more?

Candace made a clean pivot on her heels, pavement clacking beneath them as she beelined for her glittery monstrosity. She peeled out from the quiet suburban street and was gone in seconds.

It took Daisy half as much time to miss her.

# CHAPTER 13

## *Candace*

*P* *asta Bolognese.*
*Gnocchi with vodka blush sauce.*
*Angel hair in a lemon and white wine reduction with clams.*

Candace's eyes scanned the bifold, leather-bound menu three times before she read a single word. Her mind was a million miles away, nowhere near the cozy, upscale Italian restaurant her body currently occupied. A body, she was proud to say, that did not look the least bit trashy.

It was not fair. Candace knew Daisy liked to push her buttons, and she deserved it after everything she had done. But did the prickly woman have to drive her thorns so deep?

After their rough start this morning, they seemed to be getting along. Candace did her best to be useful, and to make things fun while she learned an integral part of the business she jumped into. She thought they were connecting. The way

Daisy opened up, even if an anxiety attack spurred it, felt like progress.

Candace's heart broke hearing the confident, talented woman spiral. She watched Daisy, day by day, work harder than anyone she had ever met. However, there was only so much one person could do alone. Daisy had been fighting the tide for so long, it was no wonder she was worn down.

And the idea that no one would want her because of her traumas... It took everything Candace had not to reach out and hug Daisy. She settled for the breathing exercise, and it had been so satisfying to see the method work. To physically feel Daisy calm under her hands, at least for a short while.

Then, her uncle and his ridiculous demands had to go and ruin things.

*No*, Candace thought. She ruined things herself by giving in to the manbaby. But what choice did she have? She owed him and, worse, she would *always* owe him. It went deeper than money. Now, with her technically working against his interests, she needed to toe a very careful line.

Daisy did not understand Peter Perry the way Candace did. There was a world where he would find them working together amusing. As long as he thought they were not a true threat, he might be content to snicker from the sidelines and mock their struggle.

If he thought they might actually disrupt his plans? Daisy and Bagel Bombs! would see the full focus of a man with few limits.

Candace was playing a dangerous game. Her involvement could save Bagel Bombs!, but it could just as easily destroy it.

So, she would suffer through a date. An awkward one, at that. Candace knew from her end why the atmosphere was so stilted. Her tiff with Daisy, along with the little fact that she was not attracted to men, put Ted Cando in a tough spot. Still, she graced him with her best, lady-like air, and treated him like a premier business client from the moment she sat down across the candlelit two-top from him.

Candace was perfectly pleasant. Cordial, without invitation for more. Her date seemed inclined towards the same.

Lowering the menu so that she could peek over it, Candace observed the man. It was a bit of a shock; Ted had come out of his All-American shell. In high school, he'd been a very conservatively acceptable young man who looked like a love interest from a *Dawson's Creek*-type show. Tall, clean-cut, with blonde hair and baby blue eyes, he dressed in all the popular brands you could find at the local mall.

Now? He was still clean-cut and well-dressed, but there was something different. It was not just his fashionable earrings, his neatly-tailored floral-patterned shirt, or stylish chinos that matched his belt.

As a young man, he'd been a loudmouth and a bit of a bully. This older version was nothing but polite. Unlike other dates with the opposite sex she'd been subjected to, he tried to make conversation rather than talk about himself. When Candace could not muster the will to chat, and he did not seem to want to delve into his personal life, they drifted into a silence broken only by the occasional interruption of their waiter.

Candace mused aloud, "You've really changed, haven't you?"

Ted set his menu down and flashed an almost shy smile. "I could say the same about you. I didn't think you'd ever come back to Wonderwood."

With a light tilt, Candace told him, "That was the plan, but here we are. For the time being, at least."

Ted let loose a genuine-sounding laugh as he shook his head. Behind him, Candace made eye contact with a gorgeous woman who glared at the noise.

"You never were one to hold back, Candy. Even when you were pretending to fit in, you were good at standing out."

*What's that supposed to mean?*

Candace took a sip of wine to cover her frown. Thankfully, their waiter came to check on them, buying her time to think of a response.

"I never pretended," she corrected once they were alone

again. "I let people see the version of me they wanted to see. Their biases aren't my fault."

"No," he agreed with a conciliatory shrug. "People will think what they want, that's for sure. You know, I don't blame you for not wanting to come back. In a South Jersey town like Wonderwood, especially when we were younger, there's a lot of backwards thinking. But it's getting better."

"Is that so?" Candace asked. She rested her chin atop bridged fingers and considered the man. "My friend tells me the town council still won't approve a Pride parade down the boardwalk. It might be better, but not for everyone."

Ted nodded, and his amiable expression turned serious.

"You're not wrong. But if all the people who want it to change leave, this is how it's always going to be. I want to help the ways I can. My dad might not be police chief anymore, but our name carries weight."

"I suppose it does. Even my uncle wants a favor from him."

"And my dad wants a favor from your uncle. I guess they both think they're helping each other out by setting us up. Not that it isn't a pleasure to see you," he added in a tone that made her believe it. "But this wasn't exactly something I could say no to."

"Likewise. To both." Pausing, Candace sighed as the weight of the day—all that she had been through since the moment she found out she was being fired from the job she worked so hard for—settled on her shoulders. She caught her slouch and straightened. Fixing Ted with a true smile, she admitted, "Regardless of why we're here, it's nice to see a friendly, familiar face."

"Been seeing some unfriendly ones?"

Snorting, Candace told him, "You could say that. This place makes me feel like a teenager, drama and angst included."

"Well," Ted offered, looking as sincere as a person could, "allow me to be your no-drama friend? I come with the benefits of a charming personality and my old man's credit card."

"Ha! What a coincidence! I'm *also* charming, and my uncle told me to send him the bill."

At that moment, their waiter delivered their meals. Again, out of the corner of her eye, she caught the woman behind Ted watching them. She was a statuesque figure, with an intense, dark gaze that looked remarkably similar to Daisy's. Or, maybe they just had the same glare. Ravenous as she was, Candace bit her lip before digging in. For herself and for the person she was trying to be, she decided to be honest.

"Ted, I should make it clear: 'friends' is as far as it can go for us. You seem like a great guy. But I'm—"

Holding up his hand, Ted stopped Candace. "You don't need to explain yourself to me. I know how your uncle is. Him, my dad, and their friends with that Wonderwood Works political party are the ones who have managed to shoot down the Pride parade every year."

There was sympathy in Ted's voice; sympathy, along with understanding. The man leaned over the table with a conspiratorial smile. "I'll tell you a secret: this year the parade is happening, approval or not. I'll make sure to send the details if you want."

Candace beamed. "I'd like that."

It felt as if a massive, dark cloud moved on from its place over Candace's head. There did not seem to be a hint of subterfuge in Ted's demeanor. In fact, if anything, he looked... *relieved.* They settled into their meals and a normal conversation, as if they were old friends.

Ted, it turned out, followed in his father's footsteps to join the police. He had worked his way up to lieutenant, and was aiming for a run at sheriff in the near future.

"Hmm," Candace plotted as she twirled up another nest of spaghetti. "From lieutenant to sheriff, then you take your stab at Wonderwood's esteemed mayor seat."

Flashing a toothy grin, Ted confided, "You've found me out. I'll see if I can earn your vote."

A glass of wine in, Candace felt comfortable enough telling

Ted about her work at Bagel Bombs! He was surprised, but wished her luck.

"After everything she's been through, DeMarco deserves a win. She's lucky to have you."

Candace forced a smile. "Let's hope that's true."

From there, Candace was grateful they moved on to lighter topics. Ted showed her pictures of his fishing boat. Modest and well-maintained, it was a far cry from the leisure yachts Candace had seen (or been on) at the local marinas. The little vessel was an old, converted police rescue boat—a tank of a craft, best-suited for choppy waters and catching flounder in the bay.

Candace told Ted about Demi and her yoga studio, which, as it turned out, he was already familiar with.

"It's a nice place," he said, his voice taking on an odd tilt. "My... er... friend... goes there."

Candace cocked her head. Once more, she caught the woman behind them fixated on their table. Almost imperceptibly, Ted threw a backward glance as if he were aware of her.

"Do you know that woman?"

"What? Who?"

Ted made a show of looking around, but Candace was not buying it. And was that blush on his cheeks?

"The one behind you," Candace clarified. She met the woman's now impossible to miss stare head on. "She's been staring at us the entire—"

The woman sprang to her feet, her face a mask of nervousness. She started to make a break for the exit, but Ted caught her.

"Maddie, wait!"

The woman, Maddie, did stop. As she and Ted locked eyes, his hand drifted from her forearm to her hand.

It was hard to misinterpret *that*.

"You're together."

Casting a shy, but undeniably proud smile, Ted corrected her. "Engaged, actually. As you can guess from this date, my dear dad doesn't approve."

Without missing a beat, Candace insisted that Maddie join their dinner. If they were going to be forced to play this game for their families, they would make them regret it.

Candace flagged down their waiter, saying, "Let's turn these wine glasses into bottles and unpack some issues."

Against all odds, Candace's date turned out to be a pleasant affair. She did not even mind that she became the third wheel for a loving, committed couple. Maddie was understandably on guard. Yet, once she realized that Candace was not after her fiance, she eased up enough to talk about herself.

Maddie was lovely.

Tall and refined, she wore a long, yellow spaghetti-strap maxi dress that showcased her toned frame and looked stunning against her dark skin. As a physical therapist and personal trainer, bodily health was a strong passion of hers. She not only attended Demi's yoga studio, but taught spin classes once in a blue moon.

With a bashful, weighted expression, Maddie said, "Demi's a saint for putting up with me. I wasn't my best self back in high school when we dated. It took me a while to sort out who I was."

Hearing that snapped everything into place for Candace. While she had not recognized Maddie, Ted said they attended Holy Mother Prep together. They talked about shared memories, mutual acquaintances, and Maddie even mentioned sitting next to Candace in a class or two. But the cast of people who matched that description, and had also dated her best friend, held only one possible solution.

Back then, Maddie had gone by a different name.

It was difficult to not feel furious. Not at Maddie and Ted, of course, but at the position his father put them in. Her transition was why he did not approve of them getting married. Why he joked about Candace 'setting Ted straight.' She did not know the specifics of why Ted and Maddie needed to go along with his father's charade. If it was anything like her own complicated familial relationship, she could empathize.

Someday, Candace hoped Ted could be the change he planned.

The rest of the dinner went by like it was the most normal situation in the world. Just a sweet couple and their loveless lesbian friend. After the day she had, Candace needed the chance to let loose and the pair were happy to join. They paid the impressively sizable bill they managed to wrack up, left their waiter a ridiculous tip, and parted with the promise to go out again soon.

Candace was glad she did not have far to drive back to her room at the Comfort Clam. With a belly full of carby goodness and feeling a pleasant buzz from the wine, she was ready to pass out.

The figure she saw looming by her car woke her right back up.

It was nearly 11pm. They had been one of the last tables in the restaurant, meaning that the few remaining cars were of workers closing up for the night. There was no one else around.

The parking lot was not too well-lit, but headbeams from passing traffic gave her the occasional glimpse. Had Candace not recognized the man, she might have turned tail and run. As it was, taking in the sight of her uncle's fixer, she slowed her approach. If he was keeping tabs on her, it could not mean anything good.

Vinny Lamarka cast Candace a lazy grin once she got within conversational distance. "Candy, Candy, Candy... This car of yours sure makes it easy to spot you around town. Did you have a nice date?"

"It was. Ted Cando and his fiancée are good together."

The man gave her a regretful shake of his head.

"Your uncle is going to be disappointed. He would have preferred you two hit it off. It would look a lot better for him if you—"

"I don't give a damn how my love life looks to anyone," Candace snapped. She was not in the mood to play polite princess with a slimeball. "I did what my uncle asked. Ed Cando should be happy until he sees the bill. Now, I don't care if you do or don't mind, I've had a long day, so I'm going home."

Since the man propped himself up on her driver's door, Candace went for the passenger side. Lamarka charged around and blocked her path.

"I'll bet you have," he continued in a suggestive drawl. "You've been busy."

Candace froze, bolt straight. Instinct made her shift her keys between her knuckles. She retorted, "I'm trying to get my life back in order. You'd be busy too."

A smile cocked Lamarka's thick moustache. He mocked, "It's a shame about that career hiccup. Funny how that happens to difficult little girls, isn't it? Then, they come running back home to daddy–or *uncle*, in this case–to save them."

"You don't know me."

"That's hurtful. Without me expediting the process for your guardianship paperwork, who knows how long you would have been in the system after your grandparents gave up on you. I know you better than just about anyone else. So, I'll give you a piece of advice: be careful."

"I haven't done anything wrong," Candace argued. But even she heard the waver in her voice.

"Fibbing is for children. You want to be a big girl, don't you? That means taking responsibility."

"I am," Candace growled. "I'm not perfect. I've made mistakes, and I'm sure I'll make some more. But I'm doing my best."

"Is that so?"

The man leaned into her space. One hand pressed over the door to prevent her from opening it, and the other hooked casually to his belt. The scent of pungent aftershave and sweat made her head pound.

"Doing your best for who, exactly? Your uncle is a generous man. Even after you turned your back on him, the man who raised you when your own father failed, he welcomed you back with open arms. Don't test his patience too much... and don't get in his way."

There was some awful, ugly insinuation behind the look Lamarka gave Candace. Despite the warm late-spring air, his regard chilled her to her core. She felt herself shrinking under the man's threat, but tried to hold her ground.

"I'm helping my friend, that's all."

"I hear you," Lamarka soothed. "But it's not good for the resume to cling to a sinking ship, is it? Some businesses are meant to end up at the bottom of the bay."

Candace did not want to dignify the words with a reply, and Larmarka seemed content to let the metaphor hang. He shrugged.

"Best luck, Candy. When you're ready to be good, let us know. Otherwise... There's a lot more to lose than a silly career."

With that, Lamarka stalked off into the darkness. Candace was able to hold her sobs in just long enough to get her car started and on the road.

# CHAPTER 14

*Daisy*

C andace called out sick the next day.

Talking to her on the phone, Daisy thought she sounded convincing. The woman was good at playing a part, after all.

It was for the best. Whatever the truth was, today called for some space.

If Daisy could stop hating Candace, it would be so much easier. Then, though, she would hate herself for giving in. Maybe if she pushed Candace enough, the problem would solve itself.

Eventually, Candace would leave like everyone else. Why not speed up the process? Because Daisy knew, deep down, she needed her

—and not just as a business partner.

The shift dragged on as usual. Customers came and went, buying the bombs Daisy had made just the day before with

Candace. She had to force herself not to grimace as she handed off a baggie of peanut butter bombs to a boy and his mom. Norman showing up towards the end of her shift was her one bright spot, and, even then, he pouted that Candace was not working.

"You're stuck with me, old man. Don't look so disappointed."

He told her in a prodding tone, "Things have been a lot more lively around here since she started coming around. *You* seem a lot more lively. She's a gem, that one."

Daisy snorted. "More like glass. She's got her uses, but I'm trying not to get cut again."

Norman did not reply. He watched Daisy with a thoughtful expression until he moved on with his day.

By the time Daisy left Bagel Bombs! in Rio's care, she was in the worst mood imaginable. She did not go home. When she was so distracted, inventory prep and baking with precision measurements was a recipe for failure. One of the few things that could mellow her when her thoughts turned so dour was going to her favorite place, Higbee Point.

It was an old speakeasy spot on the far point of the island, covered in wooded marshland. Although there was a small beach, tourists tended to avoid it since the cove was only accessible by way of a trail that cut through a quaint copse. This time of year, the area was bursting with colorful blossoms, from elegant swamp mallow rose bushes to silk trees with their fanning, fragrant pink petals.

By the time Daisy reached the beach, it was nearly sunset. She walked along the sandy strip, lost in a mess of thoughts, soaking in the shimmering glow. Occasionally, her path was blocked by beached horseshoe crabs left behind from their egg-laying as the tide pulled back. One by one, she flipped the helpless creatures and placed them carapace-up in the reaching wave runoff that rushed the shore. It was a small mercy, but it saved them from being seagull food.

Daisy continued her habit of picking up junk treasures. Opaque sea glass that somehow still glimmered, shells, funky pieces of driftwood, and even a barnacle-covered, tarnished silver spoon. She ended up sitting near the remnants of a moldering dock, where her hands moved of their own accord to arrange her finds. She used to do this often, making a sculpture for the next person who came walking along, or, more likely, to be reclaimed by the sea.

Watching dusky darkness descend on the bay beyond her, Daisy felt herself relax. Her thoughts and feelings were still a confusing swirl. Yet, as her phone chimed with a message from Candace, she did not feel her usual pang of annoyance.

*Candace: Demi said we can meet tomorrow morning after her beach yoga class to go over the designs. Can Dotty cover BB?*

*Daisy: Shouldn't be a problem*

*Candace: Great*

The conversation could have stopped there. Before she could talk herself out of it, Daisy sent another text.

*Daisy: Feeling any better?*

The text indicator disappeared and reappeared half a dozen times before Candace's response came through in a barrage of staggered parts. A corner of Daisy's mouth cocked as she pictured the woman's fretful face.

*Candace: A bit*
*I worked on some social media stuff*
*Don't worry. I'll send anything over before I post it*
*See you tomorrow*

*Daisy: Sounds good. See you*

Daisy blinked at her phone. The bright white of the chat screen blared back at her, its emptiness daring her to add more. Her thumbs flew atop the keyboard and typed out the words she could not bring herself to say out loud.

*Daisy: Thanks, Candace*

When Candace told Daisy they would be meeting Demi after yoga, she did not realize the woman meant after *taking* yoga. She said that Daisy could wait off to the side while they completed their practice. There was no challenge in her tone, but Daisy found one anyway. She grabbed an emergency beach towel from her cart and threw it down next to Candace's.

It was an odd experience.

Daisy had never taken a yoga class before. Demi guided the practice,starting with a breathing exercise similar to the one Candace had shown her the other day. Then, she led the group through a series of poses that ranged from simple to how-is-that-possible.

Daisy was in reasonable shape, she thought. She lived a fairly active life that included biking around town, being on her feet, and even some lifting with all the boxes she hauled.

Yoga was a whole different animal. She bent and contorted her body to (poorly) match what Demi was demonstrating, using muscles she did not know she had. Not to mention the difficulty of balancing on sand. But, according to Candace, Demi's beach classes were a huge shoobie draw.

Daisy knew very well that you had to give the shoobies what they wanted.

By the end, Daisy was gasping like a fish. Candace and Demi, meanwhile, looked like... well, Goddesses was the first word that came to mind, and she quickly shoved the thought down. They packed up their gear and said their goodbyes to the other yogis with pep in their steps, while Daisy slogged behind them.

Dressed in hot pink, coyly cropped Lycra that conformed to every contour and curve, blonde locks tied in a tight side braid, Candace led the way to a nearby beach bar. Her leg muscles flexed as she picked her way over the shifting sand. Under the hot morning sun, the barest sheen of sweat dappled her skin. One bead dripped from the nape of her neck, down between her shoulder blades, to be absorbed by her sport-cut top.

Daisy gulped.

Beside Daisy, Demi cast a knowing side-eye.

"Gets the blood pumping, right?"

"Sorry?"

"The yoga, I mean. It's good to see you outside of a random bump on the street, Zee. I've been looking forward to a chat with you..."

For 11AM on a Wednesday, Beachy Ben's was surprisingly busy. The bar—placed far up on the long beach to avoid the tide but close enough to be in sight of the rolling ocean waves —was a hive of activity. Just about every stool of the central ship galley-themed wrap-around bar was filled. Thankfully, nowhere was off limits to Candace Perry.

A few words to the hostess, and the eager-beaver manager himself was guiding them over to one of the bar's private, reservation-only cabanas. Daisy huffed, but even she had to admit the preferential treatment was nice. Sitting in plush-lined wicker chairs that overlooked the water, strawberry daiquiris in hand, they planned Bagel Bombs'! future.

Since Daisy was keen on the initial designs, they started in a good place. Her lease was very specific about the type of renovations she could make on the space. Nothing structural, but, for the most part, anything was fair game. This time, Peter Perry's cheapness and desire to offload building upkeep onto his tenants worked in their favor. Overall, Daisy added a couple of necessary changes and a handful of aesthetic ones, which Demi was able to plug right into her laptop's design program. Before her eyes, a potential future was coming into focus.

Apart from the occasional comment, Candace took a back seat while Daisy and Demi workshopped. The other woman had a fair amount of practical kitchen knowledge thanks to working at the diner. It was fun to consider paint choices and look up shiny, new industrial ovens. Daisy felt like a teenager excitedly poring over a fashion magazine with a friend. The idea of a countertop that was not laminated, peeling plywood was a dream. Yet, as the improvements added up, Daisy could not help noticing the price tag.

"This is great, but I've gotta be honest. Between labor and materials, there's no way I can pay for any of this." Daisy gestured at Candace. "I can barely pay you."

"I have the money," Candace told her. "Don't worry about it."

Daisy ground her teeth. "Don't 'don't worry about it' me. What happened to keeping me in the loop? You told me you were broke."

With prim decorum, Candace set her empty glass on the table and folded her hands atop her lap. Her attempt at a soothing voice had the opposite effect.

"You're in the loop, I promise. This is a one-time cash infusion."

"Oh? Did you go on another 'date' with one of your uncle's friends?"

Daisy could not say why that was the question she asked. Or why she wanted an answer more than anything else. But her words hung heavily between them as they stared each other down.

Candace was difficult to read. All morning, she'd been quieter than usual. Now that Daisy was thinking about it, not a single expression reached the woman's weary eyes. She was pleasant, but reserved. Even the hurt Daisy expected to see was absent.

Candace gave a simple, "No," as she got to her feet and started for the cabana steps. "I need to use the restroom."

An awkward beat passed.

The stuttered chords of an indie band attempting to get

through a rendition of *"Margaritaville"* filled the air around them, along with natural sounds of the rushing wind and waves. Daisy busied herself taking a long, loud draw from her empty drink. Even so, she could feel Demi's gaze on her.

"If you have something to say, say it."

Demi pursed her heart-shaped, coral pink lips. Yoga seemed to have done well by her; aside from the barest hint, she looked like she had not aged a day since they graduated. Her bond with Candace had also not changed. She crossed her arms over the airy romper she'd thrown on and fixed Daisy with a reprimanding look.

"You know, I was worried when Can-can told me about this whole idea of hers. Don't get me wrong, Bagel Bombs! is a Wonderwood institution, and I'd hate for you to have to close. But you two have a complicated history."

"We're good," Daisy grunted. "We talked it out."

"Mm-hm. That sounded real good just now."

Cringing, Daisy could not dispute reality.

Demi relaxed her posture and let loose a softened sigh. As she went on, though, her tone was no less serious.

"Look, Candace is my best friend. If she'd let me move her into my house and help get her life back together, that's what I'd be doing. But she didn't want that. For some reason, *this* is what she wants. I don't know whether it's about setting things right with you, winning over her uncle, or proving that she can pull a business from the brink—maybe it's a combination of the three.

"Whatever it is, don't take her for granted."

Daisy did not like feeling like she was being scolded. Or that a part of her agreed with the defensive friend. She shot back, "I was *literally* minding my own business until she showed up. Don't make me the bad guy here."

"I don't think there are any 'bad guys' here," Demi said with a shake of her head that bobbed her messy auburn bun. "Well, Peter Perry and his goons, for sure. But you? I think you're like most people, trying to figure yourself out. Just make sure to not hurt my friend in the process. She's been through enough."

"Yeah, right," Daisy mocked. "We've both got dead moms. Must've been real hard growing up getting whatever she wanted."

Demi shook her head, her expression dangerously dark compared to her yogic, serene self from moments before. "You don't know anything about her. What her uncle is like... She deserves better."

"I—"

Daisy was grateful Candace chose that moment to return. Truthfully, she had no idea what was going to come out of her mouth next. She only knew the guilt gnawing at her, and her frustration at its source.

As she plopped three fresh drinks onto their table, Candace deadpanned, "I sold my car."

"*What?!*"

Daisy and Demi made eye contact as they echoed one another.

In a disbelieving voice, Demi repeated, "You sold your car? But why? You *loved* her."

Standing tall, Candace played with her drink's umbrella. She shrugged, saying, "I did love her. She was also a limited edition and worth a nice house down payment. The collector I found was practically begging me for the sale."

"What about the loan I was going to give you?"

"You're already helping more than enough with these designs. Really, it's okay. This is a golden parachute I should have pulled a while back." Candace paused. It was almost imperceptible, but she seemed to shudder. "Besides, I forgot how awful it is to have a recognizable car in a small town. You couldn't pick the car I traded it for out of a lineup."

Demi shook her head with wonder. "That's crazy, Can-can. We—"

"We should run the numbers for the design," Daisy cut in. For a moment, she caught eyes with Demi again. The woman wanted her friend to not be taken for granted? Fine. Daisy would gladly take whatever Candace wanted to give. They were all adults. Daisy was not going to let herself feel guilty over a choice that was not hers to make.

Not too guilty, at least.

To Candace, Daisy said, "If we're going to get the work done in time for the height of the season, we need to talk about timelines and get moving ASAP. Right?"

Candace nodded. For the first time all day, her seafoam eyes showed some spark.

Cocking a grin, Daisy said, "I assume you already have some of this worked out. Maybe a sticker-covered binder?"

That spark grew to a full, gorgeous glimmer. Daisy's heart burned in response.

"Well, since you asked…"

# CHAPTER 15

## *Candace*

June came crashing in like an impossible-to-escape tidal wave.

It took a full three weeks to plan, organize, and execute Bagel Bombs'! renovations. From paint swatches to particleboard, every detail mattered. Their progress was simultaneously warp-speed and too slow, which left Candace in a constant state of anxious flux—all that, plus the paradox that was her relationship with Daisy.

A shift happened.

Daisy only frowned at Candace half as often. And, most times, it turned to a begrudging, dimpled smile. Her cutting comments dulled to snarky ribbing, or even the rare compliment.

But it was impossible to say why.

Maybe it was the sheer amount of time they were spending

together. Along with the cafe shifts they co-worked, Candace started helping Daisy with inventory. They ran errands and baked bombs, shared mundane moments like debating which *Simpsons* episode to watch, and talked business strategy late into every night. Candace would get into her (far from) new Nissan Altima, drive back over the bridge to the illustrious Comfort Clam, and sleep like the dead.

Then, she would start the day all over again.

To say she was tired would be an understatement. Not a minute passed where Daisy, Bagel Bombs!, or the future of both were not on her mind. It was exhilarating, too, because little by little their plans were coming together.

Candace just had to break her current trend of messing things up, which included keeping her uncle off their backs. He called her at the most random times, 'checking up on her,' he said, when it was more like keeping her emotionally hostage as he ranted about various topics. Candace swore the man was in love with the sound of his own voice. But, she listened, and did her best to keep him happy... while reassuring him that her work with Daisy DeMarco was a flippant, unserious effort.

Uncle Perry probably did not believe her. When she was young, he made a habit of interrogating her. He seemed to enjoy making her lie, like it was some kind of game, and her secrets were his to collect. Candace would keep playing—and lying—until she won.

Bagel Bombs'! renovation came in two parts: demolition and reconstruction. Stripping back the stubbornly stuck, crusted layers with a combination of power tools and raw elbow grease was a process. There were decades of grime in unreachable places, and even a picture frame (filled with a photo of Bagel Bombs'! opening day) that was rusted to the wall. Candace was glad they opted to close during the messiest parts, considering some of the horrors they unearthed.

Closing the cafe, however, put them in a tight spot. Their window to complete a very long checklist was nail-bitingly narrow. It would have taken Candace and Daisy ages to do by themselves. Thankfully, they were far from alone.

Demi swept in like a benevolent tornado with a cadre of cousins borrowed from the family restaurant. Despite bickering the whole time, they did the bulk of the demolition in a single afternoon.

Ted Cando stopped by while he was on boardwalk bike patrol. He let Candace borrow a spare crowd-obscuring privacy fence, which allowed them to contain their construction chaos. It was kind of him, especially since Daisy was rude once she found out he had been Candace's date.

Even Rio and Dotty insisted on lending a hand, despite Daisy's best efforts to give them the days off. In return, all everyone asked for was a discount going forward.

Candace was so grateful, her heart was ready to burst—along with other parts. Every bit of her felt like jelly. The hammering, lifting, bending, painting, and myriad of manual labor they undertook in such a short period was more brutal physically than anything she had ever done. The harsh fluorescent glare from the industrial work lamps was making her head hurt, and she'd ruined multiple outfits.

But it was so, *so* very worth it.

Tomorrow morning, they would unveil the new Bagel Bombs! to the world. Candace had been posting online like a pro influencer, trying to drum up interest with sneak peeks and teasers. Their growing "BagelBabe" fans were metaphorically eating it up. Now, Candace just had to get them to literally stuff their faces.

It was late by the time they finished the most important tasks on Candace's checklist. Or very early, depending on how you looked at it. Dotty was long gone, and Rio got a ride with one of Demi's cousins after some sparks flew between them during the whirlwind of activity. It was Demi, Daisy, and Candace left, with all three of them running on fumes.

"Can-can," Demi said around a yawn, "don't you think it's about time to wrap up?"

"Almost," Candace promised. Their new special of the day

sign was refusing to cooperate. "Would you hand me that level?"

She did, quipping, "That sign couldn't be any straighter if it were a Sears catalog."

"Are they even still in business?"

"Barely, but you sure are. Look at this place! You're going to have a line all the way to the other side of the boardwalk onto that rusting pier."

Demi threw an arm around Candace's shoulders (closer to her back because of their drastic height difference). She spun them in a pan-around of the work they'd done. When she saw Daisy hovering by the new, solid oak backroom sliding barn-style door, she grabbed her, too. They did not seem to get along overly well—more than once, Candace caught Demi looking at Daisy with unusual scrutiny. But, for her sake, they seemed to have a truce.

Demi told them, "Wonderwood isn't gonna know what hit 'em." She gave another squeeze, then released. "I, meanwhile, need to hit the hay. I'm bushed."

Candace was about to tell Demi how grateful she felt. She had been agonizing how to thank her friend for going above and beyond. Of all the people who had come in and out of her life, Demi was the one person she knew she could count on. Before she could get the words out, though, Daisy beat her to it.

Arms crossed, looking adorably embarrassed, Daisy thanked Demi.

"Look… Back in high school, I avoided you because we ran in different crowds." Both women side-eyed Candace, who had the grace not to huff. "As an adult, I could be kind of a jerk, ignoring you around town. You've never been anything but nice to me, though, and now you've done this. I guess what I'm trying to say is I'm grateful. Thanks, Demi."

"You're welcome. Just remember, you're on the hook for catering my studio's holiday brunch. And no skimping! My yogis eat like horses."

"Heard," Daisy promised. "Get home safe."

"I will. Well…" Demi trailed off. Her smile turned thoughtful as her eyes bounced between Daisy and Candace. "Don't stay up too late, crazy kids. You've got a big day tomorrow."

Demi went to leave through the back. She paused to grab her pouch of a purse and let out an exclamation. "I almost forgot! Leo and Rex found this when they were moving that tetanus-trap file cabinet out of the office. Here."

It was an old, unlabeled VHS tape. Daisy inspected it with a puzzled expression.

"Thanks."

They said another round of goodbyes, and Demi left. Candace wrapped up the last few things that needed doing—she knew Morning Candace would be grumpy if Night Candace left her any messes. Daisy, however, continued to study the unexpected find.

"Do you know what it is?"

"No," Daisy told her. There was something in that no, though, that sounded like she might.

"We should watch it! That old TV in the back has a player. I'll go get it!"

"I don't know," Daisy wavered while Candace lugged the portable relic on the shiny stainless steel prep countertop.

"What's the matter? Not *all* mysterious, unlabeled VHSes are sex tapes."

Daisy snorted. A smirk quirked her lips.

"Don't lie, you'd like that. But fine. Let's give it a look."

Candace was too caught up in the moment, too giddy from the lack of sleep, that she failed to notice the hesitation in Daisy's voice. She unplugged the worklights. Moonlight and the glow from boardwalk lamps filtered in through the gaps in Bagel Bombs! security shutter, but it took a moment for her eyes to adjust. She groped for Daisy in the darkness and guided the woman's tape-clutching hands to the TV's slot. Together, they pushed it in.

A catchy musical jingle blared out from the little TV. Grainy, potato-quality images of a bygone 1990s Wonderwood boardwalk flashed over the screen. Women with big, permed hair, rollerbladers, and giant boomboxes were all hilarious blasts from the past. A man's voice said:

*"Spending your vacation at the Jersey Shore? Don't let it be a bore. Visit Bagel Bombs!, where every bite is an EXPLOSION of flavor."*

Candace's eyes widened as the video centered on the old Bagel Bombs! Cafe. The vibrant, weird-looking place that drew her in all those years ago while she wilted at her uncle's side. A mouth-watering display of baked bounty she could not wait to try. The gawky girl who stood at the counter, looking like nothing could tear her down. It was all exactly as Candace pictured in her memories.

Child-Daisy, who could not have been more than five or so in the video, was joined by her parents at the counter. They sang while Daisy did a familiar dance on the counter.

*"Bagel bombs, bagel bombs, bite a burst a' fun! Bagel bombs, bagel bombs, you can't stop at one!"*

The tape abruptly cut. It was not done, but Daisy was. She pressed the eject button and stood facing the TV. In the inky blackness, she looked like a statue standing so still that she scarcely seemed to breathe. Then, with a clean pivot on her heel, she bolted out the back.

Worry surged inside Candace as she scrambled to lock up and chased after Daisy. Her partner did not head to the little back lot where their vehicles waited, but instead, looped around to the boardwalk ramp. She walked so fast, she might as well have been jogging. Candace had to dodge around a pair of wobbling boomers to keep sight of her.

There were not too many stragglers out this late. Technically, the boardwalk was open 24 hours, but Wonderwood's nightlife was more dive bars than hopping clubs. The people they passed were either too drunk or tired to pay them much mind. Which, thankfully, meant no one noticed as Daisy hopped the boardwalk railing down to the off-limits beach below.

Candace followed. Sand kicked up with their fast movements, stinging her like daggers wherever it hit exposed skin. She tried calling out, but Daisy did not stop until they reached the shoreline. With the icy waves lapping at their sandaled feet, they stood side-by-side facing the pitch black ocean span.

"Daisy," she started carefully. "We can talk about it, if that would help. I know what it's like to—"

"*You don't!*"

Daisy's shout was swallowed up by the crashing waves, carried deep into the Atlantic's churning depths. Then, the ocean's pull dredged it back up. Her pain, the guilt she bore, came rushing to the surface.

"You don't know the whole story. No one does."

"Tell me, then. Please."

Daisy let loose a breath that rattled her whole body. Her voice was a quiet rush as she went on, talking to the watery void.

"The day they died, I was supposed to pick up ingredients at the corner store on my way home from school. I didn't. I got caught up working on some stupid art project, and by the time I got there, Mr. Grant had closed. Couldn't have been more than ten minutes. He'd changed from his summer hours, something that happened every year, but I forgot. So, my parents had to drive off-island to the all-hours big-box store. I offered to go, but they were worried since it was raining and I'd just gotten my license. They were worried about *me*, but they were the ones who—"

As Daisy choked on the next word, Candace placed a featherlight hand on her shoulder. Daisy did not shrug the contact away. She concluded, "It's my fault they were out that night. It's my fault they're gone. I ruined everything."

"Oh, Daisy... That's not right. It was an accident. You didn't ruin anything."

"I did. And now I'm stuck here, living out their dream. I hate it. I hate myself for hating it even more. And I hate *you* most of all for waltzing in, all perfect and put together, making me think things could be different. My parents are gone. Nothing we do will ever make this place what they thought it could be."

"Whoever said we had to?"

"What...?"

Daisy's expression was difficult to read in the muted moonlight. Even so, Candace could not help smiling at the slack jaw she knew the woman wore.

"Who said you had to make it what they wanted? It's yours now, so you do what you want with it."

"You're oversimplifying things."

"And you've complicated things so much you convinced yourself you hate it when I know that couldn't be further from the truth."

"Typical," Daisy spat. "You would be the type to tell someone else what their feelings are."

"I won't ever tell you how to feel. But hate is a strong word, and I don't believe you mean it."

Beneath Candace's hand, Daisy's bicep flexed with her clenched fist. Still, she did not move away.

"The little girl dancing in that commercial," Candace told her, "the one I met who was so proud of her new peanut butter bombs... the one who poured her heart and soul these last few weeks into renovating the whole cafe... I've seen real, repugnant hate, and none of that seems like it to me. Burnt out, maybe. Resentful. But I know you love what you do. I think you just need to not feel like it's the *only* thing you do."

Daisy sucked in a sharp breath as if Candace's words dealt a physical blow. Candace's heart broke for her, but it needed to be said. The truths people actively denied themselves were the most painful, she knew.

"You're allowed to live for more than bagels, Daisy. You're allowed to live for yourself and pursue what you want. There's nothing to feel guilty about."

Despite Daisy's tense posture, she had not shrugged herself free from Candace's hold. She did not stop that same hand from moving to brush away the tears that had started to streak her cheeks.

Daisy let loose another hitched breath. In a voice that was barely audible over the wind and waves, she admitted, "I don't know how to stop feeling this way. Part of me has always resented how my parents leaned on me, even when I was too young. But they're also some of my most cherished memories. I remember when we made that commercial. It was such a long day, but we had so much fun and we were so happy... How could I forget?"

"You've been hurting this whole time. It's easy to forget things when you're in pain."

As Candace finished her tear-gathering, she stroked a lock of hair that escaped Daisy's bandana back into place. It could have been her imagination, but the woman seemed to lean into the touch even as it drew away.

Candace admitted, "You know, I feel like I ruin things, too. They told me I wasn't cut out for 'serious" work, and made me feel so guilty for not appreciating the easy life I could have if I just married some rich asshole. I ignored them, I kept on pushing, until I ran face-first into a wall. But, just because I hit one wall, doesn't mean I won't go through the next one."

Daisy made a thoughtful sound, almost like a hum.

"For me, I think the pressure got to be too much and I just... gave up. I'm not even sure when I stopped believing I could do more. I accepted this was how things were, and there was no point in hoping for more. My life was only going to get worse."

Candace promised Daisy and herself, "It doesn't have to."

"No. Maybe not. Ever since you came back to Wonderwood, you've been making me think that. Pushing me."

Guilt bubbled inside Candace. "I don't mean to force you, Daisy. I know I can be a steamroller, but I swear, if you want me to stop, just say it and I'll leave you alone. I—"

"Don't go."

There was a definitiveness to the words that set Candace's heart pounding. A wrenching, pleading needfulness, too. The hands that moved to grip her sides and turned them chest to chest were steady, somehow, despite their trembling. Slowly, as if one wrong move would scare the woman away, Candace looped her arms around Daisy.

"That settles it, then. Hate me, but I'm here to stay as long as you want."

A hot puff of breath scorched Candace's neck as Daisy agreed, "Hate... is a strong word."

# CHAPTER 16

*Daisy*

Getting home last night, Daisy did not sleep a wink.
How could she after such a moment like *that* with the last person she wanted to show such vulnerability to? Which ended with a hug so intimate, so soul-twining, it made her blush more than any sex act. But, an internal voice whispered, if she did not want Candace to see that side of her, why did it feel so *good*? The relief she felt letting it all out was wild. Not only that, but Candace's response was cathartic.

It was like seeing the world from a whole new perspective. Daisy did not hate Bagel Bombs! Her feelings were more complicated than that, but she had been so wrapped up in resentment that she lost sight of anything else. Candace Perry, though, was hard to ignore. Her keen, kind insights... the gentle touch that grew tighter when she was sure it was allowed... her lilac scent mixed with the salty tang of the sea.

No, Daisy did not hate Candace, either. Not anymore, if she ever even truly had. The revelation hit Daisy with a full-body rush as she lay wide awake in bed. She vibrated beneath her covers as thoughts of the smartly-dressed, high-ponytail-sashaying woman paraded over her mind. So, if she did not hate her, what *did* she feel?

And why did the reverse question make her so nervous?

What must Candace think of Daisy after last night? After all the explosions of negative emotion she bore with a smile? Exchanges where Daisy had once felt justified flashed before her mental eye. Now, they were colored by an ugly, embarrassing lens.

Demi's words echoed in her head. *"You don't know anything about her... She deserves better."*

The sentiment was hard to argue against. Especially as Daisy watched Candace the next morning at Bagel Bombs'! grand reveal.

There had to be some kind of mistake.

Even before they opened, well before dawn, a surprising amount of people gathered around the shuttered cafe. More showed up while Daisy, Candace, and Rio did their final prep work. Looking at the online chatter, people were pumped. When it was time, Candace went out with a portable microphone and started the show. Everyone, including Daisy, fell under the Pier Princess' spell.

It was incredible to watch. Candace had mentioned being forced to participate in beauty pageants when she was younger, so she worked a crowd with ease. Along with her wit and oddball humor, she had no trouble connecting with people. Wonderwooders and shoobies alike chatted about their favorite bagel flavors over steaming hot coffees. Free samples, bagel-themed games, and the pep of a whole cheer squad wrapped into one person made for an electric atmosphere despite the early morning hour. And, as the day went on, the excitement only grew.

Somehow (probably thanks to a friendship with Ted Cando

that Daisy *definitely* was not jealous over), Candace had managed to convince the Wonderwood PD to let them put on an eating contest. At noon, five contestants sat at a borrowed fold-out table that supported several heaping plates of plain cream cheese bagel bombs. It took them a whole night just to make the contest bombs, in addition to the figurative million other ones they made in anticipation of extra business and samples. But, as always, Candace got her way, so they went through with it.

Now, holding up her phone to record the spectacle, Daisy had to admit it was worth it. A buzzing crowd was openly placing bets and buying their own special "spectator variety packs" from Rio, who dutifully helmed the till. Demi stopped by after her beach yoga class and never left; she floated around with a coffee pot, topping people off. When Candace handed the microphone to Dotty and took the final contestant seat, everyone went wild.

Daisy mouthed at her, *"You're not?!"*

Candace winked in response and sat waiting like the prettiest, most proper girl at a ball. Then, she shattered the illusion.

To put it lightly, the other contestants were in a different weight class from Candace. Yet, when they tapped out, she kept going. One after another, she popped the bombs into her mouth and vanished them into the pit that was her stomach. The only time she paused was to grab a different flavor cream cheese for dipping. Meanwhile, microphone in hand, Dotty reverted to her old days of announcing at the Atco racetrack as she commentated the whole thing.

It was hilarious.

Organic.

The kind of thing that made you feel special for being there. Daisy, though, felt special for a different reason.

Candace was the last left at the table not doubled over, clutching their middle. Candace, who forced herself under the spotlight despite preferring to keep to herself in front of so many people. Candace, whose grin blossomed when she found Daisy through the crowd.

How could Daisy ever hate someone who looked at her like that?

Dotty belted out, "Theeeeeere we go, folks! Coming out from Barbie's Dream House and every man's fantasy, Candace Perry wins by a mile! What didja win, I don't know! But good job, kid!"

As they planned, Daisy passed out gift certificates and mini googly-eyed bagel trophies to the other contestants. Candace pouted when Daisy had nothing to hand her.

"What?" Daisy said, "You should have asked me to make more if you wanted one."

"I know! But aren't you proud of me? I feel like I deserve *something*."

From the crowd, someone who sounded suspiciously like Norman's meddlesome self suggested, "Give 'er a kiss!"

A chorus of whooping and wolf-whistles egged them on. Were it for any other reason, it would have been funny how fast Candace's expression dropped. A fierce, impossible-to-miss flush burst over the fair skin exposed by her Bagel Bombs! tank top.

Daisy felt her heart kick up to a sprint. For a split second, they were teenagers back on that beach, their first kiss exposed to the world's cruel scrutiny.

This was now, though, and they were both in a different place. Candace angled up from her seat, leaned forward, and closed her eyes. Her lips were painted her usual bright pink, so sweet and soft, they looked like sugar taffy; like they would melt into the mouth of anyone they touched.

Daisy arched over Candace. She let the moment breathe, relishing the feel of control. Maybe that was why she was compelled to do what she did next. Feeling in control, feeling so free, brought out Daisy's flirtatious side. As she brought her mouth right up next to Candace's, she purred, "How about we save it for the bedroom?"

*"Wha–?!"*

It was almost too perfect. Candace reeled back, eyes wide and mouth agape in a perfect ring. Quick as lightning, Daisy popped a cinnamon bagel bomb right in. She quipped, "Something sweet to tide you over."

While the crowd around them hooted and hollered, Daisy held Candace's gaze. The shock she saw, the embarrassment mixed with begrudging want, made Daisy push further. She licked the cinnamon dust from her fingers as she imagined doing the same thing to the woman before her in *many* other places.

It finally felt like summer to Daisy, and she was determined to heat things up.

From the grand reopening in the middle of the month to its end, the rest of June smashed every expectation Daisy had and more. Even in its heyday, Bagel Bombs! had never seen such booming business. Just like Demi promised, they had lines across the boardwalk daily.

Life was busy managing the cafe and making bombs. However, with Candace taking on her share of the duties, Daisy somehow had more free time than ever. She got even more after they hired a new employee. Tina, one of Demi's cousins, was a bit of a clutz, but she barely needed training thanks to her time spent working at Zeus' Torch.

One change at a time, the pressure lessened.

Everything was working out like Candace laid out in her cute, color-coded binders. The business was humming along, corrections made and course set. Candace and Daisy were, as it turned out, excellent partners. Unfortunately, the same could not be said for whatever was happening between them as people.

Ever since Daisy's teasing at the reopening, Candace was jumpier than a rabbit when they came into close proximity. Accidental physical contact made her yip. And, she flushed whenever they made eye contact for more than a single second.

Unfortunately for Candace, her reactions only goaded Daisy. Thanks to the woman's own incessant social media posting, Daisy had the perfect excuse.

"C'mon," she cooed. "Your #BagelBabe fans will love this."

Lips pursed, cheeks puffed up in defiance, Candace avoided Daisy's bagel-poised hand. However, since her back pressed against the wall, there was nowhere she could go. Rio and their weeboo-self would have called it a "kabedon" moment, and with Candace blushing beneath her, Daisy could see the appeal.

"It's embarrassing," Candace grumbled. "And people will keep getting the wrong idea about us…"

"Oh? And what's the right idea? Business is booming, and there's a whole line watching, so let's give the people what they want. Now, say 'ahh….'"

Staring daggers all the while, Candace popped her mouth open. Her tongue unfurled in a slow slip. Then, as Daisy was distracted wondering what magical things that muscle could do to her, Candace flipped the script. She snapped the bagel up like a feral animal, nearly taking a piece of Daisy with her.

Eyes shining with challenge, she warned, "I bite."

Daisy grinned. Taking her phone back from Norman, he told her, "I think I recorded it the wrong way."

"Oh no," Daisy mock-lamented. "We'll have to do it all over again."

It would have to wait, though.

Tina was in dire need of bailing out. They had the briefest of lulls during shift change where Daisy thought it would be a good time for some promotional teasing. Out of nowhere, though, they were swamped.

The 'wrong idea' or whatever Candace wanted to call it, was damn popular. By the grace of the Algorithm Gods, their rainbow bagel Pride month post was shared by popular lesbian and LGBTQ+ influencers. In addition to a growing number of followers, they now had *fans* who dissected every post.

Were the *#BagelBabes* a couple? People asked about Candace and Daisy's relationship even on regular bagel posts. They were becoming a "ship," as Rio explained, a couple goal without even being together.

Daisy was more than happy to lean into it. Candace, though... She fled to the back without meeting Daisy's eye, saying that she needed to do a freezer tally. Before Daisy could think too long on it, she lost herself to the customer chaos.

Sometime later, while Daisy was working the register, a man reached the front of the line. His face was unfamiliar to her, but the bland-looking older man greeted her by name.

"Ms DeMarco," he said with a warm smile underneath his thick moustache. "How are you?"

With a pointed glance at the line behind him, Daisy replied, "Busy building a bagel empire. What can I get you?"

The man ordered a small coffee with cream and extra sugar, and pointed out a couple bomb flavors seemingly at random. As the bagels toasted, he waited off to the side, watching Daisy. It made her skin crawl. After she'd taken her next customer's order, he kept talking.

"I'm not surprised you don't remember me. It's been a long time."

Daisy forced an easy tone. "Yeah, sorry. I see a lot of faces. Give me a hint?"

"I handled some legal papers for your parents a while back," he elaborated with a smile that seemed to mock her.

Daisy had no idea what he was talking about. Growing up, her parents had shared little of the practical, paper side of the business. It was part of why she had such a difficult time taking over with their secretive records and bookkeeping. Hackles raised, she gave Tina a silent look that told her to take the register.

The man went on, asking, "Is Candy around?"

"No," Daisy lied, internal alarm bells at full blast. "She left."

Shrewd eyes bore into Daisy, but his mouth was still all smiles.

"Hm, too bad. That girl can be so flighty sometimes... Her uncle is worried about her."

Of course the man was a Peter Perry lackey. Daisy shot back, "Candace is a grown woman. She's doing just fine."

"Is she? From working with Fortune 500 companies in New York to selling boardwalk bagels... No offence, but that's quite the fall."

As Daisy opened her mouth to retort with something she'd regret, Candace emerged from the back. She retrieved the man's bombs and thrust the paper baggie at him.

"Shouldn't you be barnacled to my uncle, Vinny?"

Daisy blinked. The open, seething disdain she heard in Candace's sweet voice was foreign. But, she had heard of Peter Perry's lawyer Vinny Lamarka, and none of it was good. With his collared polo and high-waisted Dockers, he looked like a Church deacon riding his high horse. He tut-tutted them with a shake of his head.

"You're a smart girl, Candy. I thought you'd pick your priorities better. You have a chance to make things right if you go tonight."

"I've already told him, I don't have time."

"You should make time. Don't forget what we talked about before."

Whatever the threat meant, it made Candace shrink. Daisy saw red.

"This isn't a Starbucks," she growled. "Fuck off."

Vinny let loose a joyless chuckle. "Feisty! Just wanted to pass along my concerns as a friend of the family. And, support a small business, of course. Have a nice day, ladies."

While Tina continued to bustle around them, Daisy watched

Candace's gaze follow Vinny until he disappeared into the boardwalk throng. She was good at keeping her composure, her expression schooled, but the shortness of her breath gave away her feelings. Daisy started to reach out, yet pulled back at the last second.

*She deserves better.*

Thick tension swirled between them. It was broken by Norman's frank assessment of the situation. "Crooked bastard. Lawyers like Lamarka ruin the profession."

Daisy snorted and refilled her favorite regular's coffee. "I don't care what he does or how crooked he is. Knowing he's friends with Peter Perry tells me all I need to know."

"He's like Mike from *Breaking Bad*."

Daisy faced Candace, hands on her hips, and tried a joke. "You *know* I don't know any shows outside of *The Simpsons*."

"He's my uncle's fixer," Candace explained seriously. "Anything that needs doing, Vinny handles. And don't let his looks fool you. He's more than happy to get his hands dirty."

"What's this thing he was harassing you to go to?"

Looking down at the new neon pink and green tile she had installed herself, Candace bit her lip.

"There's a gala at the music pier tonight. My uncle wanted me to go as his date."

"And you told him no."

Candace lifted her gaze to meet Daisy's as she nodded. With confidence, she promised, "I know what my priorities are."

There were not many times in Daisy's life when she could claim to have her breath taken away. Most instances had been caused by one singular woman. Candace Perry had a unique power, and now was no exception. Candace was choosing *her*, and everything in the world made sense again.

"You should go." The words wanted to stay stuck in Daisy's mouth, but she spit them out like the gravelly truth they were. "Things are going well for us... for Bagel Bombs!. You said before that your uncle would make things harder for us if he felt slighted. If you stand him up tonight, what're the chances he'll throw a tantrum?"

"High," she replied with a tired sigh. Her arched brows pinched with worry and disappointment. "But what about helping you with inventory? We were finally going to order from that Vietnamese place, and I—"

"I know," Daisy told her. Winking, she said, "It's okay. I'll take a rain check."

"I won't be able to stay too much longer, then. I need to go back to my room and change."

"Their loss. I think you look perfect."

This time, she brought her hand to Candace's shoulder. Her thumb worked what she hoped were comforting strokes along the strap of the woman's tank top. She'd been wearing their Bagel Bombs! branded merch ever since they ordered a new batch for the reopening, and it suited her. Everything suited her, really, but the fact that this was what she picked filled Daisy with the oddest sense of pride.

Daisy wanted to say more. Maybe offer some words of encouragement or lighten the mood. Before she could swim up from her thoughts, Candace got moving.

"Thanks, Daisy. I'll see you tomorrow."

It was the fastest she ever moved; in a blink, Candace was gone. Dazed, Daisy fell back into helping Tina with the onslaught of hungry customers. When Norman spoke up again, she nearly dropped the order she was bagging.

"Don't you have an invite?"

"What?"

"That shindig your partner is going to. If I'm not mistaken, it's the Chamber of Commerce's yearly small business gala. I read about it in the *Wonderwood Word* this morning."

Naturally, Norman had his newspaper close at hand. He leafed it open and showed the article to Daisy. She snorted.

"Funded by Wonderwood Amusements and Peter Perry. Figures. He's throwing a party for himself and his friends."

And, for some reason, he wanted Candace on his arm. Badly enough to send out his fixer, too.

*Why?*

The question gnawed at Daisy.

Memory hit her. She *had* gotten an invite; she got one every year and had never bothered to go. Yucking it up with a bunch of self-important, rich types was not her scene. But if it meant she could keep an eye on Candace…

"Sorry," she told Tina, who did not look at all surprised. "I've got a party to crash."

# CHAPTER 17

## *Candace*

Galas and public events were Candace's personal hell. Along with the ones her uncle forced her to attend when she was younger, she had to go to a fair number for her professional career as well. They were a blur of schmoozing and mediocre finger foods.

At least there was an open bar at this one. Candace was able to sneak away while Uncle Perry chatted up a couple of representatives from a local private equity group. No doubt, he was trying to get their buy-in for his fun pier expansion. If Candace were in the right frame of mind, she might have tried to slyly approach them on Bagel Bombs! behalf. Now, though, the bar was far more appealing.

While Candace waited in line, she was thrilled when Demi appeared beside her. Her friend descended like a gorgeous, terrifying force of nature, taking attention wherever she walked in a swirl of style and earthen allure. She wore a cleanly cut, burnt umber romper suit that complemented her auburn locks. With her hair tamed into an intricate side-plait, she almost looked like a different person. Yet, the familiar, full-body bear hug she gave Candace was all Demi.

"I didn't think you were coming!" Candace returned Demi's hug just as tightly, adding, "You look incredible!"

"Of course I came! I wasn't going to leave you to the jackals. And forget about me, look at *you*. What cursed runway did you step off of?"

Candace flushed. She was not sure what had come over her. An hour before, fresh out of the shower in only a towel with sopping hair, Candace surveyed her outfit options. She had a couple she knew Uncle Perry would approve of without a second glance; conservative, classy, but fuckable. Things she would wear if she was going to be a "good girl."

Even so, Candace hesitated. Daisy's compliment earlier, her entranced eyes as they roved from head to toe, played on repeat in Candace's head. Of their own volition, her hands assembled a Frankenstein-monster's outfit unlike anything she had ever worn. But, she thought, it was perfect.

Black fitted slacks and a matching chic blazer brought the business side of Candace. For fun, she wore an eye-catching gold spangle belt to go with her bright pink eyeshadow, aiming for a punk-pop look with her makeup and accessories. The flats were because her feet were tired after standing all day. And, to show where her priorities were, a fresh, tucked-in, Bagel Bombs! tank top as her blazer shell.

Candace wished Daisy could see her. She was probably home, arm deep in dough. The fact that she encouraged going along with this was as confusing as the rest of her actions lately. The covert smirks, the flirting, the "accidental" touches while their customers watched... all of it was for show.

*Right?*

It had to be, because Candace could not dare hope for more.

Demi, with her best friend's intuition, knew precisely where (or, to whom) Candace's thoughts drifted. They retrieved their free merlot drinks, courtesy of a local vineyard, and moved their chat to a private corner.

The Wonderwood Music Pier was not the most glamorous of venues. It was more of an open auditorium space, dull and lacking much architectural flair, that could be rearranged to suit whatever function was renting it out. The one thing it had going for it was a wrap-around balcony and cathedral-height windows around the entire building. Poised over the roiling waves, it made for a spectacular view during a rainstorm.

Candace and Demi floated towards one of the balcony exits, just off the designated dance floor. On the stage, a local silver-haired band of retirees-turned-amateur musicians struggled through the opening chords of some bygone *BeeGee Boys* beach anthem.

"I haven't seen you around the studio much," Demi said as she nudged Candace with her elbow. "I miss seeing your scrunched up face during chair pose."

"You and me both. I've had a knot in my shoulder for weeks that I've been dying to wring out."

"When was your last day off? Like, a real day where you're not slinging bagels and being hounded by the Gluten Garcon? She wasn't mean to you for coming, was she?"

"Who?" Candace feigned dumb, but the woman eyed her over her drink. "She's been nice, I swear. We're busier than I could have ever dreamed of. Things are going well for us, Demi. *Really* well, which is why I'm here."

"Uh-huh," Demi hummed. One elegant, thick eyebrow cocked, she said, "And I'm sure dressing like a Bagel Bomb! influencer won't poke the bear at all. Don't get me wrong, you look hot, but..."

"I know." Candace tossed her free-hanging blonde locks over her shoulder, saying, "That I'm hot, and that it might not be the best idea. To be honest, I only just unbuttoned the blazer, so he hasn't seen the tank top. I'm not that brave."

Demi shook her head, her expression earnest.

"Don't say that, Can-can. You're one of the bravest people I know."

"Yeah, right. Call me Xena, I'm a regular action star."

Candace broke from Demi's over-serious gaze to take a deep drought. The merlot was from young grapes, bitter and immature, and burned on the way down.

"You are," Demi insisted. "Anyone else thrust into the privilege and pressures that you were would have turned into a miserable, insipid witch. Christ, do you remember the inspections? The responsibility talks? The 'camp—"

"*Of course I do!*" Candace hissed.

She jerked her arm, and wine sloshed over the rim of her glass. Cursing, she set it down on a nearby table and tried to keep the drips from getting on her clothes. If Uncle Perry saw wine stains on her hands, he'd get angry at her for being 'messy.' Demi grabbed a handful of cocktail napkins from a waiter passing out crab rangoon and helped Candace contain the damage.

"I'm sorry," Candace told her. "I appreciate you so much. You're the only one who understands how weird my life is."

"I know. So please, be kind to yourself. I just want you to be happy."

Demi continued to hold Candace's hand after she cleaned her up, clasping one in both of hers. She squeezed, her gaze filled with adorable worry. In her heels, she almost reached Candace's chin.

It was sweet of her to come tonight. Candace had texted her about how Vinny Lamarka and his slimeball self came around Bagel Bombs!. She'd needed to freak out a bit, and Demi was the only one who would get it. But for her to spend her Saturday night coming out to keep Candace company was why she was her dearest friend.

Candace returned Demi's grip. "What is it you say to your yogis? 'Happiness is a practice?' I'm working on it, promise."

As if on cue, Candace's phone buzzed with a social media notification. She slipped her hands away from Demi's to check it. Norman, as it turned out, had filmed her and Daisy's "kabedon" moment like a pro. The reaction from their followers had been nothing short of thirsty, with all the usual questions asking about their relationship status. Flushing, she shook her head and slipped her phone back into her pocket.

Demi, who saw the phone screen, did nothing to hide her disapproving frown.

"This *BagelBabes* hashtag of yours... Don't you think it's going a little too far?"

Candace shrugged.

"It's marketing. People like watching hot women do things. They like watching them do things together even more. Nothing we've posted is lewd. Well, *too* lewd, and the bagels take center stage."

Demi crossed her arms beneath the flattering V-cut of her romper. She repeated, "'Marketing?' Is that what you call the video that went up today? What flavor was the bagel she fed you?"

"It was sesame. And Daisy is having fun with it."

"She's messing with you."

The words were said gently, in the same tone Demi used when correcting a yoga posture. Still, they landed like a slap.

"What does it matter?" Candace replied as nonchalantly as she could manage. "Our followers are eating it up. What's the harm?"

"Your heart, for one. We're not kids anymore. You can't put on an air and pretend it's just some summer crush. We both know how hopelessly in lo—"

Candace made a strangled sound as she choked on her own spit. Demi's gaze enveloped her with steady support.

"I don't want you to get hurt. That's all."

"I can handle it, really. You worry too much."

In truth, Candace would be lying if she said there was not some part of her that enjoyed the attention. She could do without the audience, online or in person. But, even if it was to tease, the woman's newfound attitude was unbelievably hot.

The way Daisy's eyes blazed into Candace's melted her. Every touch was a delicacy she savored with greed. Their chemistry was so palpable, she could practically taste the fingers Daisy licked each time she acted out their little game.

So, what did it matter if Candace got hurt? For at least a little while longer, she was happy pretending that it was real. Once Daisy moved on, she could figure out how to be happy without her.

From across the venue, Candace eyed Uncle Perry looking for her. She gave Demi an apologetic smile.

"Go on," she encouraged. "I don't want him to send some health department friend of his to the studio for a surprise visit. Hold on." Smooth as a stagehand, Demi fixed Candace's blazer so that the Bagel Bombs! tank top was plain to see. "You're right. If this is what you want, don't back down."

Standing tall, Candace sucked in a final bracing breath. Then, she made her way over to the man who could ruin her with a handwave.

Candace noticed that Uncle Perry's lifestyle was catching up to him. From the pictures she saw, he was once handsome; it was from his side that she'd inherited her full blonde locks, her height, and face that had been asked to model. Now, though, he was an example of what not to do.

After decades of living in a shore town, refusing to wear "fake liberal" sunscreen, he looked like old jerky stuffed into ill-fitting, designer clothes. Excessive alcohol and rich foods he indulged in during his social outings had not helped either. The spray tan he used to try and even out his skin's blotchiness showed on his suit collar like he was an actor. Or a clown, with his poof of thinning, comb-over hair.

It was ridiculous. Uncle Perry expected everyone to look at him like he was an Adonis, and they would because *money*. To Candace, he looked like a hot dog at a funeral. The thought gave her courage to keep her chin raised as she came up beside him, despite the menace he exuded.

"*There* you are, Candy!" He looped a thick arm around her

shoulders and jerked her closer. "I was starting to think my niece abandoned me!"

The group he was speaking to were unfamiliar to Candace. They were all well-dressed, put-together people, but there was something plastic-y about their appearance. Their greetings were bright and fake, like morning news TV hosts.

Candace forced an apology, saying, "Sorry, Uncle Perry. I had to use the restroom and ran into a friend."

"You've always been such a social butterfly." He gave her shoulder a not-so-gentle squeeze. "I've been waiting to introduce you to these nice people..."

Candace's guard raised even higher. These "nice people" were from a conservative think tank that was connected to several dark money investment groups. They threw the names out quickly, expecting her not to know them, and she gave no indication to prove them wrong. If her uncle was getting involved with this group, it could not mean anything good. They eyed her with suspicion, giving her outfit obvious appraisal.

A man with a flop of dull brown hair and a checkered bow-tie gave Candace an overly enthusiastic grin with his too-bright shark teeth. "The Pier Princess herself! Your uncle has been telling us a lot about you. Faith and family are beautiful things, yours is an example for the rest of us."

"Er, yeah. Thanks."

Candace could not remember the last time she stepped foot into a church or talked to family outside of her uncle.

"The Lord tests us with adversity," he droned on as his companions nodded like bobbleheads. "The tragic death of your mother, an alcoholic, unavailable father... It's a miracle that you had your uncle to step in and keep you on the right path. Denying the devil is a full-time job for a Godly woman."

Again, Candace forced out a thank-you despite her rolling nausea.

"It's been a long road with a few bumps," Uncle Perry said with gravitas. "But family stands together, and that's what tonight is about. If you'll excuse us, it's about time."

*Time? Time for what?*

Candace's uncle steered her away from the God Squad and started walking them towards the stage. The band had stopped playing, and a man—Tim Burgson—was standing front and center holding a microphone.

While Tim introduced himself, Candace demanded in a hushed voice, "What was that about? What's going—"

*"How dare you?"* Uncle Perry's vise grip on her shoulder rent divots that would surely bruise. They stood at the bottom of the stage steps, hidden from general view by a thick, red velvet wing curtain. His eyes bore into her as he hissed, "I turned around and you were gone, cozying up with that Greek tart. You made me look like a fool."

"Don't talk about my friend that way. You never said you expected me to be glued to your side all night."

"Listen here: you don't have 'friends.' You have people *I* allow you to see, and I think it's about time I remind you of that. I've let you make a scene with that Bagel Bitch for too long."

"No," Candace begged. Impossible-to-hide terror leached into her voice. "Please, leave her alone."

"Why should I? She's nothing. A depressed, low-class loser with no prospects. I won't let you tie our name to that filth."

"You're wrong. The renovations, all of our hard work... It's going to pay off. Daisy is going to meet that dumb lease clause, and then—"

"Then?" Uncle Perry sneered down at Candace, looking at the Bagel Bomb! tank top with particular disdain. "No. There's no 'then.' First, I call my friends at the health department. Cooking out of her own kitchen? I'm sure there are violations and, if not, they'll find some. Next, I'll handle those disgusting social media posts with the same company I pay to take care of the pier's online presence. Your pages will be down in a day. I'll make it my mission to destroy that cafe, its brand, and anything else that urchin attempts to accomplish—unless you do what I say.

"Just remember, you asked for this. Now, smile and act fucking grateful."

A numbness spread throughout Candace as her uncle hauled her on stage. They stood behind Tim Burgson with fake grins plastered on their faces while the man introduced them.

It was gag-inducing fluff. Tim presented an aggrandized caricature of Peter Perry, a "visionary entrepreneur" and "Wonderwood's wacky uncle." You'd think the man built the boardwalk plank by plank himself, rather than the real story of buying an already-developed fishing pier and dumping some carnival games onto it.

Then, Tim's introduction got personal. He talked about Candace, echoing the God Squad's tone, talking about her like she was Little Orphan Annie. How her uncle swept in like a white knight to save her back then, raised her despite Candace being a rebellious, "confused" youth. And, now, he was seeing to her future.

Giving Candace one final look, Uncle Perry took the mic. He boomed, "My Candy is one of a kind, isn't she? Falls into a closet for her outfit and still looks like a million bucks. How about a hand?"

The smattering of polite applause buzzed like a hornet hive in Candace's ears. It grew worse as he went on.

"Family, folks. A family that sticks together can accomplish great things. It makes our community a stronger, safer place. It makes us *great*. So, when Candy here asked to work with her dear old uncle, I knew great things were on the horizon.

"Wonderwood, I'm thrilled to announce the expansion of my amazing fun pier, along with a very special partnership with my niece. It's going to be a whole new boardwalk when we're through with it."

Candace couldn't breathe. The buzzing turned to a sharp, stinging tone. She looked out over the swimming sea of faces. So many strangers clapped along, except for one lone, still figure.

*Daisy DeMarco.*

She wore an impossible-to-miss crimson dress. Backless, it bore a deep diamond view of the woman's front, with sides that cinched behind her neck in an elegant curve. The A-line hem split high, giving an incredible frame of her long legs and black lacing gladiator heels. Her hair was styled and textured, slicked back from a face touched with makeup as bold as her dress. She was the most gorgeous person in the world, a hibiscus flower in a sea of gray.

The smouldering amber eyes that looked back at Candace were filled with hatred.

# CHAPTER 18

*Daisy*

T he last time Daisy needed to dress up was Halloween two years earlier. Rio's friend group threw a party, and Daisy ended up getting dragged along as their plus one.

The "costume" they provided was actually a *very* nice cosplay of a character from some survival horror video game. Ada Wong, the semi-love interest of Rio's costume character, was known as "the woman in the red dress." Daisy rolled her eyes when she saw the satin-smooth, blazing crimson garment. A qipao-wearing, zombie-killing femme fatale was a nerd fantasy, for sure. However, she looked so good that she ended up keeping it. Now, she was as grateful as she was mortified.

Walking around as a sexy secret agent at a nerdy party was one thing. At this kind of event? Daisy wanted to fling herself into the ocean. She'd forgone the costume's gunbelt and grappling hook accessories, yet eyes followed her the moment she stepped through the doors.

Occasionally, conventions or craft fairs would set up in Wonderwood's Music Pier. The last time Daisy was inside the place was for *Puffcon* pastry convention—a fun afternoon filled with people doing their best *Great British Bake Off* recreations. Dotty's friend was running the ticket booth and had snagged them a pair.

Tonight, the vibe was markedly different. It felt, and looked, like a bougie vampire masquerade populated by members of the local golf club. Gaudy gold accessories and red velvet accents dominated the space.

Daisy spared no time locating one of several bars and got herself an Old Fashioned to sip. The pimply waiter tried to pawn off his quick-to-pour wine, but she recognized the label as a local dud.

Drink in hand, it did not take long for Daisy to find Candace. She watched from afar as the woman chatted with Demi. They were close. Closer than close, with a bond that made Daisy—and her increased desire to *also* be close to Candace—uneasy. It was not (wholly) jealousy. Faced with someone who loved Candace, the pressure of understanding her own feelings nagged Daisy.

Feelings that were, at the moment, dominated by *other* thoughts. It was hard to think objectively about Candace Perry when the woman looked like that. The slacks that hugged her perfect ass... the boss-girl blazer... *Her tank top.* When the dazzling woman left Demi for her uncle, she crossed the room right past Daisy without realizing it.

Lilac trailed in her wake.

Dazed, Daisy gravitated to Demi. The yogi eyed her like she was coming in half-way late to a class.

"Hello, Zee. Don't you look nice."

The word "nice" was a loaded one, but Daisy decided to take it as a compliment. She returned it, saying honestly, "That color suits you."

"Thank you."

Daisy cringed at their mutual stiffness. She kicked back a sip of mulled, malty orange and tried to loosen up.

"This is one weird party, huh?"

"Have you ever been to one of these?"

"No," Daisy answered. "Not exactly my scene. You?"

Demi let out a musical chuckle. "Every now and then. I believe in community engagement, but this is a bit much."

"You mean bull?" Daisy commented with a snort, "Look at 'em, just patting themselves on the backs for making money off people."

"You're a part of it, too. The whole cycle of owning a business, growing it, is a balance of give and take. Although, yes. Most of the people in this room are on the 'take' side." As she played with the rim of her glass, Demi gave Daisy a measured survey. "Candace tells me things are going well. That you're having… fun."

Daisy crossed her arms. In her periphery, she continued to observe Candace; she looked uncomfortable, speaking to a group of people who had an uncanny-valley, over-polished vibe. But, *damn*, Daisy could not stop herself from thinking again how beautiful the woman was.

She heard herself say, "What's wrong with fun?"

"Nothing," Demi admitted with an edge. "As long as it's in the right spirit. Like I said, Candace—"

"Deserves better," Daisy finished. Breaking her fixation to face Demi head-on, she added, "I know."

"Do you? I love that woman with all my heart, and the thing I want most is for her to be happy."

"Why don't you date her, then?" Daisy regretted the question as soon as it came out. But she started digging and could not stop. "If you care about her so much, you make her happy."

"I tried."

Daisy had suspected it, and yet, the confirmation was no less of a gut-punch. Nodding, Demi took a satisfied sip of her wine.

When she spoke again, her lips curved into a wistful smile.

"I was so happy when she agreed to go out with me. She wasn't out-out, but I knew she had crushes... *a* crush... on a girl, so I thought I had a chance."

Around the lump in her throat, Daisy asked, "What happened?"

"Well, I wasn't her crush, for one. It was always 'Demi, let's go get bagels,' or 'Demi, have you seen so-and-so around school lately? What's she like?' 'Demi, have you ever thought about cutting your hair short?' It was so annoying, I ended things before we even kissed."

Daisy reeled at the implication that was slowly dawning on her. Without ever knowing it, she had been the third point on a love triangle. She mumbled out, "That wasn't cool of her."

"No. It wasn't. But we were dumb teenagers, so I forgave her. I could never stop loving her. It just changed. I've been with her through everything. *E-ver-y-thing.* You know, her uncle used to do daily inspections of her room? Her schedule, her internet search history... her *periods.*"

"She was a kid!" Daisy tamped down her anger as several nearby gala attendees looked up at her raised voice. Across the hall, Candace was gone. Demi shrugged, but it was more like a shiver.

"He's sick. I don't think he sees Candace as a person, just another *thing* for him to control. When he can't, he punishes her. Like after he found out about her crush on that other girl. See, the man isn't religious, but his image hinges on him appearing to be. Candace being gay isn't appealing to his circles."

"That *fucking* piece of shit. It's *her* life!"

Looking up at Daisy, Demi said, "Until she was eighteen, legally, it was his. I think he misses that power over her. Being able to bend her to whatever he wanted. But he couldn't break her. Do you... Maybe remember not seeing her in the summer of our junior to senior year?"

"I... yeah, I noticed." To anyone else, Daisy might not have admitted it. "I always wondered."

"Candace's uncle sent her to a 'leadership camp.' For over a month, they drilled her on conservative values, etiquette, and being a subservient, traditional wife. It wasn't a conversion camp, thank the Goddess, but I was so worried... You know what she asked me when she got home?"

Daisy shook her head. A resigned, happy smile curved Demi's lips.

"She asked when we could go get bagels. Back then, I encouraged her to ask you to the beach party. I was so, *so* disappointed by what she did to you. But I understood. What about you, Daisy?"

"... Me?"

"You. Normally, I'd keep this kind of information to myself. You're a part of it, though, so I feel like you deserve to have the whole picture. So, Ms Bagel, now that you know the real Candace Perry, what will you do?"

A surge of emotions crashed over Daisy. She wanted to find Candace and steal her away from these monstrous people. She wanted to forget the pain from their past and move on to their future. She wanted to—

The hall quieted as a mic tapping sounded from the stage. A man introduced Peter Perry, and then Perry himself took the mic.

*"... Wonderwood, I'm thrilled to announce the expansion of my amazing fun pier, along with a very special partnership with my niece. It's going to be a whole new boardwalk when we're through with it!"*

Daisy heard the words and filed them away under *"what the fuck"* for processing. Her gaze shot from Candace to Peter Perry, watching his putridly self-satisfied grin as he dragged his niece to the dance floor. Something clicked inside Daisy— *this* was what real hate felt like. Handing her drink to Demi, she stalked after the pair.

The band was halfway through a rendition of Frank Sinatra's *My Way* by the time Daisy caught up with Candace and her uncle. It was a good thing they were in a public place because being within arm's reach of the ugly excuse for a man made her blood boil. In a viper-strike, Daisy latched a hand around Peter Perry's suited arm.

"I'm cutting in."

Roving Daisy's body, the conman's eyes shone with excitement. Rage roiled with disgust as she realized he did not recognize her *and* that he thought she was asking *him* to dance. He released his hold. Before he could blink, Daisy took Candace and swept her away.

*But where...?*

Daisy scanned the hall, looking for an exit that would not take her past Peter Perry or his circling cronies. With one arm looped around Candace's waist, the other raising their clasped hands high, Daisy spun them around an out-of-step conga line. Candace's panicked pleading reached her ears over the music.

"I swear, I didn't know! Please, believe me. I don't want anything to do with him or his—"

With a gentle squeeze, Daisy assured her, "Fuck him. I'm getting you out of here, princess. *Left!*"

They made a hard pivot to avoid dancing into Vinny Lamarka's line of sight. In a far corner, Daisy caught sight of her favorite pimply bartender coming back inside from a service entrance. She led Candace through the pungent haze of a recently smoked joint, onto the music pier balcony.

Outside, it was like a whole different world. Sound from the party muted as the door shut behind them. They were at the furthest end of the building, near the looming shadow of one of the many major bulwark concrete columns that supported the whole place. Wind whipped around them, punctuated by the harsh, successive slaps of the waves breaking beneath the pier.

Arms crossed, Daisy leaned back against a column facing the dark expanse of the sea. Candace did the same. It was hard to tell how long she had been crying. But, fast, silvery streaks fell down the woman's cheeks. Her words were labored.

"I'm *so* sorry, Daisy. This is all my fault. I never meant for any of this to happen."

Gently, Daisy knocked their elbows.

"Hey now, remember? Let it be and ride the sea. It's not the end of the world. You can tell him to shove it, and we'll—"

"I can't." With furious swipes, Candace removed her tears. Steadier, she explained, "He said he'll throw everything he can at ruining Bagel Bombs! if I don't start working for him Monday. Not just the physical location, all of it—the brand, our online presence, *you.* Everything your parents worked so hard for, that we tried to fix, he'll ruin because *now* I'm useful to him. Or, maybe he was planning this the whole time, waiting for us to get nice and comfortable before he pulled the rug. *Fuck!*"

Daisy flinched as Candace slammed a fist against the concrete. When she went to do it a second time, Daisy stopped her. With care, she worked the woman's balled fingers through her own. Their eyes met in the low light.

"What do you mean 'useful to him'?"

She let loose a growl of a breath.

"There's a conservative investment group he's been trying to catch the eye of for a while. Apparently, they never saw him as Godly enough to sink their money into... until I gave him the idea to play up a family partnership. They loved that, especially after they heard all about how he *saved* me."

Daisy snorted but was not the least bit amused. "Those types do love a good fake sob story."

"They do. And it'll all be for show. I doubt he'll even give me any real work. He'll just stick me in some closet. Again."

"Screw that. We'll lawyer up if we need to."

Candace shook her head. She pulled her hand free and clutched it to her chest.

"This was a mistake. I'm sorry. I just got so obsessed with the idea of being the hero, of being *your* hero, I didn't realize how much worse it would be if I got involved. You were right. I really am the worst kind of garbage."

Daisy felt the word as if it had been aimed at her. How could she have been so wrong?

"I should have never said that. You're not garbage. You're…"

Daisy trailed off. In her mind, she sifted through the pieces that were labeled "Candace." The old ones, dusted off and seen in a new light… The oddly shaped ones that now seemed to fit… The ones from the present, so spectacularly shining…

Daisy told her, "You're sea glass."

"I'm *what?*"

Kicking off from the column, Daisy retrieved a dirty wine glass from a bus tray by the door. She smashed it against the side of the building and picked out a few shards. Showing them to Candace, she said, "Look. It's been broken, so it's sharp and dangerous. It gets tossed away and ends up drifting, lost at sea. Then you know what happens? Over time, the edges get worn down. They smooth and, before long, you have…?"

"Sea glass."

"Treasure," she corrected. "Someday, someone is going to pick these pieces up. To them, it'll be treasure."

With her hand extended over the high balcony rail, watching Candace, Daisy let the shards fall into the sea.

"That's littering," the woman admonished with a wry tilt. She peeled from the column and approached the railing like a wary cat.

"I've picked up enough, the ocean owes me a few. And you, washing up on my shore a second time… I don't want to lose you again, Candace. We'll figure this out. Together."

She murmured, "None of my binders planned for this."

"No, we'll have to get creative. Lucky for you, I've been feeling that in spades lately."

"Hm?"

Daisy licked her suddenly desert-dry lips. She had not expected to bring up her recent free-time exploits, not without more practice. But Candace needed to know what she had done. She pulled out her phone and thumbed to the photo gallery.

"I've been making art again. Nothing special. Just some drawings and a couple sculptures with random things I find. But thanks to you, I wanted to try."

"Oh, Daisy... These are beautiful."

Candace grew quiet. Her expression was difficult to read, even illuminated by the phone's glow as she continued to study the images. She looked at one, a rough pencil sketch of the newly renovated Bagel Bombs!, longer than the others before handing the phone back.

"You can have that if you want. I still owe you a prize for the eating contest."

"You do, don't you?"

It was just bright enough that Daisy could see Candace's gaze flick to her lips. And was that... *lust*? Memory of the other prize Daisy almost gave to Candace thrust into her thoughts. How on that day, the gorgeous woman before her had closed her eyes, waiting.

Would she have let Daisy kiss her then? What about now? Pulled by their shared heartbeat's pulse, she found herself leaning forward to find out.

Candace went the other direction. She let loose a soft curse and yanked Daisy along with her, back towards the column. One hand on Daisy's arm, the other over her mouth, she pressed them into the darkest shadow.

In the next instant, Vinny Lamarka power-walked past. They were hidden thanks to the columns' curve and Candace's quick thinking. His fast footfalls pounded against the pier planking, echoing further and further away.

Seconds trickled by as Daisy and Candace stayed as they were. Moving was the last thing on Daisy's mind with this woman against her.

In a slow drift, the hand that covered Daisy's mouth moved to mirror the other one gripping her forearm. Candace's head rested in the crook of her neck, and every breath she took was like a searing caress. Her thigh, nestled in the valley between both of Daisy's, tensed.

Stars steamed over Daisy's vision. She held in a gasp that came out as a whimper. Her hands shot to Candace's waist, diving under her jacket to dig at her tank top.

*Goddamn*, Daisy wanted to rip these clothes off. Before she could, Candace pushed back.

"I think he's gone."

"Yeah," Daisy agreed in a delayed, dusky huff.

Stepping back into the light, Candace's expression was serious. "It's not because I don't want to be seen with you. It's just... I hid because I didn't want this to end yet."

"It doesn't have to," Daisy told her. She closed the distance between them once more, but resisted reaching out. "What do *you* want?"

"I want..."

In flats compared to Daisy's heels, Candace had to look up to meet Daisy's eyes. Her regular seafoam shine was so dark, it was like looking into the deep ocean. It threatened to swallow Daisy whole, and she would gladly let it, diving in head-first.

Instead, Candace pulled out her phone.

Keeping the annoyance from her voice, Daisy asked, "What're you doing?"

"I never did get a chance to eat. I'm seeing if that Vietnamese place is still open. And, they are! Would you, maybe..."

Daisy cocked a grin.

"Best idea anyone has had all night. Banh mi, my place, a little strategizing, and the *Simpsons*?"

"You read my mind. But I swear, someday, I'm making you watch something else."

Linking arms with Candace, Daisy started to lead them around the balcony. Thankfully, they could saunter right out to the boardwalk and avoid going back through the world's worst party.

"You can try," Daisy told Candace.

And she would succeed. The woman was good at getting what she wanted.

The evening seemed set. Daisy decided once and for all that she wanted to get closer to Candace. She might even try her luck at a kiss. A little planning, deep confessions, followed by some oh-so-necessary stress release.... Where else could things go?

Then, on the way to retrieve their takeout, Candace texted Demi and Rio for 'planning backup.' She seemed shaken after the stunt her uncle pulled, so, of course, Daisy was not going to stop her from reaching out for support. And, equally predictably, both helpful humans jumped to the princess's aid. Demi was excited for an excuse to leave the gala, and Rio happened to have the night off from their Wetlands Institute duties. They met up at Daisy's house, looking like two happy clams as they shared a joint from Daisy's hidden porch stash.

The charged, borderline romantic mood died with Rio's greeting of, "What's up, buttface?"

Daisy would be lying if she said she was not disappointed. Sharing Candace was bad enough, but having to split her sandwich added insult to injury. She cut hers lopsided and kept the bigger portion. They sat out on the porch where the screen wrap-around partition and flickering citronella candles (mostly) shielded them from the mosquitoes.

Daisy's general lack of company meant that there were not enough chairs. Demi staked her claim on the two-person loveseat, and Candace took the place beside her. Rio had already been lounging atop Dad's old Adirondack, which left Daisy to plop down on a cooler. While they tucked into hoagie rolls stacked with chargrilled pork strips and pickled vegetables, Candace recapped her uncle's demands between bites.

Afterwards, Rio asked the obvious question.

"If he's known this whole time you were working at Bagel Bombs!, why is he making a stink now? Seems like he would have put his foot down sooner."

"Well," Candace admitted, "he sent his lackey to try and scare me a little while back. And he's been calling... threatening in his own, roundabout way by exerting pressure he knew I couldn't refuse."

The echoes of disbelief, including Daisy's unfiltered curses, made her flinch.

"Why didn't you say anything? You should have told me."

Daisy hated the whine in her voice. She knew the real issue was that Candace omitted an important piece of information. Instead, Daisy was hurt by the fact that she had not come to her for support.

Candace murmured, "I know. I was stupid."

"I didn't mean it that way. You don't have to deal with these assholes alone."

Daisy's instinct was to reach out to Candace's hunched figure. She chickened out when she remembered their audience and turned the motion into a weird, wiggling gesture as if she were swatting a bug. Thankfully, Candace's attention was on her plate. It seemed like she might descend into another self-deprecating spiral.

Instead, she took a page out of Daisy's book and let loose some anger.

"I hate him. I hate that I'm related to him, that I look like any version of him, and that when people think of me, he's in their head, too. That ugly smile when he knows he's lying. The way he pretends to be all about family, when it's really about controlling people's perception of him because he has a *massive* inferiority complex. He's the fucking worst. A cruel, entitled grifter who has stolen or cheated to get ahead, no matter who he had to hurt."

There was silence following Candace's rant. Only the sounds of nature, the cicadas and grasshoppers, along with croaker frogs who lived in the nearby bay reeds, filled the air. Until Rio asked another question.

"I mean… Are there receipts?"

"What?" Candace was confused, but Daisy knew exactly where Rio was going. They always did say that they played rogues in their *Dungeons and Dragons* sessions.

"We're bagel people, not blackmailers," Daisy answered. "He's not going to have a manila envelope labeled 'crimes' lying around."

Candace made a thoughtful hum as she munched on a bean sprout that had escaped her sandwich. "Maybe nothing that blatant, but… Demi, do you remember those ancient computers we nearly ruined downloading music off *Limewire*?"

The other woman snorted. "I remember a lot of virus-filled porn. But yeah. Why?"

"The pier office is *still* using them. My uncle hates technology and has always insisted on paper records. His secretary even prints out his emails. It's possible there's some kind of paper trail… The problem is knowing what to look for. It'll have to be something big, enough to make him back off for good without leaving him room to retaliate."

"So, what…?" Daisy asked with bewilderment that was undercut by a *very* sexy mental image of Candace in a skin-tight spy suit, "You'd be my double agent or something?"

"I suppose you could say that. It's a long shot, but I don't know what else we could do. Either I find some real, bottom-of-the-bog muck, or…"

Or, Daisy's thoughts filled in the blank, they were finished.

"Maybe it's for the best," Demi theorized hesitantly, like she was poking at a bruise. "Candace, if you're a part of this major pier expansion, it could set your career back on track. You might even be able to move back to New York. Isn't that why you came to Wonderwood in the first place?

"And Daisy, if Peter Perry follows through on his eviction threat, my *theia* has a lawyer who would be happy to represent you. She'll make sure you get a fair payout, and then you can set up shop somewhere else. Sue him for libel if he goes after your brand. No harm, no foul, you can both move on with your lives. Right?"

"No," Daisy decided without a second thought.

"'No?'"

"Nope. Not good enough." Daisy took in a deep breath of the dewy nighttime air. To Candace, she deadpanned, "This is your fault."

"W-what?"

"I think you've rubbed off on me, and I've gotten greedy. I don't care if we can get what we originally wanted. It's not enough if it means my partner gets taken away."

"Daisy…"

Candace bit her lip and tried to hide her watery gaze. She was so adorable that Daisy could not help going on.

"We've had to play that jabroni's game this whole time, so let's change the rules and take him down. If you're in, I am too. Okay?"

"Yes. All in."

It was hard to say what Candace was thinking. She looked like she was holding her breath, holding back what she felt or wanted to say. Yet, the smile that curved her lips was pure mischievous joy. Leaning forward, she propped her elbows on her knees with her chin atop her folded fingers. The insecurity that filled her eyes gave way to determination as her business side took over.

"That being said, we're going to have to play this smart. Let's talk details…"

From there, the group discussed the nitty-gritty of their plan. Candace would start working at the pier on Monday. She would do whatever her uncle asked and fit in as best she could, while using her access to find the dirt they needed. No more shifts at Bagel Bombs!, grocery store trips, or baking help.

At the end of the day, it had to look like the *#BagelBabes* 'broke up.'

They would use their social media platform to sell the separation, letting people draw their own conclusions through vague posts and a distinct lack of Candace-content. Daisy would make sure to play up her punk persona, acting like a jilted ex to anyone who directly asked about her former partner. Rio said they were available to pick up some slack at the cafe, and Demi offered to help with the occasional inventory run or batch bake. Things were going to get harder for Daisy once again, but this time, she was not alone. By letting old friends further in and trusting new ones, they had a chance to take Peter Perry down—a chance Daisy would need to take if she was ever going to get closer to Candace.

It was well past midnight by the time they had their con worked out. Candace tried, and failed, to hold back a yawn. With a glance at her phone, she said, "I think we'd better call it here. I need my beauty sleep if I'm going to play super-spy."

"Stay over." Three pairs of wide-eyes were suddenly on Daisy like floodlights. She stammered out, "I mean, if you want. It's not safe to drive when you're tired."

For a moment, it looked as if Candace might accept. It was the last time they could share the same physical space together for the foreseeable future. The last night they could spend as friends, or whatever their relationship was turning into. However, with untraceable disappointment, Candace shook her head.

"Thanks, but I'll be alright. My laptop is in my room, and I'll need it to get started on those social media posts ASAP."

"I'll follow behind you just in case," Demi offered. "It's not too far out of my way."

It was, Daisy knew, but she kept the comment to herself as Candace agreed to the escort. If it meant everyone got home without getting into an accident, she could keep her jealousy in check. At an amble, they headed out from the porch to the cars parked along the sleepy suburban street. Demi said her goodbyes and hopped in, while Candace lingered by her driver side door.

Did she feel the same lead weight in her stomach? Daisy wondered. There was only an arm's length between them, yet the distance seemed to expand by the second. Soon, it became an impassable void.

"Well—"

"Yeah—"

They spoke at the same time, cutting each other off. It was hard for Daisy not to laugh... at the absurdity of their situation, the bittersweetness of it all, and the cowardice that kept her from making her move. Candace was about to put everything on the line for her, but was it out of guilt? Or something more? If Daisy was wrong about her feelings, it would make things supremely awkward. So, she laughed. Candace did, too, though it was more of a sigh.

Ever formal, the princess extended a slender, manicured hand. Daisy took it and pulled her into a full-body embrace. Candace squeezed back. There was too much to say, more than either of them could manage at the present moment. For now, this would have to be enough.

"See you around, Perry. Text me when you get home."

"I will."

Then, like she was never there at all, Candace was gone. Daisy dragged herself back to the patio and flopped into the Adirondack. A light spark and distinctly skunky smell reminded her that Rio was still hanging around, watching the whole sordid scene.

"That sure was embarrassing. Wanna talk about it?"

The old Daisy would have threatened to fire Rio. Kept boundaries and bolstered her emotional wall. Present Daisy was desperate for advice. She gestured for the joint and bogarted it for a good minute.

"I like her."

"*No! Really?!*"

Rio did their best Kevin McCallister impression and slapped

their palms against their cheeks. In contrast to Daisy's gala wear, they were dressed for comfort in baggy cargo shorts and a printed tee. It was their day off, after all, yet here they were. Taking the joint back, Rio managed a smirk while they took in a toke.

In an exhale, they mused aloud, "You like her. You think she likes you. But you're afraid to shoot your shot because of how much of an ass you've been?"

"I… Yeah. What should I do?"

"Hm. Seems to me like you've gotta grind out some rep."

"*What?*"

"Reputation points. Like in *Stardew Valley*, or some dating simulation. You were picking the worst conversation options for a while, and now you need to make up for it."

Daisy glared. Still, stripping back the nerd veneer, the take made sense. She asked, "How?"

"Well, the normal stuff. Talk to her daily, give gifts from her favorite list, do quests… Although I guess she's the one on the stealth mission. You outta come up with a good reward since you skimped her last time."

Dumbfounded, Daisy wondered, "How is it *you're* the one with a steady girlfriend?"

At Rio's dual fingergun flash, they both broke down in a riot of smoky giggles. For a little while longer, they burned the night away chatting about life and love. Eventually, Daisy's phone buzzed with a burst of texts. Rio snickered as they read over her shoulder.

*Candace: I'm back!*

> *Sorry again for everything. I'm going to do my best to make things right. Let operation Bad Candy begin!*
> *Also… I didn't get a chance to say it earlier, but you looked gorgeous in that dress. Goodnight, partner.*

Daisy hid her face behind her hands, fighting a fierce blush. It was not fair. Whether or not Candace had romantic feelings for her, she was sure making it difficult to stop Daisy's from growing.

# CHAPTER 19

*Candace*

July on the Wonderwood boardwalk was a sight to behold.
It was the busiest part of the summer season, with shoobies swarming like locusts upon the small shore community. From the Fourth of July, with the town's bombastic celebration, to annual festivals like the Country Music Beach Jamboree and the Mega Monster Truck Rally, you couldn't go a week without some big event going on.

Bagel Bombs! capitalized on the influx of spenders with themed deals and promotions. Their red, white, and blue dyed bombs, along with their limited-time double-size 'monster mounds,' were huge hits. Every day, it seemed like Daisy whipped up a new, creative take on the humble breakfast food.

In addition to walk-up business, their online presence was helped by an unlikely source. Along with their love of nature, Rio had a passion for programming and web design. It turned out that they had been doing some solo tinkering since even before Candace came onto the scene. With a fair amount of ego, they unveiled a basic but customer-friendly app. A rewards system, plus mobile ordering, brought a whole new edge to their game.

Then there was Dotty's friend who worked with the local news station. Mid-July, right in time for National Bagel Day, Dotty's friend got the cafe featured for a puff piece. Daisy looked so cute and nervous talking to the sophisticated news anchor. She even did the dance from her parents' commercial, which took off spectacularly with their #BagelBabe fans.

Times were great for the renovated Bagel Bombs! cafe, and everything was coming together.

But Candace could only watch from afar.

As she suspected, Uncle Perry stuck her in a closet—literally—with a mountain of busy work. He did not intend on using her expertise to help with his expansion or to manage his accounts. No, aside from trotting her out for the occasional visit from the Solid Rock investment team, AKA the God Squad, Candace might as well have been a ghost. Her uncle left her in a moldy old office beneath the Manta Coaster, stuffed to the brim with disintegrating documents and a paper shredder.

"*Straighten up,*" he told her with a sneer.

Some papers had not seen the light of day since the early 90s, before her uncle bought the pier. Just like Candace hoped, he kept most of his records the old-fashioned way. So, one document at a time, Candace did as she was told, all while keeping an eye out for anything incriminating.

Could she find the magic piece of dirt they needed to shut Peter Perry up for good? It seemed impossible. But, then again, so did her relationship progress with Daisy. The woman wanted to save Bagel Bombs! *and* be Candace's partner. What *exactly* the word "partner" meant to Daisy was a gnawing question. But, with the reassurance she was wanted at all, Candace had to try.

So, this paper pushing purgatory was her life now. Flyers for

1995's Doo-Wop Summer; inventory purchase receipts from places that no longer existed; employee timesheets written by hand. Candace learned more about the pier and its inner workings than she ever thought she would. Yet, almost a full month in, countless boxes of manila folders later, all she had for her troubles was eye strain and tiny cuts on her fingers... along with a severe case of missing a certain someone she was not supposed to see.

Candace and Daisy had stuck to their agreement to avoid one another. On and off the boardwalk, they were careful not to cross paths in case Vinny Lamarka or anyone else was tailing her. Knowing her uncle, it was more than possible. Still, every day she woke up to a 'good morning' text from Daisy. Every night, they spoke on the phone, watching new shows together, or talking about whatever came to mind, until one of them fell asleep. In spite of the physical distance, they kept getting closer.

It felt like an illicit affair, communicating with Daisy like she was some kind of dirty secret. Guilt and desire warred inside Candace. She wanted to be with Daisy. To be wanted by her. Yet, the closer they got, the worse Candace's dread became. She had messed things up before, and now their situation was even more complicated. Potentially dangerous, since blackmail was in the mix. If she were to come clean about her feelings, it could be catastrophic.

Meanwhile, Daisy was thriving without Candace. Between Bagel Bombs! and a renewed passion for making art, the woman glowed like the most vibrant sunset. It might be from afar, but Candace would do whatever she could to catch a glimpse.

On the last day of the month, taking a break from document destruction, Candace escaped the damp pier underdepths to take lunch outside. It was "soupy," as Daisy liked to call it. The weather had been horribly humid all week, and today was no different.

Norman said the Farmer's Almanac was calling for a biblical

storm at the end of the season, and Candace believed it.

Today, a blistering haze hung in the air, making the beach look like a desert. The shoobies who weren't baking on the sand scurried from air-conditioned spot to air-conditioned spot. The boardwalk had its fair share of passersby, but, with the sun raging overhead, the outdoor parts of the fun pier were dystopianly empty and would stay that way until nightfall.

Alone, Candace sat at the themed Bayou Shack lunch counter outside the Haunted Swamp Mansion ride. The netting overhead was not the greatest sun cover, and the food was a mock-imitation of the authentic stuff. Even so, this was her favorite spot. With her mind a million miles away, Candace spooned up another bite of jambalaya and rolled it around in her mouth until she could bring herself to swallow.

"Jambalaya?" Demi's voice grew closer as she crossed from the boardwalk to the fun pier. "When you said you could meet for lunch, I didn't expect this place. You hate spicy foods."

Shrugging, Canace lied, "I'm expanding my palate."

"Mh-hm, I'm sure that's it." Sitting next to her at the counter, Demi followed Candace's line of sight right across the boardwalk to Bagel Bombs!. "Nothing at all to do with the view."

"Nope. No idea what you're talking about."

Candace's gaze betrayed her, though. She could not stop herself from glancing in Daisy's direction. Despite the oppressive weather, the place was in the middle of a lunch rush, and Daisy was handling it like a pro. She had not yet noticed that Candace was on her break. Sometimes, when she sat here, they would catch eyes and make faces at one another. With text conversations, it was almost like they were sitting side by side.

Almost, but nowhere near close enough.

Candace forced down another bite, to her stomach's immediate regret. She set her spoon down and passed the offensive dish to her friend.

"Thanks, but I'm not a masochist."

Demi ordered herself an iced tea, saying she would eat real food at the diner, and they set to catching up. Outside of brief chats before and after yoga class, they'd had little time for their friendship. While Candace was keeping up with her uncle's demands and her secret investigation, Demi had her own plate full. Running the studio and playing errand girl for Daisy was hard enough. But, thanks to Candace's renovation needs, Demi had also gotten drawn back into family restaurant drama.

"I'm sorry," Candace apologized again. She felt like the worst kind of person, focusing so much on her problems and wants that it blew up on her friend. "It was a big ask getting your cousins involved. I didn't mean to make you open that can of worms."

"It's alright. Living in the same small town, pretending everything in the family is hunky-dory, there's bound to be drama. It's the South Jersey way. They just needed me to pick up some shifts. I could do it in my sleep."

Demi's tone was easy, and a smile lifted her apple cheeks, but Candace could sense her stress. During class, her usually impeccable balance postures like tree and dancer were as wobbly as her state of mind. When it came to her family, nothing could throw her more.

"Are things with your aunt still the same?"

Demi winced.

"Yes. She's perfectly polite, like I'm some sunburned shoobie right off the boards. I can't blame her. I'm the one who blew up her marriage."

"That's not what happened. Just because you discovered the affair and told her about it, it's not your fault. Your uncle is the one who cheated."

"With my instructor and the class card I gave him for Christmas. I think *Theia* Thea would have preferred the air fryer."

Despite turning it down, Demi took a baleful scoop of sad-looking, poorly seasoned fish-rice and ate it. Her scrunched-up face was worth the amount Candace suffered through.

"How about you gave her the gift of getting rid of a cheater?" Candace reached out and gave Demi's shoulder a squeeze. "It's only been a year. Your aunt will come around, give her time."

"You're right," Demi said in a poor attempt at a chipper voice. "It's hard to ignore me when I'm standing in front of her waiting for my table's order. 'Business first, bitching later' might as well be the family motto."

"We'll crochet that on a pillow," Candace said, making them both laugh. "At least you and your cousins seem close as ever. I can't thank them enough for all their help."

"Are you kidding? You heard *theia*. You're family to me, Can-can, so you're family to them. They might come with some baggage, but they're always there to help."

Candace did not know what to say. Having so little blood family of her own, she had always looked at Demi's with awe. The idea that she could be considered a part of it was special to her beyond words.

Rather than address any of those more complicated feelings, Candace observed, "Katina really seemed to hit it off with Rio."

Demi snorted.

"They're still hitting it off. Katina had to coach my *theia* on pronouns, but she adored Rio as soon as they praised her spanakopita. For some people, food is a love language."

"Yeah," Candace agreed wistfully. "I know what you mean."

Demi's eye roll might as well have been audible. With a smirk, she added, "Speaking of... *Someone* is trying to get your attention."

Candace got whiplash from how quickly her head snapped to look across the boardwalk. The snicker it drew from Demi only stung a little. Waving at them, Daisy held up their special of the day chalkboard sign. She'd drawn a giant arrow that pointed towards the ground.

"An arrow?" Candace pouted, "I don't get it."

Daisy's waves turned to frantic downward gesturing before her attention was taken by a customer.

"I think she wants you to look around near here," Demi

guessed.

They both set to seek-mode, investigating under the bayou shack's polished wood countertop and enamel swivel stools made to look like curled up shrimp. Taped to the underside of the stool Candace habitually sat on, they found a tissue-wrapped package. She held it in her trembling hands as her brain forgot what she needed to do next.

"Well?" Demi urged, "Open it! Doesn't look like flaming dog poo to me."

Candace cast her unhelpful friend a look. Sucking in a breath, she broke Daisy's carefully placed tape seal, peeled back the paper layers...

—and gasped.

It was a sea glass flower pendant—a daisy, to be exact. Six dainty, milky white oblong shards for petals, and an amber lump made up the middle core. The pieces were connected with intricately woven copper jewelry wire that also formed the stem and a curling leaf. If Candace wanted, she could attach it to a necklace or keychain. Now, though, she held it cupped in both her hands as if it were gold.

*Nonono, this isn't good!* Candace's inner monologue went haywire as she struggled to come up with a platonic explanation for the gift.

"Wow," Demi whistled. "Zee always was great with her wirework, but I never thought she could be sweet. Seems like she's come around."

"We're friends. I think, maybe..."

"Friends, huh? So, when are you going to tell her you want more?"

"*What?!* Are you crazy? I can't do that."

Demi took a long, languid sip of her tea. "Can't, or won't?"

"Both," Candace grumbled. Her thumb swept across the amber center's smooth surface, marveling over it. Softer, she continued, "Things are going so well for Daisy. If I bring *that* up, it could ruin everything. I won't mess up her life again."

"She might not let you have a choice on that one. Giving

you meaningful flower presents… Asking you to sleep over after late-night planning sessions… the goofy look she's giving you right now… That woman is dropping some cosmic-sized hints."

"You're reading into things. We haven't even been in the same room together in almost a month."

"Mm-hm. Yeah, and she was *really* hoping you would stay longer."

Candace was feeling hot, and not in a good way. The sweltering, thick air was making it difficult to breathe. She argued, "It was late. Daisy gets worried about me crossing the bridge at night, that's all."

Winking, Demi finished, "Because she cares about you. Zee hasn't ever asked *me* to stay over, you know. Whenever I see her, you're all she talks about. It couldn't be any more obvious how you two feel about each other. Why deny it?"

Through the crossing boardwalk crowd, Candace and Daisy locked eyes. In her usual Bagel Bombs! tank top and aqua blue athletic shorts, her fresh undercut complementing the longer length of her hair, the woman looked as confident as she had on the first day Candace came back to Wonderwood.

*Strong. Self-assured. Sexy.*

She was Daisy—*no*, Candace reminded herself—**Zee** DeMarco. And Candace would always be the person who hurt her most.

Apologizing to Demi, Candace made up an excuse about her break being over. She fled from Daisy, and the feelings that were growing impossible to fight.

Throughout the first half of August, Candace did her best to cut back contact with Daisy. She stopped answering her good morning texts, and pretended to be too busy for their nighttime chats. Communications were kept professional. Despite Daisy's best attempts to steer their conversations to 'fun' topics, if it was not about Bagel Bombs! or business-related, Candace did not engage.

It was beyond difficult. Candace wanted to talk to Daisy about her art, her day, what she thought of the show they had been watching... if they could forget about everything and run away together...

But this was how things had to be if Bagel Bombs!—*and she*—was going to make it through the summer. Candace just needed to focus on finding their golden ticket to take down her uncle. She promised Daisy that she would fix things, and she was determined to keep good on her word.

No matter how miserable it made her.

The worst part was that Daisy noticed the emotional pull back. She asked if something was wrong, and Candace flopped out a fib about how she was exhausted. That she was trying her best, and everything was fine. She encouraged Daisy to focus on the cafe and herself. Candace was no stranger to playing oblivious when it came to placating hurt feelings with others. Yet, lying to Daisy only made the pit in her stomach deepen.

Candace felt anchored by her past. It dragged her down, and she was letting it. For all the hurt she had caused, it was where she deserved to be. Daisy was the only one who could set her loose. Yet, Candace, mired in self-hate, kept pushing her away.

Until she could not.

The minute Candace arrived at the fun pier offices on another soupy late-summer morning, she was greeted by Janice. The woman was, in the kindest terms, Uncle Perry's sycophantic secretary. Janice had been around longer than any of his other employees, and it was a sure bet that she knew where all the (hopefully) metaphorical bodies were buried. She was a devoted Christian, the type who believed 'imperfect vessels could produce God's perfect works.' So, of course, she worshiped Peter Perry.

For as long as Candace had known her, the woman looked the same with her endless supply of knit sweaters worn even on the hottest summer days and long, ankle-length skirts. Today, it was the ugliest combination yet of puke green and a busy bathroom curtain of a floral pattern.

Practically bouncing with excitement, Janice told Candace, "The Solid Rock Group is stopping by today to work out some final details with Mr. Perry. He asked you to be at the meeting."

"Why? That has nothing to do with me."

Candace was a prop in those meetings. They never spoke to her, and only looked her way to leer. She was sick of it.

The woman's eyes popped behind her glasses. She pushed them up the bridge of her pug nose with a disapproving look. She would never think of questioning Peter Perry's wisdom, but she was too much of a coward to talk back to Candace, either.

"I didn't ask. He's a very busy man, Candy. I sent the details to your calendar."

Flatly, Candace thanked her. Bending her schedule for a narcissist (anymore than she already was) had not been a part of her plan for today. Candace had bigger fish to fry, and she was running out of time.

In her desperation, Candace had even broken into Ernest Leary's old office to root around. The deceased accountant had always been a bit of an odd duck. He was friends with her uncle, and a part of the boy's club and Wonderwood's regressive political sphere. Yet, when Candace went off to college with aspirations in his field, Leary encouraged her. The rigid values his type stuck to could bend in very odd places. Unfortunately, there was nothing useful in the abandoned space, nothing important, as if anything consequential had already been cleared out.

For the rest of her day, up until the meeting later that afternoon, Candace continued her fruitless 'straightening.' She lost track of time and was the last to arrive at her uncle's office. The place was located off-boardwalk in a *very* nice colonial-style building on Wonderwood's main street. It was a historic building, an old ship captain's mansion with a gorgeous widow's walk balcony that overlooked the town below. Peter Perry cared nothing for the history, of course, but enjoyed the prestige of doing business there.

Unlike his dank, mildewy space beneath the pier, this place was meant to impress. Separate from his private study, business was conducted in a hall of a room that was gilded to the nines. It had artful crown moulding, gaudy Victorian-style wallpaper, and ornate French salon furniture in a mock imitation of grandeur. Candace had always thought her uncle decorated the place like a funeral parlor.

Meeting eyes with her glowering uncle, Candace took the open seat next to him. On his other side, Vinny Lamarka gave her a cringingly upbeat hello. The God Squad was seated on the opposite side of the oversized table. Spread out between the two groups were an array of documents.

"As I was saying, I believe this is everything your firm asked for," Lamarka told the group. "All of our records are in order. What you see here are our current plans for renovating Perry's Pier and a significant portion of the adjacent boardwalk properties. With your investment, it could become the greatest, most exclusive beach front resort on the east coast."

"Super," the bow-tie wearing man gushed. "We're thrilled about this partnership and bringing a little wholesome family fun to the shore. Once our lawyers verify everything, we'll be able to work out more details."

Candace tried not to be obvious as she strained to see everything she could of the documents before they were shuffled away into a manila folder. Her heart dropped.

"The permits," she murmured, "you already have them?"

Somehow, Uncle Perry already had the official building plans stamped and approved. Bagel Bombs!, along with the entire building on that section of the Wonderwood boardwalk, was slated for demolition. In its place, he wanted to build a behemoth resort that would make Mar-a-Lago look humble. So much of their hard work was going to be for nothing.

Uncle Perry seemed to enjoy watching the realization hit Candace. Leaning back in his kingly leather chair, he said with a smug tilt, "It helps to have friends move things along. Wonderwood officials know not to stand in the way of progress."

"What about your renters? They have multi-year lease agreements. You can't—"

"I can and will. Agreements change all the time, especially with something as trivial as this. It's business, Candy."

"But you said Daisy—"

"Screw the DeMarco girl! She can stay if she wants, but that building is coming down."

Rage made Candace clench her teeth so hard she feared they would crack. Was this really it? After everything they had been through, Bagel Bombs! was finished by her uncle's whim?

Across the table, the lone woman of the group (who, to Candace's annoyance, was wearing a duplicate of her cherished seafoam suit) leafed through the papers. She seemed like the analytical type, doing most of the work for her peers.

"DeMarco?" She asked, looking at one particular document, "As in the original owners of the property?"

"Erm, yes," Uncle Perry replied. "Their daughter still rents a unit from me."

"A bit cruel to evict her, but it can't be helped. Beachfront real estate is prime property, and it looks like you snagged this for a song after the '08 recession. How unlucky. I'd never speak to my parents again if they'd lost such a valuable investment."

Candace felt the floor drop out from under her. Was she understanding that right? Her uncle had bought the land and the Bagel Bombs! building from Daisy's parents? He got some kind of deal?

Did Daisy know?

Uncle Perry twisted the ring on his finger as his dark gaze

met Candace's. There was a warning, there, but also the trace of unease. He was nervous. Beside him, Lamarka smiled with an edge as he moved the conversation forward.

"One person's loss is another's opportunity. And here, Mr. Perry and I see a great opportunity for Wonderwood. Why don't we discuss some logistics? Candy... Make us some coffee."

When she hesitated to move, her uncle barked her name again. "Don't be difficult in front of guests."

"Oh, don't worry," bowtie-boy eased. "We're just about partners here. You take your time, sweetheart."

Stumbling from her seat, Candace went to the far less opulent kitchenette down the hall. Her hands auto-piloted making a pot, which she dolled out like the good little niece Uncle Perry expected her to be. All the while, warning bells screamed inside. She had finally found a thread to pull on that might lead to her uncle's misdeeds, one that would lead right back to Daisy.

*How much pain had the Perry name inflicted on that poor woman?*

Candace needed to learn more. She kept her focus despite wanting to flip the table over. Halfway through that pot of coffee and an hour into the meeting, Candace's phone rang inside her purse. She silenced it without looking.

It rang again. And again. Ignoring the glares, she took a covert peek at the screen.

*Daisy.*

While the phone continued to ring in her hand, Uncle Perry asked, "Don't your friends know better than to call when you're in a meeting?"

Candace stared at the screen. Something was wrong; she could feel it.

Deadpan, Candace lied, "It's my gynecologist. I need to take this."

Without waiting for a response, Candace lightning-stepped outside onto the busy main street. She apologized as soon as the call connected, saying, "I'm sorry! I was stuck in a meeting, are you—?"

Daisy's sob made her freeze in the middle of the sidewalk. People looked annoyed as they went around her, but she did not care.

"Daisy, what happened? Where are you?"

Broken and watery, she replied, "I'm... I'm at my house. It's Norman, he's—" She cut off, letting out a stuttering exhale. "Please, just get here. I need you."

Candace was already halfway to her car.

# CHAPTER 20

*Daisy*

Norman had an epilepsy-induced seizure. He was alive, but he had been hospitalized thanks to a head injury he sustained during his fall.

Daisy only found out days later, when she called the local senior center to check up on the man after his unusual absence from the cafe. The very next call she made was to Candace, who now sat at her kitchen table consoling her.

"It's going to be alright," she soothed. Her palm worked circles around Daisy's back, alternating from little to big. Drawing goosebumps along their path, shifting thoughts from concern to—

*No*, Daisy thought. She thrust up from the table, away from Candace. Why did she call her? She was *frustrated* with her and this infuriating hot-and-cold dance.

Daisy knew she was not wrong; there was still something

between them. She dropped so many hints about her feelings, tried to force the truth out of Candace, but the woman pretended to be oblivious.

Then, when Daisy gave what she hoped would *finally* get her intentions across, Candace responded with more distance. She said that she was tired, but was that all it was? Had Daisy pushed her too hard?

It was difficult for Daisy to make sense of any of it. So, like always, she threw herself into work. With or without Candace, BagelBombs! was turning into the success Daisy's parents wanted it to be. These last few weeks should have been a victory lap for her.

Even so, the news about Norman sent Daisy spiraling. Rio was away for a science coop, and Dotty was sweet but too batty herself to be helpful in stressful situations. As thoughts of guilt and traumatic memories clawed their way to the surface, Daisy needed a lifeline.

The one she reached for was Candace.

Forcing all that aside, Daisy told her, "I need you to take me to visit him."

"What? But isn't he at Mainside Hospital… Off-island?"

Candace whispered the last word like it was a curse. The concern in her gaze was too real.

Growling, Daisy shot back, "I know. But he doesn't have any other family. I'm all he's got, and he's just been sitting there alone in that room, thinking no one cares. He came to visit me after my parents. He's *been* there for me this whole time. I need to do this."

"Oh, Daisy…"

"Look, I don't want to ask for help, but I don't have a car. If you could… I mean, if it's not too weird…"

With her eyes squeezed shut, her mind going a million miles a second, Daisy did not realize Candace got to her feet until she felt the woman in front of her. The hands that clasped hers were warm and already holding keys.

The truth of Daisy's golf cart was that she did not do well in the confined space of cars. Windows up, doors shut and locked, she felt like a caged animal. The panic would grow and grow until she was ready to burst.

This time was no different.

The soft suede of Candace's passenger seat filled Daisy's fists as she held the sides in a death-grip. She tried to measure her breathing like she'd been taught, but each one came in faster. A raking ripple pulled down her spine as she listened to the tires scrape along the asphalt. She could sense Candace glance over at her from the driver's seat, however, her vision stayed locked straight ahead.

Wonderwood's main street passed by on either side, with the bridge on the horizon coming closer and closer.

"Daisy," Candace asked, "do you want me to stop? I can pull over and we can—"

"No," she forced out through gritted teeth. "Keep going."

Reading Daisy's mind, Candace rolled the windows down. It helped. The dual blast of cold AC air and hot August humidity shocked her senses. Even so, as their car joined the single-lane queue towards the bridge, she felt like invisible walls were closing in.

The gentle incline of the ascending road might as well have been a ninety degree angle. Any second, they would reach the point of no return. She was going *upupup*; just a little more and she would fall back, straight down into the bay. Thoughts of her parents, horrific visions of their final moments, played on repeat in her mind's eye.

Air came in, but Daisy could not hold it. Great, gulping gasps wracked her body. She clamped her eyes shut, unable to look any longer.

The car sped up. A series of horns made Daisy squeeze her eyes even tighter. Then, the car stopped.

Completely.

Not over the bridge, but at a pull-off right beforehand. It was a tiny beach, popular with crabbers like Marin and her fisher friends. With cars rushing past on the bridge overhead and some old, industrial buildings nearby, it was not the most picturesque spot. For Daisy, it was like making beautiful landfall during a torrential storm.

Relief warred with the adrenaline surging inside Daisy. She demanded, "What are you doing? I told you to keep going!"

"But you seemed–"

"I'm fine!"

"You and I have very different definitions of 'fine.' This isn't a Band-Aid you can just tear off."

Candace reached for Daisy's hand over the center console. Daisy snatched it away.

"You're not a fucking therapist."

"No, not with what you're paying me. I'm your partner, which means I'm here to help. But, please, don't ask me to help you hurt yourself. I can't do that."

The authority in her voice was so absolute, so very *Candace*, it brought Daisy back to herself. She touched her cheeks and realized they were wet with tears. Wiping them, she slumped back against the seat with exhaustion.

"I'm sorry. I shouldn't have called you. This is so embarrassing."

"It's alright," Candace told her with gentle acceptance. "I'm glad you did. And there's nothing embarrassing about facing your fears for someone you care about."

Out of the corner of her eyes, Daisy chanced a glance at Candace. The woman was back to wearing her business wardrobe. Which, if Daisy were being honest, part of her had missed. Today, Candace was dressed in the same outfit she had worn on her first day working at Bagel Bombs!, flared white slacks and a lavender sleeveless button-down shell.

She swore she was not ogling the subtle swell of chest. But a glimmer between Candace's bosom caught Daisy's eye. Sweet, savor-worthy relief washed over her as she realized what the object was.

"You kept it."

"Of *course* I kept it! It's my favorite gift anyone has ever given me. Just don't tell Demi. She spent a fortune on those Lady Gaga tickets for us."

Daisy did not reply. She stared at the sea glass pendant dangling from that eye-catching gold ribbon around Candace's neck, and her mind wandered to distant shores.

After a beat, Candace asked, "Would you... be willing to try something else?"

Daisy cocked an eyebrow, feeling too drained to muster a front. Did she *look* like she could try something else? Maybe, with Candace, she could.

"I trust you."

A small, satisfied smile curled the woman's lips. "Let me make a call."

To Daisy's chagrin, the call Candace made was to her former 'date' and local narc, Ted Cando. They met him close by at some residential docks set along the bay.

Prior to his latching onto Candace, the last time Daisy saw him, he'd given her a ticket for smoking a legal joint behind the cafe. Now, he greeted her like they were old friends.

"Hey there, Zee! Long time no see! I hear you gals need a lift?"

"Yo, Cando. Yeah, you could say that. But wait... You mean for us to ride in *that*?"

Daisy crossed her arms. Her gaze bounced between Candace and the old police boat she expected to make it across the bay. To be fair, it was not the worst vessel Daisy ever saw. Ted seemed to clean his boat, at least. But this was her grand plan?

"Just think about it," Candace urged. "We'll wear life jackets, no bridges or heights. If you fall in, we'll fish you back out. Easy peasy."

Ted suggested, "But maybe don't fall out. It's a choppy one."

Candace shot the man a searing look that would have made Daisy laugh at any other point. Numb terror won, stealing her voice as she considered the wild proposition.

Around them, it was a regular summer day. Families loaded up with hoagie and beer-packed coolers bustled past them on the bobbing dock, heading for their own boats. A little girl wearing rainbow unicorn swimmers charged past. Dogs trotted about unleashed. This was no fancy marina, but more of a working-class shove-off point. For everyone else, it was a fun, sunny occasion.

Daisy locked eyes with Candace's assessing eyes. "Alright. But if I go overboard, I'm taking you with me. Partner."

"Naturally."

The boat itself was a simple craft, with driver and passenger bucket seats portside behind the wheel and center console. Its belly was flanked by bench seating, and there was a single fisher's perch on a platform atop the stern.

Nestled within their blocky life jackets, Daisy and Candace settled on the bench. The woman might have gone to the other side for weight distribution. However, with her hand trapped in Daisy's vise-grip, they sat thigh-to-thigh. She squeezed back.

In the driver's seat, wearing aviators and a beat-up rotary volunteer club shirt, Ted flicked the radio on. Buffeted by salt wind, they made their way.

The final notes of a divorced dad rock classic, *Drops of*

*Jupiter,* played out over the radio. Ted had on Wonderwood's local station, and Wild Wally took to the air once the song ended. He brought up the recently-named hurricane headed their way sometime in the next week.

*"Mandy,"* Wild Wally said in a suggestive drawl. *"I had a girlfriend named Mandy in college. Sounds like this storm is gonna throw my stuff onto the lawn the same way she did, OOOoooooooh yeah. So, make sure to have a plan, folks. Invest in plywood, 'cause those boards should be flying off the shelves onto your windows. And remember, if Wonderwood calls for an evacuation, Cape Crest High is the spot to be. Get ready to cozy up and get frrrrrriendly with your neighbors...."*

Casting a look over his shoulder, Ted spoke over the radio and boat motor. "People are getting real antsy about this storm, calling it the next Hurricane Sandy. I bet it'll peter out, myself. But we're gearing up over at the station. You doing anything special at the cafe?"

"Mandy Munches," Daisy yelled back. Beside her, Candace giggled and looped her free arm around the one she was already holding. Sounding more like a normal human, she added, "We're selling Mandy Munches at the cafe—everything bagel with matcha cream cheese. They're a hit, so far."

Candace praised, "As they should be!"

They made more idle conversation, but before long, the ride was over. Despite the bay's supposed choppiness, it was smooth sailing to the other side. Candace even showed off her boating skills by docking the vessel, the sight of which unlocked a latent pirate queen fantasy inside Daisy.

When they reached the posh marina on the other side of the dock, Ted helped them disembark. Then, with the promise to take them back to Wonderwood whenever they wanted, he went on his way.

The hospital was not in Cape Crest, but another twenty minutes by car in the next town over. Feeling like she could handle it without the bridge, Daisy had Candace order a ride through her phone app. It was only as they went to get into the backseat that she realized they were still holding hands.

Daisy did not let go, and neither did Candace.

Leaving Wonderwood for the first time in over a decade was surreal.

More than surreal, it was like coming out of a deep sleep. Growing up, Daisy had come through Cape Crest with her parents often. It was one of the many semi-industrialized suburban municipalities that dotted South Jersey's rural stretches; a collection of single-level strip mall plazas, apartment blocks, and cul-de-sacs anchored by some chain establishments right off some major interstate highway. There was a chaotic quaintness to the mismatch of it all.

On their way to the hospital, Daisy saw familiar places like the Adventure Putt Putt or Candace's Comfort Clam Inn. Holy Mother Prep was empty for the summer, but it was just as posh as she remembered with its gated access and sculpted hedges. The mega big-box store on the edge of town was packed with shoobies and locals alike, shopping for storm supplies.

Daisy made a mental note to start her preparations. Normally, such a wipeout end to the season would have ruined her. Yet, they were so far ahead that they could afford to weather whatever the storm brought.

Bagel Bombs! officially hit the revenue goal for Peter Perry's lease clause. Against all odds, they met their original target and then some. However, thanks to Candace being stuck elsewhere, what should have been a roaring celebration hit like a lead balloon.

Daisy needed to tell her. But, then, would Candace decide their partnership was through? In their stilted conversations over the last few weeks, Daisy managed to avoid mentioning specifically how well they were doing. However, the summer was not going to last forever, and she had to come clean.

At the hospital, they navigated their way around the hotel-like corridors to find Norman's room. To no one's surprise, they found him chatting up a nurse about some article from his daily paper. When he saw them in the doorway, his jovial expression dropped.

"Lil bit," he croaked, looking so small and frail in his hospital bed. "You came all this way for me?"

Daisy fished a paper bomb baggie from her cross-body bag and gave it over to the stunned man. "Special delivery."

Once the emotions simmered down, Daisy asked about Norman's prognosis, which was stable, and then she caught him up with all Wonderwood's goings-on. Of course, with his paper, he was more connected than she was. The only thing he did not know about was Bagel Bombs! success. When Candace, who had been quietly empathy-crying in the corner, left to get some water, she told him the good news.

"Your parents would be so proud of you," he assured her. "With everything they had going for them, things should've been so much easier for you. But you're still kicking life right in the tuckus. *I'm* proud of you, too."

Daisy sniffed back another round of tears in a lovely sounding snort. "Don't go trying to butter me up, old man. I know you can afford full price."

"Right, right..."

Scooting up, Norman leaned forward to peep out into the hallway. Aside from one grayhair knee replacement patient wheeling their way along, it was empty.

"So," he prodded, "you finally womaned up and called her, eh? Bout time, with all the moping you've been doing."

"It's not like that. I needed her car. And a boat."

Norman tisked Daisy. "What you *need* to do is fess up how you feel."

"It's not that easy. I've been trying. But I'm not sure she feels the same way anymore."

"Have you asked?"

As she scrubbed at the nape of her neck, she grumbled a "no."

"Use your words, girlie! Take it from an old man who's lived a full life. The people you let in, the ones you want to keep... make sure they know it."

The steady hum of medical machines and intermittent beeps answered when Daisy did not—the truth and gravity of mortality made into tonal melodies.

"Now, as much as this old man appreciates a visit, take that girl on a proper date."

How could Daisy argue?

Promising to return with more bombs, it was late by the time they left Norman. Too late to ask Ted to drop what he was doing to come and get them. Blushing furiously, Candace invited Daisy to spend the night in her motel room.

The Comfort Clam lived up to its reputation as a less-than-reputable establishment. Daisy was not one to put much stock in 'vibes,' but the whole feel of the place was off. The u-shaped two-story strip was a collection of building code violations and repairs done by a questionably sober maintenance person. Loitering around, the other guests of the inn were, nicely put, *rough* types.

As their car pulled into the central parking lot, the driver asked if they were sure about staying there. Brushing him off, Candace paid the man and led the way inside.

"Um... It's been a long day. I'm going to shower and change out of my work clothes."

Becoming a blur, Candace disappeared into the bathroom on the other side of the small space. The rattling vent fan and sounds of running water came through the door.

Daisy was not sure what she expected of the place Candace Perry lived. The woman oozed class, so it was only natural for her to be surrounded by the finer things in life—not this musty mess.

The room was... eclectic. Nothing was thrown about or misplaced. Yet, it was like standing in a clash of personality as fashion and financial forms warred to dominate the space.

Just about every surface was covered in the guts of Candace's binders, from stickers to spreadsheets. A closet was filled with all of her office clothes and Bagel Bombs! tanks, plus an overflow rack beside it. There was an old, fat TV wedged within a rickety wardrobe cabinet along with a mini fridge and a desk that had clearly been the site of many brainstorming sessions. The hot plate she had on the edge was a fire hazard, but there was nowhere else it could go.

This was where Candace went back to every night? A place where roach traps were a part of the decor, and there were Rorschach mystery stains on the drop ceiling?

Wide-eyed, Daisy perched on the bed's edge, absorbing every detail.

It was a while before Candace emerged in a cloud of floral-scented steam. TV remote in hand, Daisy had just turned it on.

"Hey," Daisy asked, "how was your—"

*"Oh yeah, baby! Give it to me!!"*

The sounds of enthusiastic fucking burst out from the TV. In a thumbnail on the pay-per-view screen, a woman was being pounded by a man wearing a delivery uniform. Candace dove and snatched the remote from Daisy's hands.

The silence was loud as she flicked the TV back off.

"This is... more of an hourly establishment," Candace explained.

Something about the way she said the words—embarrassed, but with the utmost decorum—made Daisy crack up. Once she started laughing, Candace broke, too, and all the tension drained with it.

Thinking aloud, Daisy asked, "Do you want to go get ice cream? My treat."

"That is, I stress, never a question with me."

"Noted. Lead the way, princess."

The Adventure Put Put right down the road had a side soft serve stand, Scoopy-doopies. The big brown dog mascot painted over its sign was, what one might call, copyright adjacent. It boasted an impressive twenty flavors, from standard favorites to ones made with local berries and more adventurous fare.

Daisy and Candace got their frozen treats—a cup of banana soft serve topped with walnuts and a cone of salted caramel-fudge respectively. Then, they walked to the nearby playground. Sitting on a pair of swings, the pair caught up on all the little mundane things they had missed over the last couple of weeks.

Candace told Daisy more about her uncle's secretary, Janice, and the woman's awful fashion sense. It sounded as if she drove her up the wall preaching nonsense and praising Peter Perry. Being cooped up in the pier under depths with her seemed like its own special kind of torture.

Daisy only died a little of embarrassment as she showed off her most recent artistic creations. She tried to make one thing a day, finding inspiration in whatever she could. Caricatures of boardwalk passersby... sculptures with the washed-up treasures she found on her beach walks...

Lately, though, her main source of inspiration was playing hard to get.

Candace ate her ice cream one small, savoring lick at a time. Similarly, Daisy was in no rush. They both wanted more. More deliciousness. More time together. More—

"Can I try some of yours?"

"Sure." Daisy scooped up a bite. Instead of handing over the spoon, she poised it next to Candace's mouth. "Open wide."

The other woman did as she was told, looking annoyed and eager at the same time. Daisy loved the feeling of control she had dipping the utensil into Candace's mouth, the way her lips caught and bounced as the spoon pulled back out; the satisfied sound she made, her eyelids fluttering with contentment.

"Mmm... That's tasty."

"Yeah," Daisy agreed in a puff of breath. "My turn."

Dropping her spoon, Daisy took hold of the hand Candace used to steady her cone. She stole both towards her mouth. From the edge of the cone to the curled, soft-serve tip, she drove a deep divot into the cream with her tongue. She slurped up her spoils at the top, locked with Candace's gaze the whole time.

It was more than she intended to take, but Candace did

not seem to mind. She looked at Daisy with the same kind of hunger.

"Yours might win," Daisy admitted as she released her grip and thumbed a drip from her chin.

"I thought you weren't a fan of sweets."

"I never said that. To be honest, I have a real bad sweet tooth. I thought they weren't good for me, so I tried to stay away. But I'm through with that."

Flushing, Candace looked down at her feet dangling over the fresh, fragrant cedar wood mulch.

"You should listen to your instincts. Everyone knows sugar is bad."

It was her Candy voice, airy and filled with disaffected humor. Meant to brush off the emotions building so steadily between them. Yet, Daisy knew Candy was not Candace. The persona was as much an act as it was an armor.

*So*, Daisy thought as realization dawned on her. *That's what it is.*

Candace was afraid of hurting Daisy again. The hesitance, the distance, was not because she wanted it, but because she thought it was for the best.

Daisy would have to prove to her it wasn't.

Thrusting off the swing, Daisy downed the rest of her ice cream and tossed the cup in a nearby trash can. Under the buzzing streetlamp, she faced Candace with her arms crossed.

"Screw everyone else. I know what I want. Winner buys."

Those big, bright eyes blinked with confusion. "... Winner?"

Daisy grinned. In a challenging tilt, she ticked her head towards the mini golf stand. "You don't think I can handle my sugar? Seems to me, the only way to settle this is with a game. Pick your putter and get ready to lose."

Candace hesitated. In a slow stream, what was left of her ice cream began to drip from her cone. Cursing, she devoured the whole thing in monstrous, gaping bites.

"Fine. But wipe that smirk off your face. You're going down."

"Really? Don't tempt me with a good time."

As it turned out, Candace was telling the truth. She was a mini golf pro once she shook the rust off after the first couple of holes. Daisy, not so much. By the time they reached the trickshot windmill at the midway point, things were looking dire. Daisy wildly misjudged her swings, over or underpowering each hit. Granted, the last time Daisy went mini golfing, she was the same age as the young, cranky kids being shuffled away from their final fun activity of the night. Even so, she thought she would be able to hold her own.

The counterperson yelled at her, "It's putt-put, not the PGA!"

Daisy and Candace both broke into laughter, which made aiming even more difficult. Win or lose, Daisy did not care. Candace's joy, seeing her at ease, was the best prize. They came to the last hole and started a whole new game with a declaration of "best two out of three."

It was late by the time they finished their victory ice creams. Daisy and Candace were left alone while the place closed up for the evening, with the sound of cicadas chattering in the wooded backdrop. It would have been the perfect moment to "woman-up" as Norman advised and make her move. Yet, she decided to wait. Planning was Candace's forte, but Daisy wanted to do this right.

As they walked back to the Comfort Clam, Daisy noticed that Candace seemed nervous. She unlocked the door with a hitched breath and stood there, blocking them both from entering.

Daisy said, "What's the prob–"

*Oh.*

A smirk curled Daisy's lips. It was hard to keep things PG when there was only one bed. She sauntered forward, ducking around Candace, and flopped down like she owned the place. Ancient mattress springs protested every movement. She could only imagine what it would sound like if they actually put the bed to work. As it was, she patted the place beside her.

"Unless you're gonna sleep there, that is."

Without turning on the lights, Candace latched the door and

made her way to the bed. Ambient motel fluorescents broke through the curtain panels and, turning her into a fidgeting silhouette. She offered, "Um, I have pajamas you can borrow, or —"

Stripping down to her bralette and bottom briefs, Daisy asked, "How's this? Nude sleeping is the way to go, but I can keep some propriety for your delicate sensibilities."

"... It's fine..."

Candace was either too distracted to change or did not bother. She settled in under the covers beside Daisy, as far away as she could manage on a bed that was just barely meant for two people. While Daisy was propped up on her side, watching the woman, Candace lay stiff as a board facing the ceiling. She was so awkward and nervous, it was beyond adorable.

Daisy made conversation, hoping to ease the tension.

"You know, I haven't slept off-island since I was a kid."

"Really?"

"Yeah. My parents used to close the cafe during the winter months. We took a lot of road trips, visiting all sorts of places. My dad was a history buff and my mom loooved art museums, so picture a bored kid getting dragged around a battlefield reenactment. I'm grateful, though."

In the low light, Candace's expression was impossible to read. Likewise, the emotion in her strained voice was complex. "They were good people. They didn't deserve what happened to them."

"Most people don't deserve the shit life throws at them. That's how it is. It just makes savoring the good things important. At least, I'm starting to believe that."

"You're right," Candace agreed with a sigh. Fabric rustled as she looked towards Daisy. "Are you okay? Will you be able to sleep?"

Around a not-entirely-feigned yawn, Daisy assured her. "I think I can manage. The weirdest part is how not-weird it feels. But maybe it's present company."

"What do you mean?"

"I guess I feel safe with you. Thanks for picking up earlier. I wasn't sure you would, but I'm glad you did. I hope it doesn't get you in any trouble."

"I'll smooth things over," Candace said. And yet, there was hesitation in her tone. She went on slowly, as if each word was a considerable choice. "Daisy... the meeting I was in earlier... I saw..."

"What? Did you see something that'll finally shut that asshat up?"

"I—"

Springs screeched in protest as Candace thrust onto her side, towards the wall. She finished, "I saw something to look into. I'm going to figure this out, I promise. Goodnight."

"Thanks, Candace. G'night."

Daisy was not sure what else to say, or why something that should be good news filled her with unease. Maybe because she cared less about taking down Peter Perry, less about Bagel Bombs!, than preserving this peace with the woman she wanted to be with. How could she make Candace understand?

The warmth that radiated from her, the sheets that were tinged with her sweet scent, threatened to lull Daisy into a deep slumber. She stayed up as long as she could, piecing together their first real date.

Candace Perry was a princess, and princesses deserved perfection.

# CHAPTER 21

## *Candace*

There was no doubt about it.

Candace was not a good person. If she were, she would never have gotten herself into this position. She would have stayed on her side of the boardwalk and left Daisy DeMarco alone.

Instead, she kept getting closer.

After visiting Norman, their not-date ended as platonically as any outing could. They were just two sexually compatible adults who happened to sleep in the same bed. Candace was fine with that; glad, even.

She could not bring herself to be honest about what she saw at the meeting about Daisy's parents, or Bagel Bombs! imminent doom. She needed more information before she let herself take the bait Daisy so deliciously dangled before her. For now, visions of Daisy licking that ice cream cone—of long, lieth curves atop her bed cast in neon glow—would have to be enough to satisfy her.

And yet, Candace was greedy.

As they returned to their separate lives, Daisy and Candace went back to texting at their old frequency. Maybe more, as her phone did a vibrating dance every couple of minutes from its place atop her desk. The rusted, hollow metal made an impossible-to-miss *vruuuuum* sound each time, catching Janice's ire.

The woman huffed, saying, "You kids and your cell phones. Always stuck in your screens, never in the *real* world. Don't you know there's a hurricane heading this way?!"

"Really? I thought we were just doing a little cleaning."

Hurricane Mandy was due to make landfall within the next day. Uncle Perry planned to keep the park operating as usual until the evacuation order went out. No concern for the employees he forced to work or the park-goers he tempted. Presently, Candace and Janice were in the midst of packing away the office area's non-essential computers along with a stone-faced IT person.

Janice glared at Candace with a puckered lip.

"After the stunt you pulled the other day, running out on that meeting, I can't believe your uncle was so forgiving. You should really be taking this job more seriously."

"Of course, yes. Everyone knows that fun piers are serious business. My uncle is a saint for putting up with me."

At least, that was how the Solid Rock Group saw it. Her 'tantrum,' as her uncle called it, made the investors more sympathetic to him. The man continued to fail upward. She, meanwhile, had her eyes on the prize.

With a mock salute, Candace went back to packing. Janice muttered under her breath about 'ungrateful, spoiled girls.' As soon as the woman's back was turned, Candace swiped up her phone and checked her messages.

*Daisy: Ask the IT guy if he's been to the Matrix. I've actually seen that one!*

> *Candace: Just x1000 more things until you're caught up ;p*
> *And he's more of an Agent Smith-type than a Neo*
> *How're things at BB?*

> *Daisy: Not sure*
> *I asked Tina to come in early today*

Candace's heart skipped a beat as she re-read Daisy's text. Was something wrong? That afternoon, while Candace struggled through yet another bowl of jambalaya, Daisy looked fine in all senses of the word as she watched her across the boardwalk. She'd been texting since then like normal.

> *Candace: Is everything okay?? Are you alright? Where are you?*

> *Daisy: Aw you \*do\* care*
> *I'm peachy*
> *What time do you think you'll be able to escape that death-trap?*

> *Candace: Soon. Why?*

> *Daisy: Come to my house after and let me know when you're on your way. I've got something I need to show you*

From there, Daisy stopped responding when Candace asked what was going on. It was cruel.

How was Candace supposed to focus with that thread left dangling?

With fumbling hands, for the next hour or so, she followed along with what she was supposed to be doing. She might as well have been sleepwalking with how little she paid attention. More than once, the IT guy or Janice had to fix her shoddy work. But she did not care.

Daisy DeMarco had *something* to show her.

Once Candace became enough of a liability, Janice decided they were better off finishing without her. She bolted before they could change their minds.

Outside, Candace took a moment to re-tie her hair as a gust whipped it into her face. The tempestuous August air was heavy with pressure from the impending storm. Clouds had been churning overhead all day, fighting with the sun. A discerning person could sense the ominous weight of destruction on its way.

Yet, the pier was packed as ever. Candace had to press her back against the souvenir shop window as a group of kids ran past. It was the end of the main summer season, with the shoobies and locals alike getting their last bit of fun. Her uncle —and the rest of the boardwalk entrepreneurs—were happy to give it to them.

Candace wondered what kind of fun was in store for her.

The drive to Daisy's house was over before it began. Candace knew she followed the rules of the road to a robotic T, but she could not describe a moment of her route. However, once she arrived, she found the place empty.

And, a piece of paper taped to the front door.

It was a treasure map. In stylized, scratchy ink strokes, Daisy drew Wonderwood with a dotted line from the bungalow to an unknown destination. In one corner, she scrawled a poem:

*Sea glass sugar*
*Sweet and bright*
*Would you dine with me tonight?*

-    *D*

It was impossible to say how many times Candace re-read the words in front of her. Enough that her eyes began to blur from ping-ponging back and forth. The fact that instead of marking the treasure with an 'X,' Daisy drew a heart meant nothing. She was being sarcastic, as usual.

*Dinner,* Candace told herself. *That's all. She wants to celebrate the end of the season.*

Shoving down the intrusive thoughts, Candace returned to her car and set to following the sudden side quest. The journey was easy thanks to Daisy's map accuracy. While things were not exactly to scale, using landmarks and street names, she was able to find her way. It brought her to a secluded car lot outside of a thick copse by the island's northside bay.

A few cottages with bold DO NOT DISTURB signs posted on the trees were visible through the surrounding evergreens. There was a state park trailhead marker beside a sandy, pine needle-covered pathway that led into the copse. Walking closer, Candace found a single daisy tucked into the plexiglass cover.

Her heart kicked up to a steady pound. She plucked the flower free and started on her way.

The sun was beginning its descent. Beneath the tall pines, oaks, and spruces, it was so shaded that it was almost dark. Candace hugged herself tighter, wishing she had worn something warmer than a halter dress.

It was a less conservative article she would not normally wear to work at the pier, as much to avoid Janice's scrutiny and the leering looks of teenage boys. Still, on the off chance she saw a certain someone...

Deep royal purple, it fell mid-thigh with a flared, side-split hem. Like most halter styles, the front of the dress clinched up and around Candace's neck with a thin collar. However, it bore a distinctive split down the middle that gave an eye-catching view of her cleavage. Without sleeves, her toned arms (along with all the chaturangas Demi queued during Vinyasa class) were on full display.

Candace thought—no, *knew*—she looked incredible.

Even so, a shawl would have been a smart inclusion.

*Damn layering weather...*

By the path's end, her teeth were chattering from her nerves and the chill. Then, as she stepped out from the shade onto a beach, she warmed right back up. Not thanks to the sun, but the sight that greeted her.

The spot was a hidden gem. It was clear that the place did not see the same kind of traffic as the main boardwalk beach. This one had no amenities and the bare minimum landscaping, with tall, difficult-to-navigate reeds and driftwood clumped by mystery sea greens all around. There were no shops or pier, just the dilapidated, soon-to-be-driftwood remains of an old dock, and a rock jetty down the way.

The beach was not that large, either. At high tide, it seemed the bay might reach all the way up to the treeline. Now, it was about twenty or so paces away, lapping lazily closer with each slip against the shore. On the horizon, the setting sun cast the storm clouds overhead aglow, turning them to cotton-candy pink and orange. The water beneath was a veil of shimmering fire, so bright it was difficult to look at.

But Candace stared nonetheless. She had never seen the sky cast with so many colors, a spectrum of hues with the most subtle and dramatic differences that vibrated against the land and sea.

No, this beach was not a tourist spot. It was a gorgeous piece of the Jersey shore's natural wonder, made even more special by the woman who brought her here.

Multi-colored lanterns, lit by tiny, electric tea lights, were placed with haphazard artistry. They were planted within grass clumps, hung from driftwood, and nestled atop sand piles. Candace's gaze followed the path they laid out, towards the woman who waited for her.

Daisy sat beside a picnic spread that would have made Martha Stewart proud. A big red blanket was weighted down by lanterns in each corner. It was set with a traditional wicker basket and two serving sets, each including a fluted champagne glass.

As Candace slowed her approach, Daisy sprang to meet her.

The bagel-trepreneur had most definitely not come straight from her cafe. With her usual flip-flops, Daisy wore fitted, darkwash jeans looped by a stylish gold and black leather belt. A peek of her tanned, belly-ringed navel showed thanks to the creamy white crop top she wore, and the look was tied together by her chic black blazer jacket. Her hair was styled and textured with pomade, with the long half pinned behind her ear, aside from a few wind-plucked locks.

Candace was so distracted taking the woman in that she nearly toppled on the uneven sand.

"Don't trip at the finish line, Perry! You finally made it. I was starting to think I needed to go fight that Janice-woman."

"I–" Candace cut herself off as she regained her footing, needing a moment to speak around her suddenly thick tongue. "Please don't. She has park security on speed dial. What is this place? It's so peaceful."

Daisy's smirk turned wistful with a glance around.

"This is Higbee Point, one of Wonderwood's lesser-known beaches."

"That's an understatement. We're the only ones here!"

"People tend to give this place a wide berth. A couple of those bungalows down the way were speakeasies back during prohibition, and this point has never really lost its seedy reputation. It's also a horseshoe crab nesting ground, so it's an important habitat for them."

"Is that right..."

The latter point was fairly apparent, as the gull-eaten carapaces dotted the beach here and there like macabre rocks.

*Horace has it good compared to her relatives,* she thought.

"For me," Daisy went on, "it's my favorite spot on the whole island. I've wanted to bring you here for a while."

In a small voice that scarcely sounded like her own, hitched and breathy, Candace could not help voicing her disbelief.

"You have?"

"Yeah. Longer than I realized, I think. Here."

Reaching out, Daisy offered Candace a multi-colored bouquet of flowers to match the one she found at the trailhead. Magenta and yellow, white and orange, pink and red, they were arranged in a familiar sunset color scheme.

The lace-tied plants felt like a 50–lb weight in Candace's hands. She did not—*could not*—resist as Daisy guided her to sit across from her on the blanket.

"C'mon," Daisy insisted. Like a food magician, she began to pull a ridiculous amount of edibles from the basket. "Let's dig in. I *know* Candace Perry needs more than some sad jambalaya to get her through the day. Try this."

Candace's mouth, which had popped open to protest, was filled by Daisy with a pimento spread-covered cracker. It was delicious, like everything else the woman made. Next thing she knew, she had eaten another, and a juicy green grape followed. The fizzy champagne Daisy handed her washed it all down.

While she chewed gourmet crostini, Candace chanced a glance at Daisy. The woman was cattish as usual, all grins and swagger, but there was something else, too. There was a gravity when their eyes met, unnamed but *so very* tangible, it was silly to ignore.

Candace choked. She turned away to get herself under control, her vision trained on something, *anything*, else. Meanwhile, Daisy dropped a bomb that sent her sputtering even harder.

"Bagel Bombs! made its target revenue."

"*What?!*" Once she managed to even out her breathing, she demanded, "When?"

With her attention on the mini empanada she was selecting, Daisy shrugged.

"When some woman decided to make a crazy gamble and devote all her effort to saving it. But, technically, two weeks ago."

"Two weeks?! Why didn't you say anything?"

Daisy did not answer right away. She finished chewing and took a drought from her champagne. Simply, she deadpanned, "I am now."

Candace's stomach twisted. In her head, she had known they were close. However, she never had access to accounts and relied on Daisy for raw numbers. Why would she hide something so important?

Guilt and shame doused the thrill she felt at reaching their hard-fought goal. She needed to tell Daisy about what she learned in the meeting with the Solid Rock Group. But how could she explain it if she barely knew the details herself? She had not been able to find anything about the land sale from Daisy's parents, or dirt that would stop her uncle from tearing the whole place down. She failed.

Unable to hold back any longer, Candace burst.

"Your parents used to own Bagel Bombs!. Not just the cafe, but the whole place, land, building, and all. I don't know how, but my uncle used some kind of shady tactic to buy it from them for next to nothing right before their accident. He has demolition permits for the whole block and the new building plans ready."

"Huh."

Daisy looked thoughtful as she chewed on a celery stick, with an elbow poised on her upturned knee. She took another sip of champagne, then fished her colorful bottle from the basket.

She offered it to Candace. "I brought water, too, if you want it."

Candace gaped. "Daisy, don't you get what I'm saying? It should be yours! Instead, because of that monster I'm related to, you're going to get kicked out. Now that he's secured the funding he needs for the project, there's nothing stopping him from evicting you. You might get some settlement cash if you took him to court, but that's it."

The breath Daisy let loose was carried away by the persistent wind. Nodding, she concluded, "Bummer. We gave it a good fight, though."

Candace could not believe how nonchalant Daisy sounded. *Bummer?!*

Like she had no care in the world, the woman continued to munch on her meticulously prepared picnic.

"How can you be so calm? It was pointless. Everything we worked for, all of it, was for nothing!"

Mid-bite, Daisy paused. She looked at Candace heavily, and, even full of food, her voice had just as much weight.

"Do you believe that?"

"But… Saving Bagel Bombs! is what this whole partnership was about."

Daisy swallowed. Her lips curled into something that was not a smile. Even so, the expression's warmth sent a sirocco coursing through Candace.

"Was that *really* all it was?"

"I… It was…"

"Aren't you the one who told me my life didn't have to revolve around bagels?" While Candace continued sputtering for a response, Daisy revealed, "I've been looking into classes."

"Classes?!"

Candace felt like a parrot, squawk-repeating what she heard. Yet, she was on an emotional roller-coaster, clinging for life, and could do little else.

For the first time that evening, Daisy fidgeted with apparent bashfulness.

"Yeah. I'm still not sure what exactly I want to do, but I was thinking about a trade. I enjoyed working on the renovations for Bagel Bombs! It was like a practical art application, if that makes any sense. Rio was helping me look into the certification programs and apprenticeships the local county college offers."

Grinning, Candace's thrill for Daisy outshone her own tumultuous feelings. She praised, "That's an amazing idea! Good, reliable contractors are always in demand. You could be Wonderwood's top handyperson."

"We'll see. If I keep myself open, there are a lot of possibilities. You showed me that. So, don't stress about the rest, okay?"

"How can I not? Aren't you angry with me? That property is worth *millions*. You should be set for life, not struggling like you have been all these years. My uncle—"

With more exasperation than edge, Daisy cut in. "Stop talking about your *damn* uncle. Last I checked, you're not him.

Now, for the love of *Jeebus,* eat some more, or I'm gonna start to take it personally."

Candace could not breathe. Here she was, bearing the truth of their dire situation, and the person affected most... the one who should be furious with her beyond measure... was cracking deep-cut *Simpsons* jokes. Blinking, with fresh eyes, Candace took in the scene around her.

In a murmur, she asked, "Daisy... Why did you bring me here? What is all this?"

The look Daisy gave her before answering was long and pointed.

"Don't be Candy, Candace. Not with me. You know *exactly* what this is."

The sun had dipped beneath the horizon. While the world at large muted, their little plot of beach stayed lit by lantern light. The rhythmic waves played their ocean song, accompanied by the wind's whistle. This patch of sand, the blanket they sat on, was its own island separate from time, space, and reality.

And Daisy wanted to be here with her.

Candace cried. Like that very first day she returned to Wonderwood and made a fool of herself in front of Bagel Bombs!, a torrent descended her cheeks. Ugly and uncontrolled, the emotions she tried so hard to bury burst free.

Although Daisy stayed where she was, her features knitted with concern.

"I'm difficult," Candace blubbered. "And when I get an idea, I steamroll. I have self-esteem issues, and I need constant validation. I'm materialistic and greedy. Nothing would be easy with me. I might mess up even worse than before."

For an extended beat, neither woman spoke. Candace's tears continued to fall, and Daisy continued to observe her. When Daisy did talk, the flatness of her voice was undercut by her nervous smile.

"Are you about done? I know what I'm getting into by now. It's a relationship, not a warning label. Do you wanna be my girlfriend or not?"

*Girlfriend.*

That word launched a javelin from the moon straight through Candace's heart. *"Yes"* left her mouth before she had even finished processing the question. She wanted to be Daisy's partner, and girlfriend, and *so many* more things she could scarcely name them all.

How could she lie about such an intrinsic truth any longer?

"I want that. I really, *really* want that."

Daisy's mouth moved into a full, goofy grin.

"Well, Candace Perry gets what she wants, right? And what about me? Can't I get what I want, too?"

Again, in a slow concession, Candace said, "Yes."

That one word was all it took to break the final barrier between them. The moment her lips completed it, Daisy's were on them like the waves crashing on the shore. Fierce and fast, decades of desire spilled over. The figure that pushed her to the blanket and arched over her was almost unrecognizable.

One hand raised Candace's overhead, while the other held her jaw, firmly but with near-possessive care. Heat and friction built as their bodies melded into place.

*Pulling.*

*Grinding.*

*Pressing.*

They moved in chaotic tandem in a desperate bid to feel.

Pleasure flooded Candace as Daisy's thigh nestled between her legs. She gasped into the mouth locked on her own. The sound was muted by the tongue that found its way inside, seeking soft sighs and moans made by measured ministrations.

Fizzy champagne, along with the lingering trace of earthy taste from a smoked joint, teased Candace's taste buds. She was taken by the bittersweetness, made ravenous as the smell and taste worked in delicious dichotomy to overwhelm her senses.

The hand that gripped her jaw trended down. From Candace's neck, sweeping through the valley of her sensitive collar bones into the slit between her dress, Daisy's touch staked her claim. With searing softness, it slid up and over Candace's breast to curl around her side and back. There, her palm splayed wide, drawing them even closer.

When they parted for breath, Daisy's dark, succubus-stare bore into Candace like hot coals. *So hot.* There was no doubt of what she wanted or that she intended to follow through.

The realization of where things were going hit Candace hard. She'd been expecting anger, even an end to their partnership. This was... not that. The tempest that churned inside of her broke, and so did she.

Once again, Candace's emotions poured out in tangible form.

The mood flipped in an instant. Daisy let go and sat back on her heels, fretting as if she were the problem.

"Fuck... I came on too strong, didn't I?"

Candace shook her head even as her outpour said otherwise. She got up and mirrored Daisy's position.

"No, it's not that! These are happy tears, I promise. I'm sorry. I can't seem to keep it together when I'm with you."

"I love that you can be yourself around me," Daisy told her. "When you lose control, when you eat a whole mountain of bagel bombs or wear so-called trashy clothes, I'm glad I get to see you. So don't apologize for that, or anything else. I don't want there to be any more regrets between us."

As she spoke, Daisy inched forward. This time, her kiss was far more chaste; a peck before she went to look for something inside the basket.

"You're a foodie Mary Poppins," Candace said through a sniffled giggle. "What else could you possibly have in there?"

"Plenty. I'm pretty sure the way to your heart is through your stomach, so I came prepared. And I wasn't going to come without a couple of these."

As Daisy passed her a bagel bomb, Candace knew without asking which flavor it was. She took in a shaky breath and squinted away more tears. Ripples of memory from that summer's day drifted between them.

"You come off cool and collected, but you really are sweet, Daisy DeMarco."

"This is a taste. Just wait until you've had a whole bite."

It was a corny line, said with humor. Even so, the promise made Candace lick her lips.

Eating her own bagel bomb, Daisy's face shifted from contentment to annoyance. Her hand went to her blazer pocket. Inside, her phone's insistent vibration could be heard over the sea sounds.

Candace asked, "Who is it?"

"If they're not you, they don't matter."

"It could be important!"

"If it is, they'll call back."

They did, and it was, unfortunately, very important. The new oven at Bagel Bombs! was sending out an error code and needed to be reset, but Tina did not know how.

Candace could hear Tina apologize over and over to Daisy in between apologies the girl shouted at, presumably, a line of waiting customers. Although she kept it from her responses, Daisy's disappointment was plain. They packed up the picnic in record time and hightailed it back to Candace's car.

In an unspoken bit of growth, Daisy settled into the car's passenger seat with ease despite her anxieties. The woman's renewed artistic passion and her drive for progress were incredible to witness. Bagel Bombs! might be forced to close, but Daisy had grown beyond needing to build her life around that place.

Daisy had learned to live for Daisy, and Candace was so proud. It was difficult not to stare at her adorably pouting *girlfriend* and pay attention to the road.

For her part, Candace was sad to leave the intimate picnic. Yet, she bounced with excitement over what could come next. The night was young, and she was about to show the woman she loved off to the whole world.

# CHAPTER 22

*Daisy*

By the time Daisy and Candace arrived at the boardwalk, Tina was almost in tears. She was eighteen years old, one of the babies of Demi's big family. This kind of crisis, and so many people cross with her, was a new experience.

Daisy did her best to hide that she was one of those people and instead focused on solving the problem. Thankfully, a simple internet search told her what she needed to do. Ten minutes after they arrived, the oven was fixed and filled with the first batch of back-orders.

It was funny; Daisy felt the familiar, nagging urge to stay and help. There were customers, and customers meant she had to work. But, as her gaze shifted between the line that Tina went back to handling, and Candace's patiently waiting face, she knew to leave it. Her life had been on hold long enough, and it was time to order up.

*But, what now?*

Daisy planned for a romantic picnic, not a maintenance call. She stood on the corner of the boardwalk and the off-ramp that led to Wonderwood's streets, hands in her blazer pockets, debating.

Candace, it seemed, had her own idea. She hooked an arm through one of Daisy's and tugged her forward. The look on the woman's face, dimples high with her grin, was infectious. And, worrisome, once Daisy realized where they were headed.

"Hey, we're getting a little close to enemy territory. Aren't you afraid someone will see?"

"Afraid? No, silly, that's the idea. I want them to see."

Winking back at Daisy, Candace pulled her even closer. She added, "Plus, we're on a date at the boardwalk. I think one of us is legally obligated to win the other a stuffed animal."

"Is that right? Well, fine. Take me to whichever of these games is the least rigged and I'll give it a go."

According to Candace, all of the boardwalk carnival games were rigged in some way or another. The balloons for dart toss were underfilled, making them difficult to pierce with dulled metal tips, and the milk jug rims were slicked so that the waxed softballs would roll right out. A round of water guns would have gotten them a prize, but they conceded it to their younger opponent. The kid's face was worth it, and so was watching Candace's smile giving it away.

Then, that let Candace have the chance to show off her crane machine skills. As they walked past the pier arcade, Daisy saw a stuffed Horace the Horseshoe Crab that she had to have. Candace zoned in on one, lined up her claw, and grabbed the plushie in one try.

"Yes," she said while tossing back her shining tresses, "I *am* that good."

"Show off. Bet you can't beat me at *DanceDanceRevolution*."

Candace could, in fact, beat her. Grumbling, Daisy blamed the song choice and its 2000s hyper-electronic fast-paced beat. Or, her flip-flops.

"Yeah, because pumps are sooooo easy to jump around in."

She stuck her tongue out and, naturally, Daisy could not let that challenge go. They played three more rounds before giving the machine up to the bemused-looking gamers waiting in the wings. With breathless giggles, hand in hand, they scurried from the metal dance platform to their next mischief.

Zombie shooting games, air hockey, and skee ball heated up their impromptu competition. Daisy even managed to win a game by distracting Candace with a kiss on her neck while she lined up her shot. It was a dirty tactic, but Daisy was done holding back. She was having too much fun.

Unfortunately, it was getting late. The arcade and pier at large were starting to close. As they exited outside, the door locked behind them. It was a slow mass exodus with people filing out from the half-lit amusements. Nearby, Daisy watched the last lingering lines file into their seats on the Mouse Kart.

In a wistful tone, Candace said, "I guess that's it, then. We should—"

Daisy grabbed Candace's hand and dragged her to the coaster.

"One more thing!"

There was no one else left queuing for the ride. Still, they were breathless as they ran up the zig-zagging metal ramp to the ride attendant.

"Wristband," the teen asked with a bored wave towards the barcode scanner.

"I don't have a wristband," Candace told him with a smile, "but my uncle owns the park."

Dead-eyed, the boy blinked at her.

"Uh, Mr. Perry owns Perry's Pier."

"Yes. I'm Candace Perry, and I also work here. Peter Perry is my uncle. Can we get through?"

Again, he blinked. It was unclear if he did not believe her, or did not understand.

"Does Candy Perry ring any bells?"

"Uhhhh…."

Huffing, Candace tore her pier worker's badge from her wallet and scanned the barcode. "There. She's with me."

"Actually," Daisy corrected, "I have a ticket."

Her hands were steady as she drew the single ride ticket she had gotten from Peter Perry. She'd held onto it all this time in a forgotten fold of her wallet; a token kept out of habit long past sense. Even so, in this moment, its presence and release felt so right.

Flatly, the teen said, "It's five tickets."

"Oh, for the love of—!"

Candace ushered Daisy past the teen, who did not make the barest attempt to stop them. His fly-trap mouth had not closed the entire exchange.

As they squeezed into the compact, two-person mouse vehicle, Daisy cast a nervous glance back.

"He's not the one driving, right?"

"It's automatic," Candace assured her.

It was a tight fit in the little car, especially for two tall women. Both of their knees butted up against the front metal panel, and the lap bar jabbed down onto their middles. But, wiggling, Daisy found that there was no way she was going to fall out—that was a comfort.

With a *clankclankclank,* the gears started up, and the mouse jerked forward. In sync, Daisy and Candace's hands linked atop the plush, cheese-themed foam that covered the lap bar.

Halfway up the first and highest incline, it dawned on Daisy how trapped she was. She couldn't get out. Familiar anxieties mounted with each upward inch. Daisy sucked in one breath after another of the heavy air, buffeted by more wind the higher they went.

It was only as Candace urged her to open her eyes that she realized she'd pinched them shut.

"You need to see Wonderwood like this," she yelled over the machinery sounds. "Trust me. I've got you!"

In a squint, Daisy managed to peek out and see what it

looked like at the top. Her eyes popped.

Wonderwood was her home and her prison. She'd been stuck here all her life and explored every inch of the marshy land. But she'd never seen it from this view.

It was eerily gorgeous. Even as lights began to dim, they were beacons in the thick, late-night haze. The far-off clips of carnival music and bursts of laughter were distantly dreamy.

Everything looked so tiny, too. The people leaving the pier, going about their lives... the boardwalk, where she could glimpse Bagel Bombs!, and the city beyond... all of it was small. For the first time in her life, Daisy felt herself rising above it.

Then, the coaster dropped.

Their mouse dipped, zipped, and whipped along the rickety track at a snappy pace. Screams and delighted laughter belted out of them both. Since the ride was designed for younger children, it had nothing too death-defying like loops or corkscrews. Even so, it made Daisy's heart pound with excitement.

As their car pulled back into the ride queue, Candace took one look at Daisy's face and knew she wanted to go around again. She sweet-talked the attendant into indulging them, and he did not seem to care either way.

Two runs later, they stumbled from the exit in a tangle of limbs and laughter. The boardwalk was a ghost town, with even Bagel Bombs! shuttered up by Tina. However, as they left the pier, the women did not return to Candace's car. Daisy led them to the beach, where they ambled along the vacant shore.

They walked and walked, beyond the boardwalk to the beach outside one of Wonderwood's premier resorts. Peter Perry would make a fair penny if he managed to build his muck-mansion right on the boards. With access right from people's rooms to his pier, he would have his market cornered. Like a mini, mouldy Disney World by the shore.

But Daisy did not care about any of that. Peter Perry could have his money and Wonderwood. The idea that he might have pulled one over on her parents nagged at her. Yet, none of it mattered if she had Candace. Even if he used his lofty power to make them live in a box, they would be richer.

"So," Daisy asked, continuing her train of thought aloud, "what do you think you'll get up to now? With no Bagel Bombs!, there's no reason for you to be held hostage over at the pier anymore. You could try to start fresh with a job around here. Or, maybe you could go out on your own. There are a lot of other struggling small businesses out there who need a money-minded savior."

Scrunched up to Daisy's side to ward against the chill, Candace shrugged.

"You know, I'm not sure."

"Really? I thought you'd be planning your binder colors."

"Maybe the stickers, at least. Some motivational sayings and that kind of stuff. Demi gifted me a bunch of yoga-themed ones a while back that are super cute."

Candace's easy tone turned thoughtful, and her grip on Daisy's arm tightened.

"It's funny. When I was stuck here, I planned for years how to get out. I thought if I could just do that, I would be happy. I wasn't, though. Not at all. I planned my life around some vague idea of success, using my uncle's warped notion of what 'making it' looked like to measure my own. No wonder I was so miserable."

Quietly, Daisy said, "But you got out. You were living in New -Freaking-York on your own and killing it. Sounds to me like you planned pretty damn well."

Sighing, Candace leaned her head against Daisy's shoulder. In a murmur, she answered, "Too well for something wrong. How could anything I planned have been right when it didn't involve you?"

Daisy could feel Candace's sidelong gaze on her, even though she could only see the barest hint of her silhouette in the darkness. If they were not walking together, she might have swooned.

"So," Candace concluded, "for now, I'm not going to worry.

I'm going to enjoy our date, and let it be. Right?"

"Yeah," Daisy agreed as her heart melted. "I think you're onto something."

They ambled for a while longer. Their imprints in the sand were left side by side, in perfect step. Out of the blue, Candace pointed ahead.

"What's that?"

Daisy peered through the inky blackness. A tall, but not overly large, stilted structure stood at the very edge of the shoreline. With the storm clouds overhead blocking out the moon and stars, the night was particularly dark. It was only as they came right up to its base that Daisy knew for sure.

"It's a lifeguard stand. One of the covered ones they bring out when it's supposed to rain. They must've forgotten to wheel this one back."

Daisy urged Candace to the front of the ladder. It was about ten rungs up, high enough for the lifeguards to have a decent vantage point but low enough for them to make a quick descent.

Without giving it too much thought, Daisy started to climb.

"What are you doing?!"

"Trespassing. C'mon, my legs could use a break."

At the top, Daisy pulled her way into the plywood construction. The vague smell of lumber and paint told her this was one of the newer boxes that her lifeguard regulars had been excited about; something about lights, seating, and a lack of mildew. Sure enough, as she groped along the half-wall ledge, she found a switch.

"Nice! Our tax dollars at work."

Wrapped around the counter lip of the half-wall, a thin strip of LEDs came to life. A warm, yellow glow filled the small space. It illuminated a bleacher bench along the back but, apart from that, there was nothing else. Wonderwood did not want its lifeguards distracted from their duty.

As Candace's head popped up at the floor's base, Daisy reached down to help her the rest of the way. Her eyes gave the place an unimpressed assessment.

"Is this thing even safe?"

"Not good enough for the Pier Princess, hm? From the woman who just rode a rickety roller coaster three times."

Daisy, who had not yet released Candace, tugged her close. Her grip sailed from the woman's wrist to cradle the base of her neck.

"Yes, well... I guess there are worse ways to go."

*Fuck*, Daisy thought as she observed the beauty in her arms. Candace was gorgeous. In the warm, low light, even with her hair wind-mussed and dress disheveled, she looked like an actual princess.

And Daisy was the baker about to defile her.

Surging forward, Daisy took Candace's mouth. There was no question, no hesitation, in the crash of their lips and tongues. No gentleness or careful caress, either, as they both fought to take lead.

Unlike before, Candace did not seem to be holding back. Her kisses were urgent—unrefined yet wholly focused. Short springs of mallow fluff, sweetly coy, followed by languid, wet molasses drips.

Soon, it was all Daisy could do to keep up.

The hands that delved under Daisy's blazer smoothly slipped it from her shoulders. Then, without missing a beat, they went for her belt. Her pulse skyrocketed, listening to the woman deftly work the clasp free.

Drawing in a breath, Daisy braced herself against the half wall. She could not believe it; *Candace Perry* was stripping her in a lifeguard stand. She managed to pull back just enough to question it in a breathless gasp.

"*Here?*"

"What?" Candace giggled, teasing, "Not good enough for you?"

"It's not that. It's just—ah!"

A sting, followed by shivering pleasure, coursed through Daisy as Candace nipped her neck. Fast and devouring, the woman sucked and nibbled the exposed skin along the bust of Daisy's crop top. As she spoke, the vibration of her voice sent shockwaves through each spot.

"You told me that I could taste you. So, *can't I*?"

*Toss me in the oven and cook me, please.*

Words beyond her, Daisy's head bobbed. Rough, hard wood filled her grip. She held the wall ledge as her jeans' zipper was undone, one tooth at a time.

A sharp breath filled her lungs at the fingers that skimmed inside the new gap. They trended along her underwear, tracing the edge of the cloth as if it were a starting line. Her whole body clenched with anticipation at the single digit that slipped under, heading towards—

"*Ouch!*"

Daisy jolted, and not with pleasure, as Candace accidentally pinched her labia. Lack of moisture would do that; Daisy's body and mind were not on the same page. She felt like the dog who caught the car. She had Candace exactly where she wanted her, was *desperate* for her, yet her biological response was... lacking.

Candace pulled back. Brows knitted, she searched Daisy's face.

"Now I'm the one going too fast. Should I—?"

"*No!*" Daisy licked her swollen lips and deflated with embarrassment. "I fucking *need* this, it's just... been a while. And I'm not really used to being on the receiving end. I think my body is catching up."

"Hm..."

Nodding, Candace's nervous expression softened. Her touch returned, wrapping around Daisy's hips and hooking into the loosened jean waistline. She paused like that and met Daisy's gaze.

It was not permission Candace Perry waited for; no, she knew she had that in spades. The smile that curled her lips was equal parts devilish and demure. As she eased Daisy's pants down with one hand, she hiked her dress up with the other.

"I need this too," she breathed.

Then, with their legs fitted like puzzle pieces, she curled against Daisy.

*Oh, shit.*

Candace Perry—the prim, pristine model of conservative grace—was going commando.

Hot, sticky wetness trailed along Daisy's thigh. The heady scent of lilac steeped with honey wafted up like an aphrodisiac musk. Her muscles throbbed in response. She found herself moving along with Candace, meeting the lips that sought hers and flexing to improve their position against the wall.

"You're not *receiving* anything," Candace corrected in a taunt broken by fervent kisses. The hitch of her breath, the desperation of her continued thrusts, was undercut by the command in her tone. "I'm getting what *I* want, and what I want to do is fuck you, any way you'll let me. Is that alright?"

"Candace Perry gets what she wants."

Daisy took one of her hands from the ledge to raise Candace's leg from below. She loved the gasp it drew and how her fingers sank into springy flesh. The woman's rear was as perfect as Daisy always thought.

In languid, luxurious draws, Daisy rocked Candace along her thigh. She gorged on cries and whimpers, the needful sounds that increased with each subtle shift.

Wild with want was the best way to describe Candace. There was vulnerability in her assertiveness, too. Guilt and shame that seemed to haunt the woman were absent as she let herself come undone.

It was not long before Candace reached her release. Shuddering and sweating, she collapsed against Daisy; she might have fallen without the extra support.

In a steady, rhythmic pulse, Candace's pussy drummed against Daisy. As they stayed there, molten drips seeped between them. She could not stop herself from reaching down and taking a taste.

"What do you think?" Candace asked, panting, "Am I as

sweet as you thought I would be?"

Daisy greedily sucked her fingers clean.

"Even sweeter. Thanks for the dessert."

Candace let loose a breathy chuckle. She relaxed against Daisy, molded to her like putty. One hand found its way under Daisy's crop top to idly grope. Her fingers played circles along the sensitive skin, blazing trails with goosebumps. The touch was pleasant, but nowhere near enough.

Daisy might not have been ready before Candace's display, but now, she was rearing to go. Impatience drove her. She stole one of Candace's hands and plunged it beneath her underwear to her own sopping heat.

"What about me? How do I taste?"

"*Oooh,*" Candace purred. "You've caught up…"

A groan escaped through Daisy's clenched teeth. She bucked as Candace swept along her entrance in one long, slow slip. With pressure placed at the base of her wrist, most intense right over Daisy's throbbing clit, it felt like a rolling tsunami.

Candace's withdrawal was as maddening as it was seductive; the way in which she inspected her slick-covered hand, smelling and licking it, was nothing short of feral. Her lidded gaze held Daisy's the whole time.

Husky, she begged, "Can I have another sample, please?"

There was no way Daisy could even pretend to deny the pleading princess before her. Nor did she resist Candace guiding her to sit on the bleacher bench. With her crop top and underwear removed, she was exposed in the nighttime air. Yet, as Candace fanned Daisy's knees apart and settled between them, she felt powerful.

Being between a woman's legs was rivaled only by having a woman between your legs. And this particular view of this particular woman was something truly magnificent.

With annoyance, Candace muttered, "One second…"

Fast and weaving, she re-tied her hair.

Mesmerized, Daisy watched how Candace's biceps flexed as they raised over her head, how her hands twined and wrists flicked, tightening her locks into a neat tail in one smooth, deft motion. She was like a warrior suiting up for battle.

Daisy struck out first.

Thinking nothing and wanting everything, she grasped the ponytail and twined it around her hand. Her grip was secure, not tight; the last thing she wanted to do was cause Candace pain. However, wrapping the woman around her fingers, literally and metaphorically, felt incredible.

Seeing Candace's wide-eyed surprise, followed by her submissive acceptance, felt even better.

The hot breath at her front contrasted with the cold bleacher beneath Daisy's rear. Anticipation was undercut by wanting to savor the moment forever. But she could not wait any longer.

"Go on. It might not be a 5-star meal, b—"

Whatever quip Daisy had been about to make was lost in her throat. Instead, she convulsed, gasping as Candace went to work.

There was nothing shy about the way she suckled and lapped. Her mouth moved with an almost selfish urgency, exploring with a voracious appetite. Velvety lips hummed with her muffled moans, drawing out the same sounds from Daisy.

"*God-d-damn, Candace,*" Daisy heard herself utter. "Didn't I just feed you?"

A muted whine of "*More*" came from between her legs.

With a subtle ponytail tug, she slowed the woman's pace while urging her deeper. She exhaled a cross between a laugh and a cry as Candace tongue-fucked her one swirling probe at a time.

A hand gripped around Daisy's back, pressing her forward. The other joined Candace's tongue and thrust along with the muscle. Those long, delicate fingers took over filling Daisy, stirring her, while Candace's mouth migrated.

From little licks to full kisses, she showered every inch of Daisy's pussy with reverence. It was hard to tell if it was to tease or savor, but she took her time. The wait—here and the entire time it had taken them to be together—was worth it.

Whiteness blanked Daisy's vision as Candace's lips fell over her clit. She could not help clenching the hand ensnared by golden coifs, but Candace did not seem to mind; it spurred her faster. Daisy leaned back and sank into satisfaction.

It really was a beautiful night.

The carnal crackling of Candace's fingers through Daisy's slick blended with the distant crash of ocean waves. Outside, the persistent gale buffeted the plywood frame, pounding harder and harder just like her heart. Her eyes fluttered shut so that she could let the sounds and sensations wash over her.

There was no great cresting as she came.

Since riding that roller coaster, Daisy had already been at the top. Now, she was falling. Taken by a delicious, downward spiral of desire spun by the woman between her legs. *Downdowndown* diving into depths she never thought she would reach.

When the touch became too much, Daisy gave the slightest tug, and Candace pulled back. She released the locks bundled in her fist. Observing Candace, the way she sat back on her heels, looking so proper; her messy, sweat-matted hair; the mingled juices that sheened over her mouth; the silvery trails that sleeked down her long neck, past her halter collar, to gather in her cleavage and the seaglass daisy nestled there...

Daisy's breath caught at the sight of this Candace, who was meant only for *her.* She shuddered as contractions tensed her center, and yet another orgasm rippled throughout her body. The plywood shook as she fell back, utterly spent.

"*Holy hell,*" Daisy puffed. She was so numb with pleasure, she did not even care that there was a splinter jabbing her back. In her hazy periphery, she was aware of Candace's chuckle while she went about the space gathering Daisy's clothes.

Sitting beside her, Candace nuzzled Daisy's neck. Hot breath tickled as she said, "What can I say? I've wanted to try that flavor for a while. And I want it again... and again... and..."

The words turned to butterfly kisses, drawing contented sighs from Daisy's throat with each one. Turning, she caught Candace's jaw and her lips. The taste of her, of herself *on* her, was the sweetest flavor of all.

If it were possible, Daisy would have stayed there forever. However, breaking into their blissful moment, reality came crashing in.

It had been a bad idea to turn on the light strip.

Beneath the lifeguard stand, there was the sound of a car coming to a stop. The engine cut, and a door creaked open.

Daisy and Candace shared a look of panic. They scrambled to their feet while the first ladder rung creaked with their interrupter's weight.

A grumble came over the floor ledge. "Damn horny teenagers... can't get a room..."

Candace hissed, "What do we do?"

There was no other option. Daisy grabbed Candace's hand and urged her to climb atop the bench. From there, they could reach the halfwall lip.

Or haul themselves over it.

*"Abandon ship!"*

Together, Daisy and Candace leaped down. Truthfully, Daisy landed with more of a scramble, while Candace, in her yogi balance, managed a far more graceful tumble. As they ran away, though, there was no finesse to be found.

The beach patrol person gave a half-hearted attempt at chasing after them. However, as they hunkered down in a thicket beside a dune, he appeared to give up. The tension melted with the sound of his footfalls turning back towards his vehicle. If they hightailed it back to the boardwalk, he would never find them.

As Daisy started to emerge from their cover, Candace stopped her.

In a whisper, she suggested, "Much as I enjoy the view, you might want these."

It was only then, as the adrenaline died down and the cold

set in, that Daisy realized she was buck naked. She was not sure why, but a wave of embarrassment coursed through her. With shaking hands, she took the bundle of clothes Candace offered. Sheepishly, she met the woman's gaze, expecting her to be even more ashamed at being caught.

Instead, Candace burst into happy giggles. Helping with the blazer arm holes, she told her, "You're so cute. Hurry up, or I might be tempted to take another 'sample' right here."

It was as much of a threat as it was an offer. Adulthood, and not catching public indecency charges, won out. Daisy finished clothing herself at a record pace, despite the sand caked in all sorts of unpleasant places.

The faster she dressed, the sooner she (with Candace's help) would be able to undress.

Daisy took Candace's hand as they emerged from the thicket. Overhead, the barest bit of moonlight broke through the storm clouds, casting them in a mysterious glow. Like echoes of a summer's dream, they fled into the misty night.

On the way back to Daisy's house, it was a trial to keep their hands in polite places. The pair made it as far as the outdoor shower. Crashing into the confined wooden stall before the water had even begun to heat, they warmed each other.

Daisy lost herself to the feel of taffy-smooth skin, etching her claim with caresses soft and rough across every place she could touch.

Candace Perry was *hers*.

To kiss.

To adore.

To build a life with, even if that life was as simple as being together.

When the shower started to run lukewarm, they went inside. Wordless aside from stuttered gasps and moans, thumps as they bumped against walls and furniture, they landed in Daisy's bedroom. There, they traded in all the secrets their bodies and souls could share. A discovery and a dedication built on a love that was, at last, let flourish.

Daisy was desperate not to let the evening end. She watched the woman, who nestled against her as if it were the most natural state in the world, fall into a deep slumber.

*What if this was all a dream?*

Yet, when Daisy woke the next morning to the pitter patter of rain on her window, Candace was still there—adorably snoozing and cutting off the circulation to her arm. She wanted to stay like this all day. Unfortunately, Bagel Bombs! was not a rubble heap yet, and someone needed to make sure the place was boarded up tight. She would not put it past Peter Perry to charge her if the storm took the whole roof off.

A giddy smile wobbled Daisy's lips as she untangled herself. She did not mean to wake her. Even so, Candace's eyes fluttered open, looking like sapphires in the pre-dawn muted grays.

"Morning," she greeted Daisy in a sleepy, smiley mumble. Bundled under the discount-store appropriated comforter, she snuggled closer.

"Sorry. I was trying to let you sleep."

"More like trying to get out while you can, hm?"

"It's my house." Laughing once at the joke and again in bewilderment at her life, Daisy shook her head. "My Bagel Bombs! duty calls."

"I'll come with you."

Candace started to sit up, and Daisy's attention flew to her newly exposed cleavage. *Boobs.* Candace Perry's, with their peach-pink nipples marked with love-bites that were just starting to show.

Daisy gave her head another, harsher shake.

"No. It looks like Hurricane Mandy is on her way, so Beach Patrol'll be clearing the boards soon. I'm just gonna make sure things are buttoned up. If you come, it'll take twice as long because I won't be able to keep my hands to myself. You have off from the pier, right?"

Flopping back down onto her belly, Candace let loose a cat-like yawn.

"Doesn't matter. I'm sure my uncle flagged my badge scan at the coaster and checked the security footage. I bet he threw a fabulous fit, shame I couldn't see. I'll type up a formal resignation once I get my laptop. And coffee."

"I can handle the coffee part, plus breakfast if you're okay with something fast."

"Eggs and toast?"

"Woof, steep order, there." Daisy took on a mock-indignant tone. "I bet you'll expect some butter and jam, too? Typical. If that's what it takes to make her highness happy, I guess I'll have to find a way to manage."

"*Egg*–cellent! You're setting yourself up for girlfriend of the year already."

*Girlfriend.*

The word took Daisy's belly and did somersaults with the organ. She was the one who first said it, but hearing Candace so casual about the title was different. It was real.

It was a good thing Daisy had the eggs to focus on. Otherwise, she would have been in real danger of saying screw it, and throwing the woman right back in bed. Eggs kept her on task. The hardest part was not moving slowly.

Daisy wanted to sear the image of Candace hanging out in her kitchen, wearing only a borrowed tank top and shorts, into her brain for eternity. Obligation moved her, but the promise of picking up where they left off when she got home was what finally got her out the door.

Circumstances kept her there.

The state of emergency declaration was imminent, and the town was due to officially close the boardwalk by midday.

Even so, as soon as Daisy opened, Bagel Bombs! was swamped with customers. The little cafe was one of the only places not completely boarded up, so the storm lookie-loos, weather station crews, and Beach Patrollers all flocked there.

Daisy wished she had brought Candace with her for the extra pair of hands alone. She did not even have time to respond to the sexy selfie the woman sent from her bed until hours later. Her reply went unread.

When she finally had a break around noon, she sent another text that also went unread. She tried again minutes later.

*Daisy: Were the eggs that bad?*

A jolt shot through Daisy's chest as a notification came through.

The text did not just go unread.

It was undeliverable.

# CHAPTER 23

## *Candace*

C andace was no stranger to comfortable beds.
In luxury hotels and resorts all around the world, she had slept in some of the most high-end beds, nestled in sheets fit for royalty. The Comfort Clam's musty linens had been a steep downgrade. Even so, she slept like a baby most nights thanks to sheer exhaustion.

Daisy's bed, though?

Candace conked out so hard, she might as well have been dead. Multiple, mind-blowing orgasms would do that. But, also, with Daisy's acceptance came a different release. They could *finally* move forward, and in ways Candace had only ever dreamed.

After eating the simple, yet ridiculously delicious, breakfast Daisy prepared for her, she almost fell right back asleep. Instead, she contented herself basking in her girlfriend's domain.

Daisy's bedroom was the most *her* space in the whole house, an eclectic mismatch of treasures and things that resonated with the prickly woman. Like the rest of the home, the bedroom was compact by modern standards. However, with the bed pushed to one wall, there was room for an impressive art drafting table. All kinds of projects, from the makings of another wireframe seaglass flower to the evidence from her map-making for their date, were strewn about.

Candace smiled to herself as she ran a hand along the seaglass and polished shells strung from the window curtain rod; her girlfriend was a magpie. Shiny, pretty, colorful things dominated the small space, with elements from her beloved seaside home and a strong preference for blueish green. No wonder she wanted to collect Candace, too.

The thought made her tumble with joy. Candace rolled herself up in Daisy's sheets, inhaling their earthy, toasted flour scent. She only pouted for a short while after the sexy selfie she sent was ignored. Unfortunately, she had her own business to handle and far less fun communications to draft.

Resigning from the pier and her uncle's "partnership" was not a thread she wanted to leave hanging. Screw his image with the God Squad or his Boy's Club. Candace wanted out. No matter what he threw their way, Daisy and Candace would figure it out together.

And, maybe someday, she would thank Uncle Perry for being so horrible. That way, she had no choice but to see him for what he was and run straight into Daisy's arms. Easiest decision she ever had to make.

Easy in theory, though, did not mean easy in practice. Candace had never formally resigned from a job. The cafe she worked at in college had come to a natural conclusion once she graduated, and her last job had ended with security looming over her while she threw her desk belongings into a too-small box. She fretted over the proper language to use, whatever ended things as unequivocally and quickly as possible.

No emotion. No bargaining or apologizing.

In a surprise turn, it was Uncle Perry who came to bargain. Or, Vinny Lamarka on his behalf. A little before noon, Candace saw the man in his red polo and tan Dockers walk up to the porch. She should have pretended not to be home. However, feeling bold, she went to the locked door and yelled for him to go away.

"Fuck off," she ordered, borrowing one of Daisy's favorite phrases. "I'm not dealing with my uncle's bullshit anymore. You can tell him—"

"That his niece is a dirty whore? He knows that, but the rest of the world will find out just how depraved you are if you take that tone with me again. Open the door, Candy."

Warning bells blared in Candace's head. She knew that if she opened the door, she would not get it closed again. Even so, her pulse jumped as familiar, unmistakably *erotic* audio came from the other side. Her face burned hot as she thrust the door wide.

Vinny's smirk made his moustache lopsided. He held up his phone, angling it for Candace to get a clearer look.

But she already knew what he had.

Pictures of Daisy atop Candace at Higbee Point after they'd declared their feelings; voyeuristic, black and white stills taken from below the lifeguard stand, with Candace's pleasure-contorted face visible over the half wall; the close-up, overhead video of them inside the shower stall could have been professional porn.

"You followed us on our date... Put cameras around her house...? What is *wrong* with you?"

"Me? What do you expect, acting out the way you have? Mr. Perry has been patient. Last night, parading all over the pier in sight of customers went too far."

Candace was grateful for the doorframe. She gripped the solid wood, steeling herself.

"We haven't done anything wrong. No one, aside from shitty people like you, cared that we were at the pier. If you publish that video, we'll take you to court so fast—"

"And the damage will be done," he concluded with a shrug. Slipping his phone back into its Boomer belt holster, he leveled his gaze at her. "Once this kind of content ends up on the internet, it never goes away. You can put on a brave face here and now, but what about when you're looking for that new job? There are only a handful of places that will hire on based on your O-face... no matter how impressive it was."

Swift and reactionary, Candace slapped the weasel in front of her. She did not regret it one bit. It felt like thousands of fire ants marched over her skin as she tried to hold her ground. Yet, Vinny looked at her like she was a petulant child.

"Last chance," he told her, sounding like a shady car salesperson trying to close a deal. "You might be able to stand the attention, but what about Ms. DeMarco? Word around town is that she had a rough go of it the last time her love life fell under the spotlight. Oh, that was your fault too, wasn't it? How long do you think you would have before the hate and resentment set in again?"

*She wouldn't*, Candace thought. Daisy had forgiven her for their past. It would always be a part of what brought them to where they were, but their relationship was not defined by it.

This, however, was not the past. This was a whole new problem Candace had caused. She spat, "What does he want?"

"To talk."

"Talk," Candace repeated. "There's nothing to talk about. I'm done making him look good for his cess-pool friends. I'm seeing Daisy, *intimately*, and nothing he says will change that."

The man looked at Candace. With an impassive expression, he pulled his phone out once more and thumbed to a prepared social media exposé. As his finger hovered over the post button, her conviction wavered. She stopped him at the last second.

"Alright. Fine. Delete your perv collection, then I'll go."

"Good girl. Give me your phone."

"What? No way."

"Mr. Perry doesn't want any interruptions. Non-negotiable."

Again, Lamarka stared her down. It was clear one of them would have to budge. She thrust her phone into his waiting hand and watched him flick it to Airplane Mode.

Candace pushed past Lamarka for his car. She let her frustrated tears fall, unbothered by him seeing her emotions. She did not care what he thought; the only person whose opinion mattered was Daisy.

And Candace was determined to fix things before the woman had another reason to hate her.

As Lamarka drove to Peter Perry's off-island mansion, Hurricane Mandy's strength grew.

Howling wind shook the frame of the man's Mercedes all the way over the bridge. Fat droplets drummed with a dull roar against metal and almost completely drowned out the radio. The car's low undercarriage struggled with the sheer volume of water pooling in the streets. Overall, the drive was a harrowing experience for reasons entirely separate from her situation. Candace was almost grateful when they reached the hidden, white gravel driveway despite what awaited her there.

When she left Wonderwood on her eighteenth birthday, she thought she would never see this place again. Just like the man himself, Peter Perry's home was an empty shell. It was a wooded plot, an acre of once-protected pineland forest that had formerly teemed with wildlife, which he carved out for his personal kingdom. He liked it because it was situated out of the way from the rest of the world and the 'shoobie mouth-breathers.' The stucco stone behemoth was a monster of a residence that loomed out of the natural world like a mausoleum. Flowerless, geometrically sculpted hedges made for a muted aesthetic. On such a rainy day, maybe always, grayness seemed to sap every bit of color.

It was also where Candace spent most of her time after her uncle took custody of her. When she was not on the boardwalk with Demi or at school, she was stuck miles away from anything or anyone she cared about. She had not been a princess in a tower, but she had been as isolated—yearning to work up the courage to talk to the other princess whom she had a crush on.

Lamarka parked in the garage in one of the few available spots. There was a Michael Bay movie worth of Maseratis, Lambos, a new, ugly-as-sin Tesla truck, and more, all meticulously stored in the sprawling space. Peter Perry loved cars because they were more things he could show off. When it came down to it, the man was a simple creature.

His entire, sad existence revolved around obtaining bragging rights.

Candace's pumps slipped on the polished concrete floor, but she growled at Lamarka's attempt to offer a hand.

"As if I'd ever touch you."

"You feminist types hate gentlemen, don't you?"

"Don't kid yourself, you're a henchman."

"And you've always been a brat. It's about time Mr. Perry dealt with your embarrassment."

Lamarka's genial front dropped. He drew back, loathing in his dark eyes plain, and left Candace to follow. Fine by her; she didn't like pretending to be someone she was not. Why should he do the same? As far as she was concerned, it was far easier when bigots let their brain-dead flags fly.

As they entered the main house through a reinforced door, he keyed in a code to the electric lock. Candace feigned fixing her hair while she scoped the digits. She rolled her eyes, realizing that it was Peter Perry's birthday backward.

They walked in through the kitchen, with all its high-end equipment that would have made Daisy drool. Not that Uncle

Perry ever cooked in his life, but, again, bragging rights. When his friends and their wives came over, he wanted them to know he had it all. He could go on endless diatribes about how special his imported Calacatta marble countertops were, sourced from the most exclusive quarry, bold veining, blah, blah, blah... He did not give a single shit about the marble. To him, it was something expensive he had that someone else did not.

From the kitchen, they made their way through the cavernous central living area. The floor-to-ceiling glass along the back wall gave a terrifying view of the storm's continued raging outside. Hurricane Mandy shook the tall pines along the property's perimeter like they were matchsticks. Candace flinched as she watched a whole branch snap free to be whipped away into the fury. She was so distracted she did not notice Uncle Perry until he spoke.

"Over here. Now, Candy. You know I don't like waiting."

Of course he was already safe and hiding away. There was no need for him to go take shelter with Wonderwood riff-raff over at the public school. He sat in his favorite leather recliner, bourbon in hand, dressed in his usual neatly pressed slacks and collared shirt. Even in his own home, the man did not look comfortable. He was always trying to put on a show, she realized, and had taught her to do the same.

Not anymore.

Candace stood before him in her rain-dampened tanktop and sweats. Unafraid, unhidden, and wholly herself. The disdain in his regard, the undercurrent of covetous filth as his gaze lingered on her exposed flesh, only made her stand taller.

She answered, "No one likes waiting. But you called me here to talk, and now you can sit there while I do."

To her surprise, Peter Perry did wait. He watched her over the rim of his glass with the barest trace of interest as he downed a sip. Candace drew in a steadying breath. She'd mentally rehearsed what she wanted to say on the way over, but, in truth, the words had been on the tip of her tongue for far longer.

"When you took me in, I had no other options. I was a child, and I needed someone to protect me. You didn't do that. I was a burden from the moment I arrived, an embarrassment and reminder that your family was not perfect. You never saw me for me, but as another thing to control. I've had enough. From here on out, I don't need or want you in my life.

"Whether you like it or not, I'm dating Daisy DeMarco. Yes, I will be public about it because I'm madly in love with her. We know you did something underhanded to take that beachfront land from her parents, and that you'll do whatever you can to ruin the Bagel Bombs! brand—go right ahead. You can't scare us apart. When we get married, don't expect an invitation."

Candace let that sink in. Then, she pivoted to face Lamarka.

"We're done here. I'm going to order a car, but if I can't get someone to pick me up in this weather, one of you is going to drive me home. My phone."

Candace held her hand, waiting. Lamarka looked to her uncle, and a silent communication passed between them. A pit opened up inside her stomach. She knew that look. They were humoring her. Too late, Candace realized her mistake. They never intended to let her go.

Calling out to a side room, Uncle Perry said, "Didn't I tell you she was difficult?"

Another man, someone Candace did not recognize, came into sight. He looked like a medical professional in his teal scrubs and gloves. The logo on his shirt and badge read Pleasant Meadow Recovery. Nodding at Perry, the man began to write on a clipboard.

"What is this?" Candace demanded, hoping the terror in her voice sounded like anger, "Who the hell is he?"

No one answered her. Instead, the scrub-wearing man subjected her to a series of humiliating questions.

"Has the patient always displayed such contempt for authority?"

"Is the patient a risk to herself or others?"

"What is the patient's sexual orientation?"

"Does she have a history of seeking out dangerous sexual situations?"

It went on and on, while Perry answered in half-truths and exaggerations. When Candace tried to escape, Lamarka's vise-grip held her in place.

"Why?" She begged, "Why can't you leave me alone? I don't want your money or anything else. Please, just let me live my life!"

Scoffing, her uncle complained, "See how dramatic she is? No, I can't 'leave you alone.' No matter what *you* want, you are a Perry, and what you do reflects on me. You're right, though. I'm tired of policing you. This situation calls for professional help."

"You can't," Candace argued. Searing panic ran through her veins as she began to understand his insinuation. "Dr. Long—"

"Patricia? Yes, I've been in contact with your doctor for some time. She faxed over your file, along with a detailed write-up on the toll your career has taken on your health. The nervous breakdown you had was particularly troubling. And you've stopped taking your mood-balancing medication."

"What? I didn't have a breakdown. I don't take any meds other than aspirin! I... No. This isn't right!"

"According to Dr. Long and signed witness statements, it's been a drawn-out, sordid affair. I warned you, Candy. The working world is a harsh place. You can do everything right, and your coworkers will still throw you under the bus for client recommendations or a little bonus cash."

Candace shook her head. Tears fell unbidden as she went limp in Lamarka's grasp. She recalled what the henchman said when he first threatened her after her date with Ted: 'Hiccups' happened to difficult girls, and she had 'more to lose than a silly career.' He'd been taunting her with the truth.

"You did it, didn't you? You're the reason I was let go... Why I couldn't get a new job, no matter how many applications I put in... It wasn't my fault. It was *you* this whole time. You hate me that much."

Peter Perry did not need to say it. Candace could see it in his eyes—the same seafoam blue as her own, but so very cold—how he wished she were gone.

"Why? Can you at least tell me that? We're family. Why can't you care about me?"

"Care?" He said with venom, "I care that you're not normal. You *won't* be normal, no matter how much I've tried to help you. I can't let you ruin the Perry name."

"I… I don't understand. That's what this is about? My name?"

"*My* name," he repeated in a yell, like a toddler claiming a toy. "The Perry name is *mine*. I built it up from nothing, with no help from your dead witch mother or anyone else. She had no right to keep that name after she hitched herself to your useless father, much less give it to *you*. I'm not going to let you jeopardize my reputation any more than you already have. So, if you won't behave, I'll have to make you."

Disbelief warred with revelation within Candace. She had always thought his hate came from some nebulous, undefinable place. But he knew, and she could hear in every word his righteous conviction. Hated for who she was not *and* for who she was through no fault of her own. His reasoning was so illogical, so unrepentantly *disgusting*, she could not think of any way to defend herself.

Uncle Perry turned his attention back to the man from the "recovery" center. "When can your facility take her?"

"Well, there's a waitlist, and—"

"Janice sent over my donation earlier today, correct?"

"Erm, yes… Thank you. It was very generous, which is why I'm here in person to do this evaluation. There is also the issue of your conservatorship paperwork. Once you've…"

*Conservatorship.*

A loud, tonal ringing filled Candace's ears as that word echoed inside her head. It drowned out the rest of what the men said, their thinly veiled haggling over how much more Perry would need to bribe for the exchange to move along.

For just a little extra, some missing paperwork would not be a problem; a little more for a woman's freedom. Hurricane Mandy was her only saving grace.

"I'll send a transport over once the arrangements are complete," he told Perry. "It may take some extra time for them to arrive depending on how the roads are, but—"

"End of day, or I'll find a more cooperative facility."

"Y-yes, alright. End of day it is."

A single, satisfied nod bobbed Peter Perry's head. With a flippant wave, he added, "In the meantime, give her something to keep her quiet. I've heard enough tantrums."

"Fuck you!" Candace thrashed in Lamarka's hands as her mute shock slingshotted to wild indignation. The man underestimated her strength. She managed to land a good blow to his ribs, but he held tight. "You can't do this! Daisy will find me and we'll… we…"

It was only belatedly that Candace felt the needle pierce her neck. The man from the recovery center came up behind her and jabbed her skin with expert precision. Heaviness tugged her whole being, wiping her will to fight… or run… or do *anything* to save herself. She fell into Lamarka's hold and drifted into darkness.

# CHAPTER 24

## *Daisy*

P ossibilities raced through Daisy's mind.
    She stared at her phone, willing the undelivered notification to change. Wondering *why?*

It was not about last night. The bitter, angry past-Daisy would have jumped to abandonment, and blamed Candace for running away again. She would have thrown a fit, been sullen and withdrawn. That wasn't her anymore. Daisy knew something had happened, and she was not going to sit on her ass doing nothing.

Outside in the raging torrent, with one last hammer-twack, Daisy finished nailing the final plank to Bagel Bombs'! fortification. The storm was coming in faster and heavier than any of the forecasts had predicted. Any minute, the evacuation sirens would sound and the police would start clearing the boards. She needed to figure out where Candace was before the whole place went into lockdown. If Peter Perry was planning to use the confusion around the hurricane to do something to her...

*No.*

She wasn't going to let him hurt her anymore.

First, Daisy needed reinforcements. She called Demi, who picked up after three rings, sounding very distracted.

*"Zee?"* In the background, there were people yelling and the buzz of power tools. *"Are you okay? I'm a little busy. It's not the best time right—"*

"Candace is missing," Daisy cut to the chase. Before she could even begin to explain, Demi interrupted.

*"Meet me at Zeus' Torch. We'll find her."*

Daisy sprinted.

With the wind flying every which way, she barreled down the boardwalk like she was on stilts. It was practically deserted now, aside from a small group of people standing outside the restaurant. She recognized a couple of Demi's cousins who had helped out during the renovation, along with Tina and her wispy, shaking frame. The group stood huddled in the downpour, anxiously looking up.

Following their gaze, Daisy noticed people—including Demi, with her big hair whipping from her bun—atop the restaurant's roof. It appeared that they were trying to dismantle the place's iconic neon torch, the big, custom beacon sign that had decorated the restaurant since the place opened in the '60s.

'Busy' was an understatement. Daisy might have been out of her mind with worry, but she knew better than butt in. Hanging back, she waited and watched while her foot tapped a hole into the boards.

An older woman who could have been Demi's mother with her shared lion's mane hair muttered to herself in a different language. The umbrella that was clutched her hands was lopsided. A sheet of rain angled down her leopard-print cardigan, but she hardly seemed to notice with her attention so fixated above.

As she steadied the umbrella, Tina told her, "It'll be okay, *Theia* Thea. They're almost done, and then the sign will be safe!"

"I don't care about the sign! I should have told her no! What if they—"

A roaring gale tore by, making them all stagger. Metal creaked as the newly-detached torch was nearly blown away. Together, though, Demi and her cousins weighed it down. Once the coast was clear, they rigged up a rudimentary pulley and lowered the relic down.

The woman, *Theia* Thea, practically melted with relief once all of her relatives were safely on the ground. She rushed them at the boarded-up restaurant front entrance, pulling each of them in for a hug. Demi, Daisy noticed, she squeezed tightest of all.

"I told you we could get it," Demi bragged. She slicked back her sopping locks, looking triumphant. *Theia* Thea crossed her arms and snapped something back in Greek, sounding less than pleased. The other cousins shuffled nervously in the cramped, damp alcove.

Demi looked hurt. Wide-eyed, she argued, "Just last night you were crying, '*The torch is going out! What're Nona and Papau going to think? It's the end of their dream!*'"

*Theia* Thea shook her head. "I was being dramatic. You should know better than to take me seriously!"

"Of course I take you seriously! I hate seeing you like that."

The woman sputtered out a mix of English and Greek insults. "Reckless! Foolish!"

"Why are you upset? I was trying to help!"

"Because it's just a thing."

It was Daisy who spoke. She said it, watching this woman who so clearly loved her niece lose all composure at the thought of her getting hurt. In *Theia* Thea's fierce love, she was reminded of her own parents. How they celebrated her, how they worried for her... In that moment, if it was what she wanted, she knew they would be okay with her letting go. The neon flame and Bagel Bombs! were objects. They were important, with sentiment and memory attached. However, they would always come second to the people who made them.

"Zee?" Demi and everyone else's attention turned to her.

Sure of herself, Daisy nodded. "She's upset because you put yourself at risk for a thing. You're upset because you did it for her. It's fucking adorable, and you should probably talk things out more when you're not standing in the middle of a hurricane."

A beat passed where it was hard to tell what *Theia* Thea thought. Her shrewd eyes bore into Daisy as if she were reading a Terminator-style stat breakdown.

Demi explained, "*Theia*, this is Zee DeMarco. She's the owner of—"

"I know who she is," the woman answered in a flat tone. Then, like a coin flip, her entire aura brightened. She reached out (and up, thanks to her short height) to pinch Daisy's cheek. "How could I forget such a cute face? You were probably too young to remember, but back in the day, your parents used to bring you to the restaurant for our Boardwalk Business Association meetings. You and Demitra once spilled a whole pitcher of orange soda all over table 12."

In unison, Daisy and Demi exclaimed, "*We did?!*"

*Theia* Thea nodded, and a wistful smile tugged her bright red lips. "You two were so bad together, Demi, your parents stopped bringing you. I always liked how lively it made things." Taking Daisy's hand, *Theia* Thea added, "Rose and Robert were good people, and they loved you *so much*."

"Yeah," Daisy said thickly. "They did. Thanks."

*Fuck.*

Daisy was glad every inch of her was soaked, masking the couple of tears that sprang from her eyes. Even so, the older woman gave her hand another squeeze before she let go. Daisy drew in a deep breath and tried to right her emotional rudder.

*Candace.*

Locking eyes with Daisy, Demi read her thoughts.

"Catch me up."

Thankfully, Daisy did not have to explain about the date or where it had ended. Candace had sent a series of descriptive emojis to her best friend shortly after her last text to Daisy.

"It sounded like things went, ah, *well*," Demi commented with a knowing grin. Her brow furrowed as she went on, and her tone was laced with worry. "Candace isn't exactly clumsy, but maybe she broke her phone somehow. Are you sure she isn't just—"

"*No.* I called my neighbor. Her car is still at my house, but she's not. It's that bastard Peter Perry, I know it."

"He'll have to evacuate the island like everyone else," Demi pointed out.

Sure enough, the sirens began to blare all around them. The group shared nervous glances, while Daisy's pulse jumped. *Theia* Thea made a motion for everyone to get moving down the boardwalk ramp for their vehicles.

Quickly, Demi continued. "I doubt he'll evacuate to the high school. If Candace is with him, they'll be at his mansion in Keller's Grove."

"And if she isn't? Where else would he have stashed her?"

Daisy knew she sounded desperate, most likely looked it, too, but she did not care. Demi shook her head.

"I don't know. He has property all over, friends, and business contacts. She'll be safe, wherever she is... He wouldn't do anything drastic."

"*Drastic?!* He fucking kidnapped her!"

"We don't know that for sure," Demi reasoned. But, by the waver in her voice, Daisy could tell she suspected nothing good.

The clattering of a police cart sounded down the boards, clearing the last few stragglers. They were out of time. From the boardwalk ramp, *Theia* Thea called out for Demi.

"Be right there!" To Daisy, she pleaded, "Come with us. We'll get to the shelter and figure out our next step. Ted will be stationed there, I'm sure he'll help."

Daisy held in a growl. She didn't want to wait for Ted Freaking Cando to waltz in and save them. Beyond the police cart, far down the boardwalk, the fun pier loomed in her sight.

"Zee? We need to go!" She almost had to shout over the chaos. Slowly, Daisy shook her head.

"No. I... I'm supposed to get a ride with Rio. They're meeting me at my place."

Demi hesitated, holding back her whipping hair as she studied Daisy's face. "Are you su—"

"Go on. I'll meet you there."

*Theia* Thea yelled something that made Demi jump. With one last backward glance, she left. Daisy, meanwhile, headed off to pay Janice a visit.

# CHAPTER 25

## *Candace*

It was dark when Candace finally woke. She thought that she was still trapped in that dreamless nightmare, drifting down into the depths of nothingness. However, as thunder rumbled the sky, she felt it in her bones. Primal, like an animal responding to danger that stalked just out of view. The lightning strike that followed snapped her to focus.

Sort of.

Candace groaned. Her head felt like it was stuffed with cotton balls, heavy and lolling as she rolled atop a soft surface. At a molasses pace, she managed to move onto her side and prop herself up. Memory of what happened, of her confrontation with Uncle Perry and the "help" he arranged, came back to Candace like a face-slap.

He would hide her away forever if she let him. Locked in some facility with the legal and medical system weaponized against her, she would never be free.

*No fucking way.*

Candace pawed the sleep from her eyes and surveyed the muted space of her would-be prison. It was her old bedroom. She could tell by the familiar feel of her smooth satin covers, along with the trace scent of the cucumber-melon perfume she (and a million other teenage girls) used to wear. She had always hated this room. It figured that she would need to escape this place one last time.

On the second floor, overlooking the back hedge garden and pool, it was not the steepest drop. She could make use of the classic bed-sheet rope trick and jump the rest of the way. In staggered, jelly steps, she hauled herself over to the window.

*Woah… shit.*

Whatever they dosed her with was wearing off, but not fast enough. She felt like she'd just ridden the teacups at max speed. Breathing deeply, Candace pressed her forehead against the cool glass.

It was difficult to tell the time. Far darker than when she arrived, the roiling mass of purple clouds overhead shut out the sky. Intermittent lightning flashes provided glimpses of the apocalyptic outside. Running into the torrent with nothing aside from the clothes on her back, trekking through miles of Pineland forest where she could trip into a creek and drown, was not the most appealing plan. Somehow, though, she needed to get to Cape Crest High School. Wonderwood would have evacuated by now, and Daisy… Candace prayed that she was safe.

Over the crashing chaos of the storm, Candace heard a different sound. The doorbell's merry chime was like a starter's pistol. It was now or never.

Candace decided on misdirection. She set the stage by throwing the window open and kicking out the mesh screen. However, she did not climb through. Without the time to make herself a rope, there was no way she could get down unless she wanted to break a leg. Instead, she made it *look* like she had escaped. Then, she wedged herself under the bed and waited.

Minutes passed. Her heart thrummed painfully in her chest like it wanted to jump free. She breathed it back into place, just like Demi taught her. Not fighting the feelings that swelled within her but keeping the parts that served her and letting the rest flow through. When she heard voices outside the door, she went corpse-still.

"—wants you to take care of this quietly," Lamarka told someone as he unlocked the door. "Your facility came highly recommended for its discretion. Make this go away, and—"

The man cursed. Candace tensed as she watched his loafers through the gap between the bed skirt and the carpet. He rushed to the window, with two facility workers close behind him.

Lamarka growled, "That *bitch.* Help me search the grounds. She can't be far."

On top of Uncle Perry's "donation" to the facility, these individual workers seemed to have some incentives. They followed Lamarka outside in clipped steps without a word of question.

Candace, meanwhile, went the other way. Balanced on the balls of her feet, she padded down the cavernous hallways as stealthily as she could while her mind raced. Searing betrayal stung Candace. So many relationships manipulated by lies and greed—her doctor, her coworkers, and, worst of all, her own blood. The tears she shed were not for sadness or self-pity, but a cleansing rage. She had her truth, now, and could move on.

First, Candace needed wheels. The garage with its lineup of getaway vehicles was on the far side of the mansion. Thankfully, her years of tiptoeing about to avoid her uncle's wild moods left her a pro at navigating in the dark. She made it back to the keypad-locked door between the kitchen and the garage, where she punched in the code. As her fingers grazed the icy metal latch, warning prickles ran along her spine.

Candace chanced a glance over her shoulder. At the far side of the kitchen, Uncle Perry wavered with another rim-filled bourbon. His surprise was clear; the glass slipped from his hand and landed before him in an explosion of boozy shards. A lightning strike showed his shift from shock to fury, like caricatures of emotional range. He lunged.

The sprawling center island was a buffer between Candace and her uncle. Before he could maneuver around it, she threw her way into the garage. A pushbroom handle jammed under the door latch bought Candace time, but not much. Successive crashes reverberated against the other side as he tried to get through. Her eyes scanned the room until she found the mounted car key lockbox.

Standing before it, Candace guessed that her uncle used the same passcode and was correct. She did a quick survey of her options, and grabbed the key to a bumblebee yellow Land Rover. Her movements were calm yet quick as she belted into the driver's seat, locked the doors, and thumbed the overhead garage door button. She was not going to let anything stop her.

Not even Peter Perry. He barreled into the garage, disheveled and huffing, right into Candace's path. His attempt at an intimidating posture was anything but as he squinted under the high beams' spotlight. Even so, Peter Perry thought he had won. He planted himself between Candace and the garage's gaping exit, looking satisfied with his victory—

—until she gunned it.

Peter Perry dove out of the way just in time for Candace to miss clipping him. She did not look back to see his face, or even if he followed. Her attention was on the road and the woman who waited for her at its end.

The drive to Cape Crest High was like something out of a disaster movie.

Even so, Candace's stolen SUV cut through the hurricane like the tank it was always meant to be. Reinforced tires crushed whole branches like twigs, and sturdy handling let her navigate through the flooded streets.

Once she made it to the center of town, she reached the high school in no time. The main lot was packed with buses and evacuee cars, plus a fair amount of emergency support vehicles. After Candace knocked on the bolted front entrance, a very surprised-looking patrol officer let her inside. He directed her to the gymnasium, but she was already off one squeaky stride at a time.

People hardly glanced Candace's way as she passed them by. She was far from the only dripping, dazed wanderer. The whole place was packed to the brim with Wonderwooders and unlucky shoobies worrying their night away while Hurricane Mandy raged.

*"So much for fun at the shore..."*

*"Damnit... My car is going to be ruined where I had to leave it."*

*"Poor Horace! She escaped from the nature center staff while they were evacuating, and now she'll be washed away!"*

Misery was the theme for the evening, it seemed. No one was having a good time. Candace, meanwhile, had her own reason for worry.

*Where are you, Daisy?*

In the swirl of faces, she began to feel overwhelmed. So many people, so many potential threats thanks to her uncle's wide web of contacts... As she spotted Demi's cousin Rex chatting with some friends near the locker rooms, she nearly burst into tears. Then, catching eyes with Demi herself, she broke.

*"Candace?!"*

In a blur, Candace fell into Demi's arms. Her adrenaline hit its peak, and she came crashing down into a puddle of tears and blubbered explanations. Demi wrapped her up in a dry hoodie, holding tight while doing her best to make sense of everything.

"That disgusting toad! He's evil, but I never thought he would try to pull a Britney Spears on you. You're okay now, we won't let them touch you."

Rex promised, "How about we touch them some with our fists and make things even, yeah?"

A couple of the other cousins chorused in agreement. *Theia* Thea warned, "No violence. Unless you can make it look like an accident."

Candace laughed, but she was not entirely sure the woman was joking. The friendly, familiar faces gathered around her, forming a sort of protective barrier. The Panopoulos family, from Demi to her *theia*, reliable clutz Tina and the rest of the extended relatives... Rio was there with Katina, too, in their classic overalls and graphic tee... Dotty ambled over, along with a fresh-out-of-hospital Norman and some of his senior friends... Even Ted Cando, with his fiancée Maddie at his side, joined the commotion.

For the first time in a long while, maybe ever, Candace remembered what it was like to have people in her corner. However, one person, the one who mattered most, was missing.

"Where's Daisy?"

Demi and Rio shared a long look. The pair explained that Daisy had been looking for Candace, and had lied about having a ride.

"But that was hours ago," Demi worried. "And she's not picking up her phone. It just keeps on ringing."

Ted interjected, "I let the Coast Guard know we may have people still trapped on the island. If we figure out where she is, they can send a rescue boat out for her. The best thing we can do is stay put, and..."

Candace nodded as Ted went on. Yet, the textbook platitudes went in one ear, out the other. The chant of denial that filled the space was not much better.

*Nonono...*

This was a nightmare. But she was awake, and, as always, she needed a plan. Candace sucked in a breath while she surveyed the faces around her. So many people gathered to help, offering encouragement. Except for one.

Spying on them from behind a bleacher, Janice tried to hide and only made herself even more obvious. Candace charged. Thanks to backup from Rio, Katina, and the linebacker-sized Panopoulos cousins, the woman could not slip away. She trembled in her ugly floral sweater as Candace greeted her with a feral grin.

"Hey there, office buddy. Texting my uncle?"

Without waiting for a response, Candace plucked the woman's phone from her hands. She confirmed her suspicion and sent out a quick *"fuck you"* before handing the device back. Janice scowled.

"You need help, Candy. Mr. Perry is a good man. He only wants what's best for you."

"What's best for me?" Candace laughed at the complete conviction before her. It was all she could do in the face of such upsetting ignorance when she knew nothing would change the sycophant's mind. Instead, she clapped back, "What's best for me is a tall, tanned, gorgeous grump of a woman who bakes like a goddess and fucks me better than any man ever could. So unless you know where Daisy is—"

The way she showed emotion, Janice would have made a fabulous stage actor. With her eyes bulging outside her thin rectangular specs, face white as a sheet, and mouth pursed tight, she was the personification of guilt.

"Spit it out. You've seen her, haven't you?"

"T-that woman," Janice sputtered, "she's trouble, always has been. It's about time Mr. Perry ended her lease. Bagels... Too much carbs will make you fat, you kn—"

Candace slammed her palm against the bleacher. *"Where. Is. She?"*

"It's her fault! She came barging in right as we were

evacuating and demanded that I tell her where you were. Of course I wouldn't! Then pier security came, and—"

Realization crashed into Candace.

"You left her there." Growling, shaking the woman, Candace repeated, *"You fucking left her at the pier!?"*

"There was a lot going on, and…"

While Janice continued spouting excuses, Candace turned to Demi and the others. She was as hopeful as she was devastated. Daisy was locked in the fun pier offices, trapped where drunks and mischievous teenagers were held until the police could deal with them. If the place was not flooded, or *worse*, it would be soon.

"I'll call the Coast Guard."

Pulling his radio from its holster, Ted power-walked to the adjacent corridor. Candace followed. She listened to his conversation with the very distracted-sounding Coastie, biting her tongue until the end. Then, palm up, she put her hand out in front of him.

"Hm?"

"Keys. The roads are flooded, so I need to borrow your boat."

Understanding dawned on the man. He shook his head, saying, "NO… Not a chance, Candy. I can't let you do that for so many, many reasons! That's a terrible plan."

Demi, Rio, and some others filtered in from the gym. They waited off to the side while Candace threw the tantrum of a lifetime.

"I don't give a damn! Right now, a terrible plan is all I've got. You heard the Coast Guard, they're dealing with a million other catastrophes. How high do you think Daisy is on their list? They won't find her in time, but I know exactly where to go. I can save her! It has to be me."

"But my boat—"

"I swear, even if I have to claw my way back from a watery grave, I'll buy you a new boat! The freaking Taj Mahal of boats! Ted, please… I love her. If something happened to her because of me, I'd never forgive myself. And now it's on you, too, so give me your keys."

Candace could see the waver in his conviction. If nothing else, Ted understood fighting for the person he loved. Shaking his head, he muttered something about her being a spoiled, heroic brat as he fished the keys from his pocket. "The far boathouse."

However, before Ted could hand them over, Ed Cando's familiar voice called out.

"Now, son, you can't let a little lady go off and get herself hurt." Ed sauntered between Ted and Candace. Hands on his hips, he scolded, "Candy, this behavior is why your uncle is so concerned. Let the good people from Pleasant Meadows evaluate you, that's all he asks."

"Have them evaluate you, you prick," Demi spat. She threw out a rude gesture, which prompted Rhonda Moss and some of Peter Perry's Wonderwood Works political friends to jump to Ed's defense.

"There's no reason for insults! Aren't yoga teachers supposed to be calm?"

"We've been calm for too long," *Theia* Thea chimed in. She stood beside Demi, proud and firm. "Peter Perry has treated this town as his personal toy box for years, putting good people out of business by being a bully and a cheat—with help from people like *you*."

It was a sight to behold. Two sides of the shore community devolved into passionate arguments. Candace was caught in the thick of it all, with Ed Cando and others blocking her way.

*"Babe, catch!"*

Ted threw his keys to Maddie. She caught them with ease and feinted around her father-in-law-to-be. "Sorry, pops. Girls's gotta do what a girl's gotta do!"

Thanks to Maddie, Demi, and a few others, Candace managed to break out from the swell of people. She booked it for the exit. As she threw the door open, Demi's call for her to be careful could barely be heard over the storm's roar. It was an impossible promise to make, so Candace settled on blowing a kiss. Then, she was in her stolen Land Rover once more, gunning for the Cape Crest Marina.

*Hold on!*

This time, Candace was running towards Daisy, and there was no time to lose.

# CHAPTER 26

*Daisy*

T his was not how Daisy wanted to go. Not that she wanted to do any kind of going, but drowning in a drunk tank was nowhere on her metaphorical "I'd be cool dying like this" list.

*Fucking Janice.*

The woman's sweaters were as ugly as Candace claimed. After meeting Demi, Daisy went to shake Perry's secretary down for information. Before she could get more than a word out, the woman called security, and they tossed her into a glorified closet. Then, clearly, they had forgotten about her.

A minor inconvenience turned deadly thanks to the hurricane that flooded the pier offices. Whether it was rain or ocean, water found its way inside, and it was surging. Daisy, meanwhile, was trapped. Kicking the reinforced entryway gave her a jammed toe. There was a door window; however, it was too small to be useful. Her phone sat within sight atop a desk right outside of her cell, but there was no way she could get it. As it vibrated, each missed call was a gut punch of someone trying to reach her. Demi was the only one who might have any idea where Daisy had gone, and it would be a Sherlock-level guess.

"Goddamnit," Daisy yelled. "I don't have time for this!"

It was hard to gauge how long it had been. Every second was one that took Daisy further away from saving Candace. She *needed* to rescue her; to prove, after everything they had been through, she would try. By now, that bastard Perry could have stashed her anywhere.

In the end, there was nothing Daisy could do. While the water continued to pool under the door over her feet and up her ankles, she wallowed in dread. *Why?* Just when she'd found drive—found *love*—life had to hit her with a new, fresh tidal wave of bullshit. As the water rose higher, and her breaths grew shorter from panic, Daisy clung to thoughts of Candace.

Candace, with her pouty, pink lips when she was trying to get her way; all her meticulous outfits that so perfectly toed the line between professional and sexy; those eyes...

If Daisy had the choice, she would do it all over again. From that very first bagel to now, she only regretted that they had not gotten over their stupidity sooner. Candace was the one for her. Spoiled, adorable...

And, as it turned out, wildly reckless.

*"Daisy? DAISY?? Are you—?"*

"Here!" Rushing to the door, Daisy let loose something between a sob and a laugh. "Holy fuck, I'm in here!"

Candace's face appeared on the other side of the window. She was drenched, shivering in an oversized hoodie and the same shorts Daisy lent her that morning; she never looked hotter, like some kind of magnificent mermaid girl-next-door.

"Dummy," Candace chided, though the love in her voice was obvious. "I warned you Janice would call security!"

"What can I say? My girlfriend was in trouble, and I wasn't about to let some assholes take her away again."

"Well, she wasn't going to let them either."

Candace mirrored Daisy's giddy smile. However, separated by two inches of steel-plated plywood, their happy reunion turned serious.

"You wouldn't happen to have that employee key card on you?"

"I don't, but…"

Candace's attention drifted to the side. In tandem, they had the same idea. Thank *goodness* for home renovation knowledge. They owed the Property Brothers a fruit basket. If you could not unlock a door, take it down.

In a single breath, Candace promised, "There's a maintenance closet down the hall—be right back!"

Daisy waited and did her best to keep calm while the water continued to climb up her calves. The lights flickered until only a few struggling emergency bulbs remained. Under her feet, all around, she could hear the waves beating against the pier's foundation. How long would the bulwark supports withstand the violent undercurrent? She forced visions of falling deep into the ocean depths, sharing the same fate as her parents, from her mind.

As Candace returned, screwdriver in hand, she set to work on the hinges. From the top down, she removed the bolts until the door fell under its own weight. Daisy stumbled over it and into Candace's embrace. She wished they had the time for a passionate kiss or a repeat of last night's activities. Instead, Daisy was distracted by the sand castle pail Candace lugged onto her shoulder.

"*What the—? Is that…?*"

Inside, looking none too pleased as she scuttled against the side of the bucket, was Horace the Horseshoe Crab. Daisy blinked down at the crab and swore she flipped the finger with her needle tail.

Candace explained, "I saw her clinging to the boardwalk right where I docked and couldn't just leave her there. Now, c'mon! We've got a rough ride back!"

"Ride??"

Together, Daisy and Candace stumbled through the flooded office halls to the exit. They burst out onto the pier in an alcove near the Manta Coaster's line queue. Outside their shelter and its emergency lighting, it was difficult to make out much of anything. Sideways rain that was littered with debris ripped past at a roaring volume. Mountainous waves crested up over the pier guardrail and even broke through loose boards to burst up like geysers.

Candace pointed.

"There! I tied Ted's boat right to the pier, it's—"

*Gone.*

Whatever boat Candace came in on was nowhere to be seen. Daisy did not feel particularly upset about sticking to land. Same problem, same plan: *stay alive.* Holding Candace's arm, she tugged.

"Screw it! We'll go to the cafe."

"No," a genial voice told them, "you won't."

Steady despite the howling wind, Vinny Lamarka rounded the corner of the building. The gun he held was trained straight on Candace and Daisy. They froze at the edge of the coaster alcove, facing the man as he advanced on them.

A spitfire even in the face of certain doom, Candace snarled, "I should've known you'd follow me. You'll do whatever your boss wants, won't you?"

The smug upturn of Lamarka's moustache spoke loud and clear. He did not feel remorse for what he had done or what he was going to do. This was a job, one he enjoyed doing.

"You know why your uncle and I get along? We're both traditional. Everything I've done has been for family."

"*I'm* family," Candace argued, and Daisy heard real pain in her voice. "All he had to do was accept me for who I am."

"Selfish as ever. It's not all about you. Mr. Perry, see, he understands... sometimes, family as an institution trumps blood. Here in Wonderwood, we're making a place for the *right* kind of family. If I have to get my hands dirty, I'll be a man and do it. You and the DeMarcos, those annoying, hippy Panopouloss, gays and gender-whatevers—don't belong here."

Daisy surged a step, yelling, "Who the fuck are you to decide? All you assholes say the same bull and act like Wonderwood is falling apart... No shit, a lot of places are for a lot of different reasons. You're sure as hell not helping."

Lamarka shifted his aim to Daisy. She gritted her teeth and did her best to not give him the satisfaction of showing the fear that jolted her insides. The man took a few strides closer, gesturing at Daisy with his piece.

"Right now, I'm the one with the gun. On your knees."

With no other choice, Daisy complied. She grimaced as the rough concrete pad bit into her skin.

Candace rushed forward, only to stop dead in her tracks as Lamarka turned the pistol on her. She threw her hands up and dropped Horace's bucket straight down with a plunk beside Daisy. Despite the waver in her voice, Candace mocked him.

"So, what? You'll murder us, and tie things up for him in a neat, little bow? Go home to Sue and the kids, pretending to be such a nice, family man after you wash the blood off your hands? Is it really that easy for you?"

The man shrugged.

"It's never easy. I've had to extort the coroner to play nice. There's usually someone who gets suspicious and needs bribing. And don't get me started on getting rid of the bodies. Thankfully, the ocean should take care of that last part. Reminds me of your parents going over that bridge, DeMarco."

The man looked down at Daisy as he finished speaking. His words, their implication, fell over her like an icy mantle. In a horrified murmur, Candace put the pieces into place.

"You don't mean... What happened to Daisy's parents wasn't an accident, was it?"

"They really should have sold. Mr. Perry came to them with a good offer, and they were ready to accept. Something about downsizing to fund their daughter's college tuition."

"*What...?*" Daisy blinked, shaking her head. "But they never said..."

As she thought back, she recalled working more hours as her parents went to 'appointments.' They mentioned making changes over the next year. Daisy always thought they were going to have her take over the business, not get *rid* of it. A tornado of regret and bitter realization ripped through her emotions.

"The paperwork was all but signed," he went on. "But, when the DeMarcos heard about Mr. Perry's future plans to build a world-class resort, they reneged on the deal and decided to look for more 'environmentally conscious' buyers. Mr. Perry was very disappointed."

"So you killed them," Candace concluded with a crack in her voice. "You destroyed a beautiful, loving family because they wouldn't do what you wanted. You had access to everything. All you had to do was forge the dates and signatures to make it look like my uncle made the purchase before their deaths. Between his friends in the county clerk's office and the PD, he had all the right angles to slip a shady deal like that through. Daisy, I'm so sor—"

As Candace reached to comfort Daisy, Lamarka cocked his gun. She sucked in a bracing breath. "You're monsters."

"I told you before: it's just business, Candy."

"You're not very good at it if it's taken you all this time. You deserve to fail."

"These kinds of projects don't happen overnight. The pier was hit hard during Hurricane Sandy, and for years, the town's politics were more split. Now, things are different. Funding from the Solid Rock Group was the final piece. Although the rent Ms. DeMarco here has paid over the years has been greatly appreciated. We–"

Daisy had enough. Out of the corner of her eye, inside Horace's bucket, she saw the screwdriver Candace used to free her from the pier office. In a viper-fast snatch, she grabbed it and thrust the shaft into Lamarka's foot.

"Appreciate *that!* C'mon!"

Lamarka flailed in pain. While he struggled to pull the screwdriver free, Daisy and Candace took their chance to run deeper into the Manta Coaster loading depot.

"This wa—*woah!*"

Daisy staggered back as a *"Are you tall enough to ride?"* sign flew past like a spear-toss. It landed in the wall right in front of her with a reverberating twang. Candace ended up further ahead, towards the ride operation booth. Lamarka bull-rushed right behind Daisy. He tried to shoot her, but missed. The bullet ricocheted off a metal line divider that Daisy ducked behind and went wild, almost hitting the man himself. She tried to lose him between the lone coaster left on the track.

Unlike the little, sit-down Mouse Kart, the Manta Coaster was a big, top-down contraption that latched onto its riders like a claw crane. With five cradle-like seats across, six rows down, it rocked back and forth at the wind's violent pull. Daisy wove around the seats, narrowly avoiding Lamarka's reaching grasp.

"*Shit!*"

Daisy's ankle caught in a gap in the floor grating. She managed to pull herself free, but it gave Lamarka time to catch up. Sandwiched between two seat rows, with a barrier rail blocking her rear, Daisy was trapped.

Down the way, Candace stood with her hands hovering over the ride controls. She urged, *"Push him!"*

Daisy shoved without thinking, without realizing *why*, until she was mid-motion. When she understood, she put everything she had into forcing Lamarka back into the coaster seat. As soon as he was in place, Candace proved once and for all that she was the claw-machine master—she slammed the pressure restraints down and locked Lamarka in.

"Shall we send him on a ride?"

Lamarka thrashed impotently while Daisy picked up his gun. She stepped back, nodding with grim determination, and cleared the way. As reality set in for the man, he became enraged.

"Don't you dare, you *bi—AGHHH!!*"

Lamarka's insult turned into a scream as he was launched forward. In addition to being larger than the Mouse Kart, the Manta Coaster did not start out at a gentle climb. This roller coaster was for thrill seekers. It launched its riders straight up at a tongue-swallowing pace, before careening them back down into a series of loops and corkscrews.

It was one of the East Coast's favorite coasters. By the sound of it, though, Lamarka did not have very much fun. They let him do one lap before leaving him at the depot. After what he did to her parents, and who knows how many other innocents, there was a part of Daisy that wanted more bloody vengeance. Even so, she was merciful enough to give him a sliver of survival.

Then, Daisy and Candace (with Horace in tow) bolted for shelter that was not over the ocean. Thanks to Wonderwood's healthy duneline, the water seemed to be holding at the boardwalk level. However, with the chaos around them, they deemed it too dangerous to go far. Instead, they managed to break into Bagel Bombs! through the back entrance Daisy had forgotten to board up in her panic over Candace. While the storm buffeted the whole building so hard it shook, they did what they could to bunker down.

With a flashlight upturned for light, and beach towels spread out over the backroom floor, they made themselves comfortable. It was almost cozy. Daisy leaned back against a chest freezer, and Candace leaned against her. She listened to the discordant *dripdripdrips*, hypnotized by nature's fury.

Candace nuzzled her head against Daisy's shoulder like a cat. She said, "I won't ask if you're okay, because there's no version of the word that covers this. There's no way to make up for what they did. But… I'm here for you, whatever you need."

"I need *you*," Daisy begged. She did not even realize she said the words until they left her tongue, did not register the want until it was voiced, yet it came like a tidal force. She caught Candace's chin between her thumb and pointer finger so that she could turn her face. As their mouths met, her lips tasted like ocean, rain, and tears—of truth and lies untangled to the very last thread until their essences were bare.

One tender kiss turned to several, each one more urgent than the last. Gentle caresses became needful pulls. Piece by piece, their clothing littered the floor. Before long, it was not the sounds of the storm that Daisy focused on, but Candace's building pleasure.

It crested along with the adrenaline still pulsing from their escape, leading to a gasping release. They collapsed back onto beach towels and bagel bags, blissfully spent. While Hurricane Mandy continued to wreak havoc, the world outside was cast to ruin, in this tiny corner, there was only contentment.

Daisy was not sure which of them fell asleep first. She was glad, though, that Candace had the foresight to throw a towel over their naked bodies. It made the scene a *small* sliver less awkward when the Coast Guard came bursting in for their heroic rescue. Thankfully, and with a fair amount of eye-contact avoidance, they all made it back to inland safety with relative ease.

A small crowd was waiting for them at the marina.

"Demi?! Rio? How did you find us?"

Smirking, Rio pointed to Horace. "You can thank her for that."

Daisy smacked her forehead, saying, "The livestream! Wait, does that mean...?"

Demi nodded and, to her credit, at least tried to hold in her laughter. "People saw the whole thing. The attempted murder, Lamarka's confession, and er...Let's just say the nature center cut the feed off before it turned too X-rated."

Daisy found Candace's hand with her own. The gentle pressure of her squeezing back was better than a thousand verbal reassurances. There was more to be said, so much to unpack emotionally, but the marina dock in the middle of a hurricane was not the place. As Ed Cando charged up with some of Peter Perry's other friends to call for Candace and

Daisy's arrest, they ignored him. Ted, meanwhile, had a car waiting to take them to a hotel.

"You two deserve rest after the day you've had," he said, speaking over his blustering father. "If the station is still there after this storm blows through, you can come down and make a report once you're up to it."

While Demi and Rio went back to the high school with Ted, Daisy and Candace went their own way.

And they always would.

# EPILOGUE

*Three months later*

## *Candace and Daisy*

T raditionally, the fall season was Wonderwood boardwalk's last hurrah before its winter hibernation. From harvest celebrations featuring local farmers to beer-fueled Oktoberfests, the town tried to keep the shoobies coming as long as possible. This year, though, the vibe was markedly different.

For one, Hurricane Mandy left the town in shambles. The storm tore a path of destruction along the whole New Jersey coastline, and Wonderwood bore the brunt of it. Many of the old, unfortified speakeasy bungalows along Higbee Point were ripped to splinters. Beachy Ben's was blown away, and the Wetlands Institute on the bay that Rio interned at was flooded with two feet of marshy water. Worst off of all was Perry's Pier.

Late that night, after Candace and Daisy made their harrowing escape, the hurricane's full power pummeled the poorly maintained structure. Whole pieces of it washed away, including the offices where Daisy had been held. The Mouse Kart even pried up from its supports and drifted half a mile down the beach. Despite the losses, with insurance payouts and government assistance, it's possible Peter Perry would have been able to come out of the ordeal stronger.

Instead, people finally saw him for the monster he was.

Thanks to Horace the Horseshoe Crab, Lamarka's attempted murder was broadcast to the whole world. His first words after being rescued by the Coast Guard were to demand a lawyer. A precinct move, since the Feds had already been building a case thanks to information turned over by Ernest Leary's widow. As it turned out, the former fun pier accountant's death was as untimely as it seemed; the man had grown a conscience about the many misdeeds he had a hand in, and they killed him for it. However, not before he bundled up everything he knew in a binder so nicely organized that it rivaled Candace's.

What Peter Perry and Lamarka did to Daisy's parents was only the tip of the iceberg. Their business dealings over the decades were rife with coercion, bribery, and murder, ranging a wide web of conspiracy between their many contacts. Under the law's Eye of Sauron, it did not take long for the rats to start jumping ship; Janice's information was particularly helpful, Ted told Candace.

Peter Perry, Wonderwood's fun, wacky uncle, became the weird one you didn't want to invite to family holidays. He was not in jail (yet) thanks to the slow wheels of justice, and it was possible he would never actually see the inside of a cell. But his reputation was ruined. In the end, that was the greatest victory they could have.

Although the payout Daisy was due would be a welcome bonus. Her lawyer was not clear on the exact sum, but soon, Peter Perry would be the one handing her a check. Most significantly, the land Bagel Bombs! was built on—a whole block that included several other storefronts—would be returned to her ownership. Lamarka's begrudging testimony helped.

However, it was luck that clinched their claim.

During the storm and subsequent clean-up, they discovered a surprise inside Bagel Bombs! A framed picture of Daisy and her parents outside the cafe on its opening day, the same one they had been unable to remove during renovations, turned out to conceal a hidden safe. They cracked it open and found that Daisy's parents kept a copy of the original deed inside. With that document compared to Lamarka's forgery, the proof was impossible to deny.

Or, so Daisy hoped. She did not quite believe everything that was happening. The idea that she might never have to work a day in her life again, that she could wake up and do whatever, wherever she wanted, was almost too daunting to face. It would have been, without Candace by her side. Together, they went to every lawyer meeting, every deposition and court appointment, slogging through the muck of bureaucracy.

As far as relationship-starts went, theirs was tumultuous to say the least. While Daisy reeled from her world growing much larger, Candace's shrank. Her uncle had been evil, but he was one of the few blood relatives she had left. Plus, she was now once again unemployed and broke. She picked up shifts at the diner and helmed the front desk at the yoga studio to keep her bills paid (despite Daisy being happy to cover her expenses). Without her uncle stymying her career, she could try to find something in her field once more. However, she was in no rush. For the first time since she was young, she operated with only a loose plan, and she was just fine with it.

At Demi's insistence, Candace left the waterlogged Comfort Clam and took up residence in her spare bedroom. That arrangement lasted about two weeks. One night, lying in Daisy's bed, they realized how ridiculous it was for them to be apart any longer. She moved in the next day. Since then, the little bungalow had undergone a transformation as Candace unleashed her style and sensibilities on the place. It was not easy for Daisy to change things from the way her parents had left them. And yet, each day she woke up feeling lighter.

The future was theirs to make what they wanted of it. One change, however, was impossible to avoid.

While the fun pier would never be the same, the boardwalk itself remained largely intact. Most of the storefronts were undamaged, including Zeus' Torch. Demi and her cousins reinstalled the iconic torch sign to its rightful place, and the bustling diner returned to normal (or, as normal as things could be with Panopoulos drama) within days of the storm.

Bagel Bombs! was not so lucky.

The roof did, in fact, tear off. With the building condemned, they had no choice but to demolish the whole block. One crisp October day, while the dwindling shoobies continued about their business as usual, it happened. Daisy, Candace, Rio, and Demi watched from across the boardwalk.

As the hulking industrial crane clawed into the debris, eating away a place that held so many memories as if it were paper mache, Daisy felt a full spectrum of emotions. The expected sadness was there; frustration and bewilderment at life's winding way. But there was hope, too. The end of this was not the end of *her*. For Daisy and Candace, things were only getting started.

The loud sniffle Candace let loose cracked Daisy's stoic face. Grinning, she teased, "Don't worry. You know I'll make you bagel bombs any time you want, girlfriend-discount included."

Looking refined and ladylike even as she cast the stink-eye, Candace went stiff under the arm Daisy had looped over her shoulders.

"You're cruel. I can't help crying! Maybe I should go and grab —"

"No you don't," Daisy warned. She hauled the woman back against the boardwalk rail, embracing her from behind as they continued to look forward. "We already saved the fluorescent sign and Norman's stool. The house is full enough now with all your stuff without adding junk debris."

Demi agreed, saying, "She's right, Can-can. I think the construction workers will throw a fit if you interrupt them again."

"Ugh. I liked it better when you two didn't get along."

"Too bad," Demi told her. "We're the next great partnership. My yogis are loving Zee's seaglass art at the studio, and her bagels are selling better than hotcakes at the diner. I'd say I'm in danger of making your *#BagelBabe* fans jealous, but they got all the confirmation they needed about you two the night of the hurricane."

"And in front of poor, innocent Horace," Rio added in a mock-aghast voice. "I did *not* help set that feed up to get high-def video of my boss getting lucky."

The irony was not lost on Candace that in trying to stop compromising material from leaking to the internet, she ended up throwing more on the pile. *Let it be, ride the sea,* she told herself. Shifting in Daisy's grasp, she met the other woman's wry gaze and murmured as she closed the distance between them.

"How about a live show?"

Candace trailed her lips from the nape of her lover's neck, up her jaw, to her lips. Light and drifting, like grains of sand filling the container of Daisy's heart. She did not care who saw, and, by her pleased purrs, neither did Daisy. Their fans, their foes, and friends were all important, but the one who mattered most was already kissing her breathless.

Rio and Demi shared a snort.

"Well, I'm off to get some lovin' myself," Rio bragged. Their relationship with Katina was going strong, and they took every opportunity to flaunt it. "Smell ya later, nerds."

Demi said, "I should get to the restaurant for my shift. *Theia* Thea has *finally* come around enough to stop calling me 'Demitra,' so I want to stay in her good graces. We're still meeting tonight?"

Candace met Daisy's eyes. Her gaze was searching, trying to find hesitation where there was none.

"Hell yeah," Daisy answered with a confident tick of her chin. "Let's do this."

"Are you sure?" Candace pressed, "We don't need to jump right into planning the reconstruction. There's plenty of time to wa—"

"Nope. I've spent enough time doing nothing. Whether we rebuild Bagel Bombs!, or something new, I want to figure this out. So, market research and gyros it is. As long as my smarty-pants girlfriend is still willing to help..."

"Of course! I was just reading the coolest article on hybrid models for shared spaces. It involved—"

Demi cut in, "Save it for the binders, Business-Candace. Zee, see you later!"

With that, she bounded off down the boardwalk in a rush of boho skirts and jangling bangles. Daisy and Candace lingered, basking in the background construction cacophony. It was incredible how fast the professional demolition crew worked. Before long, the crane machine strained, pulling at the last wall until it crumbled like the rest.

Daisy let loose a small breath. Hands in the pockets of her hoodie, she propped a flip-flop against the boardwalk rail and leaned back. Candace, in her matching hoodie and scandalously casual joggers, mirrored the pose.

"Say," Candace mused, "we're friends now, aren't we?"

"Uh, considering the things we did last night—and the night before that *and that*—I'd say we're a bit more than friends."

Biting her lip, Candace shuffled. The eyes she leveled at Daisy were as demure as they were accusatory. "If that's the case, don't you think it's time you let me call you Zee like everyone else?"

"You want me to treat you like everyone else?"

"What? That's not what I—"

Daisy kicked off the rail and spun, pinning Candace against it. She did not wait before kissing her, brief but biting. When she pulled away, the woman's fair skin was bright crimson because, somehow, she was still flustered whenever Daisy made a move. It was adorable, and Daisy hoped to keep on flustering her for years to come.

"My friends call me Zee—people who know me around town, and strangers on the internet. After my parents died, it was a way to reinvent myself because the people who knew me best, the ones who loved me most, were gone. But you came back, Candace. You called my name, and it pulled me from the miserable depths I didn't even realize I'd sunk to. So, please, don't stop."

"Okay," Candace promised. She leaned forward, pressing their foreheads together, and relished the closeness of the woman she never thought she could have. "I'll keep on calling you Daisy, and loving you because I do—I love you, Daisy DeMarco."

"I love you, too, Candace. No matter what your last name is, the only thing I care about is that you're here with me."

*Candace Perry.*

Daisy's first crush...

First heartbreak...

And, if she said yes, her future wife.

**THE END**

# AFTERWORD

Thank you so much for reading my book!

For longtime Nat Paga fans who know me from my Weird-Western Adventure series, *Ashe and Dez*, this book might have been a bit of a surprise. A normal, modern setting? No evil cults? Only *some* murder and sex?!

However, with *Beaches, Bagels, and Babes,* I wanted to challenge myself to write a slower-than-slow burn. I'm so proud of my *#BagelBabes*, and how much they grew from my initial draft. You might want to shake them and yell "JUST KISS ALREADY" by the time they do, but I hope I made it worth the wait. They say authors sometimes write pieces of themselves into their characters, but for Daisy and Candace, that's definitely true. I hope their flaws and foibles make them as special to you as they are to me.

Wonderwood was a joy to write about. As a lifelong Jersey Girl Millennial, the setting was inspired by the South Jersey shore towns I know and love. When I spent soupy mornings hosing down the hermit crab cages for my first-ever job, or worked at my stepdad's shop on the Ocean City Boardwalk, I used to dream up the books I would write (or, be actively writing while I was supposed to helm the register). That bored teenager would be so excited to know that she had finally done it. I'd tell her to appreciate the present a bit more. Stress less, enjoy the moment—let it be and ride the sea. Summer doesn't last forever, but the memories are gold.

# ACKNOWLEDGEMENTS

This book would not have been possible without some amazing people. Lila and Emily's beta-read insights went so above and beyond what I ever expected or hoped for. I can't begin to thank them enough for their kindness helping to make BBB the best it could be. I'd also like to thank the online sapphic community for being so endlessly supportive. The world can be dark, but you make it a brighter place. Most of all, thank you to my partner in crime, DJ. You champion every word (and always encourage more). Thank you!!!

# AUTHOR BIO

Nat Paga is a full-time Hobbit and cat mom from New Jersey. She writes about sapphic women who like to kick and touch butt in equal measure. From humor to real heart, her stories straddle a line that will leave you breathless. She can usually be found writing (in an uncomfortable position thanks to her cats using her as a bed), practicing yoga, doing nerdy things, or making mac&cheese that will knock your socks off.

# BAGEL BOMB RECIPE

INGREDIENTS

- **375 grams all-purpose flour**
- **14 grams sugar**
- **8 grams diamond crystal kosher salt**
- **3 grams instant yeast**
- **225 grams warm water**
- **226 grams brick-style cream cheese**
- **1 egg (for egg wash)**
- **⅛ cup bagel toppings (optional)**

INSTRUCTIONS

1. **Mix.** Mix flour, salt, sugar, and yeast in the bowl of your stand mixer. Pour the water into the middle. Start the mixer on a low speed and give the dough a minute or two to incorporate, pausing and scraping down the bowl as needed until the dough comes together in a messy ball in the bowl. *If your kitchen is humid, hold back ⅛ cup of water and add it 1 teaspoon at a time only if the dough isn't coming together or seems very dry.*

2.   **Knead.** Increase the speed to low-medium and let the mixer run for 3-5 minutes, dusting in more flour only if the dough is sticking to the bowl. You're looking for a dough that is smooth and elastic and just slightly tacky to the touch. It shouldn't cling to your hands or the bowl.

3.   **Rise.** Shape the dough into a smooth round ball, and place it in a lightly oiled bowl. Let it rise for an hour in a warm spot or until about doubled in size. When you press a finger into the dough, it should fill in partially but not completely.

4.   **Cream cheese.** Divide the cream cheese into equal portions of about 18 grams each. Scoop onto a parchment-lined quarter sheet pan and place in the freezer to chill while the dough rises.

5.   **Deflate.** Turn the dough out onto a clean counter or work surface, gently deflating it with the pads of your fingers.

6.   **Divide and pre-shape.** Use a kitchen scale to divide the dough into twelve equal pieces (about 50-55 grams each). Flatten the dough gently against the counter, tuck the edges up, and pinch them together on top. Flip the dough over and cup your hand around it. Drag your hand toward your body against the counter to create surface tension and shape the dough into an oval. Rotate the dough 90 degrees and repeat to create a circle shape. Repeat with the remaining dough. Cover the dough balls with a damp paper towel and let them rest for 15-20 minutes.

7.   **Assemble.** Starting with the first dough ball you shaped, flip it over so the seam is facing up. Gently flatten it out with your fingers. Place one of the frozen cream cheese balls in the middle and pinch all the edges of the dough together to seal the cream cheese inside. Flip the dough ball over so the seam is facing down, cup your hand around it and scoot it around in circles to tighten up the seam at the bottom. Cover the dough balls again and rest for another 15-20 minutes.

8. While the stuffed bagels rest, preheat your oven to 400°F and fill a wide, high-sided skillet with at least 2 inches of water. Bring it to a low boil on the stove. Line a sheet pan with parchment paper or a silicone mat and set aside.

9. **Boil.** Boil bagel bombs in batches for about 30 seconds with the pinched together bottoms facing up. Remove to a lined sheet pan, flipping them over so the seam side is facing down.

10. **Egg wash and toppings.** Brush each mini bagel with egg wash (1 large egg + 1 teaspoon water, whisked together) and sprinkle with add any desired toppings.

11. **Bake.** When all the bagel bombs have been boiled, egg washed, and topped, transfer the baking sheet to the oven and bake them for 17-19 minutes, until golden brown and shiny.

12. **Cool.** Remove the bagel bombs from the oven. Let cool for a few minutes on the sheet pan, then transfer a wire rack to finish cooling before slicing.

13. Enjoy!

*Recipe Notes*

- *You can add up to 36 grams of mix-ins (bacon, everything bagel seasoning, chives, grated cheddar cheese, etc.) to the cream cheese before scooping it; aim for no more than 21 grams of cream cheese per bagel bomb.*
- *If you need to let the bagel dough rest or relax at all during the shaping process, cover it with a damp paper towel to prevent it from drying out.*
- *Once cool, store bagel bombs in an airtight bag in the fridge with as much air pressed out as possible for 4-5 days. To reheat, microwave for 10-15 seconds or in the oven at 350°F for 5-7 minutes.*
- *Frozen mini bagel bombs can be stored in an airtight bag with as much air pressed out as possible for up to 1 month.*

*Reheat in the microwave for 15-20 seconds or in the oven at 350°F for 10 minutes.*

# DON'T FORGET!

If you want more stories from Nat Paga, be sure to leave a review on Amazon, Goodreads, post on social media, or yell about her to a stranger. Follow @natpaga on social media for info on upcoming projects. Your support makes magic happen!

www.ingramcontent.com/pod-product-compliance
Lightning Source LLC
Chambersburg PA
CBHW070533260626
47161CB00002B/368